# THE SAXON WARRIOR'S CAPTIVE BRIDE

MEDIEVAL BRIDES: BOOK TWO

EMILY ROYAL

TWINKLE PRESS

The Saxon Warrior's Captive Bride

**Medieval Brides: Book Two**

**Emily Royal**

Text by Emily Royal.

Proofreading by Imogen Howson.

Cover Design by Wicked Smart Designs.

ALSO BY EMILY ROYAL

**Medieval Brides**

The Saxon Lord's Unwanted Bride

**Headstrong Harts**

What the Hart Wants

Queen of My Hart

Hidden Hart

The Prizefighter's Hart

**London Libertines**

Henry's Bride

Hawthorne's Wife

Roderick's Widow

**Lyon's Den Connected World**

A Lyon's Pride

**Dark Highland Passions**

The Sins of the Sire

**Standalone Novels**

Her Dark Seduction

**Anthologies**

Upon a Midnight Dreary (featuring Haunted Hart)

Star of Light (featuring All I Want for Christmas is My Hart)

The Wedding Wager

Want to know more? For a free, exclusive novella, plus news, teaser scenes and cover reviews, sign up to my newsletter via my website www.emroyal.com. Your details will not be passed to third parties.

# DEDICATION

*for Frankie*

# PROLOGUE

*Leaside Hall, England, 1080*

"Lady! Lady Arlette!"

Arlette pulled a face at her nursemaid, then leaned over the balustrade overlooking the main hall.

"Hush, Esme," she said. "I want to hear!"

Plump fingers circled her wrist. "What would your father do if he caught you eavesdropping? Or Lord Henry? You think he'd deem you a suitable match for his son? A lady must show dignity."

"I want to look at him," Arlette replied. "If I don't like him, I don't have to marry him—Papa said so. Perhaps he won't like me either."

"Orson Greywell will fall in love the moment he sets eyes on you," Esme said.

Arlette snorted. "He'll shackle me to the marriage state, to service him as a wife must. The moment I utter my vows he'll demand I surrender my sword and replace it with an embroiderer's needle."

"He may not. After all, your father permitted you to train with his men as if you were a son."

"Until Guillaume's birth gave him that son. Now, I'm reduced to chattel—to be sold in marriage."

"Be thankful your father values you enough to seek your opinion," Esme said. "Your mother didn't have that luxury—widowed during Duke William's conquest, forced to marry the man who'd killed her husband..."

"Mama loves Papa," Arlette said.

"Perhaps now," Esme replied, "but at first, he was her conqueror, and she the spoils of war. Be thankful you'll not suffer as she did, on *your* wedding night."

*The wedding night...*

Arlette shivered as bright, painful red flashed across her mind's eye —droplets falling to the sound of screams, a blood-soaked nightshift, the white face of a young bride, twisted with fear while the baying crowd congratulated the man who violated her...

Raised voices echoed across the hall, followed by angry footsteps. Papa came into view, followed by a tall gray-haired man, and a younger man with thick black hair that fell to his shoulders.

The young man tipped his head up and Arlette shrank back into the shadows. His muscular build was evident beneath his tunic. A slight shadow of a beard dusted his firm, square jaw, above which a straight nose defined his features, flaring slightly at the nostrils.

His eyes—a clear gray—radiated sharp, angry intelligence, and Arlette's breath caught in her throat. What might those eyes look like when he smiled?

"We've never been so insulted!" a deep voice roared.

"Neither have *I*, Lord Wulfson," Papa said, his voice shaking with anger. "You deceived me! I will not shame my family by wedding my daughter to a bastard, particularly one who's already fathered a bastard child himself!"

The young man drew his sword, and Arlette let out a cry.

"Be silent!" Esme hissed. "Do you want a thrashing?"

Lord Wulfson raised his hand. "Orson, stop! Apologize to Lord Reynaud."

"No, Father. He's insulted us." A rich, strong voice snarled in anger.

"The devil take you, de Villiers—and your daughter!" The young man sheathed his sword, then strode out of the hall.

"Forgive my son," Lord Wulfson said. "He does not take insults lightly."

Papa inclined his head.

"But," Wulfson continued, "I warn you, de Villiers. Cross my path again, and you'll pay for your insult. Few men call my son bastard and live. From this day, we are enemies."

Lord Wulfson followed his son out of the hall.

Arlette sighed. "It seems I'm not to be married today."

# CHAPTER 1

*Six years later*
*Leaside Hall, England, 1086*

ARLETTE LEANED over the unconscious young woman on the cot. Sweat glistened on her face. Eyes closed, her breathing came out in ragged gasps.

"Rosa's gravely ill, Esme. I cannot leave her."

"Your cousin was adamant you meet him by the stables at moonrise," Esme replied. "He said it was of the utmost importance."

Arlette let out a snort. "Let him rot!"

"Lady!" Esme exclaimed. "Why must you curse like a man?"

"Fulbert's a strutting peacock," Arlette said. "He only cares for land and wealth. Until Papa settled my dowry, Fulbert took no notice of me. He'd pull my braids and say I was a grubby wildcat whom no man would wish to marry."

"If you marry Fulbert, Villiers Castle will remain in the family."

"I don't want to marry Fulbert!" Arlette cried. "He's not like his father—God rest his soul. Uncle Alexandre was kind, but Fulbert has a cruel streak. He hardly mourned his first wife, and I have no wish to share her fate. Besides, Papa would rather I wed a Saxon."

"But you've found fault in every Saxon your father placed before you."

Esme was right. Arlette had rejected every suitor.

Except one—the young man she'd caught a fleeting glimpse of six years ago.

She closed her eyes to recall the image from her dreams—the tall, proud man, the warrior with the clear gray eyes that burned with intelligence and fury. Every suitor since had paled into insignificance—either preening fools caring only for lands and finery, or uncouth barbarians incapable of holding a conversation.

Was it too much to ask for a man who'd treat her as an equal?

"You could do worse than your cousin," Esme continued. "Your brother adores him."

"Guillaume's a child," Arlette said. "He knows nothing. Fulbert ingratiates himself by bringing him sweetmeats but has no genuine affection for my brother."

"Nevertheless, I beg you to meet with Fulbert. He's waiting."

"The devil take Fulbert!"

Esme frowned. "That tongue of yours will be your downfall one day."

"Not while I have my sword," Arlette said. She placed her hand on Rosa's forehead. "Her fever has lessened. The draught I gave her is working."

"Then leave her to my care," Esme said. "You've been tending to her all day."

"Perhaps I'll retire," Arlette replied. "But I won't meet Fulbert—and as you know, Esme, I always have my way."

Esme let out a sigh of exasperation and Arlette exited the room, then climbed the stairs to her chamber.

As she slipped into bed, she smiled to herself.

*Nobody—certainly not a man—will ever rule over me.*

ARLETTE OPENED HER EYES.

A sliver of moonlight stretched across her bedchamber. It was still night. Why had she woken?

She climbed out of bed, padded across the floor, and opened the door.

A clash of steel rang out followed by a familiar sound—a sound that was cut short.

Papa's battle cry.

A maidservant emerged from the shadows.

"Maude!" Arlette cried.

"Lady, we're under attack!"

"Lord save us! I must get to my sword."

"It's too dangerous," the maidservant cried. "They're all over the building—there's so many of them!"

A scream rang out from below.

"You've killed my lady!"

Arlette recognized the voice—Ivetta, Mama's personal maid.

"They're murdering my family, Maude!" she cried. "I heard Papa. Where's Guillaume?"

Maude broke into sobs, and Arlette pulled her into her chamber.

"Wait here," she said.

"You can't stop them, lady! You must get away."

"Run like a coward while my people are in danger?" Arlette cried. "Never! Do as I say—close the door and lock it. My sword's in the stables—I won't be long."

Maude nodded, and shut the door.

Arlette made her way along the passageway, slipping past the main staircase and keeping to the shadows. The smell of burning wood and smoke intensified as she reached the small spiral staircase, which led to the stableyard.

A male voice shouted from behind and footsteps clattered up the main staircase. Shortly after, she heard hammering on wood, then a splintering crash, followed by Maude's screams.

Without her sword, Arlette was no match for some murderous brute—but she couldn't abandon Maude to her fate.

She retraced her steps toward her chamber, her bare feet making no noise against the stone floor, looking for something—anything—to use as a weapon.

Then she saw it. A spent torch in a sconce on the wall—heavy enough to fell a man if she struck him in the right place. She plucked it out of the sconce and curled her fingers around the end, taking comfort from its solidity.

She might be a woman—but she was more than a match for some thick-skulled brute.

A soft footstep scraped from behind, but before she could turn, pain exploded in the back of her neck and she pitched forward into oblivion.

# CHAPTER 2

Orson surveyed the destruction. Flames curled around the building, and a plume of black smoke smothered the air. The bodies of Lord Reynaud de Villiers and Lady Emmelina lay at his feet.

Vengeance was his—but at what cost? De Villiers deserved to die, but not the lady. A native Saxon, she was rumored to suffer from poor health. And though de Villiers was a murderous swine, he had, with his dying breath, pleaded for mercy for his wife. Orson had made a promise to the cur.

But that promise had been broken.

"Where's Ulferth?" he demanded.

"Here, my lord."

Ulferth stepped forward, his eyes gleaming with bloodlust. Orson eyed him with disgust. No man should relish taking the life of another —no matter how evil.

"I told you to not to harm the women!" Orson roared. "I made Lord Reynaud a promise that I'd spare his wife."

"You said the family was to be destroyed," Ulferth said, his tone sulky.

"Not the women! We're better than de Villiers."

A calming hand touched his shoulder. Pearce—his best friend.

"Now's not the time for recriminations, Orson," Pearce said. "You've had your vengeance for Verona. Let it lie. The Lady Emmelina suffered in life—perhaps in death she'll find peace."

"Where are the rest of the family?" Orson asked. "The daughter—the son?"

"They're not among the dead."

"And the living?"

"Only servants."

Orson cursed under his breath. The Lady Arlette and her brother must have fled like cowards, leaving their parents to die. To think—he'd almost been allied to that family!

"Are we ready to leave?" he asked.

Pearce nodded. "The servants are secure, and the men are loading de Villiers' possessions onto the carts."

One of his men emerged from the building, carrying a body of a woman. Soft chestnut curls hung loose around her shoulders, not quite concealing a dark stain at the base of her neck.

"God's teeth, Brand!" Orson cried. "Did you have to hit a defenseless woman?"

The woman had a delicate heart-shaped face, a small nose, and full lips. Her pale skin almost glowed in the moonlight. Her eyes were closed, but as Orson placed his hand on her cheek, a faint whisper of breath caressed the back of his hand.

She was alive.

A knot of regret tightened in his stomach—then he remembered Verona...

His beautiful, pure-hearted sister—her blackened, charred body lying twisted among the smoking ruins. Unrecognizable save for the ring on her right hand, hanging loosely on her finger where the flesh had melted in the heat of the fire.

Verona's murderer had left Orson a message. A signet ring lying beside her body, bearing the de Villiers crest and a single stone set in gold, which winked malevolently at him as he'd roared with pain, crying over her desecrated body.

His palm itched at the memory of the raw earth on his skin as he dug Verona's grave with his hands.

He would never love another.

Not even Kendra.

Like all women, his leman was cold, heartless, and hungry for power. She'd shown an unnatural relish in the brutality of his plans for revenge on the de Villiers family, spreading her legs while he pounded into her, seeking release from the pain. But he'd found nothing but emptiness. Body spent, his soul craved the love and goodness he'd only ever seen in his beloved sister.

The girl in Brand's arms let out a groan and Orson fingered a curl of her hair.

Kendra be damned—it was time to replace her. Perhaps this pretty little thing might oblige.

"Bind her wrists and put her with the others," he ordered. "We leave immediately."

## CHAPTER 3

The ground shifted beneath Arlette and she turned her head, wincing at the stab of pain in her neck. She opened her eyes and blinked at the sunlight.

"Lady, thank the Lord you're alive!" Esme's concerned face swam into focus, and she helped Arlette to sit.

They were in a cart, along with a number of maidservants from home, surrounded by men on horseback with no hope of escape. Rosa's unconscious form lay in a corner, Maude sitting beside her. In another corner, Ivetta sat sobbing, two others comforting her. All the women's hands were bound—even Rosa's.

A second cart moved ahead, laden with trunks and bundles. Whoever these brutes were, they'd ransacked her home.

"What happened?" Arlette asked.

"H-he smashed down the door!" Maude sobbed. "He was enormous! He demanded to know where you were but I told him you'd escaped."

"What of my family?"

Esme shook her head. "I'm sorry, little one," she said. "You must be brave. Lord Reynaud and the Lady Emmelina were killed."

A cold hand clutched at Arlette's heart.

"Mama…" she whispered. "Dear Lord—no!"

"Hush!" Esme hissed. "If they discover your identity, they'll kill you."

"What of Guillaume? Did they kill my brother also?"

"I've not seen him."

"Then we must hope he's alive."

Most of Arlette's companions were crying—helpless, shivering creatures. They needed a show of strength.

She called out to the nearest rider.

"You there!"

"Lady, no!" Esme hissed.

The rider turned his head. "What do you want, wench?"

Arlette gestured toward Rosa. "This woman is ill. Unbind my hands so I can tend to her."

"Be silent!"

"I will not!" she cried. "What manner of cowards are you—to murder a family under cover of darkness?"

"Cease your prattle or I'll slit your throat!" The man drew his sword, and Arlette forced a laugh.

"Miserable creature! You're no man, if you threaten unarmed women!"

"Silence, back there!" A voice roared from ahead. "Brand—come to the front, if you can't keep those wenches in order!"

Arlette sat back, her objective achieved. Her companions now looked at her with hope, rather than blind terror.

"Have faith," she said. "I'll protect you. If they were going to kill us they would have done so already. Let us conserve our strength while I consider what to do."

Slivers of gray bled across the sky as they reached their destination—a large, impenetrable fortress that dominated the skyline.

The gray turned to light blue, and an orange glow highlighted the outline of the castle as the sun's rays filtered through the battlements to cast shadows on the road. The temperature dropped as they rode into the shadow, across the drawbridge, and into the courtyard.

"Go to the stables," the leader barked, his voice thick with anger. "Ulferth, I'll deal with you later."

"Aye my lord." One of the riders rode out of the courtyard, his horse's hooves clattering against the cobbles.

"That's the man who broke down the door," Maude whispered.

"The one they call Ulferth?"

"No—the leader."

The object of their discussion rode toward them, lifting his visor to reveal eyes the color of cold steel.

"You all belong to me," he said, his voice resonating in the courtyard—a faint echo signifying his mastery, as if the walls agreed with their master. "You're mine by right of conquest as retribution for your master's crimes."

Arlette clenched her fist, but Esme placed a warning hand on her arm.

"Say nothing. 'Tis too dangerous."

Esme was right. Arlette's stomach churned with nausea and her head throbbed with pain. Unarmed, she was no match for him. But armed…

She kneeled up, to get a better view of the other cart. Was her sword there?

The man turned his head toward her, then removed his helmet.

Arlette found herself looking at the face that for the past six years had dominated her dreams—clear gray eyes framed by strong features—a face more handsome than she had remembered.

It was the face of the man she'd secretly hoped would return to her life one day. But in a single night, her hopes were crushed.

The man who'd killed her parents was Orson Greywell.

Orson dismounted, and gestured to his men.

"Take the women to the chamber in the east wing and lock them in. Jarvis, Dudley—carry the woman who is sick."

The men obeyed and two more ushered the rest of the women out of the cart.

Pearce dismounted and joined him.

"'Tis done," Orson said. "I've had my vengeance."

"Aye, my friend," Pearce replied, "but will it lie heavy on your conscience?"

"De Villiers murdered my sister!" Orson cried. "What did he expect, if not retribution?"

"You once sought an alliance with de Villiers, through marriage."

"It was Father's wish, not mine," Orson said. "I've heard tell the Lady Arlette is a hellcat—unladylike, ill looking. And a coward—she fled, along with her brother. If I ever lay my hands on them…"

"Orson, you've had your revenge. You've killed Verona's murderer and claimed his possessions. Let that be the end of it." He placed a hand on Orson's arm. "It's time for the Bear to take his meal. I'll deal with the women later."

"Very well," Orson said. "Let us break our fast and celebrate our conquest."

PAIN RADIATED from Arlette's neck and she groaned. After cutting their bonds, their captors herded the women, as if they were cattle, into a large chamber, which was empty save for a solitary torch mounted on the wall.

A beam of sunlight stretched across the floor. Dust motes swirled in the sunbeam, dancing to a slow, malevolent rhythm as cold air circulated around the chamber, intensifying the ache in her bones.

"Have faith, Esme," Arlette said. "We'll be back at Leaside within a sennight."

Esme shook her head. "The building was in flames. All the men were killed—Leaside is no more."

Arlette's chest tightened as a wave of sorrow rippled through her.

"My home," she whispered, shaking her head. "Why?" She lifted her head and screamed. "Murderous bastards!"

"Hush!" Esme hissed. "Do you wish to be killed? We don't stand a chance against Lord Wulfson." Esme gestured toward two maidservants from home, huddled in a corner—girls who'd seen little more than ten summers. "Mylla and Giselle are terrified of him."

"Then he's a coward, to terrorize children!" Arlette cried. "What have we done to merit such cruelty?"

She shook her head to dispel the image that invaded her dreams—a face with a strong brow, square jaw, and those cold gray eyes...

"'Tis *him*," she said, "the suitor Papa sent away on account of him being a..." she lowered her voice, "...a *bastard*. That must be why he's done this. His father declared Papa his enemy."

Esme shook her head. "This has naught to do with an insult spoken six years ago. He must have another reason—and until we know what, we must keep your identity hidden. Be thankful he knows not that you're the Lady Arlette."

"I cannot hide like a coward," Arlette said. "I must fight."

"You're not a knight going into battle," Esme replied. "You're a woman—prisoner of a man with an army of soldiers at his beck and call. You cannot fight him."

"Then what must I do?"

"Perhaps Lord Fulbert..."

"I'll *not* throw myself on Fulbert's mercy. I'd rather take my chances here."

"Then, the Lady Arlette has no choice but to die."

Cold fingers caressed the back of Arlette's neck at Esme's words. "What do you mean?"

"There is no one as free as a dead man," Esme said. "If Wulfson believes you're dead, then you're safe. To survive you must become one of us—a maidservant—and control your temper."

The notion of skulking in the shadows was not to be borne—but Esme spoke sense. Rather than succumb to the urge to kill their captor, Arlette needed to be patient—to plan a strategy. A warrior used his mind more than his body. He—or she—acted rationally, in order to secure victory.

Let Wulfson think he'd won, where, in reality, he'd only taken first blood.

"Very well," Arlette said. "I'll hide—wait—and plan. But the next blood to be spilled will be *his*. And I would see it flow from his veins to soak the walls of this godforsaken place!"

"Hush!" Esme hissed.

Footsteps approached, followed by the metallic scrape of a bolt drawing back. The door swung inward to reveal the silhouette of a man.

Arlette's skin tightened as he moved into the light. He was tall, with shoulder-length light brown hair and a scar across his right cheek. His mahogany eyes betrayed discomfort—perhaps some of their captor's men disapproved of the slaughter of innocents.

"You are all the property of Lord Wulfson," he said. "Serve him well and you'll be treated fairly. Disobey, and the punishment will be severe. To ensure you don't escape, each of you is to be shackled."

"No!"

Shaking off Esme's warning hand, Arlette scrambled to her feet. The man stepped forward, and his gaze lingered on her face before lowering to her chest, a spark of lust igniting in his eyes.

She bristled with rage—how dare he!

But he thought her a servant. Most likely he considered himself entitled to look at her in any manner he pleased.

"What do you want, wench?"

"Do not shackle us."

"It's for your safety," he said. "If you try to escape, you'll be hunted down and killed—along with your companions."

Arlette's stomach clenched at the steady calm in his voice. "I give you my word of honor that none will escape," she said.

"Your *word of honor*?" His mouth curled into a grin, and she bit her lip to control her fury.

He was mocking her.

"Our home is destroyed," she said. "We have nowhere to go." She gestured toward her companions. "Look around. Some of these women are too old to run—others too young. And if any of them try to escape, I will bear their punishment myself."

His eyes widened with a flash of admiration, then he reached out his hand and touched her cheek.

"What is your name?"

Arlette hesitated. "My name is Heloise."

"What position did you hold that entitles you to speak for the others?"

"Personal maid to the Lady Arlette."

"You're bold for a servant," he said, "but you speak well. I'll consider your request."

"Might I know *your* name?"

"Impudent wench!" he exclaimed, but a smile curled on his lips. "My name is Pearce."

"Then, Pearce," she said, "tell your master, Pearce, that it's dishonorable to send another to shackle eight frightened women locked in a chamber."

He shook his head, as if in exasperation, then retreated through the door, closing it behind him. His footsteps faded into the distance, muffled by the scrape of the bolt sliding into place.

AN OWL SCREECHED outside as Orson crept along the passageway. At least the other screeching had faded—the curses of a woman, high-pitched tones calculated to cut through a man's mind like a knife through flesh.

Why did women plague a man with their demands that he do this —or that—to please them? A real woman would know her own mind and take what she wanted, openly and honestly.

And he was sorely in need of a real woman, even if such a creature did not exist among the whores and hellions.

Then why was he here—creeping about his home in the middle of the night? It wasn't just to avoid Kendra, with her too-willing body and her incessant demands...

It was to catch a glimpse of a far more delectable creature. As a lion stalked his prey, Orson relished the notion of drinking in the sight of his quarry—before he devoured her.

A tall shape emerged from the darkness.

Pearce.

"What the devil are you doing," Orson asked, "creeping about at night?"

"I could ask you the same, my friend."

"But *I'm* lord here."

Pearce laughed. "That you are. Very well—one of the prisoners bade me bring her supplies."

"She sent you on an errand? Insolent wench! And you're a fool to do it."

"She only wanted herbs and bandages—to tend to the others."

"Show me."

Pearce led him to the chamber, acknowledging the sentry with a nod. Orson peered through the barred opening in the door. Most of the women were asleep, but one tended to the others. She bandaged the wrists of an old woman before pressing a cloth to the forehead of another woman lying on the floor, who seemed to be suffering from some kind of fever.

"Is that the one who made all the demands?" Orson asked.

The woman turned her head at the sound of his voice, and he caught a flash of emerald eyes in the candlelight.

"Aye, that's her," Pearce said. "Spirited little thing."

"What's her name?"

"Heloise."

"Heloise..." Orson whispered. "Return to your quarters, Pearce."

Pearce let out a chuckle.

"Is something the matter, Pearce?"

"I know you too well, my friend." Pearce resumed his attention on the girl. "I almost feel sorry for her. I suppose there's little point in asking you to be merciful?"

"I'm a man of honor, Pearce," Orson replied. "But mercy—that's a weakness I'll never succumb to."

"I suppose that must suffice." Pearce bowed, then took his leave, and Orson returned his attention to the wench. She'd finished tending to the others and was trying to press a cloth to the back of her neck. An older woman kneeled behind her and lifted her hair, exposing the wound on her neck, and his breath caught at the sight of the creamy smooth skin. He gripped the iron bars, the cold metal on his hands tempering the fire between his thighs. Even though Kendra waited in his bed, promises of pleasure on her lips, he had never hardened as quickly as he did watching something as simple as the application of a poultice.

"I will have you under my furs, Heloise."

"My lord?"

The sentry raised his eyebrows. Orson let go of the bars and returned to his bedchamber. His appetite for Kendra was all but gone, now he'd chosen her replacement.

# CHAPTER 4

A loud crash exploded in the air, dissipating the image that had comforted Arlette's dreams—Papa's smiling face as he placed her hand on the arm of her bridegroom. She rubbed her eyes, blinking in the morning sunlight that streamed through the window.

Her heart tightened in her chest as the object of her dreams stood in the doorway of the chamber she and her companions had been locked in all night.

Orson Greywell—Lord Wulfson.

Her captor.

Some of her companions jumped in fright, nudging the ones who still slept, though Rosa remained unconscious, a sheen of perspiration on her forehead.

The brute was trying to intimidate them. But she was a de Villiers, and wouldn't be cowed. She sat up and met his gaze. Esme shifted position, moving in front of Arlette, as if to shield her from view.

Then he spoke.

"As you are now my property, I would know your names, and the positions you held at your former master's house."

Arlette opened her mouth to speak, but Esme squeezed her hand in warning, then spoke first.

"My name is Esme, my lord. I am—was—the Lady Arlette's nursemaid. The woman over there is called Tilda. She worked in the laundry. The two youngest you see in the corner are Mylla and Giselle—kitchenmaids. Rosa, the one who's sick—and Maude, who sits beside her, worked in the house. The woman by the door is Ivetta. She was the Lady Emmelina's personal maid."

He stepped inside the chamber, then addressed Arlette.

"And your name, wench?"

"Her name is..." Esme began, but he interrupted her.

"I did not ask *you*, old woman."

He fixed his gaze on Arlette, and her stomach tightened at the cold intensity of his eyes.

"Your name," he growled.

"Heloise."

"Heloise, *my lord*."

She spat out her response. "My lord."

"What was your position?"

"Personal maid to the Lady Arlette."

"How old are you, Heloise?"

"I have seen twenty summers." She curled her lip into a sneer. "*My lord*."

He fisted his hands, and for a moment, she thought he was going to thrash her. Then he addressed Esme.

"Do you know the whereabouts of the Lady Arlette and her brother?"

"No, my lord, we were all abed when..." Esme broke off, eyes glistening with moisture.

"Shed no tears for that family. They got what they deserved. My chatelaine will assign your duties. Work hard, and you'll be treated well.

He pointed toward Rosa.

"What's wrong with her?"

"She has a fever," Esme said. "She's been ill for some days."

He gestured to the sentry. "Take her away, Watt."

"Where are you taking her?" Arlette cried.

"That's none of your concern," he said. "Do you want a thrashing? If you speak again, I'll drag you out of this room and beat you myself."

"She's not well," Arlette said. "Let me tend to her."

"God's blood, woman," he said. "You're either brave or a fool. Do not question your betters. Watt—get on with it."

The sentry lifted Rosa as easily as if she were a rag doll, then the two of them left the chamber, slamming the door behind them and securing the bolt.

"Curse him!" Arlette cried. "What right have they to treat us like this?"

"They've every right," Esme said, placing a hand on her shoulder. "We belong to them by right of conquest. We must hope he's a fair lord."

Arlette snorted. "You saw evidence of his fairness, Esme. What has he done to Rosa?"

"Lady, I know 'tis hard but, I beg you, show him respect if you want to avoid a beating."

"He wouldn't dare beat me!"

"You're Heloise, a serf—not Lady Arlette," Esme said. "Trust me when I say you do not wish to attract the lord's notice. When his chatelaine comes, try to act like a servant." She pulled Arlette close, her fleshy arms circling her with their comforting warmth. "Never did I think I'd counsel you to act less like a lady."

Esme's arms still embraced Arlette when the bolt drew back again, and a woman entered the room. She looked around thirty summers. Her fair hair was all but concealed under a servant's cap and she wore a brown woolen kirtle. A set of keys jangled against her thigh.

"Stand, all of you."

Her voice was stern but her face seemed kind. The seven women struggled to their feet.

"My name is Una—chatelaine of Greywell Castle. I'll assign your duties later, but first you must eat. Follow me."

"Where's Rosa?" Arlette asked.

"Your friend is being taken care of. Have no fear—she's in good hands."

"Thank you." Arlette forced a smile.

Una smiled back. "You have Lord Wulfson to thank. He's a fair master, if a little...stern. Serve him well and he'll show leniency."

As soon as Una's back was turned, Arlette pulled a face.

"Leniency indeed!" she said. "I'll make that bastard pay for what he's done to us."

~

THE PRACTICE FIELD bustled with activity. Anxious to defend his champion's crown at the forthcoming tournament, Orson needed the diversion of a good sword fight to take his mind off the wench.

He found Pearce chatting to Seaton, a newly knighted young man of nine and ten.

"Are you ready to demonstrate your prowess, Seaton?" Orson asked.

"I am, my lord, and eager to win the tournament."

Seaton's enthusiasm reminded Orson of a puppy. His youthful good looks—wavy blond hair, and clear blue eyes framed by long lashes—attracted the attention of women, though, as the fourth son of an earl, his lack of fortune would hamper his marriage prospects.

Seaton had proved to be a skilled fighter, but he lacked the killer instinct of a true warrior. The young whelp was too gallant for his own good, and in Orson's opinion Seaton needed a good hard fuck before he could call himself a man. Perhaps one of the new wenches would appeal to him.

But not Heloise.

*Heloise...*

Why did she invade his thoughts—with her eyes like emeralds, and hair like fire? Had she secured the attention of her former master Reynaud de Villiers? Or had he been too old when that lush body had begun to ripen?

Curse that family! Always they stained his thoughts. De Villiers was dead but where were his children? Cowards, the both of them—

fleeing like rats in the dark. The son was a mere child, but the daughter—the woman who'd spurned his hand—what of her?

Perhaps her maidservant—Heloise—knew something. She ought to be watched.

And he would enjoy watching her.

# CHAPTER 5

Arlette followed Una to the kitchens for her supper. Almost a sennight had passed since her arrival. She'd been assigned to the laundry, and the constant plunging of her hands into hot water had taken its toll on her skin. But most of the servants at Greywell had shown Arlette and her companions kindness, including two young women who gave her a liniment to soothe her skin.

A harsh voice spoke from behind.

"You! Fetch me a tray of sweetmeats and some wine."

Arlette turned and came face-to-face with a voluptuous ebony-haired beauty, dressed in blue silk. Large sapphire eyes glittered with spite, and full red lips curled into a sneer. Her beauty reminded Arlette of Fulbert—pleasing to the eye but barely concealing the ugliness within.

The woman stepped forward and slapped Arlette in the face.

"Insolent serf!" she spat. "You should curtsey before your betters. Una—teach this little whore respect. I suggest a beating."

Una bowed her head, and gripped Arlette's wrist. "I will, my lady. Forgive the wench. She's new here and has much to learn."

"That she does," the woman replied. "Have the wine brought to my chamber."

She cast a look of venom toward Arlette, then turned her back and disappeared in a flurry of blue silk.

Arlette rubbed her cheek.

"Do not anger the Lady Kendra," Una warned. "She has a vicious temper when not shown proper reverence."

A flutter rippled in Arlette's stomach. "*Lady* Kendra—is she Lord Wulfson's wife?"

"Nay, lass, though not for wanting. She's the widow of one of his knights who was killed in a jousting accident four years ago. She's the master's leman."

"His leman?" Arlette asked. "What is that?"

"Heavens be, girl, you are ignorant! She shares his bed. But a pretty girl like you is bound to catch his eye, so you must be careful. Kendra's a jealous woman."

Arlette wrinkled her nose. To think, she'd dreamed of him for six years! Not only was he a murderer—but a great rutting pig with no control over his baser needs.

On arrival at the kitchen, Arlette joined two of the Greywell servants, Elvia and Dawn, at the table laden with food—leftover scraps of bread, cheese, and cold stew. Una nodded to the woman in charge.

"Prepare Lady Kendra's usual tray, Freydis."

Freydis rolled her eyes. "I've enough to do preparing the servants' meal, without pandering to her."

Arlette reached for a hunk of bread and Elvia squealed.

"Oh—your poor hand!"

Dawn nudged Arlette. "You should ask Una to reassign you. Weren't you a lady's personal maid? Perhaps you can share Hilda's duties and tend to the Lady Kendra."

Elvia snorted. "You think Hilda would accommodate another? She's Kendra's favorite and sees herself as too important for the likes of us."

"I've no wish to have anything to do with Kendra," Arlette said. "I'd rather rot in the laundry than spend a single day tending to that unpleasant creature."

"Heloise!" Una's sharp voice interrupted Elvia's laughter. "Do not speak ill of the Lady Kendra. Elvia, you shouldn't encourage her by gossiping about Hilda."

Una took Arlette's hand and inspected it, tutting at the blisters.

"Perhaps I should reassign you to the sewing room. Would that suit you better?"

Arlette nodded.

"I expect you to work hard," Una said. "We'll be very busy during the tournament next month, and the master cannot afford to take on extra hands now he's having to keep all of you."

Una's words shattered Arlette's mirth. If the Brute hadn't attacked her family home, none of them would be here. Curse him!

She voiced her anger to Esme in the maids' bedchamber when the others were asleep.

"Una spoke the truth," Esme replied.

"How dare you speak so!" Arlette hissed. "You and the others have settled here too quickly. Have you forgotten what brought us here?"

"We're treated well."

"My hands are raw, and my body aches."

"Only because you're unused to work," Esme said. "Matters will improve as you adapt."

"I don't want to adapt! I want to go home."

"This is your home now."

"It is not, and it never will be," Arlette said, choking back tears. "That brute has destroyed my family. What right has he to do this to us?"

"He has the right of a man. We are merely women—servants."

"I'm as good as any man, Esme. Did I not pledge to protect my brother as any knight would? While there's a chance Guillaume still lives, I must find him."

"You're just a woman," Esme said. "If you don't wish to place yourself under Fulbert's protection, you would do better to accept your position here as a servant."

"How can you be so unfeeling?"

Esme sighed. "I lived through the conquest, Lady Arlette, when the

Normans smashed our homes, killing the men and disposing of the women in any manner they saw fit to satisfy their base desires. I saw ladies and servants alike raped, degraded, and sold into slavery. Your fate is better than theirs. If you wish to leave I cannot stop you, but I'll not go with you."

"I cannot leave you."

"Then, you must make a choice—" Esme's voice grew stern, "—to live as Heloise, or die as Arlette."

"Lord Wulfson wouldn't dare lay a finger on me!

"He would, lady. He's driven by revenge. Freydis has told me much of him. He has been wounded many times in battles and skirmishes defending his properties but always came out victorious. A master tactician, his swordsmanship is unsurpassed and he's the most magnificent…"

"Spare me, Esme," Arlette interrupted. "I've no wish to know of his attributes. My only interest in him is whether his throat would open should I take a knife to it."

"Lower your voice!" Esme hissed. "Such words could have you killed."

Arlette sighed. "Why does he hate my family?"

"I know not, but he must have a reason."

"What reason?"

"We may never know." Esme's voice grew weary. "Forgive me for my harsh words, little one. I want you safe and happy, but if you're to survive, then you must accept that your old life is over. Sleep now—you need your strength."

Arlette closed her eyes and lay back. What had her family done to merit such vengeance?

As she drifted into sleep, an image floated before her mind's eye of a tall warrior facing her in battle, his strong, hard muscles flexing as he wielded his sword against her. Lifting his visor, he revealed a pair of gray eyes. Their gaze rendered her arms powerless as he drew her to him and began to remove her armor…

She woke with a start, biting her lip to banish the dream.

*He has destroyed my family. I hate him—hate him!*

Orson sat in his study with his steward when one of the new maidservants appeared, carrying a tray of wine. A pretty creature, she smiled seductively as he motioned her closer.

The new wenches seemed content with life at Greywell Castle. Wars and feuds had little impact on servants. They cared nothing for politics, and their loyalty lay with whoever gave them food and shelter.

Kendra's enthusiastic attentions since their arrival didn't fool him. Her jealousy festered—rot within a tree spreading from within though the tree stood tall and proud.

The steward eyed the wench hungrily.

"Have a care, William," Orson said. "Una wouldn't approve."

William colored, pouring the wine before handing a goblet to Orson. "Una and I enjoy a tumble or two, that's all."

"Women are all soft lips and caresses at first," Orson said, "but spark the flame of jealousy and you'll find your wine poisoned."

William took a draught from his goblet. "Una's not the jealous type, my lord. Mayhap you speak from your own experiences. Mistress Kendra is not the type to share."

"The wine makes you bold," Orson said.

"Wine is a great leveler," William replied. "It elicits the truth from those who would otherwise soothe and flatter. A man has no place for a jealous woman in his bed—he should send her away."

William spoke the truth. Kendra had to go, and only he, or perhaps Pearce, would dare give such counsel.

"What has Una told you of the new wenches, William?" Orson asked. "Do they give her trouble?"

"They seem content, though there's one who's unused to hard work and averse to taking orders. She's already experienced the back of Kendra's hand."

"Which one?"

William lowered his gaze. "It matters not. She'll get used to the way of things here, and..."

"Which one, William?"

"Do not beat her."

"I'll do with her what I like. Disrespect should be punished."

Orson drained his goblet, rose, and left in search of Una.

He found her in one of the guest chambers, a pile of linen in her arms.

"Mistress Una, show me the wench who gives you trouble."

"My lord?"

"William tells me there's one who does not care to be given orders."

Una's eyes widened. "She's not as capable, my lord, but if she did anything to merit a beating, I'd tell you."

"Just show me her."

Una set the sheets down and led him to the kitchen. His skin tightened in anticipation as she pointed out the wench.

It was Heloise.

She leaned over the thick, wooden table, scrubbing the surface, while Freydis directed preparations for the evening meal. Though she wore the same dress as the lowest ranking servants, an air of nobility shimmered around her form as her arm moved in graceful sweeps across the table.

A slight flush bloomed on her cheeks, perhaps from the exertion of her task or the heat in the kitchen. A curl of chestnut hair fell out of her cap. Sighing, she stopped to tuck it back in. Then, as if sensing his presence, she lifted her head and looked directly at him.

A shiver crackled at the base of his neck, radiating down his spine.

Those eyes! A deep, clear green—wide and expressive, framed by long lashes, they radiated a sharp, regal intelligence. His breath caught in his throat and heat shot into his loins, hardening his manhood, which strained against his breeches. She lowered her gaze and resumed working, but her stance had changed. Her body tensed, like the string on a longbow before the arrow is released. The slight tremble in her arms, and those lovely full lips pressed firmly together, belied her calm exterior. An air of mystery surrounded her.

She was no ordinary wench.

"Do you want me to have her beaten, my lord?"

Una's whispered voice brought Orson out of his lust-fueled dream.

"No."

Shaking his head, he left the kitchen. Rather than tame the wench at the whipping post, he wanted to tame her in his bed.

CARRYING A PILE OF LINEN SHEETS, Arlette found herself in an unfamiliar passageway. Greywell Castle was at least twice the size of Leaside. Its walls mostly unadorned save for the great hall, all passages looked alike, and Arlette had little opportunity to explore the building —or plan her escape. She had never understood how hard servants' work was. Her companions had settled into life here with such ease as to be called disloyalty.

They were happy, even.

But Arlette was not.

Drunken laughter echoed from a nearby door, and she froze. She must be near the men's quarters.

She had no wish for their disgusting attentions, but her companions weren't so fastidious. Only yesterday, she'd seen Rosa batting her eyelids at one of them—the same man who'd threatened to shackle them all.

Curse them! Why did they not hate it here as much as she?

A door opened behind her, and she quickened her pace. Her foot caught on a flagstone and she tripped and dropped the pile of laundry. Cursing, she crouched to pick it up.

"May I help you?" A male voice spoke.

A young man stood in front of her. Soft blond hair framed a handsome face with mild features and clear blue eyes that crinkled as he smiled.

"I need no help," she said, standing.

"Please? I have little opportunity to be chivalrous to a pretty girl."

His accent spoke of breeding—a nobleman, perhaps. But a man nonetheless, and therefore to be avoided.

"Flattery will not work on me," she said. "I want nothing to do with the lecherous louts who reside in this godforsaken place."

She expected a cuff, or at the very least a harsh word, but he merely offered his services again.

"Did you not hear my refusal, cloth head?"

He merely laughed. "If my head's made of cloth, then I'm best placed to help you fold a sheet of the same substance. Ah—a smile!" he cried as her lip curled involuntarily. "Then you accept my offer."

Before she could respond, he crouched before her and picked up the laundry.

"Might I know your name?" he asked.

"Heloise."

"You are very beautiful when you smile, Heloise."

"I said flattery wouldn't work," Arlette said, "and I have no reason to smile here. Lord Wulfson is a brute."

He raised his eyebrows.

Might he beat her? Or worse—take her to Lord Wulfson?

Then he smiled.

"Lord Wulfson is built for battle, mistress, and little else. But I hear he's a fair master. The servants are happy here."

"Not I."

"Then perhaps you need a friend." He took her hand and she snatched it free.

"Is this your attempt at seduction?"

He shook his head. "You've naught to fear from me—I'm not like the other men. And you're not like the other maidservants. What position did you hold in your previous master's household?"

Inwardly she cursed herself for having attracted his curiosity. "Personal maid to the Lady Arlette."

"I see," he said. "It was a pity Lord Reynaud and his wife were killed."

"You know that for certain?"

"I saw their bodies."

His words destroyed any vestiges of hope she harbored that they might still be alive, and tears blurred her vision.

"What of their son, Guillaume?" she whispered. "Did you see his body also?"

"No, he's disappeared."

The flame of hope resumed its glow and she wiped her eyes.

"You do not ask about their daughter," he said, after a pause.

Then he took her hand again. "If I were in correspondence with the Lady Arlette, I'd counsel her to remain hidden, at least until Lord Wulfson's thirst for revenge has waned."

She tried to withdraw her hand, but he pulled her close.

"Fear not," he whispered, "I'll not speak of our conversation. You have a friend here."

Her emotions swirled into a maelstrom of hatred for Orson Greywell. One day he would suffer for his crimes.

Perhaps, in this young man, she had an ally she could trust with her identity.

"Might I know the name of my friend?" she asked.

He bowed. "Seaton, at your service."

"I'm glad to have a friend, Seaton."

He lifted her hand to his lips and kissed it. A warm sensation spread through her veins. His eyes darkened, pupils dilating as he clasped her hand, fingers curling around her wrist. Kind, gallant, and genteel—perhaps he might become more than a friend.

But first, she needed to plot her revenge.

~

ORSON REACHED for his goblet and eyed it appreciatively as one of the wenches filled it. Then he motioned her to leave the pitcher at the table. Like a good woman, some wines were not for sharing among his men. Murderous bastard de Villiers may have been, but he had an excellent taste in wine, and several casks of the stuff to keep Orson in his cups for many months.

The sound of his household eating and chattering echoed around the great hall as the meal began. Pearce sat on his right and the other knights, including Seaton, occupied the places at the top table.

The knights' wives and Orson's leman sat at the next table, followed by the squires, then finally the senior servants such as Una and William, while the lowest ranked, such as the maidservants from Leaside, waited on the diners.

He took a mouthful of wine, and almost choked at the bitter taste. Bile rose in his throat and his body convulsed as he spat out the liquid in a spray of red.

Pearce thumped his back. "Has the wine turned sour?"

"No, damn it, 'tis salty!" Orson emptied the goblet on the floor and inspected the dregs.

"God's blood, the wine's been loaded with salt!" he roared. "Someone shall pay with their head for this! Bring Freydis here —now!"

A hush descended over the company, as a servant scuttled off. When he returned with Freydis, she cowered in front of Orson. A small group of servants huddled in the doorway, and Orson caught a glimpse of a pair of bright emerald eyes, glittering with mischief.

He heard a snort to the left. Seaton stared at the servants, a smile on his lips.

"Does aught amuse you, Seaton?"

Seaton shook his head. "No, my lord."

Orson rose to his feet and addressed the company.

"Someone has ruined my wine," he said. "Rest assured, I shall find out who, and have them whipped raw. I value loyalty and honesty above all. If the culprit sees fit to confess, I'll show leniency. But if not —then let it be known that I am not a man to leave an insult unpunished."

# CHAPTER 6

"The master watches you, Heloise."

Arlette looked up from her mending. Her stomach clenched in fear.

Did he suspect her?

She cursed her impetuousness at dumping a handful of salt in the Brute's wine—a wine that had been Papa's. It had been a foolish act born of anger, fueled by Seaton's words.

A warrior should fight for her freedom—not skulk in the shadows playing childish tricks. If only she could find her sword she would best the bastard and bring him to his knees.

But Elvia's words alarmed her. For the past two days she'd been plagued by a sense of being watched—her skin had prickled with it.

"How do you know he watches me?" she asked.

Elvia chuckled. "Last night, during the meal, he couldn't take his eyes off you. You'll be warming his bed soon."

"About time he replaced Kendra with another," Dawn said, looking up from her work. "Though I'd rather it were me. I had to submit to Ulferth the other night and took little pleasure from it."

Arlette's stomach tightened with nausea. "Do the men here take the servants for their pleasure? That's horrific!"

"It's what happens," Elvia said, "It is mostly pleasant, and we're at liberty to refuse—though none of us would refuse the master if he were to ask."

Dawn let out a giggle. "He is handsome, and I'll wager he's very large in girth!"

"What do you mean—girth?" Arlette asked.

Dawn lowered her voice to a whisper. "His manhood—that which resides between his legs—to give us pleasure between ours."

A rush of heat flooded Arlette's cheeks and Elvia squealed with laughter. "Oh, Dawn! I do believe she's never been tumbled. A pretty thing like you? How many summers have you seen?"

"Twenty," Arlette said. "A woman should only lie with her husband."

Elvia snorted. "Not the likes of us. It happens when the man wants it to. But, perhaps, for your first time, we can find you a considerate lover—such as Pearce, or Seaton."

"Seaton?"

"He'd be gentle in bed," Elvia continued, "though we'd have to instruct him on what goes where." She burst into laughter.

"Speak no more of it!" Arlette shook her head, unable to dispel the image of the bloodstained bridal gown from her mind. "It won't happen to me."

"Aye it will, and you'll feel much pain the first time."

"Don't frighten her, Dawn," Elvia chided.

"'Tis best she knows. But if she's a maiden, the master will wish to take her first."

"I'll not let that savage near me!" Arlette cried.

"Lord Wulfson's no savage," Elvia said. "He's a fair master—fair, and loyal. But he's driven by vengeance. Any transgression and he retaliates tenfold." She lowered her voice to a whisper. "He was born the wrong side of the blanket—his mother was a whore. When one of his squires made reference to it, he earned ten lashes. The master administered them himself before sending the squire back to his family."

"That's barbaric! Did they not retaliate?"

"Against Lord Wulfson? Nobody would challenge him or seek to anger a man of his reputation—the man who single-handedly wiped out the men who killed his father."

"His father?"

"Aye," Dawn said. "Two of the old master's allies laid siege on the castle five summers ago, killing him. The west wing is still in ruins. The master wouldn't rest until both were dead. He seized their estates and handed them over to the king. I heard the people of each household were sold into slavery as punishment for their masters' treachery. The women he set free, but the men—even young boys—were not so fortunate."

*Dear Lord—Guillaume!* Arlette's brother was out there somewhere—lost, and alone, if not already dead. What might the Brute do, if he found him?

"He's a strong warrior," Elvia continued, unable to disguise the admiration in her voice. "Undefeated in battle. You'll see for yourself at the tournament."

"The tournament?"

"Aye—to be held in a sennight," Dawn said excitedly. "The master holds it every year for his men, though he wins it every time. You'll see for yourself—he always lets the servants watch."

"Perhaps not this year," Elvia said. "Kendra may forbid it. She'll want to sit by his side now the Lady Verona is dead."

"The Lady Verona?"

"The master's sister," Dawn said. "She died earlier this year. She visited one of his properties and her party never returned. We dare not ask about it. The master flies into a rage at the mention of her name. She's the only person he ever cared about. He has no love for his daughter."

"He has a daughter?" Arlette asked.

"Aye," Dawn said. "She keeps to her room. Hilda tends to her. Her mother tried to entrap the master into marriage, but she died in childbirth before she could succeed. The master only took the child in on Pearce's persuasion. He has no love for the poor girl. And, if he marries, her days are numbered. No lady would accept a bastard for a daughter."

"Neither would she accept a bastard for a husband," Elvia interrupted.

Arlette shivered. Poor child—to be so neglected! What had driven him to such cruelty? His child might be illegitimate, but so was he.

If Arlette's two friends were to be believed, Lord Wulfson's inability to secure a wife had been driven by his birth, not his reluctance. Too many fathers would refuse to wed their daughters to men born out of wedlock.

*Such as Papa.*

Had he not been born a bastard, she might, even now, have been the lady of Greywell Castle, rather than one of the lowest ranking servants. What might it have been like?

A stern voice interrupted her thoughts.

"What are you three doing?"

Esme stood in the doorway. "It's time for your meal. Freydis says if you don't come now, you'll go hungry."

Dawn and Elvia exited the sewing room. As she followed, Arlette caught Esme's sleeve.

"Esme, did Papa and his men take their—pleasures—on you, and the others?"

Esme's eyes widened. "Why do you ask?"

"The men here are at liberty to take any woman they desire."

Esme sighed. "It's their right."

"How can that be, Esme! Why did you not tell me?"

"'Tis the way of the world, lady."

Arlette closed her eyes but opened them again as the image of bloodstains rose before her, a shrill scream in her head.

"Would that I had my sword," she snarled. "None of them would dare approach me. I cannot believe Papa treated his servants in this manner."

"He treated your mother so," Esme said, her tone stern. "When he was first granted Leaside he took your mama unwilling, to seal his conquest and ownership of the estate and all the people therein."

“You lie!” Arlette cried.

“It’s time you opened your eyes,” Esme said. “Lord Reynaud held your mother down while she struggled and pleaded for mercy.”

Arlette shook her head, biting her lip to stem the tears. “I thought they loved each other.”

“Over the years, he grew to care for her,” Esme said, “and she forgave him. ’Tis the way of the world, little one. It’s how the men view their women.”

“I’ll not accept such a fate,” Arlette said. “I’d rather die in battle.”

Esme took her hand. “Then I pray your wish is never granted.”

# CHAPTER 7

While Orson dressed for the evening meal, the solar door opened and Kendra walked in.

The wench presumed too much. She might be fit for a good hard rutting, but after taking his pleasure, he always sent her back to her chamber. He had no wish to encourage her to strike roots in his bed.

When he eventually succumbed to matrimony, he'd treat his wife the same. To yield to a woman's demands was a weakness—and he was not a weak man.

"What do you want?" he asked.

Ignoring the warning in his tone, she crossed the threshold and pressed herself against his chest. Her nipples beaded into hard, insistent points, and she curled her lips into a seductive smile.

"I've seen how those new wenches look at you, my love," she purred. "They must be shown their place."

"Their place is where I say it is."

Her smile faltered. "One of them has shown me such disrespect—I should ask Una to dismiss her."

"Your duties don't extend to the household, Kendra," he said. "You undertake them on your back with your thighs spread."

She slipped a hand into his breeches, and squeezed his cock.

Shallow creature! Did she think him a fool? Jealousy in women produced such venom. Did Kendra not realize he'd seen the look of hatred in her eyes when directed toward the new wenches—particularly Heloise?

Mistaking his sigh of irritation for one of pleasure, Kendra stroked his length. Closing his eyes to banish the sight of her, he pictured the eyes of another. Not blue, but green—a rich emerald, sparkling with spirit. He hardened at the notion of conquering that spirit.

Encouraged by his reaction, Kendra continued to service him, nibbling his earlobe and whispering into his ear—using her body to seek control over him.

All women were the same. His stepmother had manipulated his father—parting her thighs in an attempt to rule him, while she neglected and abused Orson and his sister. She hated Orson for being the son she could never have, but her hatred for Verona—her own child—arose from pure jealousy.

*I'll be damned if I let a woman rule me!*

"My love, why would you seek the attention of those whores when I can give you every pleasure imaginable?" Kendra's voice, pitched low in an attempt to seduce, made his skin tighten in irritation.

If she thought she ruled over him she would be disappointed. After the tournament he would send her back to her family and let them deal with her.

He had fresh quarry to ensnare.

~

As she cleared the kitchen after the servants' meal, the familiar feeling of being watched prickled in Arlette's skin. Wanting a period of solitude, a brief moment of peace away from servants' gossip, she'd begged Freydis to permit her time alone in the kitchen. More than willing to give the last duties of the evening to another, Freydis had complied.

A cough came from behind, and she turned. A man stood in the doorway, his huge frame filling it almost completely.

Orson Greywell—Lord Wulfson.

A cold spark ignited his gray eyes as they met her own. Rubbing his chin, he yawned, stretching his arms before folding them, the muscles bulging, radiating raw male strength—the strength of a man trained for sword-fighting since birth. He looked relaxed, but a slight tremor betrayed him—his body, poised, ready for action—a predator waiting for his prey to move when he would spring forward and devour her.

His gaze moved along her body, and she stared back. The brief glimpses of him—from that first day, six years ago, to the snatched glimpses over the past month—had not done him justice.

He was even more handsome than she had first believed—a strong jawline, and the chin of a man who commanded obedience.

But those eyes! Framed by black brows, they pulsed with a primal power. They were the color of steel—harsh, unyielding as the blades from which the strongest swords are forged. They spoke of a man who took what he wanted, because none would stand in his way.

In short, he was magnificent.

Heat flooded her body, the echo of her reaction when she'd first set eyes on him. It intensified with each heartbeat, a burning heat coursing through her—a deep, base thrill in the pit of her stomach, pulsing as a treacherous voice spoke in her mind.

*If only Papa had not rejected him...*

A knowing smile spread across his face, and he inhaled, nostrils flaring, as if he could smell her desire.

She caught her breath, awaiting his next move. Would he take her into his arms? Fulfil the pleasures of her dreams?

Then he let out a chuckle. Before she could react, he turned his back, and was gone.

# CHAPTER 8

The following afternoon, Arlette found herself in the main hall, with orders from Una to sweep the floor and scatter it with fresh rushes. Though unused to housework, her arms were strong from sword-fighting training, making the task easier than she'd expected. An uneasy feeling of being watched slithered across her skin, though each time she looked at the doorway, it was empty.

The hall was enormous—at least four times the size of the main hall at Leaside—with a high, domed ceiling. Tapestries lined the walls, depicting battles and knights on horseback, and swords had been mounted in pairs on one wall.

After looking around to ensure she was alone, Arlette moved to inspect the swords more closely. There were six in total—functional, not decorative. She lifted the smallest and tested its weight, then she made a few practice swings, the blade whooshing as it swept through the air.

How good to hold a sword again! The blade was straight, and felt sharp when she tested it with her finger. The motif of a bear had been etched into the hilt, standing upright, claws outstretched, mouth open, revealing sharp teeth, as if roaring in triumph after making a kill.

The Bear. Esme had referred to that name when speaking of Lord Wulfson's prowess in battle. It suited him well. A huge beast—hostile, merciless, and with more muscle than brains.

Perhaps the sword had been his when he was younger. How fitting would it be to use his own sword on him to exact revenge! She returned the sword to its place, and resumed her task.

After scattering the last of the rushes, Arlette rubbed her aching back and groaned. Her limbs cried out for a bath—the warm baths she had relished at home, administered by Esme's gentle hands, the soft aroma of healing lavender in her nostrils…

She bit her lip to temper the sorrow. Her home was gone. Papa and Mama were no more, and there was nothing to be gained by grieving.

Vengeance would be her consolation.

A noise by the doorway made her skin prickle—a sigh, and a footstep.

Brandishing her broom, she moved toward the door. The passage outside was empty. Shadows danced in the light of candles that flickered in their sconces.

Halfway along, a wall hanging shifted in the breeze that constantly ran along the passageways of Greywell Castle. She would have to pass it on her way back to the servants' quarters. She moved toward it, then froze.

The tip of a boot poked out from beneath the hanging. Fighting the urge to attack its owner with her broom, she retreated, until she was far enough away for her footsteps to be inaudible. Then she fled in the opposite direction.

When she slowed to a walk, she found herself in an unfamiliar part of the castle. Large, ornately carved oak doors lined the wall. This must be the living quarters where the tournament guests would be staying. A twinge of jealousy gripped her. She would have made a fine competitor had she been born a man. Even jousting—though she lacked the stamina to hold a lance for more than one run—she could unseat an opponent. She'd once sent Garret flying, to his embarrassment and the amusement of the rest of Papa's men. What satisfaction she would take from unseating Orson Greywell!

The sound of crying came from behind one of the doors. Arlette stopped and held her ear against it. Pitiful sobs rang out, which ceased as soon as she knocked.

A small, thin voice called out.

"Who's there?"

Arlette opened the door. A child sat, alone in the chamber, beside the fireplace, holding a piece of cloth in her lap. Though her face was stained with tears, she straightened her back on seeing Arlette.

"What are you doing? The lesser servants are not allowed in this part of the castle."

The child's lip wobbled, betraying her distress.

Undeterred, Arlette entered the chamber. "What troubles my lady?" she asked.

"Nothing a servant can help with."

"I'm no ordinary servant, but a lady's maid." Arlette held out her hand. "May I see what you're doing?"

The child lifted the cloth. "'Tis no good. I cannot do it."

Arlette took the cloth and inspected it. The child had been trying to embroider a flower, with little success.

Arlette smiled to herself. Despite Esme's continued assertions to the contrary, there existed at least one lady in the world with even less talent for needlework than herself.

"Don't you enjoy embroidery?" she asked.

"No." The child sniffed. "Aunt Verona used to help, but I don't see her anymore. Nobody comes to see me except Hilda who brings my meals." She reached for the cloth. "Give it back. I don't want to do it anymore."

"A lady must learn to embroider," Arlette said. "Shall I show you?"

The child eyed Arlette thoughtfully. "What's your name?"

"Heloise."

"My name's Lillian."

"What a pretty name!" Arlette said. "How old are you?"

"I have seen eight summers."

"Where's your mama?"

"She's dead. Papa says I must not speak of her."

"Your papa?"

"Lord Wulfson. He doesn't like me."

The stricken expression in the child's eyes tore at Arlette's heart.

"I'm sure he loves you very much," she said.

The child's eyes filled with tears. "Aunt Verona loved me, but she's gone. When I ask Papa about her he shouts at me. *She* would have helped me."

"Then *I'll* help you," Arlette said. "May I sit?"

The child nodded. Arlette sat beside her, then picked up the needle and thread and began to work on the cloth with small stitches, fashioning a tiny flower. She'd never possess any real skill, having devoted such little time to needlework, but the child stopped crying, her big gray eyes sparkling with curiosity.

"What are you doing?"

"See if you can guess, before I finish."

The occasional sniff broke the silence while Arlette continued to embroider. Then, the child spoke again, her voice wavering with nerves.

"Heloise—what's a bastard?"

"Lillian!" Arlette cried. "Where did you hear such a word?"

"From Papa. He says I'm a bastard, but nobody will tell me what it means."

"That's not a word a lady should utter, Lillian."

"Please don't tell Papa!" the child cried. "He'd be so angry!"

Curse him for using such an ugly word in front of the child! Gritting her teeth, Arlette finished the flower, then returned the cloth to Lillian.

"It's so pretty," Lillian said.

"It's a lily," Arlette replied, smiling. "For you."

The child curled her fingers around Arlette's hand, and her solemn little face broke into a smile.

How could the Brute treat his daughter so cruelly! When Arlette considered how much she adored Guillaume—poor Guillaume, who was lost and alone, perhaps dead, at *his* hands. Yet Lord Wulfson cared nothing for his own flesh and blood—this lonely little girl, who wanted nothing more than to be loved.

"Have you no friends here, child?" Arlette asked.

"No," came the reply. "Would *you* be my friend?"

"I'll do better than that," Arlette replied. "I have a brother who's a similar age to you. I swore to protect him, and I offer you my protection and friendship also. I can be your knight."

Lillian giggled and Arlette tutted. "That's no way for a lady to behave, Lillian. You must say: 'I graciously accept your offer of protection, Sir Heloise.'"

At this, Lilian laughed out loud, and Arlette drew her into her arms.

A harsh voice spoke from behind, full of hatred.

"What are you doing here, slut?"

Lillian withdrew from Arlette's embrace, fear in her eyes.

Kendra stood in the doorway, her beautiful sapphire eyes glittering with contempt.

"Lillian, you'll not become a lady talking to that whore."

"But, Lady Kendra..." Lillian protested.

"Be quiet!" Kendra grasped Lillian's wrist and the child cried out. Arlette pushed Kendra aside.

"Leave her alone!"

Kendra released her hold on Lillian and backhanded Arlette across the face. Pain exploded in her nose and a telltale tickle of blood brushed her lip.

"Don't touch me—slut!" Kendra cried.

Arlette pulled Lillian behind her, shielding her from Kendra's spite. "Keep your hands off this child," she said coldly.

"How dare you!" Kendra screamed. "I'll have you whipped raw!"

Arlette stood her ground, and felt a small hand slip into her own. Emboldened by the child's trust, she set her mouth into a grim smile.

"Lay one hand on me, *Lady* Kendra, and I'll break every bone in it. Lay one hand on this child, and I will break every bone in your body."

Before Kendra could respond, the door smashed against the wall with a splinter of wood, and a deep masculine voice bellowed in rage.

"What the devil is going on here?"

Lord Wulfson stood before them, his expression dark with rage. Lillian whimpered in fright, and Arlette tightened her hold on the child.

Kendra reached out to him, softening her voice to a purr. "Orson, my love, I'm glad to see you," she said, her voice breaking with false tears. "I caught this slut stealing from the Lady Lillian, and she threatened to hit me."

His gaze settled on Arlette. "Did she, now?"

Kendra shot Arlette a look of triumph before turning her adoring gaze to Orson. "Aye, my love. You must punish her. I fear for my life!"

"Mayhap she deserves a beating," he replied. "Shall we ask her?"

"She wouldn't speak the truth, my love. Listen to *me*."

"I would know why my servant has a bloody nose."

"I had to defend myself." Kendra traced a line across his jaw with her finger, then reached up to kiss him on the lips. But he pulled away.

"Why do you not speak for yourself, Mistress Heloise?" he asked.

"It matters not what I say," Arlette replied. "A whore can use her body to persuade weak-minded men to believe whatever lies fall from her lips."

"Weak-minded?" His mouth set in a hard line, but amusement flickered in his eyes.

Undeterred, Arlette lifted her chin.

"Aye," she said. "'Tis weak minded to treat your child with such disregard. She deserves love and protection, not abuse at the hands of that insufferable creature who fawns over you."

"Why you..." Kendra raised her hand to strike Arlette, but Lord Wulfson caught her wrist.

"You've done enough to my servant, madam. Return to your chamber."

"My love..."

"Now."

Kendra scowled at Arlette, but retreated, her angry footsteps fading into the distance.

As soon as Kendra had gone, Lillian stepped forward, and held out the embroidered cloth.

"Heloise speaks the truth, Papa. She came to help me, to teach me to become a lady. I want her to stay."

"Is that so?"

Arlette nodded.

"Well then," he said, "that settles your punishment, Heloise."

A ripple of fear ran through Arlette.

"Punishment?"

"Aye," he replied. "In addition to your other duties, you shall teach the child how to become a lady."

"Thank you, Papa!" Lillian ran toward him, and wrapped her arms around his legs while he stood unmoving, his face grim.

Mumbling her thanks, Arlette bobbed a curtsey and scuttled out of the room to put as much distance between her and Lord Wulfson as possible. But she heard the door slam, and heavy footsteps followed her. Two large hands grasped her shoulders, turning her to face him.

"Not so fast," he growled. "We have unfinished business."

"What unfinished b…" Arlette's words were cut short as he pushed her back against the wall, and smashed his mouth against hers.

# CHAPTER 9

Orson pressed Heloise against the stone wall, passion ignited beyond his control.

Sweet Lord—the reality of kissing the wench far surpassed the anticipation.

Her servant's cap tumbled to the floor, freeing her hair, which he grasped with one hand, and buried his face in it, luxuriating in the silky softness. Then he kissed her again, more gently, and ran his tongue along the seam of her lips, begging leave to enter. He circled her dainty neck with his free hand and she stiffened, as if expecting him to crush the life out of her. But he merely wanted to affirm his mastery.

She was so unlike the other wenches—all fire and spirit, so rare in a woman! Perhaps she was of noble birth, reduced to servitude. He would need to employ different skills to master her. But he would succeed—he always did. Caressing her skin, he coaxed her into submission, until her body relaxed at his touch—the same body he'd seen toiling in the great hall earlier that afternoon, lust surging in his veins as she stretched her limbs, pushing her taut breasts outward, as if she knew he watched her and deliberately sought to tease him.

Aye, she recognized her master. He only had to play her body as expertly as Verona had played her lute.

He cupped a breast while he stroked her soft lips with his tongue, and was rewarded as a stiff little peak pressed insistently at her palm, and she molded her body to his. She parted her lips, and a silent roar of victory echoed in his mind as he slipped his tongue inside.

She wanted him. Her hands, which had pushed against him, now gripped his arms, and his manhood surged with eagerness to be buried inside her.

"Why deny your desire for me, my sweet wench?"

His words broke the spell. She stiffened, and pulled away, white-hot fury replacing the arousal in her eyes.

"I will never desire you," she hissed.

"Your body betrays you, Heloise," he said. "I can feel the passion within you. Let me release it."

"No!" she cried. "'Tis wrong—I'm a maiden."

Saucy wench! "You must cease this pretense at coyness, Heloise," he said. "I assure you, I'll prove a more competent lover than Lord Reynaud and his men."

"How dare you!" she cried, "My f—Lord de Villiers was a faithful husband. He'd never touch the servants in the disgusting manner which you and your men indulge in."

"Did he reject your advances, wench?"

She let out a howl, and wrenched herself free, He made no move to stop her as she fled, her sobs fading into the distance.

A mystery surrounded her. Until now, she had shown nothing but courage. How proudly she had stood in Lillian's room, protecting the child, defying his leman! Any other wench would have cowered in fear. He had no doubt she would have carried out her threat to break Kendra's bones had he not interrupted them.

Yet now, distress distorted her features—eyes bright with tears, brow furrowed in pain.

Was it grief? Had she warmed de Villiers' bed? Then why did she insist upon her maidenhead?

Whatever it was, she carried a secret. And he would find out what it was.

ARLETTE STOPPED RUNNING as a sharp pain stabbed at her sides, and she bent over, fighting for breath.

How dare he! Not content with causing Papa's death, the Brute sullied his name with tales of debauchery.

A hand caught her arm, and she let out a cry.

"Leave me be, you barbaric..."

"Heloise! 'Tis I."

Seaton stood before her, concern in his eyes.

"What's happened?"

She shook her head. "I cannot say."

Seaton's face colored. "Did someone try to...touch you?"

She nodded. "It's wrong how the women are taken against their will."

"The women here aren't taken by force, Heloise."

"Aren't they?"

"Shall I speak to Lord Wulfson?" he asked.

"No—I can look after myself."

He smiled. "I don't doubt it, but I can still offer you a knight's protection."

He offered his hand. "Let me escort a lady to her chamber."

He stomach flipped. *A lady...*

Did he know her secret? No—he was merely being gallant. She returned his smile, and took his hand.

"With pleasure, sir."

His hand was warm, but soft. The hand of a man of honor, a gentle soul. She couldn't imagine him pitched in battle.

"Sir..." she began.

"Heloise," he interrupted, "we're friends, are we not? Address me by name."

"Seaton," she said. "Why are you here? With *him*? You seem unsuited to his barbaric ways."

"I had little choice," he replied. "My father wished it, and Lord Wulfson taught me well when I was his squire."

"But you're so unalike! You are kind and chivalrous whereas he…"

"…is strict, and shows no mercy?" Seaton laughed. "He rules with a fair hand, but the losses he suffered have hardened his heart."

Then he sighed, his voice catching. "The Lady Verona is much missed."

"Verona?"

"Lord Wulfson's sister. He loved her very much."

"What happened to her?"

Pain flickered across his expression. "She was murdered, Heloise. Verona—the kindest, gentlest, most beautiful creature who walked upon the earth."

"You loved her," Arlette said softly.

"No." Seaton's eyes widened.

"Your face betrays you, Seaton. Does *he* know you loved her?"

"If he knew, he'd send me away. No man was ever good enough for her. No one is permitted to speak of her. It's as if she never existed. Even her chamber…"

"What of her chamber?"

Seaton sighed. "It remains untouched since she died—as if he waits for her ghost to return. He's decreed that no one may enter it, on pain of death."

"No one?"

"One of the manservants disobeyed, and Lord Wulfson had him whipped raw. He said the next person to enter her chamber—knight, or servant—would be hanged."

Moisture glistened in Seaton's eyes—the eyes of a man unable to mourn the woman he'd loved and lost.

Arlette took his hand. "I'm sorry for your loss—sorry that you suffer alone."

"I cannot help but think that had I married her, taken her away, she'd be alive today," he said. "I will not make the same mistake again."

He lifted her hand to his lips. "If I find another woman to love, whoever she may be, then whatever Lord Wulfson says, I swear I'll protect her with my life."

He brushed a stray curl from her forehead and pressed it to his lips.

"Whoever she may be."

Then, he bowed and took his leave.

# CHAPTER 10

As Orson returned from the practice field, Seaton fell into step with him.

"Your practice went well this morning, Seaton," Orson said. "If you get a good draw in the tournament tomorrow, you'll go far. Did you want something?"

Seaton coughed nervously. "I wish to make a petition."

"Which is?"

"One of the maidservants," Season said, blushing. "I want her."

"Ha!" Orson barked. "I'll make a man of you yet. Is she willing?"

"I believe so."

"Which one has caught your eye?"

"Heloise."

A surge of jealousy rippled through Orson, and he swallowed the desire to knock the young pup senseless.

"No," he said.

"My lord?"

"Not her. There are plenty of others to take your first tumble with.

"But my lord…"

"My word is final," Orson said. "Anyone but her."

He resumed his path to the castle.

"What if I were to marry her?" Seaton blurted out.

Orson roared with laughter. "Don't be a fool! You're a knight—the son of an earl. She's a servant. Neither your father, nor I, would permit it."

"I can petition my father..."

"That's enough!"

Seaton opened his mouth to argue, then closed it again and he bowed and left.

So, he wanted Heloise, did he? That pup, who'd never been fucked.

He needed to be taught a lesson in the game of seduction.

"My love."

His skin tightened with revulsion as a hand touched his arm. That coaxing voice, once so pleasurable, now grated on his nerves. He looked at her with distaste, taking in her gown—a new gown she'd insisted on having to celebrate the start of the tournament—which he'd granted only to silence her whining. Gaudy silks, so unlike the elegant simplicity of Verona's gowns.

"What do you want, Kendra?" he asked.

"Una tells me you're permitting the servants to watch the tournament."

"It's our tradition," he said, "and I'll not change it."

"The de Villiers servants should not attend," she said. "They've yet to earn the privilege. Some of them are lacking in respect."

Ah—there it was. Subtlety was never Kendra's strongest attribute.

"Do you refer to all of them, or has one in particular been unfortunate enough to secure your jealousy?"

She pursed her lips into a pout. "'Tis a small request for the woman who shares your bed..." she ran a finger along his cheek, "...for the woman you love—the lady of the castle."

He jerked away. "You expect too much, Kendra. You'll never be lady of Greywell Castle."

"But, Orson..."

"Enough!" he said. "I'll let you preside over the opening of the tournament tomorrow, but after that you must return to your family."

"My love..." Kendra's pleading grated his senses, her falsely seductive voice causing bile to rise in this throat.

"It's time you found a husband," he said. "I'll furnish you with a dowry in return for your—*services*."

"I want only you," she whined.

"I never made you any promise," he replied. "When you offered yourself, you knew I wasn't looking for a wife."

"Is it that whore?" she demanded. "After I've given myself to you—you wish to marry a kitchen slut?"

"I've no wish to marry at present," he said.

"What about pleasure? Nobody can give pleasure as I. You'll not want to let me go."

"I will, and I do," he replied. "Now leave me. I've much to do."

"I hear she lets all the men rut her," Kendra said, spite in her voice. "Do you want to fuck Ulferth's leavings?"

"Begone!" he roared.

"As you wish," Kendra said, a scowl making her features quite ugly. "But you'll regret sending me away. And so will she."

~

AFTER SPENDING the afternoon with Lillian, Arlette set off for the kitchen. Before she arrived, she spotted Hilda watching her.

"What do you want?" she asked.

Hilda merely smiled, then scuttled away.

Rumor had it Kendra was leaving Greywell Castle the day after the tournament began. With luck, Hilda would accompany her, and both Lillian's tormentors would be gone.

Poor Lillian! To think what she'd suffered at their hands. The child needed a mother, and Arlette would have enjoyed having her as a daughter.

Where had that notion come from? The idea of being married to that brute was abhorrent. How could he have sired such a charming child? Intelligent and articulate, Lillian was blossoming under Arlette's tutelage and learning to read. Her aunt Verona had been teaching her how to read—an occupation Arlette gladly continued. Though an unusual skill for a woman, Papa had seen fit to teach Arlette, and she saw no reason why Lillian shouldn't learn. It would serve the Brute right if his daughter were better educated than him.

Lillian spoke little of her aunt, having been forbidden by her father. But from what little she said, Verona must have been the epitome of kindness and gentleness. It also seemed that Kendra—not only content with trying to force her position as mistress of the castle since Verona's disappearance—had used Lillian for her own ends, giving Orson the impression she doted on the child, though she'd treated her with cruelty.

How like the Brute—to be blinded by his baser needs!

A thick shape emerged from the shadows to stand before her. Lost in her thoughts, Arlette didn't notice until he was upon her.

Ulferth.

A crude, heavily built man—known to beat his wife regularly—who rutted his way through maidservants and whores alike.

And he was the man rumored to have delivered the blow that killed Mama.

Arlette stepped aside, but he blocked her path.

"Get out of my way," she said, eyeing him with loathing.

"There's no need to be unfriendly," he said. "I'm come to give you favors."

"I want no favors from you."

She stepped back but he was too quick. He lunged forward and took her arm in a painful grip.

"You need a lesson in obedience, wench—a lesson in my chamber."

"I will not!" she cried, trying to wriggle free.

"Ah but you will, unless you want me to fuck you here, against the wall."

He grasped her neck and thrust his face close, forcing his mouth over hers. His thick tongue battered her mouth and she almost choked, her scalp burning as he gripped her hair. Groaning with lust, he ground his groin against her. Choking at the stench of stale sweat, she reached up and raked his face with her fingernails, but he held her firm. She bit down and tasted blood, and he released his grip, howling in pain. He grasped the front of her kirtle and she pulled away, the material ripping as she freed herself.

"You little whore!" he snarled. "You'll pay for that. No woman denies me."

Arlette ran for her life, Ulferth in pursuit, murder in his voice.

She rounded a corner and slammed into a solid wall of muscle. Strong arms took hold of her. Screaming, she tried to break free, but her captor was too strong.

"Heloise?"

She looked up into the gray eyes of Lord Wulfson.

"What is the meaning of this, Ulferth?" he demanded.

"I'm taking my turn with the wench."

Lord Wulfson lowered his gaze to Arlette's torn kirtle through which one breast was in full view.

"I'll not have my maidservants taken unwillingly, Ulferth," he said. "I don't condone rape in my household."

"Others have taken a turn with her," Ulferth grumbled. "Why not I? She was more than willing."

"The blood on her lips and scratches on your face say otherwise," Wulfson said. He spun Arlette around. "Does this look like a willing woman to you?"

Ulferth grunted. "She must learn to be willing."

Wulfson pushed Arlette behind him, then he stepped forward, meeting Ulferth eye to eye—a stag responding to the challenge of another male, asserting dominance over his territory—and all the females within.

"You're not a real man if you must take pleasure in a struggling woman," he snarled. "Doubtless her screams could be heard in the tourney field. I'll not tolerate that behavior."

"She needs to be broken in."

"Do not touch her!" Wulfson roared. "I'll break her in myself. Go back to your wife."

Ulferth stepped back, glaring at Arlette.

"Whore!" he hissed. Then he turned, and disappeared down the passageway.

Rubbing her arm, Arlette began to step away, hoping she could leave unnoticed.

"I've not given you permission to take your leave." He turned to face her. "Did he hurt you?"

She shook her head, unwilling to speak lest her voice betray her distress. He reached for her, eyes narrowing as she flinched, then he drew her close. Tipping her chin, he brought his lips to hers in a soft caress. A warm hand palmed her breast, and he sighed.

Her body, at first rigid with terror at the prospect of a brutal rape at Ulferth's hands, responded to the gentle caress. Instinctively she moved closer, her breast filling his hand as if it belonged there. He pinched her nipple between his fingers and she gasped at the jolt of pleasure that fizzed through her.

He moved his hand farther inside her kirtle and the sharp sound of the material tearing reignited the fear—both the fear of him, and of her body's response to his touch.

But why did it feel so natural—so pleasurable—to be in the arms of her enemy?

"Little one," he said hoarsely, "you cannot deny your desire."

"No," she choked. "Would you force yourself on an unwilling maiden, despite your words to Ulferth?"

"But you are willing."

She loosened herself from his grip, and fled.

"I'll never be willing!" she cried.

But was she trying to convince him—or herself?

# CHAPTER 11

The first day of the tournament dawned gray and misty, but grew brighter as the sun climbed into the sky. Tents lined the outskirts of the tourney field where the competitors would prepare for battle.

An arena had been marked out, surrounded by platforms to accommodate the spectators. A high platform decorated with a multi-colored canvas had been erected in a central position overlooking the arena to accommodate the principal guests, mostly ladies in descending order of rank. Two large chairs stood in the center of the platform—one for Lord Wulfson when he was not competing himself. Kendra occupied the other.

A smaller platform had been erected at the opposite end of the arena for the servants. Arlette settled into her place among the lower ranking servants, and surveyed the field. She had spurned many a suitor at Leaside. Might any of them be competing today? Had she accepted their suit, would her position be better than it was now? Marriage might be worse than servitude, for she'd be owned by a man who viewed her only as chattel fit for breeding an heir.

But not Seaton. He saw her as a friend. He might not stir her passions, but she'd have been tempted to accept him. He had no fortune, or estate, but Villiers Castle belonged to her.

Or, at least, it had done.

A surge of envy pulsed through her as she watched the ladies on the guest platform. Which one would have Seaton as her champion?

A fanfare of trumpets heralded the start of the tournament. The competitors rode into the arena, the sunlight catching their armor.

Lord Wulfson led the procession, his tall frame unmistakable as he spurred his black destrier forward. The coat of arms on his shield included a roaring bear—similar to that etched into the sword in the dining hall. A barre sinistre slashed across the shield, signaling his bastardry.

He drew his horse to a halt beside the main platform, and the others lined up beside him. He looked every part the virile warrior as he held his sword aloft to cheers from the crowd.

Pearce sat astride his horse on Orson's left, Ulferth four or five places down the line. Seaton brought up the rear of the procession.

The cheering subsided, and each competitor rode toward the platform where the ladies waited to present their favors. Kendra held out her favor, a bright red scarf. Though Lord Wulfson accepted it, he didn't smile.

Elvia nudged Arlette. "Look at her gown!"

"It cost a great deal," Dawn whispered. "Lord Wulfson went mad when he discovered how much."

"He wasted his coin," Arlette said. "She looks like a peacock that's been dropped into a bucket of dye."

Dawn giggled. "She doesn't look happy."

"Maybe she feels out of place," Arlette said. "She's not been flat on her back with her thighs spread for at least an hour."

Elvia burst out laughing and several heads turned in their direction, including Lord Wulfson's. A sharp finger poked Arlette in the back.

"How dare you show such disrespect!" Hilda's voice hissed in her ear. "Kendra's a lady, whereas you're merely a common whore."

"That's enough, all of you!" Una admonished, "If you cannot show respect for your betters, I'll send you back inside. The master's kind enough to let his servants attend. Hold your tongues and be grateful."

Arlette sat back, watching the rest of the procession. Ulferth approached the ladies and a woman leaned forward, holding out her favor. So—that was Ulferth's unfortunate wife. She had a sweet face, with delicate features, though somewhat pale and careworn. But anyone would look haggard, married to that savage.

As the unmarried knights came forward, a number of ladies held out their favors, and Arlette laughed to herself at the sour expressions on the faces of the ladies whose favors weren't chosen. Arlette herself had never given a favor at the tournaments she'd attended. The ceremony was merely a way for women to compete for a man's attentions.

When Seaton rode forward, Arlette's pulse quickened. Whose favor would he accept? For most of the knights, three or four ladies offered their favors, but as Seaton approached, more than ten stood, their scarves forming a myriad of colors. But Seaton rode past them all.

He was only competitor not to accept any lady's favor.

A murmur of surprise rippled through the crowd.

"Did you see that? He spurned them all!"

"'Tis unheard of!"

"Lord Wulfson should disqualify him for unchivalrous behavior."

"Perhaps his sweetheart is elsewhere. He may already wear her favor."

"I see no adornment on his armor."

As the whispers died down, Arlette fancied she could see Seaton looking in her direction. She lifted her hand to wave, then noticed Lord Wulfson's eyes trained on her.

~

THE FIRST ROUND of the tournament was sword-fighting. The competitors were drawn into pairs to fight, the loser being eliminated. Seaton had been drawn against someone considerably smaller, who he bested easily. Lord Wulfson also made it through, having been drawn against Ulferth. Their fight lasted several rounds, and was the most bloodthirsty of the day, leaving Ulferth on the ground needing medical attention while Lord Wulfson held his sword aloft, to cheers from the crowd.

As the events progressed, Arlette's frustration increased. Many competitors made clear errors of judgment, either in their stance or their poor defense. Had she been permitted to compete, she could have bested most of them. She ached to feel her sword in her hand—to hold her longbow. Her frustration only deepened at the end of the afternoon when the squires and manservants cleared the field to set up the targets for the next day's archery.

During the evening, Arlette managed to avoid attending the dining hall, by insisting on helping Freydis in the kitchens with cleaning and scrubbing the endless array of dirty platters, as well as keeping the kitchen tidy while the various dishes were sent out and brought back. The drunken roars of the men echoed through the night, and she shuddered at the thought of her maidservants being subject to their attentions.

After the castle had grown quiet and she'd finished her duties, Arlette slipped outside for respite from the heat of the kitchen, and wandered toward the tourney field. The moonlight picked out the tops of the tents, pennants fluttering in the breeze. She moved toward the rack where the longbows had been set in readiness for tomorrow, picked up a bow, and checked the tension.

Then she adopted a stance, as she'd been taught, and aimed the bow at a target across the field.

It felt so good to hold a bow again!

She picked up an arrow, aimed at the target, then drew the string back before letting it go with a fluid motion, the string vibrating with a satisfying hum. The arrow whistled through the air, and hit the edge of the target.

Taking a second arrow, she adjusted her stance and tried again. This time, her aim was true and the second arrow struck the target in the center. She picked up two more, firing them in quick succession, and let out a laugh of pleasure as they joined their companion in the center.

How long had it been since she'd had occasion to laugh?

A male voice spoke. "You're to be congratulated on your prowess."

She let out a shriek and turned to face him.

"Seaton!" she cried. "What are you doing here?"

"I'd ask you the same question," he said. "Do you want to draw the attention of every person in the grounds?"

He grasped her shoulder. "Don't you remember what I told you?" He lowered his voice to a whisper. "I said that Arlette de Villiers must keep herself hidden."

Arlette's stomach clenched with fear.

He knew who she was.

Then he released her shoulder, and took her hand. "The Lady Arlette will not be betrayed by me."

He lifted her hand to his lips. "Do you know why I accepted no lady's favor today?"

She shook her head.

"Because the only one whose favor I would have taken was unable to offer it."

"You mean Verona?"

"No," he whispered, "the Lady Arlette de Villiers."

He lifted his other hand to her face, tracing its outline with his finger, down her cheek, across her lips to her chin. Then he tipped her face up, and brushed his lips against hers.

"You fought well today," she said. "I pray you'll do well tomorrow."

"May I have your favor?"

A wave of sorrow rippled through her. "Everything I had has been taken from me, Seaton. I've nothing to give you."

"I only want a token."

She tugged at her sleeve, where the cuff was frayed, and tore off a piece of material. He took it and bowed, reciting the same words the other competitors had uttered that morning.

"It gives me great pleasure to accept your token, my lady. I shall wear it with pride, and fight for your honor."

Arlette had always despised the pomp and ceremony at the beginning of a tournament. But here, the two of them exchanging a scrap of material in an empty field—not for the crowds but for each other—the little ritual became intimate and personal. This chivalrous young knight, who had known love and lost it, almost moved her to tears with his gentle affection. She pressed her lips against his and he returned the kiss—gently, not roughly as Lord Wulfson had done. She closed her eyes, anticipating a flood of passion, but her body felt nothing.

"Have no fear," he said. "I'll not betray you. But you must return inside, before you're seen."

He took her hand and led her back inside. A silhouette in one of the windows caught her eye—the tall, broad-shouldered shape of a man. But when Arlette blinked, it had gone.

# CHAPTER 12

Orson picked up his bow and looked across the field. The second day of the tournament was proving to be as entertaining as the first and, having disposed of Kendra's favor and the woman herself, a weight had lifted from his shoulders. Kendra's curses still rang in his ears as she'd left that morning.

Lord save him from a demanding woman!

But she was no longer his problem. Let her family deal with her—or the new lover that she'd taunted him with in order to make him jealous.

But there was only one man he harbored jealousy toward.

Seaton.

When he'd seen that young knave with Heloise in the field last night, Orson had to fight the urge to beat him into a pulp and claim the wench in the dirt. But she needed to be snared with finesse—coaxed into submission to heighten her pleasure, until she begged him to take her.

And beg she would.

Footsteps approached, and Pearce clapped him on the back.

"I see we're drawn against each other, my friend."

Pearce cocked his head to one side, a lopsided grin on his face. "Am

I also to congratulate you for finally having rid yourself of that shrew?"

"It was time," Orson said. "The sight of her, taking Verona's place, yesterday..."

Pearce placed a hand on Orson's arm. "Perhaps it's time you took a wife."

Orson shook Pearce's hand off. "I've had my fill of shrews."

"Then take another leman. Mayhap you've one in mind?"

Orson's pulse quickened. Did his friend suspect his growing obsession?

"I'll wager Seaton's your main rival," Pearce said.

How did the man get to be so insightful?

"My rival?"

"For the champion's crown," Pearce continued. "He's drawn against Jarvis, who's no bowman."

"Aye, Seaton should win through," Orson said. "As shall I. You're no bowman either."

"But you no longer wear a lady's favor, Orson—which is bad luck for a competitor."

"Neither does Seaton."

"That's where you're mistaken," Pearce said. "Seaton wears a favor today."

"He accepted no favor yesterday."

"Mayhap he took it last night." Pearce chuckled, then left Orson alone with his thoughts.

*Curse you, Seaton! You don't want me as a rival—I'll crush you.*

During the competition Orson watched Heloise cheer Seaton to victory against Jarvis, her voice distinguishable from the cheers of the other servants. As he stepped forward to battle against Pearce, Orson smiled to himself as an idea formed while he drew back the bow. Tonight, Heloise would be his, and that fool Seaton would desire her no more.

He released the arrow and the crowd gasped as it skipped off the edge of the target.

Pearce let out a chuckle.

"Has something distracted my friend?"

Orson nocked the next arrow and focused on the target, picturing how the arrow would spear the center—as his body would spear the wench.

His arrow hit home, and he acknowledged the cheers of the crowd.

Victory would be his. Today, he would win on the field—tonight, he would win the wench.

And she would relish having a real man between her thighs.

"HELOISE, THE MASTER WANTS YOU."

Arlette's blood froze. Una stood before her, brow furrowed, a tray in her hands with a flagon of wine and two goblets.

"Did you not hear me? You're to go to the solar immediately!"

"But the evening meal has finished," Arlette protested. "He cannot require my services."

"Her services!" Dawn giggled.

"Let me go, Mistress Una," Elvia said. "I'm willing if Heloise is not."

Una shook her head. "He asked specifically for Heloise, and said we'll all be beaten if she disobeys." She held the tray out to Arlette. "Hurry up, girl! He's in a foul temper tonight."

Arlette took the tray. A slight tinkling of the goblets against each other betrayed the maelstrom of fear swirling inside her.

The goblets rattled more loudly as she reached the solar door. The urge to flee clawed at her, but before she could retreat, the door opened.

Lord Wulfson stood before her, dressed in a loose-fitting tunic, his powerful frame filling the doorway. He reached toward her, curled his hand around her arm, and pulled her into the chamber, shutting the door.

"Set the tray down."

The solar was enormous. Tapestries lined the walls, depicting battle scenes. Candles flickered in wall sconces, the light casting sharp shadows, which danced as she crossed the floor to a table by the hearth, where a fire crackled and burned.

An enormous bed dominated the far end of the chamber, smothered in furs. She cast her gaze around the chamber, taking in the dark, forbidding colors and the aroma of musk, wood, and earth.

It was a man's chamber—the chamber of a warrior.

As she set the tray down, an arm circled her waist. Hard, unyielding muscles came into contact with her back, and his body heat seeped through the material of her gown. He lifted her hair, and her skin tightened as fingertips caressed the back of her neck. A spark of fire rippled through her, ignited by his caress, and his voice rumbled in her ear.

"Pour us each a cup, Heloise."

Huge hands enveloped her own, guiding them toward the goblets, taking control as she filled each cup with the rich, ruby liquid.

He pushed a goblet in her hand and picked up the other.

"Sit with me," he commanded.

He guided her into a chair, then drew up another and sat facing her, so close that his knees grazed against hers. The he raised his cup to his lips and eyed her expectantly. She lifted her cup, but didn't swallow.

He was a fool if he thought he could breach her defenses with wine.

"Drink," he said. "'Tis a fine wine."

She scowled and shook her head.

"I said, drink. Let me help you." He tipped her goblet up, and a splash of wine spilled onto her chin. Setting both goblets aside, he ran a fingertip along her chin, then lifted it. A fat red droplet glistened on the pad of his forefinger.

He slipped his finger into his mouth, the steel-gray orbs of his eyes darkening with desire.

"I am thirsty, Heloise."

He rose and leaned over her, nudging her knees apart with his own. His breath caressed her cheek, as the potent essence of man and spices consumed her senses.

Lust thickened his voice. "I am hungry also."

He plucked the servant's cap from her head, and tossed it aside. Then he took her face in his hands, his calloused palms rough against her skin. He tipped her head back and caressed her lower lip with his thumb. The gentle gesture sent a rush of heat through her, and she parted her lips in anticipation—but anticipation of what?

For a moment, she saw a spark of tenderness in his eyes, which called out to her soul.

Then he blinked, and the tenderness was gone.

"You want me, Heloise," he whispered, triumph in his voice.

She shook her head, but he let out a soft chuckle.

"Deny me all you wish, but your body betrays you."

"'Tis your body which betrays you," she said. "You're nothing but a brute, with no mastery over that foul thing between your legs."

He shifted his body, his manhood hardening against her thigh. "Oh, my sweet little she-cat—only you have mastery over him. Take him, and he'll serve thee well."

He captured her mouth in a swift, savage kiss, his body pinning her to the chair. As he stroked her mouth with his tongue, her body fizzed with need, and she shifted her legs, chasing the promise of pleasure that pulsed between her thighs.

An urgent need grew within her, the flame reignited, stoked by his tongue into a blazing furnace, urging her body to respond. She pulled him closer, feeding the flames with her own tongue—wanting, needing to plunder his mouth in return.

Grasping her hair, he pulled her head back, exposing her throat before planting fiery kisses on her skin, tracing a line along her collarbone with his tongue, sending spasms of pleasure along her spine.

"This lovely body was made for pleasure, Heloise," he whispered, his voice vibrating against her throat. He tugged at the laces of her gown, and her skin tightened at the rush of air on her bare skin.

"My pleasure...and yours." His tongue tickled her chest, tracing warm, wet circles, which spiraled tighter until he reached her breast.

"So pink—so sweet." He flicked her nipple with his tongue, then drew it into his mouth. She cried out at the shock of pleasure, and arched her back in need.

"That's it," he murmured. "Show me you're mine." His hand brushed against her leg and he pulled her skirt up, his knuckles grazing against her thigh. The fire in her body pulsed to a deep rhythm, and an unfathomable need surged inside her. He began to stroke her center, a promise of pleasure in each slippery circle.

"Please…" she gasped. Her mind willed her body to resist, but she parted her thighs, chasing the pleasure he offered.

"Do you want me, Heloise?"

Her body throbbed as his voice resonated in her mind, and she shifted her thighs wider as her body cried out for release…

Then three sharp knocks rapped on the door.

ORSON LOOKED up from the willing female beneath him.

"Enter."

The door opened and Seaton stepped inside. As instructed, the young man had waited for the household to retire before attending Orson in the solar. Had he arrived a minute later, Orson would have been buried inside the wench.

Seaton's expression changed from neutral inquiry to horror and disgust.

Orson's plan had worked. The wench was his.

He resumed his attention on her, and his triumph deflated. Her body, once aroused and yielding, had stiffened with tension. Her eyes, once full of passion, glistened with shame, self-loathing and fear—the most intense fear that surpassed anything he'd seen—even when she'd ran from Ulferth.

Wriggling free from the chair, she backed away, covering her breasts, tears staining her cheeks. She bumped against the table and the goblets clattered to the floor. She jumped at the noise, then let out a cry, and ran from the room.

Orson ignored the shame twisting in his gut at her stricken

expression. He'd achieved his aim. Seaton had seen her spread her legs for him—his childish infatuation was cured.

Or was it?

The disgust in Seaton's expression was aimed at him.

"You bastard."

"Come, Seaton," Orson said. "A knight must be gracious in defeat."

"You call that a victory? Summoning me to witness her violation at your hands? She was terrified!"

So—the young pup had a pair of balls after all.

"Seaton, how dare..."

"No! How dare *you*!" Seaton cried. Then he turned his back and exited the solar, slamming the door.

Orson's ploy had only succeeded in nurturing Seaton's protective nature toward the wench, and it had introduced Orson to a sensation he'd never experienced before.

Guilt—and shame.

He picked up a goblet, and flung it against the door.

"Damn her! Damn him! Damn, damn, DAMN!"

# CHAPTER 13

A hush fell over the spectators as the two finalists entered the arena. Arlette curled her hands into fists to steady her nerves. Her vision began to swirl—as if she'd drunk too much wine.

A rough hand with skin as dry as parchment closed over her fist.

"Breathe deeply, my lady," Esme whispered. "All will be well."

"He could be killed," Arlette whispered, her heart constricting as she voiced the words. "*Mon Dieu*—they could both be killed."

After a morning of jousting, Seaton and Lord Wulfson had won through to the final. What Seaton lacked in strength, he'd made up for in technique. Holding his lance steady and true, he only needed one run to unseat each opponent. In the other half of the draw, Lord Wulfson had ridden as if the devil snapped at his heels, baring his teeth at his adversaries, and bellowing with triumph as he sent each one flying with savage force. After each victory, he lifted his visor and turned his gaze toward the servants' seats—toward her.

Now, the air crackled with anticipation—the tension before a thunderstorm. Whispers rippled through the crowd as the finalists circled each other, one lithe and golden, the other dark, forbidding, and muscular.

A fanfare blew, and they rode to opposite ends of the run to a slow drumbeat. Squires rushed to hand their masters their helmets, and each man put it on, snapping the visor shut with a clang before taking up his shield and finally his lance, settling it into position.

The drumbeat stopped. Silence fell over the arena as if every man and woman held their breath. The herald held a pennant aloft, then released it.

The flag fluttered to the ground, and each competitor surged forward, the thunderous sound of the horses vibrating on the earth. Huge clods of earth scattered into the air behind each horse as they gathered speed.

Arlette's relish at the Brute's prowess warred with her loathing for him, and a spark of fear—a voice inside her mind, pleading for him not to be harmed.

With a crash of splintering wood, each man's lance hit its mark, and glanced off his opponent's shield. Seaton maintained his balance and completed the run. But Lord Wulfson was not so fortunate. He dropped his lance and almost lost his seat. He clung to his horse's neck as the animal slowed to a trot, and reached the end of the run. Though his words were indistinguishable, his voice betrayed his sentiment as he barked instructions to the squire. Seaton's squire received better treatment, a merry laugh in sharp contrast to the Brute's dark anger.

After snatching a fresh lance, Wulfson turned his horse in a tight circle, almost making the animal lose its balance, then waited for the second run.

At the signal they set off again. Wulfson's horse reared up, almost unseating him, then sprang forward. Gathering speed, he roared out his battle cry, a bearish howl that prickled the skin on Arlette's neck. Then he lifted his lance and struck Seaton squarely in the chest. The impact sent the young man flying, and he landed on his back in the mud.

Arlette screamed and leaped to her feet.

"No, lady!" Esme pulled her back. "There's naught you can do for him. Don't draw attention to yourself."

Arlette's eyes stung with tears as the squires ran toward Seaton's body. The next moment, she saw Lord Wulfson help Seaton to his feet. The two men clasped hands, then Wulfson raised his helmet to the cheers of the crowd.

They had their victor.

Seaton glanced in Arlette's direction, then, shoulders slumped in defeat, he plucked a piece of material from his chestplate, and handed it over. A cold hand of dread clawed at Arlette's stomach.

Seaton had given Lord Wulfson her favor.

~

ARLETTE STEPPED out from behind the wall hanging as the young knight limped past.

"Seaton!"

He stopped and turned. His face bore the pallor of a dead man—ash gray, rather than his usual rosy bloom.

She moved toward him, but he backed away, moisture in his eyes.

"I've not got long," she said. "I'm expected to serve at the feast. But I had to see if you were injured."

"I am well," he said quietly, "but—forgive me—I failed you."

She touched his arm, and he stiffened. "You didn't fail me, Seaton," she said. "You fought well."

"I've lost you," he whispered.

"I don't understand."

"We—that is, Lord Wulfson and I—had a wager."

"A wager?"

"Forgive me!" He took her hand. "You were the prize."

"Me?"

"Aye."

She snatched her hand away. "How could you! Am I a cow to be fought over, and taken by the strongest bull on the farm?"

"I had to accept the challenge," he said. "It was the only way I could free you, to take you away from here—as my wife. But I failed. Forgive me, lady—please forgive me."

"You can still take me away," she said. "I've a property of my own, in Normandy—where *he* cannot reach me. You can help me get there."

"I cannot," he replied. "He made me swear to have nothing more to do with you if he bested me. I must honor my oath."

"Honor?" she cried. "You talk of honor, when I'm held captive by the man who destroyed my family?"

The anger she'd kept at bay for so long threatened to overwhelm her. That brute—Lord Wulfson—Orson Greywell…

Everything came back to *him*.

Seaton drew her close, but she pushed him away. If she had her sword, she'd cut the throat of the next man who touched her.

~

ARLETTE ENTERED the main hall carrying a pitcher of ale, Esme's words echoing in her ears.

*Play the part of the servant, lady, I beg you, lest you reveal your identity.*

But her anger had yet to subside. And seeing Lord Wulfson—the victor—seated at the top table beside Seaton, only increased it.

As she worked her way up and down the tables, she gritted her teeth, as the men deliberately pushed their goblets out of her reach, laughing appreciatively as she leaned across to fill them.

One man fondled her buttocks and she jumped back with a squeal. She looked up, and her gaze met Seaton's, pity and understanding in his eyes. She glanced at the man next to him, and her skin tightened in fear. Lord Wulfson watched her, his eyes dark as a thundercloud. Though she stepped back, he continued to stare, hunger in his eyes.

A hand grabbed her breast and she slapped it away, but her assailant only laughed.

"The wench is as cold as ice," he slurred. "I'll warm her up."

He grasped her wrist and she tipped the contents of her pitcher onto his lap.

"Clumsy whore!" he cried. "I'll take my hand to you!"

He tightened his grip and pulled her to him.

"Get off me, you filthy, rutting boar!" She swung her arm back, then slapped him soundly on the face.

The laughter stopped.

"You'll regret that, you whore!" He curled his hand into a fist, then pain exploded in her head as his fist connected with her jaw. She staggered back, her head ringing, and fell to the floor.

"Jarvis!" a deep voice roared.

Lord Wulfson stood at the high table, body vibrating, his face a mask of fury.

"Come away, Heloise." Dawn's soft voice spoke in her ear, and gentle hands helped her up. The ringing in her ears began to subside, then Wulfson's voice boomed across the hall.

"Nobody beats my servants without my permission!"

*Without his permission?*

In that brute's eyes, the man had committed no sin in beating her —only that he'd not been granted leave to do so first.

Fueled by the rage that had simmered deep within her since the night he'd destroyed her life, Arlette wrestled free from Dawn's embrace, and sprinted toward the swords on the wall.

She wrenched her chosen weapon free and, with a scream of rage, she leaped onto Jarvis, forced him facedown on the table, and pressed the blade against his neck.

"Touch me again, you swine, and I'll sever your head."

"Move away from him!" Wulfson roared, "or I'll personally beat you to within an inch of your life."

"I will not!" she cried. "What right have you to treat me thus?"

"I'm your master."

"You're not my master! Nor shall you ever be,"

Lord Wulfson leaped over the table, sweeping aside plates and goblets that clattered to the floor. Fury in his eyes, he strode forward until he stood in front of her, his powerful frame towering over her slighter form.

"Put your sword down, woman, or I'll have you killed," he said. "Do it now, and I'll be merciful."

Hatred burning inside her, she raised the sword, and pointed it directly at his throat.

"I shall not," she said. "I'll never surrender to a murderer."

A voice screamed. "Lady Arlette—no!"

Esme stood in the doorway, tears in her eyes. Then she lifted her hand to her mouth, her eyes widening in horror as she realized her mistake.

*Lady Arlette...*

Before Arlette could move, strong hands gripped her wrists, and the sword clattered to the floor.

She lifted her head to meet his gaze, and cold gray fury stared back at her.

"So," he said, "the Lady Arlette de Villiers is before me, at last."

## CHAPTER 14

Treacherous little mare! She'd been under his nose all this time—laughing at him.

"Lady Arlette de Villiers."

"You big, lumbering…"

Orson pulled her to him, then fisted his hand in her hair, tipping her head back until he met her green gaze.

Anger glowered in her eyes, but he caught the flash of lust in their emerald depths. Her hands, which at first pushed against his chest, yielded, and her fingers curled into the fabric of his tunic.

Her nostrils flared and her lips parted—only by a whisper, but enough to betray her desire—the same desire that pulled at his loins.

Fighting the powerful need coursing through his body, he dipped his head, and lowered his mouth to hers, relishing the anticipation of her sweet taste. She parted her lips farther and the sight of the tip of her tongue, running along her lower lip, was his undoing. He hardened with urgency—the clawing need to claim her as his.

And she was his. A primal voice, deep within his mind, roared in triumph, as if the animal—the bear within—recognized his mate.

"My lord!" Seaton's voice brought Orson to his senses, and a flame of jealousy ignited in Orson's breast. The foolish lad had been smitten with the wench from the day she'd arrived. Had he known her identity?

But it mattered not. She belonged to him, not Seaton. The spoils of conquest—both as payment for her father's sins and from the tournament.

*You shall not have her, Seaton. She's mine, and I will enjoy taming her.*

The desire left her eyes and she struggled against him.

"Keep your hands off me, you murdering bastard," she spat.

An audible ripple of fear ran through the company.

*Bastard...*

Such a cruel word! Few had the courage to utter it in his presence.

"Choose your words carefully, madam," he said, "lest they be your last."

"I call you what you are," she said. "A murderer." Then, understanding dawned in her eyes, and her lip curled into a sneer. "Mayhap the title 'bastard' strikes a keener blow?"

He gripped her shoulders. "Let me warn you, woman—men have died for insulting me thus. You could still join them, if only to silence that foul tongue of yours."

Defiance glittered in her eyes. How spirited she was! What might life have been had he taken her as a wife six years ago? But de Villiers' words echoed from the past.

*I'll not bring shame upon my family by wedding my daughter to a bastard.*

She swung her hand back, then delivered a stinging slap on his face.

"Hellcat!" He shook her roughly. "Deceitful, dishonorable...hiding behind a servant's name...hiding like a coward!"

"You expected me to reveal myself to be slaughtered in cold blood, by a murdering brute?"

He tightened his grip. "You address me as 'my lord.'"

"And *you* address me as 'lady.'"

"Your title is forfeit," he said. "You're a serf in my household. By right, I should have you punished—along with your women."

"I've been punished enough!" she cried. "My family killed, my home destroyed, my maids enslaved. We do not deserve this—we're innocent!"

"None of you are innocent. The women you brought with you..."

"*I* did not bring them here, Saxon bastard."

He closed his eyes, struggling against his rage at the insult. When he opened them again she stared back, a flicker of fear in her eyes, though she tried to disguise it.

"You are all guilty," he said. "I shall have each of your servants whipped for disobedience."

The fear in her eyes came to the fore.

"No—you cannot!" she cried. "My servants have worked hard here."

"They concealed your identity."

"They were protecting me!"

"And, by doing so, they have earned one lash each."

She stiffened, her eyes moistening.

"Please," she whispered. "You cannot lash them—it's a punishment for men."

Aye, it was, but he ignored the protests of his conscience. To back down now—in front of the whole company—would be a sign of weakness.

A sign he could not afford.

"The punishment stands," he said. "You come from a family of cowards, where the men abandon their women to die, and the women hide under the skirts of their servants."

She set her jaw firm, as if gritting her teeth.

"There are no cowards in my household," she said. "I shall bear the punishment in their stead."

"You expect mercy?" he asked.

She smiled, though fear darkened her expression. "I wouldn't expect mercy from you. But I'll not let you punish innocent women, some of whom have barely left childhood. They acted out of loyalty to me, therefore I must pay the price."

Foolish wench! Did she realize what she was doing?

"If I agree," he said, "then you sentence yourself to seven lashes—one for each of your women."

The color drained from her cheeks but she met his gaze. Why didn't she beg for mercy? What might seven lashes do to her body—her perfect skin…

His heart ached at the notion. But he couldn't retract without appearing weak in front of the company—a company where men such as Ulferth waited for the opportunity to usurp him.

Perhaps if she swore loyalty, and begged forgiveness, he could retract.

He lowered his voice, willing her to comply. "Swear loyalty to me, my lady, for your own sake. Beg forgiveness, and I will be lenient."

But she ignored his unspoken plea.

"Never."

"I'll not ask again."

"I'm no coward," she said. "Can you say the same of yourself —*bastard*?"

With her final word she sealed her fate.

"So be it."

"Lady, please!" Seaton's voice wavered with emotion. "Stand down —he'll be merciful if you do."

She turned her head, and smiled at the young knight, her tender expression sealing his fate as well as hers.

"Seaton," Orson said. "You shall issue the punishment."

Seaton blanched. Orson's victory over the young man would be twofold. Seaton's sense of duty would compel him to obey, and in doing so, he would earn her hatred.

"You're a coward to give the task to another," she said.

Some of the defiance in her eyes had gone, and her voice shook with fear.

He pulled her close and hissed in her ear. "Yield, lady. Yield, now, and I will desist. I have no wish to harm you."

She let out a cold laugh. "Do you fear what the company will think of you, if you torture an innocent woman? Do you fear they'll see you for the worthless whoreson that you are?"

Resisting the urge to strike her, he thrust her toward his men. "Take her to the courtyard—now!"

Brand and Jarvis took her by the arms, and led her out of the hall. The old woman who'd screamed earlier grasped Orson's sleeve.

"Please, my lord! Show mercy!"

"I've passed judgment," he growled. "Speak again, and I'll double the lashes."

Pushing her to one side, he strode out of the hall.

The evening light cast a red glow on the courtyard walls. A large wooden post stood in the center, to which the Lady Arlette had already been secured. Her arms wrapped around it, wrists bound and tied to an iron ring embedded at the top. Though she stood firm, the tremble in her arms betrayed her fear.

Seaton stood behind her, his whole body shaking as Brand handed him the whip.

Orson stood in front of her, and she lifted her head and looked directly into his eyes. Then she smiled, her eyes glittering with contempt.

Fixing his gaze on her, he gestured to Seaton.

"Begin."

~

THE SKIN on Arlette's back tightened with the cold evening air, warring with the prickling sensation of the rough wood of the post against her chest. She met her captor's gaze and saw regret in his eyes. Regret—and pain.

Good. With luck, the Brute would suffer for what he was about to do.

A whistle in the air signaled the onset of the first lash, which struck the ground by her feet.

"One."

"No! You missed, you fool," Wulfson barked. "All seven must strike flesh."

"Orson…" a voice protested.

"Don't question me, Pearce!" Wulfson's brow furrowed and the pain and guilt in his eyes intensified. She curled her lip into a sneer and continued to stare at him.

The next lash caught her across the back, and a streak of fire burned her skin. Gritting her teeth, she maintained eye contact with her captor. She'd witnessed lashings at home as a child—Garret had always said they were less painful, healed more quickly, if they didn't tear the skin.

"One." Pearce's voice wavered as he resumed counting.

The next lash joined the first, and she exhaled slowly, counting under her breath to draw her focus from the pain.

She could withstand it. Just another five. With luck, none would break the skin.

Wulfson's eyes narrowed, but her triumph at his discomfort was marred by the sound of her old nursemaid weeping.

*Oh, Esme, I'm sorry you must witness this.*

"Two."

At the third lash, Arlette's luck ran out. The skin across her back ripped apart, but she suppressed her cry and fought back tears, focusing on her hatred for the man in front of her.

"Three!" Pearce's voice wavered.

"My lord..." Seaton's voice spoke, but Wulfson interrupted.

"Get on with it!"

When the fourth lash struck, she bit down on her tongue, the metallic taste of blood on her lips. The world shifted sideways and a deep roaring rumbled in the back of her mind.

"Four!"

At the fifth lash, Arlette couldn't suppress a gasp of pain. Wulfson raised his eyebrows. He had heard.

"My lord," Seaton sobbed, "surely that's enough!"

Arlette looked at her captor with loathing. How could he force a gentle soul like Seaton to carry out such a deed?

"The sentence was pronounced, Seaton. Finish it."

"Five!" Pearce's voice was hoarse with emotion.

A nugget of triumph grew in her mind. The Brute's friends were turning against him.

The sixth lash caught her unawares, and a cry erupted from her throat.

"Six!"

Wulfson's eyes widened, then he let out a groan and looked down. When he lifted his gaze again, she saw nothing but shame in his eyes—his whole body shook with it.

Her courage had won over his. She lifted her lips into a smile of triumph, then the roaring in her head increased, and her body succumbed to the darkness as she slipped into oblivion.

~

*What have I done?*

Silence descended over the courtyard except for the maidservants' sobs. Orson's men stared at him—some, such as Ulferth, in satisfaction, others in horror.

Lady Arlette's unconscious form hung, suspended by her bound wrists.

Seaton strode toward Orson, and thrust the whip into his hand.

"The lady has shown more bravery than you could ever hope to do, Lord Wulfson," he said. "You've brought shame upon yourself tonight."

Seaton should be punished for such words—but he spoke the truth. The Lady Arlette was no coward. She had the courage of a man—nay—ten men.

His anger abated, Orson saw her for what she was—a warrior, loyal to her servants, willing to suffer—and die, if need be—in their stead. He could not have believed such a woman existed. To meet his gaze, unflinchingly, while he administered a punishment she did not deserve.

No wonder he'd been drawn to her! She carried herself with an air of royalty—as if the world was unworthy of her.

*He* was unworthy of her.

Yet he wanted her. The spark in her eyes, the defiance, spoke of a warrior queen—the one woman in the world to match him.

But she was his enemy's daughter, and he'd ordered her torture in front of his household, in an act of fury, pride, and retribution.

"I leave you to administer the seventh lash," Seaton said. "As the lady is no longer conscious, even a coward such as yourself should be able to finish what you forced me to start."

Orson threw the whip onto the ground, and glared at the watching crowd, challenging them to speak.

"Begone," he said. "All of you—back inside."

The company moved toward the door, but the old woman—the one who had betrayed Arlette's identity—stood her ground.

"Have mercy," she pleaded. "Let me tend to her."

"Leave," he said through gritted teeth. "Leave now."

"I will not, sir. My lady has seen her parents killed and her home ransacked. She's been forced to work as a serf and suffer the attentions of your men. And now this—to be publicly beaten and humiliated. And for what? For defending her virtue, for protecting her servants. All at your hands."

"Get thee gone, woman!" he bellowed, guilt fueling his anger. He curled his hands into fists, and she fled, sobbing.

A hand touched his shoulder.

Pearce.

"The old woman was right, my friend," Pearce said. "I understand why you had to punish the lady, but you should have stopped after the first lash."

"Go back inside, Pearce."

"Her wounds must be tended to, before they fester."

"I said, go!"

"Very well."

Pearce returned inside, leaving Orson alone in the courtyard, the only sound the rush of wind and the cawing of roosting rooks in the surrounding trees.

Orson crouched beside Arlette. He placed his hand on her head and caressed it, burying his fingers in the soft silk of her hair.

"What am I going to do with you, my lady?" he whispered.

He drew his knife, cut the rope binding her wrists, and caught her in his arms, grimacing at her whimper of pain. He paused to wipe a tear from her cheek, then brushed his lips against her forehead.

*Forgive me, my lady.*

Two maidservants waited for Orson in the solar—the old woman and another of the de Villiers servants. He placed Arlette facedown on the bed, and as he stepped back, he caught his breath at the marks on her back.

The old woman took her hand and she stirred and gave a moan of pain.

"Be still, sweet lady. I'm here."

"Esme… It hurts…it hurts, so much…"

The pain in her voice clawed at his conscience.

"Drink this, lady—quick!" The younger maidservant lifted Arlette's head, while the elder held a goblet to her lips and tipped the contents into her mouth. She spluttered, sending droplets flying, but her throat rippled as she swallowed some of the liquid.

Then the women set to work, cleaning the wounds and spreading them with salve, tracing the angry marks. Her body flinched at every touch, but eventually her whimpers subsided and she lay still, a damp cloth covering her back, the scent of spice in his nostrils from the salve.

He stepped toward her, "I'll carry her to one of the guest chambers."

"We cannot move her," the old woman said, "unless you wish to inflict more damage. Don't you think she's suffered enough at your hands?"

"Woman, you have no right to speak so."

"I've every right," she said. "My lady will be scarred for life, by your hand, as if she were a common criminal."

"Enough!" Orson shouted. "Get out—both of you."

"But my lady…"

"…is asleep, and has no further need of you tonight. You may tend to her tomorrow."

"I'll not leave before you give me your word that you won't harm her further."

"You have it," he replied.

"How can I trust you?" she asked.

"Because I'm an honorable man and value honesty and loyalty above all," he said. "I keep my promises when others do not."

"Then I must be content with that," she replied. "Come, Maude, let us leave Lord Wulfson to his conscience."

The two women curtseyed, then exited the solar.

Orson returned his attention to the woman on the bed. How he'd longed to have her alone in his chamber! But not like this. At least her cries had stopped, the sleeping draught having taken effect.

He sat on the bed, and brushed her hair from her eyes, caressing her cheek with the back of his fingers. Then he traced a line across her forehead, and ran his fingertips down her nose to her top lip, where he traced the outline of her mouth. His skin tightened at the memory of her sweet taste. She parted her lips and sighed. Warm breath caressed his fingertips, sending fire through his blood.

*God's bones, what is this woman doing to me?*

He pulled off his outer garments, took a fur from the bed, and sat in a chair by the fireplace—the same chair she'd occupied the night he'd almost succeeded in seducing her. Wrapping the fur around his shoulders, he settled back to watch over her. Hatred for de Villiers, and the need to avenge Verona, still burned within him. But it warred with desire and admiration for the woman who'd stood up to him better than any man.

# CHAPTER 15

When Orson woke, his body ached. His neck stiff, he yawned and stretched.

*God's bones*—that chair was uncomfortable!

The morning sun stretched across the solar, illuminating the woman on the bed, and highlighting the coppery strands of her hair to form a halo. She still lay on her stomach, her chestnut tresses obscuring her face.

He rose, and crossed the chamber to his trunk, and picked up a tunic. While he dressed, the door knocked and Seaton entered. Though he bowed, the young man's face betrayed his anger as he glanced toward the bed.

"Have you ruined her virtue?"

"I've not touched her," Orson replied.

Seaton closed his eyes, and his body visibly relaxed.

"Is she being tended to properly?" he asked. "I would like to watch over her."

"You'll do no such thing," Orson said. "I'm going hunting today, and you shall accompany me. Be at the stables in one hour."

Seaton opened his mouth to protest, then murmured his assent and left. A hot flame of jealousy burned inside Orson. At all costs that young pup must be kept away from her, though, with luck, she hated him also, for it had been his hand on the whip.

Footsteps approached and the old woman appeared, carrying a tray laden with bandages.

"I'm come to tend to my lady," she said, lifting her chin in defiance, as if she expected him to refuse.

"Remain with her until I return," he ordered, "but you're forbidden to admit anyone else in to see her."

"It makes little difference to my lady who I admit," she replied. "She'll need to be drugged for the pain you inflicted, and will be unable to see anyone."

He opened his mouth to admonish her, then nodded, and left the solar, slamming the door behind him.

IT WAS ALMOST sundown when the hunting party returned. The battlements of Greywell Castle glowed a soft pink in the evening light, picking out the jagged edge of the destroyed section—the place where Orson's father had fallen.

They had returned victorious. The thrill was always in the chase, never the capture—and a boar was a worthy adversary. Cunning, powerful, and vicious, he was not to be challenged lightly. Complacency was a man's downfall—succumb to it and he'd be torn to shreds, gutted by sharp tusks.

Seaton's face was flushed with victory. The household always appreciated a successful hunt, and Orson had enjoyed a moment of camaraderie with his rival as the two of them worked together to fell their quarry. Seaton might be too gentle for warfare, but Orson would make a man of him yet.

Pearce drew alongside Orson. "I see our young friend is once more showing you respect. And he hunts well."

"I insisted he accompany us today," Orson said.

"Perhaps because you don't trust him alone with the lady?"

"Cease your prattle, Pearce," Orson growled. "You sound like a gossiping milkmaid."

Pearce chuckled. Seaton turned his head and his gaze met Orson's, a frown furrowing his brow as he curled his fingers around his mount's reins.

*You conceal your anger well, Seaton, but 'tis plain you still want her.*

But she was his—not Seaton's.

After handing his mount to the stable boy, Orson issued orders for his meal to be served in the solar, than he left the party, Pearce's laughter ringing in his ears.

The old woman was still in the solar, tending to her charge.

"Is she well?" he asked.

"As well as can be expected."

"You may go," he said. "Do not return until morning."

He caught her sleeve as she passed him, and she flinched.

"If she wakes, what do I do?"

"I've replaced her bandages. There's enough sleeping draught should she wake. She's had none since noon."

"Very well," he said, "now, leave me."

He unlaced his boots and set them on the floor. Then he threw off his tunic and chausses.

Soft moans came from the bed. Its occupant lay on her side, her body shuddering. He poured a little of the sleeping draught into a goblet, then climbed onto the bed beside her.

He brought the goblet to her lips, and sighed with relief as she swallowed the potion. When he set the goblet aside, she reached for his hand, and his breath caught at the touch of her skin. Her fingers were ice cold.

With his free hand, he pulled a fur over her body, but when he tried to move away, she tightened her grip.

"Esme..."

The need to ease her pain overcame him, and he caressed the back of her hand.

"Shhh, lady," he whispered. "I'm here."

"Don't leave me," she murmured. "I have no wish to be alone."

He lowered his head and kissed her hand. "You'll never be alone," he whispered. Then he lay beside her, careful not to touch the wounds on her back, and wrapped his arm around her body.

He'd always considered women as a means for release—the base gratification sought after by all red-blooded males. But he couldn't deny the sweet pleasure of holding this woman in his arms and giving her comfort.

He spent most of the night awake, drawing her close each time she whimpered. At one point she cried out for her mother. Torn between guilt and desire, he brushed his lips against her forehead, whispering words of comfort until she grew silent.

Unable to stop himself, he planted gentle kisses down her nose, across her cheeks, hesitating a fraction before pressing his mouth against hers. She parted her lips and sighed as he slipped his tongue inside. He would have her—and she'd come to him willing.

With these pleasurable thoughts, sleep overcame him, while he cradled her in his arms, as if she belonged there.

When he woke, sunlight in his eyes, she still slept. He hadn't needed to administer the sleeping draught again.

She was recovering.

Though he needed to see to William and the estate today, he was, for the moment, content to lie beside her. She stirred in her sleep, and nestled against him, with a sigh of contentment. He brushed his lips against her forehead, governed by the need to hold her—to cherish her.

A cough made him look up. The old woman stood in the doorway, a knowing smile on her lips.

The woman in his arms opened her eyes. Instinctively he smiled, his heart yearning to see her smile in return.

Her expression turned to horror, and she pulled away, yelping with pain as she rolled onto her back in her efforts to break free.

"You!" She scrambled off the bed, and lost her balance. As she fell to the floor, she grasped the table with the tray, and sent the contents flying. She landed with a grunt of pain, and grabbed the tray. Orson crouched down to help her up, but she swung the tray at him, and caught the side of his head with a resounding crack.

"Ouch!" he cried. "You bloody wildcat!"

"Murdering bastard!" She took another swing.

The old woman rushed forward. "Lady, take care!" she cried. "You're still unwell."

Arlette struggled to her feet, but lost her balance. Orson grasped her arms, but she struggled, and screamed.

"Be still, woman, for your own good!" He shook her, but she continued to cry out.

"Let her go, my lord," the old woman pleaded. "She's in no state to listen to you."

He released her, and she jumped back, her eyes wild with fury. She looked around and spied the cups and bowls that had been knocked onto the floor. Then she picked up a goblet and flung it at him.

He tried to duck, but it hit him on the chin. He backed out of the chamber, pulling the old woman with him, and closed the door.

A tirade of curses came from the other side, followed by clatters against the door as she flung another goblet at it, followed by what sounded like the flagon and the tray.

"Curse her—the bad-tempered hellion," he muttered, rubbing his jaw.

She hammered on the door, screaming in rage while he held it shut, until the pounding stopped, the screams replaced by sobs.

"Mama!"

"Let me go to her—I can bear it no longer!" the old woman cried, tugging at his sleeve. "She's had to conceal herself these past months and has been unable to grieve for her family."

"Then she can grieve in a locked room."

"My lord, I beg you to show mercy," she pleaded. "You know what it's like to suffer the pain of losing a beloved relation."

His muscles tensed at her words but she continued. "My lady suffers the same agonies as you, my lord. Let me comfort her. You've had your vengeance for your loss. She has nothing."

Her words pricked at his conscience. He pushed the door open and shoved her inside. Before shutting it, he caught a glimpse of Arlette, crumpled on the floor. The old woman kneeled beside her and Arlette reached out, clinging to her nursemaid, her sobs subsiding as the maidservant shushed her, stroking her forehead, as Orson had done only moments earlier.

In sleep, she had turned to him for comfort. But, awake, she hated him. He'd brought about her despair. To her, he was—and would always be—the enemy.

# CHAPTER 16

Exhausted from crying, Arlette let Esme lead her toward the bed. The pain in her back had lessened, but after weeks of concealing her identity, and her emotions, she succumbed to the grief that had threatened to engulf her since she came to Greywell Castle.

Papa had been a strict man, often a harsh man. But Mama—the gentle soul who had taken such care of her, until her delicate health had taken its toll and rendered her almost bedridden—Mama had not deserved her fate.

Arlette sank into the soft furs of the bed, and closed her eyes, taking comfort from Esme's presence. She heard the door open, then Esme cried out.

"No, sir! You're not welcome here. Haven't you done enough to her?"

Arlette opened her eyes. Seaton stood in the doorway, distress in his expression.

"Please…" he whispered.

"Leave her be," Esme said.

"No," Arlette said. "Let him stay."

"Have you lost your senses?" Esme cried. "It was his hand on the whip!"

"Seaton won't harm me."

Seaton shook his head. "I'm sorry, my lady—I came only to beg forgiveness. I'll leave you in peace."

"Stay," Arlette said. "Please."

He drew a chair beside the bed and took her hand.

"I know not what to say, Lady Arlette. You must hate me."

She placed her palm on his cheek.

"You were only following your lord's orders," she said. "You suffered as much as I."

"How can you bear it?" he asked. "Such a punishment would have broken most men."

"I must be strong for my companions, and for my family's honor, and..." she lowered her voice to a whisper, "...while there's hope my brother still lives, I pray that murdering bastard does not get his hands on him."

She squeezed Seaton's hand. "Have you heard aught of my brother?"

He shook his head. "He's not been found, but I fear Lord Wulfson would not hesitate to have him killed if he knew his whereabouts. He still grieves for his sister."

Moisture shone in his eyes, and he lowered his gaze.

"Perhaps, Lord Wulfson is not the only one to grieve," Arlette said.

He nodded, and a tear splashed onto his cheek. "My gentle Verona," he whispered. "She would accept my tokens of love with grace. Small tokens her brother never noticed—a flower from the meadow, a pretty pebble from the road—gifts insignificant to all but her..."

He closed his eyes, and his body shook. When he opened them again, the grief in his expression had turned to rage.

"You must never speak of your brother," he said. "Lord Wulfson is not a forgiving man. He loved his sister greatly, and while I cannot condone what he did to your family, I can understand it."

"What do you mean?" Arlette asked. "What does that have to do with Guillaume?"

"Not your brother," he replied, "but your father, Lord Reynaud de Villiers." He gritted his teeth as he almost spat out Papa's name.

"Sir, say nothing!" Esme cried.

A wave of dread rose within Arlette—a terrible secret that had hung over her like a thundercloud—a secret she had refused to acknowledge.

"Seaton," she said, "tell me what this has to do with Papa."

"It was he who murdered Verona."

Her gut twisted and she swallowed to stem the nausea.

"Don't be a fool!" she cried. "Esme—tell him he speaks nonsense."

Esme shook her head. "I cannot. The servants have begun to talk of it."

"How have I not heard?"

"I told them to say nothing to you."

"It cannot be true!" Arlette cried. "Not Papa!"

"Forgive me," Seaton said, "but the evidence is indisputable. Your father's seal was found by her remains."

Arlette's blood froze. "Remains?"

Seaton withdrew his hand and curled it into a fist and, for the first time, Arlette caught a glimpse of the warrior beneath the gentle knight.

"Her body was dismembered—and charred by fire, identifiable only by her jewelry. Your father's seal was found close by."

Arlette pitched forward and let out a wail. "No!"

She buried her face in her hands, and sobbed.

"Hold her, Seaton," Esme said.

Strong hands grasped her shoulders, and Esme held a cup to her lips.

"Drink this."

"No—take it away!" Arlette thrust out her hand to push Esme back, but Seaton held her firm, while Esme tipped the goblet up and cool liquid slipped down her throat. She tried to struggle, but the world faded, as if she'd been smothered by a fur blanket.

"Forgive me, Mistress Esme," Seaton said. "I thought she knew."

"Her father had a reputation for cruelty and retribution," Esme said. "'Tis time she learned the truth. I know not why he killed the Lady Verona—I'd sooner believe her cousin Lord Fulbert capable of such a wicked deed. But there's no disputing the evidence. I'd rather she heard it from you than from *him*."

"Heard what?" a deep, angry voice spoke, but before Arlette could hear more, the drug took effect and she slipped into darkness.

ORSON STOOD IN THE DOORWAY, Pearce beside him, watching the scene taking place inside the solar—the lady unconscious on the bed, the old woman holding the goblet—and the young knight with defiance and guilt in his eyes.

"How long have you been eavesdropping?" Seaton asked.

"How dare you?" Orson cried. "I am lord here, and shall do as I please. You forget your place. I told you to have nothing to do with her."

"That was when you thought her a servant," Seaton said, "but she's a lady, who commands respect. You have no claim on her."

"I care not what you say, Seaton."

"So I see."

Orson strode into the solar and grasped Seaton by the shoulders.

"Get out, you insolent puppy, before I dismiss you from my service altogether."

"If you dismiss me, nothing can prevent my offering for her. I'll no longer be honor bound to you."

"Go, damn you!" Orson roared.

"Very well," Seaton said, "but you know I speak the truth." He pointed toward Pearce. "He knows it also."

Before Orson could respond, Seaton left.

Damn that young whelp! He should have known he'd be lying in wait for an opportunity to see her.

He approached the bed.

The Lady Arlette was asleep, but her breathing was uneven, as if she'd been crying.

What had the old woman said?

*I'd rather she heard it from you than from him.*

So, the young fool had told her about Verona. Perhaps the knowledge would temper her haughtiness—a murderer's daughter had nothing to be proud of.

Though the blood of evil ran through her veins, his body yearned for her. If he wasn't careful, his soul might follow. She stirred in her sleep, turning her body to reveal the swell of her breasts, and his manhood strained against his breeches at the thought of those delectable globes in his hands.

He addressed the old woman. "You—remain with her. But if you admit anyone, I'll have you whipped. Do I make myself clear?"

"Perfectly so, my lord."

He withdrew from the solar, closed the door, and leaned against it.

Pearce chuckled softly. "Seaton seems to have found some fire in his belly."

"High time he did," Orson replied.

"You cannot blame him for wanting her, Orson—even when he thought her a servant. But now, there's nothing to prevent him asking for her hand."

"I won't allow it," Orson said. "I'll speak to his father."

"Will you speak to the father of every man who wants her?"

"If need be."

"You want her yourself," Pearce said. "What for? Revenge?"

"De Villiers took my sister," Orson replied. "I shall take his daughter."

Pearce folded his arms. "I cannot deny she'd make for fine bed sport, but she would not come willing."

"Aye, she would," Orson said. "I'll make her desire me above all others, and then I'll break her heart, so that she suffers as that bitch who married my father made us all suffer."

"Your stepmother is long dead," Pearce said, "and Lady Arlette is nothing like her. She's a tigress—a warrior. Take her out of revenge, and you'll find yourself in the marriage bed with a knife in your back."

"Then she'll spend the rest of her life in chains."

"By the saints, Orson! Listen to reason."

"What reason did her father apply when he murdered my sister?"

"Don't let your thirst for revenge destroy you, Orson. Verona did not die at the lady's hand."

"I'll have her, Pearce, and none shall stop me."

"Very well," Pearce said, "but heed my warning."

Pearce was right. The Lady Arlette was a warrior. What sons she would bear! How might her delicious little form look, heavy with child—his seed in her belly—the delightful symmetry of having her bear his bastards after her father had spurned him for being a bastard himself.

Perhaps, then, his vengeance would be complete.

"Arlette."

A voice whispered her name, but she kept her eyes closed in a bid to return to her dream—where steel-colored eyes rendered her immobile, and a sensual mouth covered hers, promising untold pleasure.

The dream disappeared, but the fire remained, pulsing to the rhythm of her desire.

The eyes had been *his*.

She rubbed her eyes and sat up.

Lord Wulfson stood at the foot of the bed. Arms folded, body rigid, he stared at her, his eyes mirroring the passion of her dream.

"What do you want?" Her voice caught in her throat.

"I have decided what to do with you."

Lord save her! How could he possibly make her life any more miserable?

"You cannot wish to remain here as a servant," he said.

"I wanted none of this, you bastard!"

He stepped forward, and fear shuddered through her at the fury in his eyes.

"Be careful what you say, woman. I have the advantage."

Aye, he did. Weak from the sleeping draught, barely clad, and in his bed—she had no choice but to listen.

"I'm a reasonable enough man to consider relieving you of your position as a servant. But I'll not grant you freedom—you're too dangerous for that."

"So, I'm to remain your prisoner?"

He shook his head. "I need a woman to warm my bed."

Disgusting man!

*But you've dreamed of the pleasure he can give you...*

Arlette silenced the treacherous voice in her mind. "What can a man who ruts his way through every maidservant in the household want with a lady?" she sneered.

He gave a cold smile. "With you, Lady Arlette, the prospect of exclusivity holds a certain appeal, provided you please me well."

Nausea clenched her stomach. He wanted to set her up as his leman—his whore—to rut whenever he pleased. She cursed her body that gave a thrill of recognition at the thought of the untold pleasures his capable hands might bring.

"Come, little one," he teased. "I remember the pleasures we shared in this very chamber—when you opened your thighs to me before Seaton interrupted us."

Hateful man! He smiled, as if he understood the shameful warmth pooling between her thighs at the memory of how she had offered herself to him.

"My body may be weak," she said, "but I'll never willingly be your whore. I shall scream every time you touch me!"

"Aye," he said, "you'll scream my name with pleasure as I take you."

His eyes sparkled like liquid silver.

Curse him! How many unfortunate women had he led to ruination? She'd die before she joined them.

"How dare you make such a proposal!" she hissed.

His smile disappeared. "You've yet to hear my offer," he said. "You shall not be my whore."

"I care not what you call it—leman, mistress, bed slave. I won't do it!"

"You will, my lady," he replied, "but you'll not be my leman."

"Then what would you call it?"

"My wife."

Arlette opened her mouth to respond, but no words came. A voice inside her head whispered what might have been had Papa not rejected him.

But her conscience dismissed it. She could never marry the man who killed her father—no matter what sins Papa had committed.

"Well?" he demanded. "Have you nothing to say?"

"I could never love you."

"Marry for love?" he scoffed. "You'll have a long wait."

"Then I choose to wait."

"You have but two choices," he said. "Marriage is better than the alternative, but I'll expect you to abide by your vows, and obey me in all matters."

"And if I don't?"

"Then I shall discipline you. If you defy me, I'll confine you to this room until you give me a son, after which I'll dispose of you as I see fit."

Ignoring the cold hand of fear clutching at her insides, Arlette let out a scornful laugh. "You're not making your offer very attractive, sir."

"It's better than the alternative."

"Which is?"

His eyes hardened. "You resume your position as a servant. Only this time, I'll not prevent my men from taking you—and the rest of your women—willing or not. In fact, I shall encourage it. A good whore can service up to ten men in a single evening. She has difficulty walking the next morning, but has no need of her legs other than to spread them."

Arlette closed her eyes to shut out his cruel smile. To be torn apart by men such as Ulferth...

She wouldn't survive it, and neither would her women—the gentle souls from home who depended on her.

"I shall leave you to make your choice," he said, giving a deep bow. "Until tomorrow, my *lady*."

He exited the chamber, shutting the door behind him. Moments later, she heard the familiar sound of the key turning in the lock.

# CHAPTER 17

Orson had not reached the end of the passageway before he curled his hand into a fist and smashed it against the wall.

Damn her for making him want her so much!

"You seem out of sorts, my friend," a voice said.

Pearce had followed him.

The guilt burning in his gut overshadowed the pain in his hand.

"I asked for her hand, Pearce."

A low hiss escaped his friend's lips, then he nodded toward Orson's hand where he'd torn the skin around the knuckles.

"I take it she refused?"

"I intended to take her as my leman," Orson said, "so she would bear my bastards and suffer the shame of it. But I couldn't do it."

"Has the lady succeeded where others have failed?" Pearce asked.

"Succeeded in what?"

"In capturing your heart."

"I have no heart, Pearce. Least of all for that hellcat."

"Then leave her be, Orson," Pearce said. "She'll not make you happy. Let Seaton have her. 'Tis time he was bedded, and if any woman could make a man out of that young whelp, I'll wager she could." He gave Orson a hungry smile. "Or—give her to me."

"No!" Orson roared, fisting his hand, as if to strike the wall again. Then, the memory of Verona's gentle smile tore into his heart and he lowered his head, no longer able to conquer the grief that clawed at him—the grief, and the guilt, that he'd been unable to prevent Verona from suffering a violent and brutal death.

"I've betrayed her, Pearce," he whispered, "by asking her murderer's daughter to be my wife."

"Orson..." A gentle hand touched his shoulder, but he pulled away.

"My sister is dead, while the de Villiers woman lives. I shall make her suffer and break her spirit—in Verona's memory."

"You think your sister would want that?" Pearce asked. "She'd want you happy—not destroyed by vengeance. Leave the Lady Arlette be—for your sake, and hers."

"No," Orson said. "I want her, and I will have her."

He left his friend and headed toward the servants' quarters. If Lady Arlette was too foolish to understand the consequences of refusing him, perhaps the old woman she doted on so much could be persuaded to make her understand.

THE KEY TURNED in the lock and Esme entered the solar, carrying a tray of food. Arlette uncurled herself from her chair, and winced as she stretched her limbs.

"What are you doing in the chair, my lady?" Esme asked. "'Tis freezing."

"I don't want to sleep in that bed—*his* bed."

Esme sighed, then set the tray down and took a fur from the bed. She draped it over Arlette's shoulders and took her hand, her fingers warm against Arlette's cold skin.

"You could do worse, lady," she said. "Lord Wulfson is a strong and capable man."

Arlette snatched her hand free.

"How dare you speak so!"

"Listen to me, lady," Esme said. "You must understand the choices before you."

"But marriage—to *him*!" Arlette cried.

"I was there the day he visited your father. I saw how you looked at him."

"That was six years ago. I was a mere child, and he had not butchered my family! It's wicked of you to suggest…"

"Be sensible, lady," Esme interrupted. "He'll not let you go. And other lives are at stake. Maude, Rosa…" Esme shook her head. "Think, child! You could live out your days as lady of this estate. Think of the good you could do!"

"But he killed Papa. He destroyed my home—our home!" Arlette cried.

"Aye," Esme said, "and now you know why. I understand your hatred, but you must turn your hate toward the deeds, not the man. He has a reputation for vengeance, aye, but that means he'll avenge any wrongdoing to himself and those close to him. Should you not want such a man for a husband? In this world, the men must be strong to survive. Women have little choice."

Fear rippled along Arlette's spine. "What if he turned his desire for vengeance against me?"

"You must give him no cause."

"What if he's cruel to me? What if he's worse than Fulbert?"

"He won't be, my lady," Esme said. "His heart may be hidden, but it beats nonetheless. Una told me that he loved his sister dearly. He protected her when she was a child against his stepmother's cruelty. Perhaps, in time, he'll love you as much. Wouldn't you want that? You must treat your father's death as if he were killed in battle."

"And what of Mama—and Guillaume?"

"Your mother's death was an accident, and at another's hands. Lord Wulfson deeply regrets it. As for Guillaume, if you married Wulfson, perhaps he may be persuaded to find him."

"So he can kill him? Never! Esme, you've lost your wits."

Esme shook her head, "I am quite sane, dear one, and I love you as my own daughter. You trust me, do you not?"

Arlette nodded.

"Then I beg you to accept him. I've never asked you for anything, but today I do. I stand in place of your mother, to give you a mother's counsel."

"You counsel me to marry him?"

"With all my heart."

Arlette slumped her shoulders in defeat.

Esme was right. Others depended on her, and it was time she placed their welfare above her need for vengeance.

"Then I'll accept him," she said, "for your sake, if not for mine."

Esme patted her hand and kissed her forehead.

"Sweet lady, I shall leave you in peace."

Esme exited the solar and the key turned in the lock once more, but not before Arlette caught her old nursemaid's whisper.

*Forgive me, little one.*

VICTORY—AT last!

Orson dismissed the old woman, and she fled from his study, but not before he saw the guilt in her eyes. She understood the benefits of her mistress yielding to him, but she clearly regretted being used as a pawn in his bid to snare the lady.

It mattered not. Arlette was his—at last.

He made his way to the solar.

As he reached the chamber, he found himself shaking with anticipation. What if she still refused him, despite what the old woman had said?

He pushed open the door and stepped inside.

She sat in a chair beside the table laden with food—untouched—a fur around her shoulders. She looked up as he approached and her eyes widened. She could not conceal the flash of desire in their expression—desire to match his.

"I'm come for your answer," he said.

"I know," she replied softly.

She might be the one barely clad—the prisoner, weakened by pain, and helpless in captivity—yet her voice held a quiet dignity he could never match.

His face warmed with shame as she met his gaze. What right had he to treat her so?

Then she spoke, and uttered the words he'd been yearning to hear.

"I accept your hand in marriage."

"You do?"

"Aye," she said, "but before I agree to it I have three requests.

He raised his eyebrows. "You have...*requests?*"

She nodded, and he leaned against the wall and folded his arms. "Let me hear them."

"First, I expect you to abide by the marriage vows."

He barked with laughter. "As you intend to? I warn you, madam, if you pay court to another, I'll kill him with my bare hands and find a far more imaginative punishment for you."

She blanched, but maintained her gaze.

"I do not fear you, sir. I will hold myself bound to my vows and request that you pay me the same courtesy."

He couldn't help be amused by the gravity of her expression. "You wish to have me all to yourself in bed?" he asked.

"I always determined to expect complete loyalty from the husband of my choosing."

"Is that why you turned away every suitor who came to visit?"

She raised her eyebrows in surprise, and he laughed. "I've heard tales of an untamed tigress who frightened many a suitor off," he said. "One such man spoke of a ruffian who turned up in breeches, brandishing a sword and threatening him with dismemberment if he touched her."

The ghost of a smile danced in her eyes, then she frowned.

"Not every refusal was my decision."

Did she refer to the day her father had rejected him six years ago? Her cheeks flushed and she looked away.

"I'll grant your first request, provided you're a faithful wife and please me well," he said. "What is your second?"

"You must give me leave to fulfil the duties of a wife, both within the household and among your tenants," she said. "I overheard your steward discussing the villagers' complaints—petty squabbles that a just lord—and lady—could preside over to maintain order. I hear many of the villagers are unhappy."

Now, she was trying his patience.

"Tenants have no need to be happy," he said. "They need to work."

"In order to do that effectively they must be content."

"Why should I care about them? I'm their lord."

She sighed. "That doesn't mean you own them. It means you're responsible for them."

He waved a dismissive hand at her. "William deals with them."

"It would do no harm if their lord granted them an audience once in a while."

"You ask too much."

"Then let the lady of the house see to it. Healing, minor disputes and so forth—I'd gladly relieve you of the burden."

He smiled inwardly. She asked a favor, yet acted as if she were granting one. But he saw the wisdom in her words. There always seemed to be too many squabbles among the tenants for his steward to deal with. Let the little she-cat try. A few visits to their filthy cottages would sully those delicate little hands enough to dissuade her from exacting any real influence over them.

"Very well," he said. "I'll speak with William tomorrow. Is that all?"

"No," she said. "I have a third condition."

"A *condition*?" he asked.

"The most important of the three," she said. "Concerning your daughter, Lillian. Her situation here is entirely inappropriate for someone of her status."

He gritted his teeth. Once again, the stigma of birth raised its head. The haughty little mare wanted rid of his bastard daughter.

"I'll do nothing you ask with regards to my daughter," he snarled.

"How can you be so cruel?" she cried. "A small act on your part would achieve so much."

Was she insane?

"What of your cruelty, madam?" he demanded. "Lillian stays where she is. If you utter one more word on the matter I'll have you lashed—and will administer the strokes myself."

"You unfeeling brute!" she cried. "You neglect that poor child, yet you, of all men, should understand her plight. Or do all fathers hate their bastard children?"

"My father loved me though I was his bastard," he growled, "'Twas *your* father who hated me for my birth, and he condemned me for my daughter's very existence."

"I care nothing for Lillian's birth," she said. "I care that she's ignored and neglected, as if she's a dirty secret. I'm not my father, and do not share his sentiments in that regard. I may never be free to make my own choices in life, but I have my own feelings and beliefs, even if the world demands I keep them to myself."

"You don't despise Lillian?"

Her nose wrinkled in disgust "I despise *you* for believing that I could. She's your daughter, and needs a parent's love as much as any child. You think I'd have rejected her had my father accepted your offer of marriage six years ago? You're wrong. I would have accepted her as my own. That is my third condition—that you let me do so now."

"With such a willful temper you're hardly fitting material for a noblewoman," he said, "or a wife."

"You think I care?" she replied. "I could never be a submissive wife."

"You consider yourself a free spirit?"

The defiance in her eyes dulled. "What woman can consider herself free? We live our lives defined by the chains and boundaries that restrict us."

"Such as the boundaries of marriage?" he asked.

"Ah, sir—that is where the length of the chain varies according to the husband's will."

"Is that why you never accepted a suitor?

"There were many reasons," she said, "but I will not share them with you."

He took her hand, the skin of her fingers cold against his own, and lifted it to his lips.

"Will you take me as your husband?"

"You leave me no choice."

"I would have you come to me of your own free will," he said,

"Will you grant me what I ask?"

He nodded. "Aye."

"Then I'll come to you willingly."

*But not gladly.*

He released her hand.

"I'll leave you to sleep here alone until we are wed," he said. "For now, I bid you goodnight." He leaned forward. "I would have a kiss to seal our betrothal."

She tipped her head up in compliance, and closed her eyes as he kissed her. He probed her mouth with his tongue, and though she parted her lips against the invasion, she made no other response—gave no sign of pleasure. Eventually, he gave up and withdrew, closing the solar door behind him.

There was now no need to lock the door. The cage could be left open, for the bird had pledged not to fly.

# CHAPTER 18

Arlette woke at a knock on the door and rubbed her eyes, puffy from crying. Ashamed at her weakness, she called out, forcing her voice to be strong. She was a de Villiers, and would carry her family's pride, no matter what Papa had done, or how much Lord Wulfson, Orson—her *betrothed*—wanted vengeance.

And she would find Guillaume.

If he still lived.

Fear of the wedding night—the bride's screams, the violation—had blackened her dreams. But she'd never betray her feelings to *him*. She would never submit.

Two women entered the solar—Esme, carrying a tray of food, and Elvia, carrying a bundle of clothes, a broad grin on her face.

Good news travelled fast.

Elvia dropped a curtsey. "Lady!"

Arlette's cheeks warmed with shame. "Forgive my deception, Elvia."

"No matter," Elvia chirped. "I always thought you different to the rest of us. And we're all delighted he didn't choose Kendra." She giggled. "Except Hilda. When she found out, her expression was sour enough to turn the milk into cheese!"

"Elvia!" Esme reprimanded. "Lady Arlette is your mistress, not your friend."

"Elvia has been a good friend," Arlette said.

"She's now your servant," Esme chided, "and Lord Wulfson has tasked us with dressing you as befits his betrothed."

Arlette opened her mouth to protest, then closed it and nodded. She had no wish to dampen Elvia's delight.

"Very well," she said. "Show me what you've brought."

Elvia dropped the bundle on the bed. There were two dresses—one green, the other blue—each trimmed with jewels adorning the collar, bodice, and hem. The image of their previous owner filled Arlette with a rush of loathing.

"How dare he!" she cried. "Would he bedeck me in his whore's attire?"

"This isn't the time to be fastidious," Esme said.

Arlette picked up the green dress. "It's hideous!" she cried. "That harlot had treasures stitched into her gown that could feed a family for months. I won't wear it."

Elvia held up the blue gown. "Is this better?"

"No. It's worse," Arlette said. "Are these the only gowns?"

Elvia's eyes narrowed in fear. "The others belonged to the Lady Verona. But no one is permitted to enter her room, much less touch her possessions. Lord Wulfson would have me whipped if I disobeyed." She flinched. "Oh, lady—forgive me."

"No matter," Arlette said. "My wounds have almost healed. And you're not the one in need of forgiveness. But I cannot wear this gown—not without removing these adornments. Why would anyone wear such a thing?"

"It was a gift from the master," Elvia said.

"Aye," Arlette snorted, "for that whore Kendra."

"And now it's yours."

"Then I'll do with it as I please," Arlette said. She held the gown up, running her finger along the jewels sewn into the fabric.

"That's why I'm here," Elvia said, "to alter the gown for you."

Arlette smiled. "Then alter it we shall. Then, I'll give my betrothed a lesson in the art of giving."

~

DAMNED TENANTS! Why did they plague him so? A man was no man at all, if he couldn't take care of himself and others. If Orson gave these people charity, they wouldn't show gratitude—they'd only expect more.

He leaned back in his chair and glared at his steward.

"William, I fail to see why you bring these petty squabbles to my attention."

"Because you're the master," came the reply. "Sometimes the flock needs to be reassured that the shepherd has their best interests at heart."

"What nonsense!" Orson said. "You sound like a woman. It matters not to me whether the farmer is too weak to till the land, or whether his neighbor has stolen a sack of grain. A man must be strong—to fight for what's his."

"He must also be compassionate."

"There's no place in the world for a man who cannot command others."

"There's every place," William said. "Would you have every man hereabouts challenge your position as lord? There's only room for one leader, and you cannot rule with your sword alone."

Before Orson could reply, the study door flew open with a crash, and William's eyes widened in apprehension.

Someone had just earned a lashing.

"What is the meaning of this!" Orson roared, turning to face the newcomer.

Lady Arlette stood in the doorway, dressed for the first time in a lady's attire. The gown accentuated her figure—the deep green complementing her chestnut hair. His cock hardened, forcing the breath from his lungs. From William's expression, Orson's steward was not immune to her beauty either.

Her eyes flashed with anger. Her spirit had returned.

Good—he relished a challenge, and had no wish for her to submit so easily.

As his gaze wandered up and down her gown, his relish at the prospect of taming her gave way to fury. The gown wasn't Kendra's. The elegant simplicity reminded him of one woman.

Verona.

He lifted his gaze to her eyes—the same eyes as her father's—emerald eyes that had widened in surprise as he'd speared Reynaud de Villiers with his sword for murdering his beloved sister.

He rose to his feet.

"Where did you get that gown?"

"As if you didn't know!" she scoffed. "It was your whore's!"

He shook his head. "I've never seen Kendra in such a dress. Tell the truth, or suffer the consequences."

"I had all that ridiculous nonsense removed," she scoffed, "not to mention a considerable amount of excess material that covered her bulk."

"Ridiculous nonsense?"

She held out her hand and opened it. A small pile of jewels lay on her palm. "I have no wish to wear these."

"Then use them as you see fit," he said.

"For any purpose?"

"Aye—for any purpose."

Rather than thank him for his generosity, she gave a sly smile.

"I wish to visit the tenants today—as per one of the conditions on which I agreed to marry you."

William let out a cough and Orson detected a spark of amusement in his eyes. She was a cunning little mare—but he had promised to grant her request, and as a man of honor, he always fulfilled his promises.

"Why do you wish to visit them?" he asked.

"Because I've no wish to spend my days idling away in your solar stitching as many jewels on my gowns as my frame can carry," she said. "I wish to fulfil the duties of the lady of the estate." She gave

William a sly smile. "Methinks your master is ignorant of what those duties might be."

William let out a snort, his struggles not to laugh all too obvious. Did Arlette mean to humiliate him in front of his steward?

"I'm fully aware of your duties, madam," he said, "and I'll take great pleasure ensuring that you fulfil them at every turn."

Fear flashed in her eyes, but she held her ground. "I wish to arrange a feast for the tenants, to celebrate our wedding."

What was she thinking? Inviting peasants to take the place of honored guests?

"That's out of the question," he replied. "Noblemen and women cannot be expected to rub shoulders with the lower classes."

"A separate feast, then—in the tourney field."

"My lord," William interrupted, "it's a means of securing their loyalty, as we discussed.

Arlette's smile broadened. "You said the jewels were mine to dispose of as I see fit, *my lord*," she said, curling her lip as she addressed him with mock courtesy. "You heard him, did you not, William?"

"My lord…" William began but Orson interrupted.

"That will be all, William. Leave us. There's something I must discuss with my betrothed."

As the door closed behind the steward, Orson took Arlette's wrist and pulled her close, dislodging some of the jewels, which clattered onto the table.

"I take it I have your permission to visit the tenants?" she asked.

"You must take an escort," he replied.

"Naturally. May I be permitted to choose my escort, if you cannot favor me with your company?"

Jealousy needled at him and he tightened his grip. "You may be interested to know, madam, that I sent young Seaton back to his father this morning, to spend time with his family—my reward for his success at the tournament."

He released her hand and she snatched it free.

"Am I not a generous lord?" he asked, "I am, after all, thinking of the young man's welfare—and yours, of course."

Her smile disappeared and she backed toward the door. She understood the threat.

"No kiss for your future husband?" He shook his head. "I can wait —I'll take what I want when we're married."

Fear and defiance flashed in her eyes, then she turned her back on him and exited the room, without bothering to close the door.

He might have won the battle, but she was well versed in the tactics of war.

ARLETTE TOSSED ASIDE her embroidery and sighed. Though her status as a lady had been restored, she chafed at the lack of occupation. She lifted her hands and inspected them. The salve Dawn provided had almost completely removed all traces of toil from her hands—though the callouses gained from playing at sword-fighting at home would always remain with her—a reminder of her past.

Tomorrow Arlette de Villiers would be no more. Lady Wulfson would take her place—a woman with a home to run, servants, tenants who depended on her. It was everything Mama had wanted for her, but it came with a price.

Her freedom.

Since announcing their betrothal, Orson had avoided her—as if having secured victory, the spoils had lost their appeal. Her fear of the wedding night yielded to relief that he didn't seek her out at night to ravage her body. But a voice in her mind whispered of disappointed hopes. A treacherous little corner of her soul yearned for the delicious sensations he'd elicited with his hands.

She glanced at the chair on which she'd sat, the night of the tournament when he'd almost seduced her—when she had parted her thighs for him. Then she looked away in shame.

*I don't want him—I cannot!*

"Arlette." A deep voice spoke and she looked up.

Her betrothed stood in the doorway. The sound of her name on his lips sent an unwelcome thrill through her. An arrogant smile spread across his handsome face. He knew she desired him.

She frowned. "What do you want?"

He arched an eyebrow. "Not the devoted greeting I'd expect."

"What do you want—*my love?*"

"I'm come to take you hunting."

"I've too much to do here," she replied.

He moved closer, and held out his hand.

"It was not a request."

The expression in his eyes told her he'd take no denial. She scowled and took his arm, and he led her outside to the stableyard.

A groom stood waiting beside two horses—the huge destrier Orson had ridden in the tournament, and a smaller, chestnut-colored mare.

"I take it you're proficient in the saddle?" Orson asked.

"Of course."

He steered her toward the mare, and helped her into the saddle. Then he mounted the destrier in the swift, smooth movement of the practiced warrior. He grasped the reins and turned his mount in a tight circle with a smile of satisfaction.

With his athletic, muscular physique, he was the epitome of male perfection.

And he knew it.

"Come, my lady." He spurred his mount forward and Arlette steered the mare to follow. What choice did she have? She'd made a promise to him—as he had to her.

They rode into the nearby forest, and did not stop until they reached a clearing, where a falconer waited, holding a peregrine on his wrist. Orson dismounted and helped Arlette down, his fingers curling possessively around her wrist as they moved away from the horses.

The falconer removed the hood from the bird.

"Come, lady," he said. Arlette approached him and he held out his arm, smiling encouragement. She reached out and ran her fingertips down the falcon's back, the feathers soft against her skin. The bird fixed its yellow eye on her.

"He's beautiful," she said.

"Aye indeed," the falconer replied, "but she's the female."

"The female hunts?"

"Aye, she does, milady. She's more proficient than the male."

He released the bird, and it soared into the air.

Shielding her eyes from the sun, Arlette craned her neck to watch its progress as it flew higher and higher.

*What it must be, to have such freedom...*

"Milady?"

She had spoken aloud.

The falconer whistled and the bird swooped toward him, wings outstretched, before landing on his wrist. She folded her wings, and deftly plucked the piece of meat he offered.

"Why does she come back to you?" Arlette asked. "Doesn't she want to be free?"

Pride resonated in the falconer's voice—pride in his skill and in his charge. "She has been trained well."

"Aye, falconer," Orson said. "You've trained her well. She recognizes her master."

He stood behind Arlette, so close he almost touched her.

"She's given freedom to fly, and in turn she gladly returns to him." He leaned forward and brushed his lips against her ear. Her skin tightened at the rush of warm breath on her neck, as he whispered—quietly enough that only she could hear.

"Perhaps one day I'll grant you such freedom. If I thought you'd always return to me."

He kissed her neck, sending a spark of fire through her blood, and she leaned toward him.

"Perhaps that day will come sooner than I thought," he said.

She started and moved away, not missing his low chuckle.

"Lady?" The falconer offered Arlette a gauntlet, and she put it on.

"Hold your hand out like this." He placed the bird on her fist and it stood still, watching her unblinkingly. Then she released her grip and the bird launched into the sky, trailing the rope between its legs, wings at full stretch, beating the air, before settling into a graceful sweep as it soared into the heavens.

The falconer whistled and the bird flew back and settled onto Arlette's hand. She gave a cry of delight as it took a piece of meat from her fingers.

"I'm glad to see my lady so happy," Orson said. "Perhaps she might bestow a smile on her betrothed?"

What was she thinking? What reason did she have to smile?

She returned the bird to the falconer, and turned her back on Orson.

The falcon would soon be returned to her cage, and tomorrow, Arlette would be placed in a cage of her own.

"MILADY, 'tis a sign from heaven that your marriage is blessed."

Arlette's wedding day had dawned dull and misty, but the sun had soon boiled away the moisture to reveal a bright blue sky.

Esme was a fool. Always she looked for signs and portents. Would that the mist had remained—oppressive and restrictive—to match Arlette's temper.

"You make the most beautiful bride," Esme clucked.

Arlette ran her hands along her body. Elvia had stitched the most beautiful gown—elegant in its simplicity—but it was the gown of a captive. The laces on the bodice she likened to chains—the Greywell family necklace a thrall collar.

Arlette shook her head. "It matters not how I look."

"Don't you want your husband to love you?"

"Esme, we both know this marriage is not founded on love," Arlette replied. "I could never love him, and I doubt he understands the notion of love. Call my situation what it is. Captivity."

Her stomach clenched at a knock on the door, marking the first step on the path to enslavement. Pearce entered the chamber and gave a deep bow.

"Your bridegroom awaits."

Arlette's breath caught and she closed her eyes. Esme took her hand.

"Courage, my lady tigress."

A crowd had gathered for the wedding, lining either side of the path to the chapel, down which Arlette walked, flanked by two of Orson's men, Pearce and Brand.

*Even now he seeks to prevent my escape.*

A girl of about six summers approached Arlette, clutching a handful of wildflowers and grasses.

Brand blocked the child's path.

"Keep away, brat!"

"Stop!" Arlette cried.

The procession drew to a halt.

"Lady, do not tarry," Pearce warned. "Lord Wulfson awaits."

"He can wait a little longer, Pearce," she replied. "I can hardly escape when I'm being led to the altar under guard."

She turned to Brand. "Out of the way."

At a nod from Pearce, he stepped aside.

The little girl remained still, eyes wide, lips trembling.

Arlette held her hand out.

"Come, child," she said. "You needn't be afraid of this great lumbering boar. If he shouts at you again, I'll send him to the pig farmer to sleep in the swill." She wrinkled her nose. "Mayhap, from the smell, he slept there last night. Shall we ask him?"

The child giggled and held out the flowers.

"Are those for me?"

"Aye, your ladyship." The child bobbed a curtsey. "I picked them with Mama."

"What's your name?" Arlette asked.

"Odella."

"And do you live in the village?"

"My father is the tanner," the child said, pride in her voice. "My older brother is one of the grooms in the castle."

"Then I shall thank him for taking such good care of my horse,"

Arlette said. "You must tell your mama she has a generous and gracious daughter."

Angry footsteps approached. Orson had come for her.

"Why do you delay?" he demanded.

Arlette winked at Odella. "It seems all men are the same today," she said. "The pig farmer will have many guests tonight."

The child let out a nervous giggle, but Pearce drew in a sharp breath. Orson's eyes flashed with menace.

"To what are you referring?" he demanded.

"My love, we mustn't tarry," she said, smiling sweetly. "Our people wish me well, and I'm overcome with rapture that they've come to share our joy and witness the moment when you make me the happiest of women."

The telltale tic in his jaw betrayed his temper, and he curled his hand around her arm.

"Let us make haste, dearest, so you, also, can make me the happiest of men." Though he smiled, his eyes remained cold and hard.

Arlette smiled to herself. If she could make sport of him, then perhaps she could bear this marriage.

Her confidence waned during the ceremony. Orson spoke his vows through gritted teeth and when it came to her turn, he curled his hand around her arm, his grip tightening when she pledged to obey him. As the priest declared them husband and wife, Orson lowered his head to kiss her, then whispered in her ear.

"You now belong to me. I expect to see no more instances of disobedience, such as that little spectacle I witnessed earlier."

Before she could reply, he led her outside to the waiting crowd.

"The Lady Arlette has made me the happiest of men!" he cried.

Amid the cheering, he claimed her mouth. His lips assaulted hers, then his tongue followed suit. He held her firm, sweeping his tongue through her mouth, claiming her lips as thoroughly as he would claim her body. Punishing her for her earlier words, he showed he could play her at her own game—and win.

He dipped his hand inside her gown, and her skin tightened as her treacherous body betrayed her need for him. She closed her eyes, fighting the vision of a torn nightshift and a pool of blood engulfing a screaming bride.

Her gown began to restrict her breathing, and the world slipped sideways as the blackness threatened to engulf her. She stumbled forward, her legs giving way, and he caught her in his arms amid raucous laughter from his men.

"She already swoons with desire for you, my lord!"

Orson's voice penetrated the darkness. "Are you well, wife?"

*Wife...*

Swallowing her fear, she nodded. "My gown was laced a little tight, that's all."

"Do not fret," he chuckled. "I shall relieve you of your gown soon enough, and more besides."

Fear rippled through her as shouts of laughter erupted from the crowd. Then her husband took her hand and led her back to the castle, each step taking her closer to the horror that was to come—her violation at his hands.

# CHAPTER 19

The trestle tables in the great hall were laden with the feast—haunches of venison, a thick stew made from boar, goblets and pitchers filled to the brim with wine. The large high table had been replaced by a smaller one on a raised platform at which Arlette sat with her new husband.

Her husband—and owner.

The jocular voices and ribald humor filled the air, as the wedding guests filled their platters. But fear of the night to come had destroyed Arlette's appetite.

Orson speared a piece of boar, then held it up, the tip of his knife blade poking through the meat.

"My love, you must taste this." He placed a gentle, but unyielding, hand at the back of her head, then held the piece of meat to her lips. With no choice, she took it in her mouth, though it tasted like sand.

"Smile," he said. "The guests expect it."

She took a sip of wine, and he nodded in satisfaction.

"I have a wedding gift for you," he said. "As you seemed so fond of the falcon, I've decided to give her to you."

Arlette set her cup aside. "Thank you, sir."

"Sir? You can do better than that."

"Thank you..." she hesitated, "*...husband.*"

"That's better," he said. "Do you know why the female falcon is larger than the male?"

Arlette shook her head. "No."

"It's so she can protect her chicks against marauders."

"If she's larger than the male, is he not afraid of her?" she asked.

"No, wife, for he knows how to master her."

"How does he do that?"

He leaned over her, his voice rumbling in her ear.

"He bites her neck to hold her still, the moment he takes her."

Her hand shook, and wine splashed onto the table.

"That's brutal," she whispered.

"But necessary, if he is to tame her."

He pulled her close, his breath hot on her neck, then he parted his lips and his teeth grazed against her skin. She turned her head to face him, and he captured her mouth in a hungry kiss, and slipped his tongue between her lips. He tasted of spices—heady, intoxicating spices—and she responded before she could stop herself.

"It seems I have already mastered you, my love," he said, "though I shall employ the falcon's technique tonight with immense pleasure."

He stood, then grasped her hand and pulled her up beside him. A ripple of quiet radiated outward as the guests ceased their chatter.

His voice echoed through the hall. "It's time that my bride and I retire."

Some of the guests made crude gestures, while others banged their goblets on the tables in appreciation.

"At last, Lord Wulfson can demonstrate his swordsmanship!" someone cried.

Arlette could delay her body's destruction no longer. Her legs grew weak, and she pitched forward. Reaching out a steadying hand, she knocked her wine cup over. Its contents spilled out, pooling into a thick, dark stain, which bled into the wood and dripped onto the floor. Echoes of screams of agony pulsed in her head with the fall of every droplet.

"It's early yet," she said, bile rising in her throat. But he merely laughed.

"Our guests will be well looked after, wife, and I shall return later."

"We'll return?"

"Just I," he said. "*You'll* be in need of your rest."

His mouth twitched at the laughter his response elicited from those sitting nearby. "Come, Pearce—we're ready."

Pearce, and five others, rose to their feet. Tightening his hold on her, Orson led her out of the hall.

"Why do they follow us?" she asked.

"Witnesses."

"Witnesses—to what?"

"The consummation of our marriage."

The food in her stomach solidified, and a cold lump of terror cramped her insides.

"Don't worry, my love," he laughed. "While many bridegrooms are happy for the deed to be witnessed inside the bridal chamber, I want you all to myself. But your screams of pleasure will be proof enough of consummation."

He winked at his companions, then led her to the solar door, where Esme and Maude stood waiting.

"Prepare my wife, old woman," he said. Then he pushed Arlette inside. "I shall return when you're ready for me."

~

THE SOLAR DOOR opened and the old woman appeared.

"She's ready for you, my lord."

Pearce slapped Orson on the back.

"Good luck, my friend. You'll need it."

Orson stepped inside. His bride sat in a chair beside the bed. Her bridal gown had been removed. Dressed in a thin chemise, she seemed to have shrunk in stature, the color in her face drained. Her fingers curled into a claw around her nursemaid's wrist as the old woman fussed over her.

"Esme—the stain…" she whispered. "All I can see is the stain."

"Hush, little one, don't think of it." The old woman stroked her forehead, then held a goblet to her lips. "Drink this."

Arlette nodded and drained the cup.

Orson beckoned the old woman over.

"Do you think to serve my wife up to me drunk?"

"It's only a potion to ease her nerves."

"God's blood, woman—what are you about?"

"Forgive me, my lord," she replied. "My lady fears the marriage bed. She's had nightmares about the…the bridal stains since childhood. I have a duty to ease her pain."

"What foolish nonsense!" he said. "She's rightfully mine, and I shall enjoy her tonight."

"I beg you, show mercy," she said. "My lady may be strong, but she is of slight build and you are a—a large man. I have given her a mild draught to relax her, so the pain will not be so severe her first time."

"I'm not an animal," he said. "Now, leave us."

She opened her mouth to respond, the nodded. "Come, Maude," she said. The two women exited the solar, leaving Orson alone with his bride.

He beckoned to her. "Come here."

She stood. The thin fabric of her chemise left little to the imagination, revealing the curve of her hips, her shapely legs, and the swell of her breasts with their tempting dark little centers. His gaze travelled downward, resting on the shadowy apex of her thighs, and his manhood surged with the need to be inside her.

*God's bones*—this beautiful creature was his, all his, to do with as he pleased.

"Are you ready to receive your husband?"

"I'm ready." Her voice was slurred, but the undercurrent of fear resonated in her words, and he saw it in her eyes. Though dulled by the potion, raw terror pulsed in their depths. Did she find the prospect of sharing his bed so abhorrent?

Her body swayed drunkenly. He reached out, but she jerked away, losing her balance, and he caught her before she fell, and lifted her into his arms. She struggled in his grip, then gave a sob of resignation as he placed her on the bed.

Hell and damnation! He had no wish to take a sobbing, unwilling woman—much less one who needed to be drugged to endure the experience.

He had his pride. She would purr like a kitten beneath him, but not tonight—and not under the influence of whatever potion that old hag had given her.

The witnesses must be satisfied—a small cut should suffice.

He pulled out his knife, and drew back the sleeve of her gown. As he placed the tip of the blade on her skin, she cried out and tried to wrench herself free. The knife caught her flesh and she screamed.

"Hold still!" he hissed. "I must have proof."

"Sweet Lord—what proof?" she cried, her voice rising with panic. She wriggled free, leaped off the bed, and ran for the door. At all costs she must not reach it—not with half a dozen men outside. He caught her chemise and they fell to the floor, knocking into a table that upended with a crash.

"Please!" she screamed, "have mercy!"

Her chemise tore in his hands. Holding her firm, he rubbed the silken material along the cut on her forearm, while she yelled and cursed. A sharp sensation bit into his face as she dug her fingernails into his cheek.

He rolled off her, taking the gown with him, and she backed away, covering her naked body with her hands.

"Get into bed and stay there," he said, fighting his desire to take her, on the floor.

She froze, staring at him, her eyes wide in her pale face.

"I'll not ask again," he said. "My men are right outside that door. Do you wish me to invite them in?"

She shook her head, then moved toward the bed and climbed in. Her eyes, though dulled by the drug, glittered with hate.

He nodded toward her arm. "It had to be done," he said. "Get some sleep. I'll not touch you tonight."

She opened her mouth to speak, but the drug finally overcame her and she sank back, her eyes closed. She would give him no more trouble that night.

Fisting the bloodstained chemise in his hands, Orson exited the solar and was greeted with cheers from his men.

"You wielded your mighty lance!"

"Did you spear your prey?"

"Did she sheathe her claws, before you sheathed your sword into her?"

Swallowing the knot of anger, he joined in the laughter. A newly wedded man should enjoy a joke with his friends after a successful bedding.

Yet his bride lay alone in the bed—a maiden still.

*Damn her!*

He strode back to the dining hall, the men in his wake, and held his bride's nightshift aloft to the applause of the guests. Then he threw the bloodstained garment onto the fireplace. Some men would hang their bride's nightgown on the wall, for the guests to view the stain. But he had no wish for his guests to inspect it too closely.

Flames danced around the fabric, and the fire hissed and spat. For a fleeting moment the flames morphed into the face of the lady Emmelina de Villiers, staring reproachfully at him. He'd only ever seen her face once, as she lay dead at his feet, killed at Ulferth's hands. Arlette resembled her, and he cursed himself for not having noticed it.

*Forgive me, Lady Emmelina—I will guard your daughter and keep her well.*

Acknowledging his guests' congratulations on his prowess, Orson returned to his seat. Pearce took the chair beside him.

"Did you take her unwilling?"

"No," Orson replied.

"I'd never judge you, my friend, but have you seen what she's done to your face?"

"I did *not* take her unwilling."

"I doubt she's into blood sports," Pearce replied. "Perhaps you did not take her at all. Was it her blood on the gown?"

"Aye," Orson said. In that, at least, he could speak the truth.

After the feast drew to a close, many of the guests slumped over the tables snoring off their ale, Orson retired to the solar. His bride slept, but she'd thrown some of the furs off the bed, despite the cold.

The wine did nothing to ease the stirring in his manhood at the sight of her naked form. He shed his clothes and climbed into the bed, settling his body alongside hers. She nestled against him in her sleep, despite his rigid member, which nudged insistently against her back.

How easily he could take his pleasures on her now—while she slept, and was unable to fight him. But he wanted her willing.

And she would be.

In time, she would beg him to take her.

~

WHEN ARLETTE WOKE, her head was still thick from the potion Esme had given her. Rubbing her eyes, she yawned and stretched, wincing at the soreness in her arm.

"I trust you slept well, wife."

Her husband stood beside the bed, fully dressed. Why did his voice send a thrill through her body?

He nodded to her forearm. "Does it pain you?"

"A little."

"Forgive me. It was necessary."

"Necessary? To mutilate my flesh?"

He sat, and the bed ropes creaked under his weight. "Do you know what happens the first time a woman lies with a man?"

She closed her eyes, but couldn't dispel the image of red liquid dripping onto a white gown.

"Blood," she whispered. "A lot of blood."

He nodded. "A bride's blood is proof of consummation—that the marriage is lawful. But we didn't consummate our marriage, so I cut your arm to produce enough blood to fool the witnesses."

Why hadn't he violated her?

As if he read her mind, he answered the unspoken question.

"I may be many things, Arlette, but I have no appetite for a screaming, struggling woman. My women have been more than willing—as you shall be when I take you."

Her breath caught at the hunger in his gaze.

"Will I bleed?"

"Aye," he said. "Now, hold out your arm."

Sweet Lord! What was he going to do?

She shook her head.

"God's teeth, woman," he said, "I only mean to bind it."

"Why did you cut me?" she asked.

"Many bridegrooms cut themselves on the wedding night as proof of consummation," he said, bandaging her arm, "usually when their wives are too hideous to bed."

Hideous? Hateful brute!

"Then why not cut your own worthless arm?" she spat.

"So that I could answer truthfully when asked if the blood was yours," he replied. "I value honesty above all."

"But not honor," she said. "If you find me so hideous, I wonder why you forced me to marry you.

He let out a laugh. "Have I offended my lady's pride? Don't despair, little one, I shall have you, and you'll come willing."

"I shall not."

"Say what you will, madam," he said, "but you want me. Your desire is so potent I can almost taste it."

He secured the bandage with a knot.

"I'm afraid you must wait for your pleasure. I've much to do today."

She tried to rise, but he placed a restraining hand on her shoulder.

"No, you stay abed, wife."

"For what purpose?"

"I have a reputation to uphold. Any woman—let alone my bride—would be expected to have difficulty walking after having me between her thighs for a whole night."

He chuckled at her involuntary gasp.

"I'll send someone to bring you food," he said. "You'll be in need of your strength, for what I have in mind for you."

He leaned forward to kiss her, but she turned her face away. Seemingly unconcerned, he rose, and left the solar.

*Barton Keep, England, 1086*

Fulbert de Villiers raised his hand until the ruby in his new ring caught the sunlight. It was a beautiful gem, though not as large as he would have liked—and at the wrong angle he discerned a slight flaw in it.

A knock on the door interrupted his study. Curse the servants! He'd asked not to be disturbed. Whoever disobeyed would be punished. He relished their fear.

They never knew whether he would ignore their transgressions, issue a beating, or have them hacked to death. It made a pleasant diversion. The ones he whipped were so ready to express their gratitude for being permitted to continue their pathetic lives. What a fool Papa had been! Always insisting they be treated with kindness. As for that imbecile Uncle Reynaud...

The door opened, and an old man shuffled in—the same servant he'd branded for stealing from the kitchen. Hunger kept them sharp—fear even sharper.

"What do you want?"

"There's a lady to see you, my lord."

"Then bring her in, unless you want another lashing."

A woman entered, eyeing the servant with dislike. Fulbert's cock twitched at her lusty beauty. Glossy ebony hair hung in two thick braids—eyes the color of ice lingered over his face with the cold, calculating expression he recognized in himself.

The foolish harlot thought to rule him. In time, he'd teach her a lesson, but for now she had her uses. She seemed to relish subjecting herself to every depravity he forced onto her, begging him to take her while she offered herself in every sordid manner imaginable. But, like all women, she was disposable—there were plenty of others in the village ripe for the taking, willing or not.

"I dislike uninvited visitors," he snarled.

"I have news which you'll find useful—in return for a token," she said, eyeing his ring with envy.

Her tongue flicked out to caress her bottom lip.

"Don't tease me, woman," he said, "or I'll have your news tortured out of you."

Her smile slipped.

"Very well," she said sweetly. "*She* is alive."

"Who?"

"Your cousin."

His stomach clenched.

*Arlette...*

"Are you certain?" he asked.

"Aye. She was at Greywell Castle all the time. The cowardly little slut made a convincing serf."

He struck her across the face, and she staggered back.

"How dare you speak of her, you whore!"

She smiled, rubbing her cheek. "*She's* the whore. She's already spread her legs for Wulfson—and half his men."

Rage boiled in Fulbert's blood. Treacherous mare!

She slipped her hand inside his breeches, her expert fingers knowing just where to rouse him. A little growl of triumph escaped her lips as his cock stiffened at her touch. With a rustle of silk, she kneeled at his feet, and licked her lips.

"Forget her, Fulbert. Think of the pleasures *I* can give you."

He closed his eyes, while she pleasured him with her mouth. As he reached his climax, he gripped her hair lest she pull away, hating her for her eagerness to degrade herself. Did she think him a fool? There was only one woman he wanted to share his empire with. And now she had, at last, been found, he needed to secure her and punish her betrayal.

The woman at his feet stood, and tried to kiss him, but he pushed her away.

"Come, my love," she purred, her voice thick with lust. "We can be together."

"No," he snarled. "Not until I've made that Saxon whoreson pay for despoiling what's mine."

"Then let me help you. There are those still loyal to me within his walls."

"Very well," he said. "Now, get out of my sight until I send for you."

"As you wish, my love." She blew him a kiss, her eyes glittering with greed, then exited the chamber.

Fulbert smiled to himself. Once he had Arlette safely under lock and key, he would deal with Kendra as he saw fit.

# CHAPTER 20

The evening after the wedding, stomach cramps signaled the onset of Arlette's monthly bleed. When Orson joined her in the solar, he waved his hand in disgust at her attempts to explain, climbed into the bed, and fell asleep without touching her.

For the next three nights, he did the same. At first, she felt only relief at avoiding violation at his hands, but, at length, frustration replaced the relief.

She found Esme unsympathetic to her complaints.

"It would be most unpleasant, child, if he forced his attentions on you while you were unwell. Your poor mother was less fortunate."

"But he ignores me during the day, also!"

"I thought you disliked him," Esme said. "Do you now desire his company?"

"Of course not," Arlette said. "He's a brute."

"He's a harsh man, undoubtedly," Esme said. "Harsh and unforgiving—but we live in an unforgiving world. Men are killed in battle every day. They accept it, and so must we. Lord Wulfson has had to fight for everything he has."

"Why can I not fight also?"

Esme took her hand. "Your battle is within these walls, child—the fight every woman faces—to take care of her household, and her loved ones. Do you really want to go out into a man's world, to face pain and death?"

"I do not fear death."

"Perhaps not," Esme said. "But now you have a husband to protect you—and he'll protect you until his last breath if you're true to him. You must learn that it's not a weakness to accept that—but a strength."

Esme spoke sense. But, as much as Arlette tried to hate her husband for what he'd done—and for the manner by which he'd secured her hand in marriage—she could not deny the need that grew within her—the need to experience the passion she had dreamed of when she'd first set eyes on him.

"Do you suppose he will take a mistress?" she asked.

"I cannot say. Few noblewomen find love—or fidelity—in their husbands. Seek solace in running the household. Heaven knows I've tried to teach you the skills of a lady." Esme squeezed her hand. "You will find love in your children."

Children—the purpose of all marriages.

Arlette shivered. What would the birthing do to her? If a bedding rendered a bride bloody and battered, childbirth might rip her body apart. She closed her eyes to control the wave of terror. At all costs, her husband must not sense her fear, or he'd have even more power over her.

She must show courage—starting today—and face him like a warrior, not hide in the solar like a coward.

She found him in the study with his steward.

"Husband, I would speak with you."

"You'll have to wait," he said. "I've important business to deal with."

"Do the tenants still express dissatisfaction with their lord?"

The tic in his jaw told Arlette that her arrow had found its target.

"That's not your concern, woman."

"I disagree."

The steward let out a gasp.

"As your wife," she continued, "I have a duty to our tenants."

He waved a hand dismissively. "Begone, before I lose my temper."

"Without hearing my request?"

"Request!" he scoffed, "You only make demands."

"I pledged to be a dutiful wife," she said sweetly, "to give healing and counsel to my husband's tenants and servants, to release him of the burden. Or have you forgotten the vows we spoke?"

Emboldened by the steward's presence, she continued. "I have some skill at healing and wish to be of use to our people. 'Tis an occupation for the lady of the household and, as such, your daughter needs to begin learning it also. I can teach her. Una has shown me a chamber I can use. She can furnish me with everything I require, so we need not trouble you."

"The lady's right," the steward intervened, "Una knows…"

"Be quiet, William!" Orson growled. "Leave us, wife, and plague me no more today."

Hateful brute! But he hadn't explicitly refused her request.

"As you wish, husband." She curtseyed, then exited the study.

Perhaps that was the way to control him—as long as he hadn't forbidden her, she could do anything she pleased.

Smiling to herself, she set off in search of Lillian. The little girl was sorely in need of love. Life as Orson's wife might be lonely and loveless, but Arlette had chosen that life. Poor Lillian hadn't asked to be born.

What had Esme said?

*You will find love in your children.*

She would start with Lillian.

~

ARLETTE PLUCKED a sprig of thyme and crushed it between her fingers.

"See, Lillian? That's how you release the aroma."

The little girl did the same, and lifted the sprig to her nose.

"Oh, that's lovely!" she cried. "Does it help cure sickness, like the mint?"

"No," Arlette said, "but it helps prevent putrefaction in wounds. Your papa and his men will have need of it after all their fighting."

Lillian giggled, and they continued gathering herbs.

"Lady Arlette." A male voice spoke—a familiar voice—and Arlette's heart leaped with joy.

Seaton stood before her, silhouetted against the sunlight.

Shielding her eyes from the glare, she looked up. The expression in his eyes—not the warm congeniality she had always seen, but cold disdain—sent a shiver through her.

"Lillian, go to your room and practice your embroidery," Arlette said.

"Must I?" the child protested.

"Please do as I ask."

Lillian frowned, then nodded, and inclined her head at Seaton, before returning to the castle building.

Arlette rose to her feet, but before she could retrieve the blanket she'd been kneeling on, Seaton picked it up and began to fold it.

"Do you remember when we folded a sheet the day we first met?" he asked.

"Aye, Seaton, I do."

"I returned this morning," he continued, "and I spoke to Lord Wulfson."

She averted her gaze from the pain in his eyes.

"Why?" he whispered.

"Forgive me, Seaton," she replied, blinking moisture out of her eyes, "I had no choice."

"There's always a choice."

"Not for a woman," she said, taking his hand. "I had my reasons for accepting him."

"A wealthy lord is a better prospect than the youngest son of an earl," he said, bitterness in his voice.

"Seaton, please—that had nothing to do with it."

"I would have devoted my life to making you happy, Arlette. I love you."

"Hush!" she hissed. "Do not say such things. You'll find someone to love, who'll love you as you deserve, and she'll be the luckiest woman in England. But I'm not her."

"I should not have left you to his mercy, lady."

"You obeyed your lord—as an honorable man."

"Then I shall pledge myself to serve you, my lady. If you cannot accept my heart, I can at least offer my sword."

"That you can," she said, "and I gladly accept. I'm sorely in need of a friend here."

He lifted her hand to his lips and kissed it. With her free hand, she stroked his fine blond hair. How different her life might have been, had this gentle soul been victorious at the tournament!

"What the devil do you think you're doing with my wife!"

Arlette's breath caught at the angry voice. Orson stood at the edge of the garden, hands on hips, murder in his eyes.

Seaton withdrew. "I-I've sworn fealty to Lady Wulfson."

"Go to your chamber, Seaton."

Without hesitation, Seaton disappeared into the building. Arlette pulled a face at her husband and followed the young man, but Orson grasped her wrist.

"You think to play me false, woman?"

"Of course not," she said. "Your jealousy clouds your judgment."

"Do not take me for a fool," he warned. "Remember who your master is."

He pulled her close and kissed her forehead.

"Come, wife—'tis time to dress for dinner and show our young knight that he's returned to a harmonious household."

She tried to pull free but he held her firm.

"Do I make myself clear?"

Arlette nodded.

"Say it, so I can be in no doubt of your understanding."

"Aye," she said, through gritted teeth, "you've made yourself clear."

He smiled. "Then I look forward to spending the evening with my beautiful wife." He bowed, then returned inside, leaving her alone in the garden.

Arlette bit her lip, fighting the moisture pooling in her eyes. She would never let that bastard reduce her to tears.

~

THOUGH HIS WIFE played the dutiful lady to perfection at the dinner table, the fire still glowered in her eyes.

She had yet to be fully tamed. And the men knew it.

Orson's mood darkened as Ulferth and Brand roared with laughter, ale fueling their voices.

"I tell you—that hellcat's claws keep him from claiming his rights. I'll wager he's not bedded her, no matter how bloody her nightgown was."

"Perhaps he prefers the maidservants to his wife."

"Unlike Seaton. Now he's returned, he can't keep his eyes off her. Look at him now—his tongue's hanging out!"

Orson leaped to his feet, knocking a tankard of ale over.

"Ulferth! Brand! Of whom do you speak?"

"A wench, my lord."

Orson's hand curled around the handle of his knife. "Might I know which wench?"

"One of the maidservants," Ulferth said, bowing his head.

"You're no man," Orson scoffed, "not if you must look elsewhere because you're incapable of satisfying your wife."

Ulferth chuckled to himself, and Brand nudged him. "Hush!" he hissed.

"Might I share the joke?" Orson asked.

"I wondered whether my lord leads by example?"

Orson drew his knife. "I'd advise you to leave now, Ulferth, before I punish you for such an insult."

"Ulferth's in his cups, my lord," Brand said. "He means no disrespect."

"I care not," Orson growled. "Get him out of my sight."

A hush descended over the party as the two men left the hall. Arlette picked up her wine goblet, her hands shaking. Orson turned his attention to Seaton who watched her, desire and disappointment in his eyes.

Damn Ulferth! He'd called Orson's virility into question, and now the whole company watched him—including that young pup.

"Wife, come to bed."

Arlette looked up, her cheeks reddening. "I've not finished eating."

"It was not a request," he replied. "Seaton shall accompany us."

Anger flashed in her eyes. It was time he conquered her—once and for all—though doubtless he'd sustain several battle scars.

She turned her head away, and lifted the goblet to her lips.

Curse her defiance!

He leaned toward her and lowered his voice.

"I shall have my way, woman, whether you like it or not. The choice is yours—come willing, or I'll carry you out over my shoulder like a sack of grain."

"You wouldn't dare!" she hissed.

"Wouldn't I?"

He held out his hand and met her gaze. Her eyes widened and she gritted her teeth as if she warred with herself. Then she took his hand, and stood.

Her face flushed scarlet as he led her out of the hall, amid roars of laughter and crude gestures from the men. He marched her to the solar, and kicked the door open.

"It's time I claimed what's mine by right."

Fear flashed in her eyes—the same fear he'd seen the night of their wedding. But, warrior that she was, she faced her fear and unlaced her gown. Then she reached for her nightshift.

"You've no need of that," he said. "Get into bed."

"You're a brute," she said, slipping into the bed and pulling the covers up to her chin. "I hate you."

"It's best that you do," he said. "If you had a heart for me, I would break it."

He undressed, and slipped into the bed beside her, pulling the covers out of her hands to expose her naked body. His mouth watered at the sight of her—the smooth, creamy skin, the perfect round breasts with their rosebud centers that begged to be tasted—a soft belly ripe for filling with children, and that tempting triangle of chestnut curls at her center.

Hellcat she may be, but, God's bones, she was a beauty! His body strained in eagerness to take her—to plunge into her softness—but he wanted his wildcat to part her thighs and purr with desire.

He placed his hand on her shoulder, and she closed her eyes, jaw clenched as if steeling herself against a siege.

"Look at me," he whispered.

She turned toward him and opened her eyes, which glistened with fear. He leaned over and brushed his lips over hers, and she stiffened. He smiled to himself. All fillies were nervous at their breaking in—they merely needed a little coaxing. He brushed her face with his fingertips and her body relaxed a little at his touch.

"Do not fear me," he whispered.

"I fear no man," she said, her voice wavering, "and certainly not my husband."

He chuckled softly. "Tonight you shall scream my name."

She parted her lips in a gasp, and he took advantage, capturing her mouth. He plunged his tongue in—stroking, coaxing—exploring her mouth, until she began to respond. Then he caressed her throat, and moved his hand lower until he reached the swell of her breasts. She drew in a shuddering breath as he cupped a breast, and the little peak at the center beaded against his palm. He teased it with his thumb to a hard point, then captured it in his mouth.

She gave a low cry as he circled the delectable little bud with his tongue, relishing the taste of her skin. Then he took a deep pull, taking in as much of her breast as he could, a groan of pleasure bubbling within his throat. With his hand, he searched for her other breast, drawing the pebbly little nipple to a peak, then he gave it the same loving attention with his mouth. A sigh escaped her lips, and he lifted his head to look at her. Her nipples stood firm and erect, glistening with moisture, waiting to be tasted again.

She arched her back, moving her breast toward his mouth. Whatever insults she might throw at him, her body betrayed her need. She wanted him as much as he wanted her. Leaning over to take her breast again, he smiled in triumph at her mewl of pleasure. He traced a path along her body, relishing the scent of lavender as he reached her belly—a belly that would soon stretch to accommodate his heirs.

When he reached the juncture of her thighs, a bolt of lust surged through him at the scent of spice and musk. He kissed her curls, and sighed against her. Faint cries escaped her throat—the mewls of a woman in need—a woman ready.

And she was ready. For him.

She lifted her hands, and buried her fingers in his hair.

"Orson…"

His name on her lips was almost his undoing, and he gritted his teeth to control the surge in his manhood.

*Not yet...*

He wanted to see her pleasure first. Then—and only then—would she be truly his.

He parted her thighs, and ran a finger along her sensitive flesh, hot and damp with her need. She gave a low groan as his fingertips searched for the little bud at the center, which turned into a sharp cry when he found it. The delicate floral scent of her skin was overtaken by that of her arousal—the aroma of exotic spices and unclaimed desires.

Soon she would accept—nay, beg for—his mastery. Nudging her knees farther apart, he continued to caress her, his movements growing slicker as her need increased. This time, when he kissed her, she responded, eagerly curling her tongue around his, little cries of pleasure rumbling in her throat as he continued to open her body to the pleasures of the flesh.

Then he plunged his finger inside her, curling it around to find her center of pleasure. Her legs shifted with her body's instinctive yearning for release, then her body began to pulse around his finger. She threw back her head and cried out, her fingertips digging into his scalp as he covered her mouth to silence her cries.

She was ready for him.

He positioned himself on top of her, and rubbed the tip of his manhood against her flesh. Then he slipped inside her until he reached the barrier of her maidenhead.

Lowering his mouth to hers, he thrust forward, and sheathed himself fully inside her. She cried out, but he held her firm.

"Shh," he whispered, "there is pain the first time—but only the first."

He eased himself out, then plunged forward again, feeling her body stretch farther. God's bones, she was tight! Her body squeezed him with a delicious friction, and he continued to thrust in and out.

Then, with a deep roar, he thrust forward one last time, spilling his seed deep inside her. He fell forward and held her close, his own body trembling with the aftershocks of his climax.

Never before had a woman brought forth such release! What might she do to him once she'd become skilled in the art of giving pleasure? She was like the finest wine—once he had a taste of her, he wanted nothing else.

He might have asserted his mastery over her, but, in turn, he had become enslaved.

As his heartbeat steadied, he became aware of soft crying beneath him. He moved off her and she rolled onto her side, her back to him. A patch of blood stained the sheet and her thighs.

Why did she cry? A little bloodletting harmed no woman. He'd given her pleasure, yet she cried as if he'd violated her! Frustrated, he rolled onto his side, and closed his eyes.

~

ARLETTE WOKE in the middle of the night, sick with shame over her body's hateful reaction to his touch. She rolled onto her back and winced, sore where he'd entered her. But her body hadn't been torn to shreds as she'd feared. After the initial sting of pain, as her husband pushed himself in and out of her, an unfathomable sensation had burned inside her, like an itch needing scratching, just out of reach. But when he stopped moving, the sensation faded, the itch unsatisfied.

"Verona!" a voice called out—filled with anguish.

Orson lay beside her. In the soft candlelight, his face no longer looked like that of the harsh warrior—he wore the expression of a distressed child. Overcome by compassion, she took his head in her hands.

"Hush," she whispered.

On impulse, she planted a kiss on his lips. His eyes fluttered open and he reached out to her.

She took his hand, and brushed her lips against his. If it eased his pain, she was content to play the part of his murdered sister.

Then he let out a sigh. "Arlette, my Arlette…"

He returned the kiss, probing her lips gently until she opened to him, and he caressed her body, stroking her arms, her shoulders, planting gentle kisses on her body. He sought out her breasts, and her stomach tightened as his warm, wet tongue circled her nipple, and he gave a long pull, drawing out the little nub. Her body shuddered with pleasure, and her skin burned where his lips left a blazing trail, on their path down her body, his fingertips playing with both nipples until she groaned with the deliciousness of his touch.

The burning itch swelled inside her once more, and she parted her thighs, her body eager for him again. Fisting her hands in his hair, she guided him lower as he flicked his tongue across her stomach. He lowered his head farther until he reached her sensitive flesh, then he dipped his tongue between her folds. A soft moan escaped her lips as he ran his tongue along her center, swirling it around the swollen, sensitive bud, which swelled and pulsed with warmth. He increased the pressure and her body burst into life as her chest expanded. A rush of air flooded her lungs, spinning her mind into a vortex.

"Orson—sweet Lord, Orson!"

Her breath came in sobbing gasps as she yielded to the pure sensation of him.

As she drifted back to earth, his mouth covered hers in a deep, lingering kiss, and she stiffened as his hardness pressed against her. Need conquered fear, and she parted her legs, driving herself upward to meet him as he thrust into her.

This time there was no pain—just the glorious sensation of him inside her. He withdrew, then plunged back in, and she lifted her hips to meet him. As he thrust into her again, her whole body rippled with an unimaginable force, and she screamed out his name.

His cries joined hers and she wrapped her legs around him. Arching his back, he gave one final cry, then he fell forward, wrapping his arms around her. They rolled to one side, panting, twin heartbeats pounding in unison.

She kissed his throat, running her lips over the stubbly growth of his beard, then she buried her head in his chest, nuzzling him as a newborn kitten. He stroked the back of her head, murmuring her name, before his body relaxed and his breathing grew deep and even.

*What have I done?*

She had determined to hate him, yet her body had betrayed her.

# CHAPTER 21

The aroma of lavender and citrus filtered into Arlette's dreams, returning her to her girlhood. She opened her eyes, stretched, and sat up.

Someone had placed a bathtub in the center of the solar, into which Esme and a number of maidservants poured buckets of steaming water.

Esme looked up, and smiled.

"You're awake!" she cried. She offered her hand and helped Arlette out of the bed, leading her toward the bath.

Arlette stepped into the water and lowered herself in. To her shame, blood stained her thighs, coloring the bathwater before it dissipated. Esme placed a gentle hand on her head.

"There, lady—'twas not so bad as you feared, was it?"

"No." Arlette flushed with shame at the memory of the night before.

"Next time will be better."

Arlette sighed. "*He* said that."

"He spoke the truth, little one."

Arlette leaned back, and closed her eyes, relishing the feel of the water on her skin. Matters had improved second time around—she'd experienced pleasures she hadn't even dreamed of.

But she'd behaved like a whore. Her parents lay dead and Guillaume was missing. She'd betrayed them all—sold herself to the enemy. No matter how he'd cried for his sister, or how tender he'd been the second time, he was still her enemy.

Her muscles began to relax as Esme lathered her hair and massaged her shoulders with expert hands.

"Mmm, Esme..." she murmured. "You always know what's best for me. I thank you for ordering my bath."

"It was at your husband's direction, my lady."

"Orson?"

"Aye," Esme said. "He was very particular about it. I believe he cares for you a great deal." She rinsed Arlette's hair and massaged her scalp. "He'll be a good husband, if only you let him."

"But, what of Papa?" Arlette asked. "Or Mama—or Guillaume?"

"Do you believe your husband to be an evil man?" Esme asked. "Or merely one who sought retaliation for his sister?"

Arlette sighed. She'd been so determined to hate him—but the glimpses of tenderness had chipped away at the fortress of hatred she'd built around her heart.

"Remember what I said, child," Esme said. "There's no weakness in letting your husband take care of you. These great warriors rarely show kindness, yet I saw a gentleness in his eyes when he asked me to bathe you today. I've never seen the like in a lord—certainly not in your father."

"What would you have me do?" Arlette asked.

"Give him a chance."

Esme spoke sense. And Arlette wasn't just Orson's wife. She was Lillian's stepmother, and the lady of Greywell Castle. Her conscience might war with her duty to her husband—but not with her duty to the people here.

She rose and stepped out of the water, and let Esme dress her, selecting a plain kirtle and overgown.

It was time to carry out her duties.

She made her way to the study Una had prepared for her. Since she'd gathered herbs with Lillian, someone had placed an array of cloths, bottles, and bandages on the table. Idle hands made for a weary heart—and solace would be found in occupation.

After spending the morning setting the room in order, her mood lifted a little. Late afternoon, Elvia burst through the door, breathless with running.

"Lady—you must come, quickly!"

"What's happened?"

"An accident in the village. The farmer's son—he's cut himself with a scythe. The priest is nowhere to be found."

"What can a priest do?" Arlette asked. "Is he expected to die?"

"Aye—he's bleeding badly."

"I must tend to him." Arlette gathered a basket of bandages, herbs, and a sturdy needle and thread.

"Perhaps I should find Lord Wulfson," Elvia said.

"You'll do nothing of the sort," Arlette replied, ushering Elvia out of the chamber. "Take me to the farmer."

The farmer's hut was only a short walk from the drawbridge. Arlette entered, letting her eyes adjust to the darkness. A young man lay on a pallet, his face ashen.

The man kneeling beside him looked up, then frowned as he saw Arlette.

"We sent for the priest, not a woman."

"Let me look at him," Arlette said.

"My son's injuries are not for your eyes."

"I assure you I have seen—and treated—worse," Arlette said. "Stand aside and let me see him."

"Who are you to speak to me so?"

"She's Lady Wulfson," Elvia said. "Mistress of Greywell Castle."

He drew in a sharp breath, then rose to his feet and bowed. "My lady, forgive me, I did not recognize you. But there's nothing you can do."

"Let me try," Arlette said. "*I* shan't condemn your son to death if he has a chance at life, however small."

He moved aside at her authoritative tone, and she took his place and kneeled beside the pallet.

The injured man was young—barely out of boyhood. A deep gash ran along his upper arm, the bed beneath him already soaked with blood.

"Sweet heaven!" Elvia cried, swaying to one side. The farmer caught her, and carried her out of the hut. Moments later, the sound of retching came from outside, then the farmer returned, alone.

"A swooning wench cannot help my son," he said.

"But I can," Arlette replied.

"You know what to do?"

"Aye." Arlette inspected the wound. "The bleeding is already slowing—see? The wound's deep, but it's not as severe as it looks, The main danger is putrefaction, but I have plenty of healing herbs. I will, however, need to stitch the wound to keep it closed. You must hold him while I perform the task—for it will hurt, and he'll struggle."

The farmer nodded, then held the boy down while Arlette threaded her needle.

"Ready?"

The farmer nodded. "Aye."

She first drove the needle into the boy's flesh, and he let out a wail of agony.

"Keep him still!" she hissed, as she continued to stitch, working quickly and confidently. The sooner she accomplished her task, the better.

When she finished, she applied herbs to the wound before bandaging it. The boy had passed out with the pain—sweat beading on his forehead.

The farmer called out. "In here, Nelda!"

A woman of about thirty summers crept into the room, crying noisily.

"My child!"

"Your son is fortunate," Arlette said, "but the wound will take time to heal. He'll need to rest, and his bandages must be changed daily."

"Thank the Lord!" the woman cried, but the farmer shook his head. "It could not have come at a worse time. We need to cut the hay."

"I'll send someone to assist you," Arlette said, "and, with your leave, I'll tend to the boy myself until he recovers."

"Lady, you're too kind."

"It's my duty—and my pleasure," she said, smiling. "I'm sure if we were in need of help, you'd give it." She rose to her feet. "I'll leave you in peace now, but will return tomorrow to see how he fares."

"Please," the farmer said. "You, and your servant must share our meal."

Elvia stood in the doorway and shook her head. Her body swayed to one side, as if she was going to pass out again.

"Very well," Arlette said, "but Elvia must return to the castle."

Elvia curtseyed and fled, and the farmer's wife approached Arlette with a bowl of broth, then retreated to a corner.

While they ate, the farmer spoke eagerly about his livestock, and how he produced the meat and grain that graced the tables of Greywell Castle. In addition to the injured boy, the farmer had three other children, all with the same sloe-black eyes. While the farmer talked, his wife nursed a young baby while Arlette bounced a child of two or three summers on her lap. To her delight, Odella, the young child who'd given her flowers on her wedding day, arrived, armed with a posy for her to take home. The farmer was Odella's uncle, and Odella promised to help look after her cousin.

Darkness had fallen when Arlette returned. Una had left two basketfuls of herbs in her study, and Arlette set to work preserving them, filling bottles of oil for some, tying others in bunches to dry, and cataloguing her supplies. Fatigue overcame her and she leaned over the table, resting her head on her arms, and drifted into sleep.

~

WHEN SHE WOKE, she lay on her back in a soft bed, wearing her nightshift. She rolled onto her side and let out a cry.

Her husband sat beside the bed watching her, eyes the color of pewter. He reclined in a chair, resting an elbow on the chair's arm, his chin on his hand. The shadows in the room played across his face, emphasizing the strong jawline and cheekbones. She felt a flush of heat under his gaze and sat up.

"How did I get here?"

He remained still, as if he hadn't heard. Then he uncurled his body, and leaned toward her.

"You were working too late."

"I had much to do," she replied.

"By avoiding me, you missed your supper."

Arrogant knave!

"Avoid you?" she retorted. "I wouldn't give you the satisfaction."

She glanced across the solar where a meal had been set out on the table—roasted venison and, if she were not mistaken, pears cooked in spiced wine and honey—her favorite dish.

"I hoped you'd join me for supper," he said. "But, alas, I dined alone. Do not disappear again without my leave."

Any tenderness elicited by his choosing her favorite dishes yielded to anger at his words. Did he think he owned her?

She rolled over, turning her back to him, expecting him to continue to chastise her.

But he didn't. Instead, he remained silent, though she sensed he still watched her. At length she heard him undressing, then the bed shifted under his weight. With luck he would fall asleep and leave her be.

His hand slid across her body to cup her breast, and her nipple stiffened in response.

"I know you're awake," he whispered. "Are you ready for me?"

He nudged her onto her back, lifting her nightshift to claim her. To her shame, her body responded as he took her to the brink of pleasure with his hands and mouth, and her cries of pleasure echoed around the solar.

# CHAPTER 22

When Orson released his wife, she pulled free, and turned her back on him. But her cries of pleasure while he was inside her belied her anger.

He wanted her as badly as he'd made her body want him, and he couldn't, now, imagine his bed without her in it.

Or his life. He may have chastised her about missing supper, but he'd experienced a rush of tenderness on discovering her in her study, bent over her work, sleeping the sleep of the exhausted. She hadn't even woken when he'd carried her to bed.

Though she still saw him as her enemy, she was proving to be a useful helpmate in the household, and on the estate—a woman who took her duties and responsibilities seriously.

Over the next few days, he began to notice the fruits of her efforts around the household. Fresh rushes were scattered in the dining hall, the smell of crushed herbs mingling with that of polished wood. Sunlight streamed through windows that had been cleaned on her orders. Even his daughter seemed happier, helping Arlette with her duties.

At night, he ignited a passionate response from her body but afterward, she withdrew, crying quietly to herself when she thought he was asleep, even though he was experienced enough of women to know he'd given her pleasure.

They had reached an uneasy alliance, but could he ever trust her?

Perhaps not. Una approached him one morning, complaining about a number of barrels of wine Arlette had insisted be brought to the cellars—wine that, according to the village merchant, had gone bad, yet Arlette had purchased the entire quantity.

She'd loaded his wine with salt before—was she planning a similar trick? Perhaps that was why she wore a satisfied smile on her lips.

Curse her! If she sought to humiliate him publicly, he'd repay her a thousandfold.

During the meal that evening, he noticed her eyes on him as he ladled stew into the trencher they shared. She nodded toward his cup.

"Do you not care for your wine, husband?"

Glowering at her, he took a mouthful of the stew, then drew in a sharp breath. Rarely had he tasted anything so exquisite. The usually tough meat was tender and succulent.

He waved a servant over.

"Bring Freydis to me—immediately!"

Freydis appeared shortly after, fear in her expression, and dropped a curtsey.

"Mistress Freydis, what is this dish?" he asked.

"Beef stew, milord, as usual."

"You are to be congratulated," he said. "I've never tasted anything so good. Surely only witchcraft would elicit such a flavor."

Beside him, Arlette smiled, and stabbed a piece of meat with her eating knife.

"I made the stew under my lady's direction," Freydis said.

Orson waved Freydis away, then turned to his wife.

"I employed no witchcraft," Arlette said, "but a consignment of sour wine. Undrinkable, but perfect for tenderizing meat."

"I thought you'd intended to serve bad wine to your husband, to sour his mood," he said.

"I've no need for bad wine to elicit such a mood in my husband," she replied. "And, as you see, I did serve it—in the stew rather than your cup."

She smiled mischievously. "Now I understand why you haven't touched your wine when I'd expect you to be on your fifth cup by now. Drink, husband, 'tis perfectly safe. See?"

To prove her point, she lifted his cup, took a sip, then handed it to him. Her eyes sparkled, and for the first time, he saw merriment in their expression.

Then, as if ashamed to be happy, she lowered her gaze and the smile disappeared.

If only she'd smile again—for him!

He leaned toward her. "Good wines are made for a man's pleasure," he said. "Did you know that the age of a wine determines its quality?"

She shook her head, and he lowered his voice.

"The same can be said for a man. His potency comes into full force in his thirtieth year."

Her cheeks turned a delicate shade of rose, and she remained silent for the rest of the meal while he served her, holding cuts of meat to her lips to taste.

At length, he stood, and offered his hand.

"Come," he said softly. "Let me show you the pleasures of a good wine."

A servant stepped forward with a flagon, and Orson waved him away. Arlette's blush deepened as she caught his true meaning—but she took his hand, and he led her out of the hall. Tonight, he would have her crying with ecstasy. Not because he wanted mastery over her body but for the sake of giving—and taking—pleasure.

~

When Arlette woke, her body was still entwined with her husband's. During the night, she'd tried to resist, but his gentle administrations had been too much for her body and mind. Yielding to pleasure, she lay on the bed, naked and pliant, as he eased her knees apart and attended to her every desire, known and secret. She blushed at the thought of her mewling cries as he'd caressed her skin and suckled her breasts, bringing her to the pinnacle of desperate, aching desire—waiting until she begged for him, before easing himself into her. Their joint cries echoed in the solar, as she surrendered to the pleasure brought forth by the hands of the man she'd secretly dreamed about since the day she first laid eyes on him.

Afterward, he held her in his arms, and murmured into her ear.

*Do not turn from me tonight, little one. Enjoy the pleasures I can give you.*

His chest rose and fell in a deep sigh.

"Arlette..."

She lifted her head to look at him. His face was relaxed, and at peace. Her breath caught in her throat as she studied his beautiful features, tracing a finger along his hairline, closing her eyes to relive the feel of his thick, flowing, shoulder-length mane, which she'd buried her fingers in as he claimed her body.

*No, I don't love him. I cannot!*

Her parents were dead. Guillaume was missing. And she could never trust her husband enough to ask him to help her find her brother—he'd kill Guillaume on sight.

If she were to have any chance of seeing her brother again, she must do it in secret, and deceive her husband.

# CHAPTER 23

After Arlette broke her fast, she resolved to take better care of Lillian—to assuage the guilt gnawing at her for not being able to help Guillaume. Several bolts of silk lay untouched in the solar—wedding gifts from her husband. It was time to put them to use.

After Esme helped her dress, Arlette sent for her stepdaughter.

The child's face lit up with joy as she arrived in the solar, and eyed the bolts of silk.

"What do you make of those?" Arlette asked.

Lillian looked at the yellow silk, longing in her expression, then she shook her head.

"They're not for one such as I," she said. "Papa's told me not to expect a grand marriage—or fine things."

"You've every right to expect a fine marriage," Arlette said, "but you'll not be married for many years yet. I merely wish to have you dressed—and educated—as befits your station."

"I have no station."

"Yes you do," Arlette said. "You're the daughter of the lord here—which makes you my daughter. I shall dress you as befits a lady, and present you to your father at dinner. Even *he* cannot object to that."

"Will he smile at me?" Lillian asked.

"Of course he will," Arlette said, her heart tightening at the longing in the child's voice, "and if he doesn't, we'll think of something else to make him smile."

Lillian stroked the yellow silk with her fingertip. Then she cocked her head to one side, and eyed Arlette thoughtfully.

"Do you play music?"

"A little." Arlette smiled at memories of music lessons—plucking clumsily at the strings of her lute, while she yearned to pick up her sword instead.

"Music always made him smile," Lillian said. "When Aunt Verona played, it would make him so happy. She told me that every time he was in a poor humor, she would play for him, because music revealed his heart. Might you play for him?"

"I doubt I can play as well as your aunt did," Arlette said.

"Couldn't you try?" Lillian turned her eager little face to Arlette. "I long to see Papa smile again. You can play for him, while I wear my new dress."

"Perhaps," Arlette smiled. "But I'm sorely in need of practice."

"I have an instrument you can use."

How could she deny the child her wish? And Arlette had to admit that the prospect of seeing her husband smile was worth a little music practice.

"Very well," she said. "I'll play for him in front of everyone—the night we present you in your new gown."

"Thank you!" Lillian's eyes sparkled with hope, and she threw her arms around Arlette's neck. If pleasing Orson brought happiness into Lillian's life, then Arlette could make the effort.

On her way to the ladies' sewing room, the yellow silk under her arm, Arlette was intercepted by a maidservant, who blocked her path.

Hilda—the insolent creature whose sharp eyes always seemed to be watching her.

"What do you want?" Arlette asked.

"I have news for you—but first you must assure me of your silence."

"How dare you!" Arlette cried. "It's not your place to..."

"It's about your brother."

A rush of hope and fear tore at Arlette's heart.

"Guillaume! Where is he?"

"I cannot speak until you give me your assurance," Hilda said. "Lord Wulfson wishes to kill your brother—and he'd not hesitate to kill anyone standing in his way."

So—Arlette's fears were not without foundation.

"You have my assurance," Arlette said, "but only if you speak the truth."

Hilda lowered her voice. "There's a man in the village who's had news of Guillaume de Villiers. He resides at the inn but is no longer able to afford his keep."

"He needs money," Arlette said flatly, though her heart thudded against her chest.

"Aye."

"Will he see me?"

Hilda shook her head, "He fears he'll be put to death. But he's willing to meet you in the empty cottage near the chapel. After sundown—tonight."

"Very well," Arlette said. "Tell him I'll be there."

"I must accompany you," Hilda said. "I'm the only one he trusts. If you go alone you'll never see him—or your brother—again."

There was no choice but to trust Hilda. Even if it was only a ruse to earn herself a coin.

"Very well," Arlette said. "Come to the solar when you're ready."

"Don't forget the money."

"I won't."

Arlette dismissed Hilda, then entered the sewing room, where she joined the ladies, and issued instructions for stitching Lillian's gown. She knew most of them by name now. Ulferth's wife sat by the window, and Arlette drew up a chair beside her.

"How are you today, Edith?"

"Well enough, my lady."

Edith turned to acknowledge her, revealing a darkening bruise on her cheek.

"Oh, Edith!" Arlette cried.

"I fell against the door again, my lady."

Arlette shook her head. "You think me a fool? I shall speak to my husband."

"I beg you do not!" Edith cried. "My husband is within his rights to admonish me as he sees fit."

"But you've done nothing wrong!"

"I've given him four daughters," Edith said, touching her belly, "I pray this one is a son."

"You're with child?"

Edith nodded, misery in her expression. "I-I should be happy, but I'm so afraid! What if I fail him again?"

Arlette sighed. Whatever she thought of Orson—there were worse husbands in the world.

"Why don't I tend to your daughters?" Arlette suggested. "Send them to me tomorrow, to be fitted for gowns of their own."

Edith gave a shy smile before returning to her sewing. Heavens above! Were all women supposed to be appeased by the promise of a gown, while they accepted the brutality of the men who owned them?

~

As soon as the sun slipped below the horizon, Hilda appeared at Arlette's door.

"'Tis time."

Arlette picked up a bag of coins, and followed Hilda to the side door leading to the tourney field. Under the shadow of the castle, the two women followed the perimeter wall until they reached the road to the village. Shortly after, the dark shape of an abandoned cottage came into view.

Hilda called out.

"Are you there, Morcar?"

A hacking cough erupted from inside and a man's face appeared at the door. He hawked and spat on the ground, the spittle glistening in the moonlight before dissolving into the earth, and Arlette suppressed a shudder of revulsion.

Hilda pushed Arlette forward.

"How dare you…" Arlette spoke, before Hilda silenced her.

"Hush! Do you want to be caught?"

Arlette hesitated. What the devil was she doing, risking her husband's wrath on the whim of a servant she disliked?

She pushed Hilda aside. "This man knows nothing," she said. "I was a fool to come here."

"What of Guillaume?" the man croaked, "I hear he misses his Lettie."

Arlette froze.

*Lettie…*

Her brother's pet name for her.

"What do you know of Guillaume?" she asked.

"Come inside and I'll tell you," he said, "but I'll have my coin first."

Arlette handed the purse to Hilda and stepped inside. If there was a chance—however small—of finding her brother alive, she had to take it.

~

DURING THE RETURN JOURNEY, Arlette's body weighed her down, concern for Guillaume turning her legs to lead as she trudged through the field. On the contrary, Hilda seemed light on her feet, her face glowing with excitement in the moonlight. Doubtless she'd earned a tidy sum tonight.

But it was a price worth paying if it led Arlette to her brother. The man in the cottage had a friend in the next village, who'd seen a young boy fitting Guillaume's description, and he promised to gather more information, for a price. He wasn't to be trusted, but while there was hope—however faint—of finding Guillaume, Arlette had to take it.

As they reached the castle door, Hilda stopped.

"This is where we part company," she said. "Wait until I'm safely inside before following."

Before Arlette could reply, Hilda slipped inside.

Insolent creature! But Arlette could bear a little disrespect for Guillaume's sake.

The building was quiet, apart from the distant footfall of a night guard. When Arlette entered the solar, she caught sight of her husband's sleeping form, and she exhaled with relief. She removed her clothes and slipped in beside him.

"What has my wife been doing in the village at this hour?"

Arlette let out a cry as a hand grasped her shoulder.

"H-husband!"

"You're shaking," he said.

"I'm cold."

"You've not answered my question. What were you doing in the village?"

"I wasn't..."

He tightened his grip. "Think carefully before you lie to me. You were seen."

Arlette swallowed the coil of fear in her gut. "I was visiting the farmer's son who I tended to the other day," she said. "I didn't realize I needed permission to leave the building."

"If I find out you've lied, I'll..."

"You'll what?" she cried. "What more can you do to me that you haven't already done?"

"I am your husband," he replied. "You answer to me."

She sighed, and closed her eyes. Arguing wouldn't help her brother.

The bed shifted as he moved against her, then he rolled her onto her back, his big body covering hers.

"Let us speak of it no more," he whispered. "Come...do your duty."

He placed his mouth over hers, his tongue pushing against her lips, and she turned her head away, willing her body not to respond. Undeterred, he continued to kiss her, his lips tracing a path across her body until his hot, wet mouth came down on her breast. She stiffened and gritted her teeth.

A low growl of frustration rumbled in his throat and he teased her legs apart. Tears stung her eyes as his thick manhood nudged against her already slippery flesh.

How could she be so weak!

"No..." she groaned.

"Yes," he whispered, his voice hoarse. "You are my wife, and I want you tonight."

"Orson..."

"You cannot deny that your body is willing."

"But *I* am not!"

She braced herself, but the onslaught never came. Instead, he withdrew, rolling away from her with a sigh. Shortly after, his steady breathing told her he'd fallen asleep, leaving her alone with an inexplicable sense of loss.

~

WHEN ARLETTE WOKE the following next morning, her husband had gone. She sent for Esme, who arrived shortly after to help her dress. While brushing her hair, her nursemaid spoke.

"I hear you were wandering about the village last night."

"You know better than to listen to gossip," Arlette snapped.

"The truth is not gossip," Esme replied, "and you shouldn't have told your husband that you visited the farm, when you were seen at the opposite end of the village."

Fear rippled through her. Did Orson know she'd lied?

"What were you doing?" Esme asked.

"Hilda took me to meet someone who has news of Guillaume."

"And you believed her?"

"He called me Lettie, Esme! Who else knows Guillaume's name for me?"

"A lucky guess, that's all," Esme replied. "He's playing you, for a coin. You're better speaking to your husband."

"No!" Arlette cried. "He would kill Guillaume. Seaton warned me of it a long time ago, as did Hilda last night."

"You'd do better to trust your husband instead of Seaton—or that creature."

"How can I? My parents are dead, and Guillaume will share their fate if he's discovered. I must find him myself and take him to Villiers."

"Don't be a fool!" Esme cried. "The path to finding your brother lies in winning your husband around, not deceiving him. And even if you found Guillaume, you could never travel all the way to Normandy without being discovered."

"I could," Arlette said. "I've been to Villiers before. It's mine by right—I'm entitled to go there."

"Obstinate child!" Esme said. "You'll always do as you wish. But you must listen to reason. If you continue to defy your husband, he'll make you suffer."

Arlette dismissed Esme, but a voice inside her mind said that her old nursemaid was right. Her husband might be a brute, but he was unlike other men. Last night, he could have taken her unwilling, as was a husband's right. But he hadn't. Though she chafed at having to defer to a man, she was, at least, spared the misery that women such as Edith—or even Mama—endured at their husbands' hands.

She opened her trunk and pulled out the silk dress she was making for Lillian, taking care to conceal the lute that the child had brought her yesterday. Perhaps, after she'd given Orson his surprise—played for him during dinner while his daughter wore her new dress—he'd see that she was prepared to be a good wife. And he would, in turn, be a good husband.

During the afternoon, Orson joined her in the solar. She greeted him with a smile, and her heart leaped with hope as he returned it.

"You're using the silks I gave you," he said, nodding in approval. "I look forward to seeing you wearing them."

"You'll see them on your daughter, not your wife," she replied.

His smile disappeared. "You'd waste silks on a child?"

"She's your child," Arlette replied. "Why can't she have them?"

"Because of her birth."

Heaven forbid! Had she heard him correctly?

"You mean…" she hesitated, "…because she…she's…"

"A bastard, yes."

Anger rippled through her.

"How can you, of all people, speak so?"

"Because, woman, I understand the way of the world. The sooner the child learns this, the better. By giving her garments meant for a noble-born lady, you set her up for disappointment. She'll forever be judged because of her birth."

"I see only one judging her because of her birth," Arlette said, "and I'll care for her as I see fit."

"No," he said, danger in his quiet tone. "You'll answer to me."

"I will not!" Arlette replied. "You have a daughter who believes herself unloved, who yearns for a smile from her father—you have a knight who beats his wife, and you do naught to stop it. You deserve no such respect."

His eyes darkened, and he took her arm. "Listen to me, woman. If I find you're disobeying me, I shall exert the rights of a husband."

He leaned over and hissed in her ear. "That includes your little midnight stroll in the village. I want to hear no more of such excursions, unless you want me to punish you. Do I make myself clear?"

A cough came from behind, and he loosened his grip. The steward stood in the doorway.

"What is it, William? Can't you see I'm busy?"

"Forgive me, my lord, you wanted to see me."

Orson released Arlette.

"Very well," he said. "William—follow me. Wife, stay here—I've not finished with you yet."

He strode away on his long legs, William struggling to keep pace.

*Curse him!* How dare he admonish her in front of the servants!

Distant laughter echoed in the background, and she looked out of the window. The men were practicing swordplay in the tourney field.

*I'll show him I won't be intimidated.*

She changed into a plain homespun kirtle, then headed toward the field.

A handful of men were sparring, including Seaton and Ulferth.

Pearce watched her approach, raising his eyebrows as she reached for a sword and shield, but he said nothing.

Ulferth curled his lip into a sneer. "Have you come to challenge a real man?"

"*You're* not a real man," she replied scornfully. "You beat your wife and force your disgusting attentions onto the servants. I'd sooner challenge a boar."

"Why, you bitch!" Ulferth stepped forward and raised his sword. Another sword appeared midair, and blocked it with a clash of steel.

"You forget your place, Ulferth," Pearce said. "You should be punished for disrespecting Lady Wulfson. Return to the castle."

Ulferth lowered his sword and retreated.

Arlette called after him. "If I see any more bruises on your wife, I'll slit your throat!"

"Lady, it's not your place to tell Ulferth how to treat his wife," Pearce admonished.

"If my husband isn't man enough to tell him, then who will?" she challenged.

Pearce shook his head, but said nothing.

Arlette tucked her skirt into her belt, and lifted the sword. "Who will fight me?"

The men shook their heads, whispering among themselves.

"Perhaps you, Seaton?" Arlette continued. "You pledged to serve me, did you not?"

Seaton shook his head, "Lady, I must protest…"

An angry roar interrupted him.

"Woman! Drop your sword—now!"

Orson stood at the edge of the field, body taut with rage.

"I shall not!" she cried.

"So be it," he said, the cold steel of his voice matching his eyes. "If you wish to fight like a man rather than behave like a lady, you shall do so—against your husband."

He strode toward the rack and took a sword—thick, sharp, and evil looking.

Her courage faltered as she eyed his sword. He could smash her to pieces with it—slice her in two. Was it the sword that had killed Papa?

Bloodlust glittered in his eyes.

"It's time I taught my wife a lesson."

~

ORSON EYED his wife as she gripped her sword, defiance in her expression. The little mare! She was a woman to admire—but did she not understand the danger she placed them in? Rumors travelled fast. A man known for being unable to control his wife was vulnerable to attack, not only from outsiders, but within his own ranks.

She must be tamed—and he'd enjoy conquering her.

He raised his sword, and she stepped back.

"If you intend to be a warrior, you must do better than that," he said.

She circled him, then took another step back as he advanced toward her.

"Just as I thought," he said. "A coward, like the rest of your family."

With a scream of rage she rushed at him, sword aloft. He blocked her with his shield, and the impact sent her sword flying. She darted to retrieve it but he impeded her path, and her eyes glowered with frustration. With nothing but her shield, she was bested.

"My wife must learn the first lesson of combat," he told the men. "Never let your emotions rule your head. That's why women will never be warriors. They have more emotions than wit."

At the final word he swung his sword at her shield. She toppled back into the mud, and before she could move, his sword was at her throat.

"Curse you!" she spat.

"That was only your first lesson," he snarled. "Defy me again in front of my men, and I'll have no choice but to punish you with my bare hands. Nod if you understand."

Her eyes, which had glittered with anger, now dulled with defeat, and she inclined her head. He helped her up, and kissed her gently on the lips.

"There," he soothed, "isn't it better when you're obedient?"

She smiled, then tipped her head up to whisper in his ear.

"May you rot in hell, Orson Greywell."

She dropped a curtsey, then turned her back and strode toward the castle building.

HE CAUGHT up with her at the top of the stairs, and pulled her into the solar.

"You're not to play the swordsman again, do you hear?"

"You cannot tell me what to do!"

"I can and I will," he said. "Must I remind you of your vows?"

"Vows I regret. I could never love you!"

He swallowed the spike of jealousy at her words, and let out a bark of laughter. "Do you fancy yourself in love with another?"

"Such as Seaton?" she taunted.

So—his suspicions were not groundless.

"You belong to *me*," he said. "Any man coming near you will find my sword at his throat."

"And one day, husband, you'll find my knife in your chest."

"Do not make idle threats," he warned.

"Not a threat, but a promise."

He recoiled at the loathing in her voice. "No man wants a shrew for a wife," he said, "particularly one who wishes to shorten it."

"And *I* have no wish to be shackled to the knuckleheaded bastard who murdered my family, yet wasn't even man enough to protect his own sister!"

Her words struck him like a body blow, and the deep-rooted pain he always fought to conquer tightened its grip on his heart.

Verona—his gentle, beloved sister—the only woman who truly loved him for himself.

How dare she sully her name! How many nights had he lain awake torturing himself over his inability to protect her?

His wife's eyes widened in fear. She understood what she'd said, and feared retribution.

And retribution she would have.

He gripped her wrist.

"Let me go!" she cried.

"Make me."

She lowered her head, and a sharp pain tore through his hand as she sunk her teeth into it. With a roar of pain he released her. She leaped back, and bared her teeth, a feral creature with bloodstained lips.

"Do that again, woman, and, so help me God, I'll have you lashed and administer them myself."

She opened her mouth to respond, but he raised his hand. "I have no wish to hear your voice any more today."

He strode out of the chamber, and slammed the door behind him, turning the key in the lock.

"Watt!" he roared. "Come here!"

Footsteps approached and the manservant appeared, panting.

"What is it, my lord?"

"You're to guard the door, and make sure my wife does not leave this chamber," Orson said, loud enough for her to hear. "Use force if necessary."

He grimaced as a volley of curses rang out from the other side of the door, then he retreated, leaving Watt standing sentinel.

What the devil had he done, wedding that hellcat? It would be a miracle if they hadn't killed each other by the end of the year.

ARLETTE LOOKED up as the key jangled in the lock. Esme entered the solar, carrying a tray, and Arlette's stomach growled at the rich aroma of stew. The door closed, the key turning in the lock. Esme set the tray down and poured a goblet of wine.

"Lord Wulfson bade me bring you something to eat."

"Where is he?" Arlette asked.

"He's with the steward."

Arlette took a bite of the stew.

"I should never have married him, Esme," she said. "He's a brute."

"You are not without fault yourself," came the reply. "I saw teeth marks on the back of his hand."

Arlette blushed with shame.

Esme tutted. "He may have the appearance of a brute, but we live in a brutal world. For all his rough manners, he's a fair and just man. He was deeply affected by the loss of his sister, and he's stigmatized by his birth."

"And I reminded him of both today," Arlette sighed. "I'm sorry for it, but I cannot condone what he did to my family. I should be able to trust my husband to help me find my brother, not fear his intent to murder him."

"Then find the key to his heart. Be a good wife, and stop defying him in front of his men. Given your behavior in the field, he had no choice but to chastise you."

"How do you know about that?"

"Seaton asked after you." Esme's eyes narrowed and her voice grew stern. "Do not be too friendly toward Seaton. It wouldn't bode well if you cast your eye over another man."

"Seaton is kind," Arlette replied. "I like his company, but could never love him."

"And your husband?"

Arlette's cheeks warmed. "Sometimes—at night—I believe I could feel something. But then I think of my family—of Guillaume. It's sinful to want my husband's attentions."

"Not sinful, but natural—the mark of a good marriage."

"How can this be a good marriage?" Arlette cried. "His thirst for revenge will never wane."

"Perhaps if you knew more about your husband, you'd understand him better," Esme said. "He's suffered much."

"I know about his sister," Arlette said, "and his birth."

"There's his father, also," Esme said. "Murdered by his former allies during a siege, because he refused to rise up against the Norman king. Have you not seen the damaged battlements in the west wing? Lord Henry was killed by a trebuchet's missile. Bloodstains can still be seen among the rubble."

"Did my husband witness it?"

"He was away at the time," Esme said. "He wasn't there to save his father, and it almost destroyed him. Imagine the pain he endured through being unable to save his sister!"

Arlette continued to eat in silence. At length, Esme rose and knocked on the solar door, which swung open.

"I'll leave you now, lady," she said, "but think on what I've said."

When Arlette finished her meal, she rose and tested the door. It swung open to reveal the sentry.

"Am I still a prisoner?"

"No, lady." The sentry bowed. "You're free to go wherever you wish."

Taking her cloak, Arlette set off in the direction of the west wing, climbing the staircase until she reached the battlements.

The ruined part was barely noticeable from the ground. Part of the wall and walkway had been destroyed, and was littered with broken masonry. A dark stain covered the stones near a gap in the wall.

*This must be where he fell.*

She crouched down to touch the stain, but it was dry—soaked into the stones years before.

What a waste of a life—a nobleman struck down for refusing to join an uprising. A man who'd wanted to live in peace, and had wished for his son to marry the daughter of a Norman to further that peace.

She closed her eyes and resurrected the image of her childhood—the tall man who'd visited Papa to petition for her hand in marriage for his son. Now that marriage had taken place, would he have approved?

Her position gave a clear view of the surrounding countryside. The village dwellings disappeared into the forest, beyond which fields stretched out, small figures of sheep and cows dotting the lush green.

At the horizon, softly rolling hills shimmered with a purple hue in the evening sunlight. She closed her eyes and drew in a lungful of air. Though midsummer was past, the sun's rays still held their heat, a gentle warmth on her skin.

"Arlette."

She turned toward the voice. Orson stood, leaning against the doorframe, watching her.

The sunlight accentuated his powerful, masculine features. He held out his hand, and his clear gray eyes drew her in, captivating her as they had on the day she first saw him.

She took his hand, flushing with shame at the imprint of her teeth on the flesh, and his fingers closed around hers. She lowered her gaze, unwilling to meet his eyes.

"You're cold," he whispered, lifting her hand to his lips.

The gentle, affectionate gesture was unexpected. Would she ever understand him?

She gestured toward the rubble. "You should rebuild this part of the castle."

"My resources are needed elsewhere."

"You should honor your father." She lifted her gaze, afraid of what she might see in his eyes.

"You place much on family loyalty, Arlette."

"Aye." She released his hand, and moved toward the gap in the wall.

"You can see for miles," she breathed. "The view is glorious." She leaned forward to get a better view.

The rubble shifted under her feet, and she slipped through the gap. With a scream, she reached out, and grasped a stone jutting from the wall. She kicked her legs, but there was nothing beneath her—only the ground, far below.

Terror overcame her as her hands began to slip. In a matter of moments, she'd lose her grip and fall to her death.

ORSON'S GUT twisted with horror as his wife disappeared over the broken edge of the battlements. With a cry, he sprang forward, his feet slipping on the stones, and dropped to his knees to peer over the edge of the precipice.

He almost wept with relief at the sight of his wife's ashen face looking up at him, her eyes wide with fear. She clung to a stone protruding from the wall, the knuckles of her hands white with tension.

Beneath her was nothing but air—a sheer drop.

"Be still!" he cried.

"Orson…"

He reached down and curled his hand around her wrist. She twisted her head around, but he let out a cry.

"No! Don't look down, woman!"

She kicked her legs, trying to get a foothold on the wall, and her wrist slipped in his grip.

"Be still, or I'll lose my hold!"

But she was beginning to panic.

"Don't let me die!" she cried.

"Look at me, Arlette," he said, forcing his voice to be calm. "I've got you. Do you trust me?"

She nodded, and stopped kicking.

"Don't look away." Keeping his gaze on her, he pulled her up, straining with the effort, until she found her footing and climbed onto the walkway. Shaking, she clung to him.

"I owe you my life."

"That you may keep, wife," he said, holding her close. "My reward will be to endure your shrewish behavior for many years yet. What husband could ask for more?"

Her body shook more violently, and he stroked her head to calm her. Then a ripple of mirth burst from her lips.

He took her face in his hands, and her laughter died. Then he captured her lips. He moved his mouth urgently against hers, to banish the image of her broken body on the ground far below. Had she fallen, he would have thrown himself in her wake, so great was his need for her.

She moaned softly as he deepened the kiss, plundering her mouth as thoroughly as he wanted to pillage her body. Releasing her, he marveled at the delicate features of her face. Her eyes were closed and her lips, swollen by the kiss, curved into a smile, parted in anticipation.

"'Tis good to hear you laugh, Arlette."

She opened her eyes, desire flaring in their green depths, then she lowered her gaze and pulled free, tutting in exasperation. One of her slippers was missing.

"I'll find your missing slipper," he said, "and if I fail, I'll have another pair made for you."

She shook her head. "It matters not."

He took her chin in his hand, stroking her face with his thumb.

"Is it so hard to let your husband take care of you, and buy you gifts?"

Her eyes narrowed, and he recalled their argument that had set today's events in motion—her defiance in defense of his daughter. He wife might be a hellcat, but she'd acted out of love for Lillian. A lesser woman would not have spared the child a second thought.

"I fear I may have been too harsh this morning," he said.

She raised her eyebrows in question.

"The silks I gave you are yours to do with as you wish," he continued. "It gladdens my heart to see how much you love my daughter."

Warm little fingers curled around his hand.

"She's *our* daughter, is she not?" she replied. "I've always wanted a daughter."

And, he hoped, a son.

"I look forward to seeing Lillian in her new gown," he said.

"Thank you, husband. I have a further surprise planned for you. But don't worry—I'm assured that you'll love it."

"A gift?"

"Aye," she said, "a gift that no money can buy. But you must wait.

*A gift no money could buy...*

His heart leaped with joy. She could only mean one thing.

She was carrying his heir.

If only his beloved sister were still alive, she could have shared his joy. He prayed that her ghost would forgive him—forgive that her murderer's daughter was the woman to make his life complete.

But while Verona's ghost lived in his mind, would he ever find peace?

# CHAPTER 24

Orson sat at the high table, his wife and daughter on his right. Lillian wore the yellow silk dress, and he had to admit his daughter looked beautiful in the gown his wife had made for her.

If Arlette cared for his bastard daughter, imagine how much she'd love her own children! Perhaps, tonight, she'd announce that she carried his son.

After the servants cleared the tables, Arlette stood, and raised her hand.

"And now, husband, your gift awaits."

His heart swelled in anticipation, but instead of cradling her belly, she clapped her hands. Two servants scurried into the center of the hall, carrying a chair and a musical instrument. Arlette sat in the chair, and the room fell silent.

Their eyes met and she smiled. Silently, he applauded her efforts to please him—he'd enjoy bedding her tonight.

She ran her fingers over the instrument and began to play. The familiar melody stirred his soul, transporting his mind to happier times—memories of his sister, sitting at her table while she played the same music for him.

The same music…

*My God, Verona!*

Arlette was playing Verona's lute.

How dare she! Nobody was permitted to enter his sister's room, or touch her things. Not only had she defied him, but she insulted Verona's memory.

"Stop!" he roared.

A discordant sound rang out, and she glanced up.

"Is something amiss, husband?"

"You know damned well there is!" He rose to his feet, and she did likewise, clutching the neck of the lute—the lute that had belonged to his beloved sister.

"I don't understand..."

"Don't play the innocent with me, woman!" he cried, his voice shaking with anger. "That instrument belonged to my sister. It was in her chamber, which has been untouched since the day your father murdered her. How dare you disturb her possessions! Do you spit on her memory?"

"I thought the music would please you."

He fisted his hands and advanced on her, but she held her ground, the confusion in her eyes turning to anger.

"You're nothing compared to Verona," he said. "Do you hear me? Nothing! I thought I made it clear that I'd beat anyone who touched her things."

"Papa!" Lillian let out a cry. "Papa, it was me who..."

"Cease your prattle, child!" Arlette cried.

"Do not speak to my daughter thus!" Orson roared. "Would you taint everything—and everyone—you touch?" He wrenched the lute from her hands, and smashed it against the floor.

"Get thee from my sight."

"With pleasure," she snarled. "I could not bear your company for another moment."

Cheeks flaming, she held her head high, and exited the hall.

Orson glared at the rest of the household.

"Begone, the lot of you."

He waved a dismissive hand at Lillian. "Child, get thee to bed.

Pearce, stay here." He motioned to the servants to bring more wine.

As the last servant scurried out of the hall, carrying the remnants of the lute, Orson returned to his seat, and Pearce sat beside him. Orson finished his wine, then refilled his goblet. His friend raised his eyebrows, but said nothing.

"Do you wish to comment on how I discipline my wife, Pearce?"

Pearce shook his head. "I'll leave that to your conscience."

Orson drained his goblet again.

"I intend to tarry here awhile before I endure her company again." He reached for the flagon of wine. "Join me."

~

THE HOUSEHOLD HAD GROWN quiet by the time Orson found himself outside the solar door. His head spun, and his mouth tasted like sour ash. He stumbled against Pearce, who'd been singing bawdy songs while they climbed the spiral staircase. He had never seen so many steps—or a staircase that turned in so many circles. Perhaps his wife was a witch, and she'd cursed the stones. Pearce had snorted with laughter at the notion, declaring that the only spell cast was due to the wine, which affected a man's cock rather than the stones of the castle.

Orson lost his balance, and fell against the door.

"Shh, my friend," Pearce whispered. "If she wakes, you'll find her claws in your face." He rattled the door handle. "It's locked."

"The door doesn't lock from the inside, you fool." Orson pushed the door, which opened a fraction. Through the gap, he glimpsed a shape on the bed, which shifted in and out of focus in unison with the pulsating pain behind his eyes.

The door was blocked, with two chairs and Arlette's trunk.

"She's barricaded herself in."

"Then you must employ siege tactics," Pearce chuckled. "Starve her out."

"Nonsense!" Orson said. "We're warriors. We must ram the door."

The two men threw themselves at the door. It flew open and, with the sound of splintering wood, the chairs collapsed under their weight.

Pearce struggled to his feet. "Victory! I'll leave you to your wife's caresses."

"You mean her claws."

"No more than you deserve."

"The wine has loosened your tongue," Orson said. "I suggest you leave, before I remove it."

"As you wish."

Pearce bowed unsteadily, then retreated, his tuneless whistling echoing off the walls. In all likelihood, he'd collapse before reaching his quarters, and would spend the night either curled up in the floor, or in the arms of an obliging maidservant, should one still be about.

His head spinning, Orson climbed on top of the bed. He fumbled at the fastenings of his breeches, then conceded defeat, and fell face forward, as the thick, wine-fueled darkness claimed him, with the promise of a sore head in the morning.

# CHAPTER 25

Arlette woke to the sound of sawing wood. Orson lay on the bed beside her. His chest rose and fell with a shuddering motion, accompanied by a deep rattling snore, and the stench of sour wine. She poked his side and, with a groan, he rolled toward her. His face had an otherworldly green pallor, and his brow furrowed in pain. He let out another snore, and she wrinkled her nose.

His breath was acrid enough to dissolve armor.

She drew back the furs and padded to the door, telling the servant outside to fetch Esme.

The old woman arrived, and glanced at Orson's unconscious form. "Shall we wake him, lady?"

"No," Arlette said. "Let him rot. It's the least he deserves after last night."

Esme tutted. "He was very fond of his sister—you know that. Nobody is permitted to enter her room. Did you provoke his temper deliberately?"

"Of course not!" Arlette cried. "We only wanted to entertain him."

"We? Did the child take the lute?"

Arlette took Esme's hand. "Tell no one it was Lillian."

Esme shook her head. "Your husband will be even more angry if he realizes you've concealed the truth."

"I'll take that chance," Arlette replied. "For the love of God, Esme, 'tis only a lute. I won't see Lillian blamed for trying to please her father. *I* can withstand his foul disposition, but the child shouldn't have to. She didn't choose to be his daughter."

A grunt from the bed made them both look up, but Orson slept on, his face—if anything—a little greener.

"Come, Esme. I've much to do today."

After dressing, Arlette left the solar, slamming the door shut with her full weight. Esme jumped at the noise, but the sweetest sound to Arlette's ears was the groan of agony from inside the solar.

Toward the end of the morning. Arlette returned to the solar laden with writing materials for Lillian's lesson. Orson was nowhere to be seen, but she wrinkled her nose at the pile of clothes on the floor, covered in wine stains.

When Lillian arrived, she wore a frightened expression.

"Is something amiss?" Arlette asked.

Lillian's voice shook. "Are you going to beat me?"

"Whatever for?"

"Am I in trouble for taking Aunt Verona's lute?"

"No, sweet baby."

"Is Papa angry?"

"Aye—but not with you," Arlette said. "He thinks *I* took it. You did it to please him, which makes you the best of daughters. One day he'll realize that."

"Are you angry with me?"

Arlette kneeled before the child and took her hands.

"I will never be angry with you," she said. "I'm sorry if I sounded harsh last night. I had to stop you from revealing yourself."

Lillian frowned, and Arlette continued. "You know we must always tell the truth, don't you?"

The child nodded. "Aye."

"But sometimes, we conceal the truth if we have good reason."

"Isn't it a sin to lie?"

"It's no sin to hide the truth in order to protect someone."

"So," Lillian said, frowning, as if in concentration, "were you protecting me last night?"

"Yes—clever girl!"

A deep cough interrupted them, and Arlette looked up.

Pearce and Ulferth stood in the doorway.

"What do you want?" Arlette asked. "Can't you see I'm busy?"

"We're looking for Lord Wulfson," Pearce said.

"He's not here—as you see."

"But we're leaving today."

"We?"

"Aye," Pearce said. "Lord Wulfson—and some of the men—are leaving to inspect his properties. Didn't you know?"

She let out a bitter laugh. "Why should he tell me what he does and doesn't do?"

Pearce stepped farther into the chamber. "What about you, lady?" he asked. "Why haven't you told him what you, or…" he glanced at Lillian, "…perhaps another—did, or did not, do?"

"How long have you been standing there?" she asked, rising to her feet.

"Long enough." Pearce lowered his voice, so Lillian couldn't hear. "So you didn't steal Lady Verona's lute, after all. I wondered if you'd done it to injure him."

"Of course I didn't!" she scoffed. "I don't indulge in childish games. If I wanted to injure him, I'd slit his throat—or cut out his horse's heart."

Pearce's expression darkened. "That's good to know."

Behind him, Ulferth stared at her, a sly smile on his lips.

"Say nothing to my husband, Pearce," Arlette said. "The child doesn't deserve to suffer his temper merely for trying to please him."

"And what do you deserve, lady? His respect—his regard?"

She gave a mirthless smile. "You know full well that our marriage was founded on neither respect nor regard," she said. "Now please leave me. If you're looking for my husband, try the field—or perhaps the alehouse, given the state he was in this morning. I've delayed Lillian's lesson for too long, and have no wish to be disturbed again."

"As you wish." He bowed and exited the solar. Ulferth followed, an expression of triumph in his eyes.

~

As evening fell, Arlette sat alone in the sewing room, finishing the hem on one of Lillian's gowns. The door opened and though she had her back to it, she recognized the footfall and tensed her body in anticipation.

"I'm leaving now, wife."

"I know," she replied, ignoring him, her needle flying in and out of the material. "Pearce told me."

"I thought you might come and bid me farewell," he said.

"I'm busy."

She sensed him approach, and her skin tightened with want. A hand touched her shoulder, and the needle slipped and pricked her thumb. Clicking her tongue in annoyance, she sucked on the small droplet that had formed on her skin.

"Forgive me," he said. "I can see you're occupied."

The weight of his hand lifted off her shoulder, and a shiver ran down her spine as his fingers brushed against her cheek. Moisture pricked her eyes and she closed them, not trusting herself to speak. She had no wish to show him that his rejection of her attempts to please him last night had cut her deeply. Emotion was a weakness. He had mastery over her body already—her heart was not for the taking.

He sighed, and removed his hand.

"I'll return in a sennight—maybe two," he said. "I leave the estate in William's hands—and the house in yours, of course. I—I'll miss your company."

He waited for her to respond, but she remained silent. She would miss him also. She thrived on their verbal conflicts during the day, as well as his touch at night.

She recalled Pearce's words. Respect, and regard—there was no shame in wanting either.

And there was no shame in making a little effort to meet him half-way. She could start by wishing him a safe journey.

She turned around to break her silence, but he was gone.

# CHAPTER 26

The household was quieter in Orson's absence. Many of his men had gone with him, including Pearce, Ulferth, and Seaton, leaving a handful to guard the building and patrol the grounds. He'd left one man to watch over Arlette—outwardly for her protection, but clearly he still viewed her as his captive.

To her shame, she often woke in the middle of the night, and reached out for him, but the bed was cold.

Were other women warming his bed? Did he love them?

Or had he loved only his sister?

*Verona...*

The day after her husband left, Arlette found herself outside Verona's chamber, having risen early.

She pushed open the door. Other than the cobwebs and smell of damp, it looked like an ordinary room. The dust had been disturbed on a table, presumably where the lute had lain before Lillian took it.

On impulse, she tasked herself with cleaning the room, snatching stolen moments over the next few days, when alone, to dust the surfaces, wipe the windows, and set a jar of wildflowers on the table. Verona deserved to be remembered, rather than pushed to the recesses of consciousness. Orson might have humiliated Arlette in the dining hall, but his anger came from heartache.

Perhaps by reminding him of his sister's life, rather than her death, Arlette could heal his heart.

Almost a fortnight after Orson had left, Arlette heard a voice call out, while she was overseeing the cleaning of the tapestries in the main entrance hall.

She turned to see a familiar figure, holding a package.

"Seaton!"

He bowed. "Your husband is on his way home, Lady Wulfson. He should arrive tomorrow evening, but some of us came ahead."

He nodded to the servants. "Leave us. And you also, Brice," he said, turning to the guard, who hesitated, then followed the servants out.

"Is my husband well?" Arlette asked.

"Aye."

"And..." she hesitated, "...you, Seaton?"

"I am well also," he said. Then he held out the package. "For you."

She took it, and removed the wrapping, then let out a cry of delight.

It was a lute—its polished wooden teardrop-shaped body smooth to the touch. She plucked a string, and a rich note resonated in the air.

"Is this a gift?" she asked.

"Aye. Your husband..." He hesitated.

"What of him?" she asked. "Does he know of this? Will he be angry that you've brought me a gift?"

"N-no, lady. I'm assured he won't."

"I know not what to say, Seaton," she said. "You are most kind—I shall play for you."

He colored and cast his eyes down. "You must play for your husband first."

"My husband is not here," she said, "and surely 'tis my choice who hears me play? The giver of any gift should be the first to witness its use."

He bit his lip, as if trying to resolve a dilemma. Then he nodded.

"Very well."

He took his leave, his footsteps echoing across the floor.

~

As Orson rode into the courtyard within the bailey wall, he glanced up and smiled at the flickering light in the solar window.

Did she wait for him? Had she missed him?

And...had she forgiven him?

As each day passed while he was away, his conscience, which had always remained hidden, came to the fore, and weighed heavily on him. For the first time, he'd seen genuine hurt in her eyes—not the anger, or the defiance he'd come to thrive on, but sorrow—as if he'd touched her heart.

Perhaps, on seeing his gift, she would warm to him again—welcome him into her arms and body. Did she like it? Or had she done what he feared, and smashed it against the door? He cursed his cowardice—but better Seaton bear the brunt of her retaliation. And, if she loved the gift, then it would show Seaton that Arlette belonged to *him*—not that young whelp.

And what of his other gift? Would she smile at him when she saw what he'd been working on—for her?

As he approached the solar door he heard music and quickened his pace. He ran a hand through his hair, full of dust from the road. Soon, *her* hands would be buried in his hair, while he buried himself inside her.

Then he stiffened at the sound of male laughter.

He flung open the solar door. Arlette and Seaton sat side by side at the fireplace, the lute in her lap, two goblets of wine on the table between them.

"What's going on here?" he demanded.

Seaton looked away, his features laden with guilt, but Arlette met Orson's gaze. Though she cradled the lute, almost lovingly, she eyed him with dislike.

"Seaton has replaced Brice as my jailer," she said.

"You expect me to believe that?"

She rolled her eyes, but he saw no guilt in her expression.

"Seaton, you may go," she said. "Now my captor has returned, I'm no longer in need of a jailer."

She set the lute aside, and held out her hand. Seaton kissed it, then rose and exited the chamber. Then she approached Orson.

"I trust you had a safe journey, husband. Do you wish to dine?"

He shook his head. "No."

"As you wish," she said. "Then I'll retire."

He took her shoulders and pulled her close, claiming her mouth.

God's bones, he'd missed her sweet taste!

He ran his tongue along the seam of her lips, but rather than melt in his arms, she remained unresponsive. With a sigh, he released her. She approached the bed, undressed, and slipped under the furs.

Hardly the warm welcome he'd hoped for. He poured himself a goblet of wine and drained it. Then he shed his clothes and joined her in the bed. He reached for her, and her body tensed.

"I'd hoped for a bath tonight," he said, "but we will share one tomorrow."

She didn't answer, and he ran his hand along her body, relishing the feel of her smooth skin against his fingertips. At length, her body responded to his caresses. The hard little buds on her breasts told him how much her body had missed him—the damp heat between her thighs showed him how much she wanted him now, and the mewls of need spoke of her surrender to the inevitable.

"Do you like the lute?" he murmured, as he dipped his finger between her thighs to tease her open.

"Very much..."

Her breath came in rasps as he caressed her.

"Was it a gift of love, Arlette?"

"I—I cannot say."

"Perhaps it was given with love," he said, "but will that love ever be returned?"

She stiffened, but remained silent, and he realized he'd been holding his breath in anticipation of her answer.

"I don't love him," she said, quietly.

"Who?"

"Seaton."

His blood froze, the familiar jealousy twisting in his gut.

"No matter what gifts I receive, I shall abide by my vows, and remain faithful," she said. "Do not punish a young man for an act of gallantry toward his lady."

Orson dug his fingernails into his palms.

Curse him—the arrogant, deceitful whoreson!

"And you're wrong, husband," she continued. "He doesn't love me —his heart lies elsewhere."

"Let us speak no more of it," he said and he brought his mouth down on hers, silencing her response.

When he woke the next morning, she'd already risen, and was nowhere to be found—not even in her study.

Where the devil was she? He'd planned to go hunting with her today. Not even Lillian had seen her.

Or had she?

The child colored as she shook her head. "Mama Arlette is in her study."

"I looked there first," he replied.

Lillian's eyes widened. "Please don't punish her! She meant no harm—she only wants you to heal. She..." She trailed off, her eyes widening. "May I go now?"

She glanced to her right, her body tense.

"Why don't you go to the solar and continue your studies?" he suggested.

She hesitated, glancing to the right again, then she curtseyed and fled.

What did she have to fear? Why did she keep looking to her right, along the passage? There was nothing there except...

Except Verona's chamber.

Verona...

God's bones! What was his meddling wife about?

Anger boiling in his blood, he strode toward Verona's room.

It was as he'd suspected. His wife stood in the center of the chamber, fussing over a jar of flowers.

"What are you doing in her chamber?" he demanded. "Woman, are you mad—or do you *want* me to punish you?"

She ignored his question, and pointed to a portrait on the wall.

"Was that her?"

"Aye," he replied, unable to look at Verona's likeness.

"She was beautiful. Why do you never speak of her?"

"Because she was murdered!" he cried.

"Is it not better to keep her memory alive, than lock away everything that reminds you of her? It's what she would want."

"How do you know what she would have wanted?" he growled. "You're merely the daughter of her murderer."

She flinched, but met his gaze. "I'd want to keep alive the memories of those I loved and lost—a beloved sister."

The unexpected gentleness in her voice soothed his heart, and his anger lessened.

"She was the kindest, most gentle creature I knew," he said. "She cared for everyone and everything—an injured bird, a lame horse, or a servant taken ill. I pledged to protect her with my life until I found a husband worthy of her. And I failed."

Bitter tears threatened to sting his eyes, and he closed them.

"She was the only person I have ever truly loved," he said, "and her blackened body lies in the ground."

At his words, his wife drew in a sharp breath.

"You also have a daughter to love..." she lowered her voice to an almost inaudible whisper, "...even if you can never love your wife."

He heard the rustle of silk, as she moved to the door.

"I see I'm intruding," she said. "Rest assured I'll not disturb this chamber again."

"Arlette?" he asked.

"Yes?"

"I wish to go hunting today," he said. "Meet me at the stables when you're ready."

The hope in her voice died, and she replied in a toneless voice.

"As my husband commands."

After she closed the door behind her, he exhaled, opened his eyes, and looked around the room. The wooden surfaces had been polished. The windows were clean, and the sunlight threw a pattern on the rug on the floor—the bright colors suggesting it had been beaten to remove the dust. A soft floral fragrance had replaced the smell of damp that had clung to the air since he'd last entered the room, a month after he'd buried Verona's body.

What had Lillian said?

*She only wants you to heal.*

BY THE TIME Arlette arrived at the stables, Orson was waiting for her, together with Pearce, Ulferth, and three others. Seaton was not there.

"See to her ladyship's mount, Will." Orson nodded to the groom standing beside Arlette's mare. The young man bore a striking resemblance to Odella, the farmer's niece she'd befriended. He must be her brother.

"Where are we going?" Arlette asked.

"Not far," he replied. "We're going farther afield soon."

She waited for him to elaborate, but he said no more.

Very well—let him indulge in riddles. She wouldn't take the bait.

As soon as they cleared the village and broke into a canter, she let out a cry of joy. To feel the wind in her hair—to be free again! She spurred her mount into a gallop, breaking free from the rest of the party, heading toward the edge of the forest.

"Men!" Orson roared.

At his command, the company surrounded her mount, boxing her in, and the party drew to a halt.

"What is the meaning of this?" she asked.

"Do not ride ahead."

"Am I to have no freedom?"

"You go where I say," he said sternly.

"I will not!" Arlette squeezed her mount's flanks but Orson was too quick for her and he snatched the reins and took her wrist.

"Obey me, woman, unless you wish me to teach you a lesson in front of my men."

"You wouldn't dare!"

Ulferth let out a low chuckle.

"Lord Wulfson ought to keep his livestock on a tighter rein…"

"…all mares need a bit and bridle…" another said.

"…the spirited mounts are more of a challenge to break in…"

Arlette bristled with fury as Orson joined in the men's laughter. How dare he demean her in front of them!

"Damn you!" she cried, wrenching her arm free. She raised her arm and struck her husband across the face with her whip.

Amid the men's gasps, he jerked back, almost losing his balance, then he righted himself and turned to her. His face bore a red mark across the forehead, and his eyes glittered with cold fury.

"I gave you fair warning," he said. "You only have yourself to blame for the reward you shall now reap."

Sweet heaven—was he going to beat her in front of his men?

Before he could take the reins, she turned her mount in a tight circle, steered between the watching men, then urged the animal into a gallop.

Orson bellowed in anger, but she ignored him, gathering speed as she approached the forest. The wind rushed through her hair and cooled her burning cheeks. How dare he deny her freedom!

Heavy footfalls pulsed behind her, and she glanced over her shoulder. A single rider followed, astride a huge black destrier. Her mare was no match for his warhorse. She must use her wits to outmaneuver him.

She sensed his approach from the right, and steered her horse sharply to the left. But she was too slow. A muscular arm snaked around her waist and plucked her from the saddle as easily as a child might pick a flower. Impervious to her struggles, he held her firm against his body, and reined his horse to a halt.

"Let me go!" she cried.

"Not until you've learned your lesson," he said through gritted teeth. "I warned you what would happen if you defied me again."

Her stomach clenched. "No, you cannot!" she cried.

"I can, and I will," he said, more calmly. "It's time you reaped the rewards."

As he dismounted, she kicked out. He lost his balance, and they fell to the ground.

"You can either make this easy or difficult for yourself," he said. "Lift your skirts, and let it be done quickly."

"I won't let you humiliate me!"

"As you humiliated me in front of my men? You cannot expect your behavior to go unpunished. I've had men lashed for less."

"Then have me lashed," she said bitterly, "you have a taste for it, do you not?"

A flicker of guilt shone in his eyes and he loosened his grip. Seizing her chance, she rammed her knee into his groin.

He let out a strangled groan and bent forward. Lifting her skirts, Arlette ran toward the forest.

# CHAPTER 27

The air grew cold as she slipped between the trees. Spangles of light dotted the forest floor, thinning to small pinpricks the denser the trees grew. Shadows slipped over the texture of the bark—gnarled faces of old men watching her, reproach in their eyes—the ancient beings of the forest.

A twig snapped ahead, and a low, guttural snarl shattered the soft whispering of the trees.

A thick shape emerged from the darkness. Pale eyes glittered malevolently as it moved toward her. It snarled again, opening its mouth to reveal sharp, yellowing teeth, to match the pointed tusks either side of its face.

A boar could rip a man in two. One of Papa's squires had met with such a fate, and Arlette would never forget the image—a mass of shredded flesh and bones, which had once been a man, screaming in pain. Papa had admonished her for looking.

Now, such a beast stood before her—thick, viscous saliva dripping from its jaws as it advanced toward its prey.

Then it charged.

Arlette let out a scream and dodged to one side, slipping behind a tree. The boar crashed through the undergrowth in search of her.

Though the animal had poor eyesight, it would be able to smell her fear. Her only hope was to run from tree to tree, using them as cover. If she remained where she was, the boar would hunt her down.

She sprinted toward the nearest tree, but before she reached her destination, the boar blocked her path, snarling with rage. She took a step back and the boar moved forward, watching her every move. Then she drew her knife. If the boar was going to kill her, she would at least die fighting.

"Arlette!" Orson's voice cut through her fear.

She turned toward him.

"No!" he cried. "Do *not* move!"

She shook with fear, her body's instincts screaming at her to run.

"Be still, my love," he spoke more gently. "Our lives depend on it."

*My love…*

The boar sprang forward. But before it reached her, Orson threw himself in its path. The animal squealed as he drove his sword into its chest. With a thrash of legs, it rolled on the ground, fighting to break free, but Orson held it firm. After a brief struggle, the boar grew still and Orson rose to his feet, a huge red stain on his tunic.

"Come here, Arlette."

Strong arms enveloped her, and a broad muscular chest quelled her trembling body. She closed her eyes and focused on the rhythmic beat of his heart, which slowed as he relaxed against her.

"Orson…"

"Hush," he whispered. "You're safe now. You'll always be safe with me."

She remained in his arms until birdsong filtered through the air, the forest creatures emerging from their hiding places now the disturbance was over. At length, he released her and cleaned his sword. Then he led her to the edge of the forest, where their horses stood, waiting patiently for their owners.

Arlette took the reins of the mare, but he pulled her back.

"Not yet," he said. "We have unfinished business."

Her breath caught in her chest. "No," she whispered. "You cannot—I know you're angry, but…"

"I'm not angry," he replied, sorrow in his voice, "but it must be done."

He drew her to him and kissed her, his tongue claiming her—teasing, probing, clouding her mind with a fog of desire until she surrendered. He hardened against her and she smiled to herself—his desire was also his undoing. He pulled her to the ground, cupping her face in his hands, then drew a line of nibbling kisses across her chin, and his commanding voice rumbled in her ear.

"Do you remember what I said about the falcon?"

Before she could respond, he nipped the skin on her neck. Then he pulled her skirts up and clamped her legs between his own.

"No!" She struggled, but he was too strong. He brought his hand down on her buttocks with a crack.

"Let me go!" She squirmed in his grip, but her struggles were met with another crack.

He squeezed her thigh and a rush of heat radiated out from where his hand had struck, igniting a flame deep inside her. Then he dipped his hand between her thighs.

His fingers drew a slippery line across her sensitive flesh. She bit her lip to quell a cry of pleasure, and he let out a low chuckle.

"You shouldn't be *enjoying* this, little one."

"I'm not..."

"You cannot deny it, Arlette." He inhaled deeply. "I can smell your need."

He slipped his finger inside her, and curled it around, until the flame exploded, and her body burst into life. Air flooded her lungs, then she cried out, her body jerking against him while he caressed her, squeezing every last drop of passion until she collapsed and lay still, her body soft and boneless.

He turned her body over and his mouth met hers in a soft kiss.

"It seems as if I've finally tamed my tigress."

His words dissipated the fog of lust, and she jerked free.

"Curse you to hell, Orson Greywell!"

"I'm already doomed to hell," he said. "Come, let us ride together."

He mounted his horse and pulled her onto his lap. She winced at the soreness in her buttocks, and her face warmed with shame at her body's reaction to his discipline.

"Why must I sit like this?" she demanded.

"The alternative is to lie across my lap like a sack of grain," he said. "I can oblige if you wish—my men are in need of entertainment."

He lifted his horn to his lips, then blew three times. Shortly after, three blasts responded in the distance.

"What was that for?" Arlette asked.

"A signal to my men."

"That you're returning?"

"Not exactly."

"That you've punished me?"

"No."

"Why should you bother to tell me?" she said bitterly. "I am mere chattel."

He sighed. "My men are poised at arms, prepared to ride hard to battle should the need to protect you arise. My signal told them I've found you safe and well, and that they may stand down."

He steered his horse toward Arlette's mare, took the animal's reins, then they set off. Arlette remained silent during the ride, trying to ignore the soreness in her derriere, exacerbated by the horse's gait.

Excited chatter broke out among the men as they returned. Pearce helped her down, and his eyes widened as he glanced at Orson's stained clothes.

"I'm glad you're safe, my lady," he said.

"Thank you, Pearce," Arlette said, straightening her back. At least she could maintain her dignity.

Orson slapped her backside, destroying her poise as she squealed in pain.

"Come, let us rest and eat before returning home," he said. "Brice, my wife will need a soft blanket to sit on after her...*lesson*."

Ignoring their chuckles, Arlette settled herself on the blanket. Orson sat beside her, placing a possessive hand on her thigh, while he ordered two of the men to fetch the boar.

As the day wore on, the men prepared a fire and roasted a brace of rabbit that Pearce had caught. Watt and Brice returned with the boar and the company ate. Orson insisted on serving Arlette, choosing the choicest cuts from the rabbit. Then he settled beside her, his arm around her shoulders, talking to the men and dropping the occasional kiss on the top of her head.

But if he thought she'd forgive him, he was very much mistaken.

As soon as they returned home, she dismounted and strode inside without giving her husband so much as a backward glance. She half hoped he'd follow her and reignite their argument. But he did not. Neither did he join her in the solar that evening—though she'd looked forward to having the opportunity to shut him out.

As the evening wore on, her stomach growled with hunger and she sent for Esme. When her old nursemaid arrived with a tray of food, she set it down and placed her hands on her hips—her expression reminiscent of days gone by when Arlette had committed a grave misdemeanor as a child.

"What's happened, Lady Arlette?"

"I married a brute!" Arlette cried. "He beat me today."

"What did you do to warrant such a punishment?"

"What did *I* do?" Arlette cried. "I only wanted my freedom—to ride unfettered without his men, but he stopped me."

"And then?" Esme asked. "He wouldn't punish you for that, surely?"

Arlette's cheeks warmed. "I may have struck him with my whip."

"In front of his men?"

Arlette nodded.

"Willful child!"

"You cannot condone his behavior," Arlette said. "How dare you side with him?"

"Need I remind you of your vow of obedience?"

"That doesn't give him the right to abuse me."

Esme took Arlette's hands. "Your husband is a warrior, with a reputation for strength."

Arlette snorted, and tried to withdraw her hand, but Esme held it firm.

"The sooner you learn this, the better," Esme said, "whether 'tis fair or not. We live in dangerous times—with rebellion and treachery around every corner. Do you want every usurper to see your husband as an easy target?"

"I fail to understand what this has to do with me," Arlette said.

"Then you're not as intelligent as I believed. A man whose wife can defy him in front of his men, without retribution or discipline, is seen as weak."

"So he would humiliate me?"

"It's not humiliation, little one," Esme said, "but a show of strength—which also benefits you. Is he joining you tonight?"

"If he does, I'll slit his throat."

Esme rolled her eyes. "Have you lost your senses?"

"My body aches," Arlette said, aware of the petulance in her tone. "I don't want his attentions tonight—or at all."

"Your duty is to him, lady," Esme said. "Imagine what would happen if one such as Ulferth challenged him?"

Arlette stuck out her lower lip, but a voice in her mind told her that Esme spoke sense.

"Why did he arrive with a bloodstain on his front?" Esme asked.

"He killed a boar." Arlette shivered at the memory of the crippling fear. "I'd run away from him—into the forest—and stumbled on a boar. I thought it was going to kill me."

"And he saved your life?"

"Aye."

"After you struck him with your whip?"

Arlette nodded.

"There!" Esme said. "You see? You have a good, strong husband to protect you. Do not deny him." She gestured toward the tray. "I'll leave you to your supper—and your conscience."

Esme dipped into a curtsey and exited the chamber.

ARLETTE WOKE to the aroma of citrus and lavender. A large wooden bathtub stood in the center of the solar, next to a box of soaps, and Ivetta, her mother's maid from home, was filling it with water.

"Lady—you're awake!" Ivetta cried, rushing over to the bed. "Let me help you."

She took Arlette's hand and helped her up. Arlette winced at the soreness in her legs, which were stiff from yesterday's ride. The lavender would soothe her skin, but the fire pulsing in her body at the memory of Orson's hand coming down hard on her buttocks was not so easily doused.

"Thank you, Ivetta," she said.

"My pleasure, lady." Ivetta smiled and led Arlette to the bath. The maidservant looked happier since coming to Greywell—and healthier. Her once-pale skin glowed with vitality and her thin frame had rounded out. At Leaside, Ivetta had scuttled along the corridors, shoulders hunched, eyes downcast. But here, at Greywell Castle, she'd turned into a confident, contented young woman.

"Ivetta, are you happy here? Happier than at Leaside?"

"Oh, yes, lady!" Ivetta exclaimed, then she colored. "Forgive me, I meant no disrespect to your family."

"Of course." Arlette placed a hand on Ivetta's arm. "Esme has told me that there's no shame in being happy here."

"Thank you, lady. Shall I help you bathe?"

Arlette shook her head. "I'd rather be alone. Send Esme to help me dress later."

"As you wish." Ivetta bobbed a curtsey, then left, closing the door behind her.

Arlette slipped off her nightshift and tested the water with her toes, relishing the prospect of luxuriating in the aromatic water. Then she eased herself into the bath, leaned back, and closed her eyes. The scent of healing herbs and spices soothed her nerves and after a few deep breaths she grew drowsy.

The door creaked open behind her.

"Is that you, Esme?" she murmured.

Soft footsteps approached, accompanied by the rustling of material. Esme had brought her clothes.

"I wish to bathe awhile yet before dressing," Arlette said. "Would you pass me the soap and cloth?"

The lid of the soap box opened and shut, then a hand caressed the back of her head.

"Mmm, Esme…what would I do if you weren't here to take care of me?"

A woody scent caressed her senses, while expert fingers massaged lather onto her shoulders, easing the tension.

"Will you wash my back, Esme?"

Gentle hands pushed her forward, then she heard a sharp intake of breath, before the hands lathered soap over her back, following the contours of her muscles. How skillful her nursemaid was! She seemed to know where the tension was, and how to ease it.

She sighed with pleasure, then leaned back. The hands continued to caress her skin, lathering soap along her arms, then across her chest in a sweeping, circular motion.

Then a hand cupped her breast, and her nipple hardened. Her eyes flew open as she heard a low chuckle.

"I see a little marital discipline has not cooled your desire for me."

The hand was Orson's.

~

Orson's wife let out a squeal and leaped to her feet, spilling water over the side. He offered his hand, but the stubborn little vixen ignored him and stepped out unaided. He picked up the drying cloth and she tried to snatch it from him.

"Nay, wife," he said. "Don't deny me the pleasure of drying you."

She scowled and covered her chest with her arms.

He placed the cloth over her shoulders. Her body was muscular, but with the soft roundness of a woman. He ran the towel across her front, gently pulling her arms away to reveal her breasts. He ached to taste them, and run his tongue across those tempting little buds that were beaded for him, but instead, he turned her until her back faced him. Once again he suppressed a curse. The scars on her back had faded but she would bear them for life. He ran a finger along one of the lines, the blemish contrasting against the smooth creamy skin. She shivered at his touch and, his conscience pricking at him, he lowered his head to kiss the scar.

His body ached to be buried inside her, but he remembered the falcon. The way to master this bird of prey—his Arlette—was to leave her wanting more.

With the cloth, he caressed every inch of her, and she let out a sigh each time he brushed against the sensitive, intimate places that brought her to pleasure in his bed. Then, he wrapped the cloth around her, tipped her chin up, and brushed his lips against hers. She opened her mouth for him and gave a groan of desire, then she lifted her hands and buried them in his hair. The cloth fell to the floor, revealing her naked body, which she pressed against him, and her hard little buds stiffened against his chest.

Ignoring the need that raged through his body, he gently pushed her away.

"I'll send for your maid to dress you."

She frowned, confusion in her eyes, followed by a flash of frustration, as he left the chamber. After closing the door, he leaned against the wall and let out a deep sigh. A moment longer, and he'd have lost control and mounted her on the floor.

But he wanted her to come to him—freely, and gladly.

And a voice in his mind told him that he also wanted her to come to him out of love.

~

Arlette didn't see her husband again until the household gathered at suppertime.

It mattered not—she didn't care to see him.

*Then why do you look for him—hear his footsteps in every creak of the door?*

Esme's words made her view her husband in a different light. If his men conspired against him, he couldn't fight them all. Some, such as Pearce and Seaton, would remain loyal, but others might not.

As if he read her thoughts, Ulferth watched her. She pulled a face, but he merely smiled, then gestured to a maidservant to refill his goblet. Hilda stepped forward and Ulferth grabbed her breast, and planted a kiss on her lips, laughing crudely.

A shiver of unease tightened Arlette's skin. Had Hilda revealed anything of her attempts to find Guillaume? She was a sly creature—most likely she would share Ulferth's bed tonight. Once again, Arlette felt a pang of sympathy for the Lady Edith, who sat with the other knights' wives, looking pale and unhappy.

Arlette had to support her husband, publicly at least. To have one such as Ulferth lead an uprising was unthinkable. Ulferth was a lumbering oaf, but his eyes glittered with cunning.

As soon as the meal finished, she rose and asked to be excused. Orson nodded, then continued eating.

After undressing, she slipped under the furs, shivering with the cold.

Would Orson join her tonight?

As time wore on, he did not come and, swallowing her disappointment, she closed her eyes and tried to sleep. What did she care if he slept elsewhere?

Her dreams were punctuated with a delicious sense of warmth, and soft hands gliding over her skin. A wave of pleasure consumed her senses, and her body throbbed with desire. The intensity increased, and she shuddered with the force of it and snapped her eyes open.

Orson lay beside her, his manhood rigid against her back. She cried out as her body shattered around his intimate caresses, and he held her firm until her body stilled.

She waited for him to take her, but he merely kissed her on the back of her neck.

"To sleep, wife," he whispered.

Within minutes, his breathing grew steady in sleep, leaving her body only partly sated by his intimate touch.

# CHAPTER 28

Arlette woke the next morning to find him standing at the foot of the bed.

"Awake at last," he said. "Get dressed—we've a long ride ahead.

"I don't care to ride today," she replied.

"It wasn't a request."

Infuriating man! But she was in no mood to fight him today.

"Very well," she said. "As my lord and master commands."

His lips twitched into a smile as she climbed out of the bed.

After dressing, they broke their fast in the solar, then Orson led her to the stables where Will, the young groom, waited with their horses, saddled and ready to ride.

Orson mounted his horse in a swift, fluid motion. With his broad muscular frame, he was a magnificent sight, sitting astride the enormous black destrier. Who would dare rise up against a man such as he? One look at this powerful warrior and his warhorse would be enough to make an army fall to its knees.

"Methinks, Will, the lady likes what she sees."

Arlette's cheeks warmed as she realized she'd been staring at him open mouthed.

"Has Watt ridden ahead?" he continued.

"Aye, milord."

"Where are we going?" Arlette asked.

"All in good time, wife."

He steered his mount out of the courtyard, and Arlette followed.

They rode for most of the day, stopping twice to rest and eat. Arlette remained silent, determined to ask her husband nothing, but each time he looked at her a smile played on his lips as if he harbored a secret. When the shadows began to lengthen, he broke the silence.

"We're nearing our destination. The terrain should begin to look familiar."

Arlette looked around her. Dear Lord! They were nearing Leaside—the home she longed to see but also feared because her husband had burned it to the ground.

Why did he persist in tormenting her?

"Follow me," he said. "I would have you pleased with what you see."

He spurred his horse on, without even bothering to see if she followed.

Her chest tightened as she rode in his wake, recognizing the clump of trees behind which her former home would have been visible.

He stopped at a turn in the road, his horse's tail swishing back and forth at a cloud of flies that danced in the evening air. From his vantage point he'd be able to see the ruins of her home—the place where her parents died, and where she'd last seen Guillaume alive. The steady beat of her mount's hooves fell into step with the rhythm of her heart, which threatened to burst with the agony of loss.

She drew alongside him, took a deep breath, and prepared to look upon a blackened ruin.

Then she glanced up, and let out a cry of disbelief.

Leaside had been rebuilt.

The hall had been extended, and silhouettes of men working on the ramparts stood out against the evening sky. A bailey wall now surrounded the building, broken by a large gate that stood open. A huge trench surrounded the wall, spanned by a drawbridge.

"Come."

Orson led her toward the building, their horses' hooves clattering on the drawbridge, and they rode into the courtyard. A man rushed forward and took their reins. Orson dismounted and helped Arlette down.

"Is the solar ready, Watt? Lady Wulfson is tired."

"Aye, my lord."

Orson took Arlette's hand. "We can dine before you rest, but first I wish to show you something."

He steered her toward the chapel. The fire had not destroyed the interior, and familiar tapestries still adorned the walls.

But the room was not entirely unaltered. Two large memorial stones had been set into the floor. Arlette kneeled beside them and read the inscriptions.

*Lord Reynaud Pierre Jean de Villiers and his beloved wife, Lady Emmelina Aelfwyn.*

"Mama—Papa..."

Uttering a prayer for their souls, she traced the letters with her fingertips. Beads of moisture splashed onto the floor, small, dark flowers against the lighter gray of the stone.

She wiped her eyes and rose to her feet. Orson took her hand and led her outside. She stumbled on a loose stone, but he caught her and drew her into his arms.

"Why?" she asked.

"Why all this?" He gestured toward the repaired buildings.

"And the tombstones..." She shook her head. "Why rebuild something you set out to destroy? The home of the man you..." She broke off, choking on her memories.

"The man I killed in battle?" He spoke quietly. "The man who murdered my sister?"

She nodded, wiping her face.

His breath caught before he replied, his voice betraying vulnerability.

"I didn't do it for him."

He turned her to face him. "I'll never regret taking vengeance upon the man who killed Verona. This you must accept. No—do not turn from me," he said, as she tried to pull away. "But I do harbor a deep regret, Arlette. I regret the deaths of my wife's father and mother. Do you understand?"

"Perhaps," she replied, her heart wilting, "You rebuilt Leaside for your sister."

"No," he said. "I rebuilt Leaside for you."

Though it might have been a trick of the light, a spark of kindness flickered in his gray eyes—kindness, and a plea for approval. She tipped her face up, and placed a kiss on his chin. His eyes widened at her gesture and he lowered his head, his warm breath drifting across her lips.

"Arlette..."

"My lord!"

A voice carried across the courtyard, and he pulled away from her.

"What is it, Watt?"

"Your supper is ready. Shall I have it brought to the solar?"

"Very well."

Orson led Arlette inside a new part of the building, and stopped at a large oak door in the shape of an arch.

"The solar."

"But the solar's back where we came."

"Nay, wife, this is the solar now," he replied. "We can never go back, no matter how much we want to. We must venture forward and embrace the future."

The new solar was larger than the original. A fire crackled in the hearth beside which a table, laden with food, and chairs were set. New tapestries lined the walls, rich autumnal colors depicting hunting scenes. At the far end of the main room was a deep red velvet curtain, which Orson drew aside to reveal an archway leading to the bedchamber.

He nodded toward a large trunk beside the bed.

"Watt came ahead with your things. Shall I send a servant to help you undress? Or perhaps you wish to dine?"

She sat on the bed, then shook her head, wanting nothing but solitude, as a surge of despondency overwhelmed her. The transformation of Leaside, as grand a gesture as it might be, marked the death of her former life. Arlette de Villiers was no more—she'd been replaced by Lady Wulfson.

Orson kissed her chastely on the forehead, then he retreated and approached the door.

"You are melancholy, wife," he said, "and I understand. The building is well protected. You are safe—but I shall leave you to spend your first night at Leaside in peace."

Only once before had he spoken so gently—the night he'd whispered her name when she comforted him after he'd cried for his sister.

At what personal cost had he restored the home of the man who had killed Verona—and laid down a memorial to him?

*And he did it for me.*

She let out a cry. "Orson!"

He stopped, and turned to face her. Leaning against the door, he crossed his arms, his stance an echo of the night she'd once caught him watching her in the kitchen. Would he forever be reminded of his sister's death every time he looked at her? Did he regret their union?

Perhaps that was why he didn't want her company.

But, though her mind yearned for freedom, her heart did not want a life without love.

And she did not want a life without him.

He raised his eyebrows and waited.

She cast her eyes down, a plea on her lips.

"I have no wish to be alone tonight."

She closed her eyes—her heart hoping he would stay, her mind expecting him to go. But she heard nothing. A small sob escaped her lips. He had gone.

As she moved to wipe her tears, a large warm hand covered hers, and squeezed it gently. She opened her eyes to see him kneeling in front of her.

"Neither do I," he whispered.

Orson tipped his wife's chin up, and placed a soft kiss on her lips. For a moment, uncertainty flickered in her eyes, then their expression turned to resolve. She stood, and unlaced her gown. The material slithered to the floor followed by her undergarments. The candlelight danced over the curves of her body, and the breath caught in his throat as he drank in the sight of her smooth skin—the full breasts with their perfect pink buds, the flare of her hips, and the tempting nest of curls where her thighs met.

He began to undress.

"No, husband, let me."

She grasped his tunic, and pulled it over his head. Then she unlaced his breeches and slid the material over his skin, her hand brushing his manhood, which surged with want.

Was she *seducing* him?

She took his hand and led him to the bed.

"How do you like your solar?" he asked.

"I have yet to notice it, for I have eyes only for my husband."

She lay back on the bed, and parted her thighs. The sight of her ripe body, spread before him in offering—a succulent feast of womanhood—was his undoing, and he mounted her, growling with pleasure as she willingly opened herself to him.

He drove himself inside her with a hoarse cry. Her body rippled around him, and he plunged in and out of her, oblivious of anything but his need. His mind exploded into a myriad of colors, and he thrust one final time, falling forward into her arms. They lay together, still joined, bodies slick with perspiration, hearts beating in unison.

She was his equal. All the women who'd come before her—hardened seductresses and paid whores—were nothing to her. Though they might scream his name, their pleasure was false. None of them exuded Arlette's raw, honest passion. Her body fitted his as if they were two halves of a whole, and with these pleasurable thoughts, he drifted into a doze.

During the night, he woke to a tickling sensation on his skin. Soft hands caressed his chest, cool little fingers exploring every inch, tracing his scars. Then a hot mouth came down on his nipple and his body jerked at the fizz of lust. She jumped at his reaction, and he smiled inwardly, relishing the notion that she thought she was stealing a forbidden pleasure in exploring his body. He looked forward to her enjoying many more such pleasures.

She continued to explore him, her light touch setting his senses on fire, as her fingers traced a line along his torso, past his navel, inching closer to his now-flaccid cock. She hesitated, and he sensed, rather than knew, that she watched him, to see if he was awake. He kept his breathing steady, eyes closed, and waited, his nerves screaming with anticipation.

He sensed her uncertainty and wanted to reassure her, but the thrill of having her explore him for her own pleasure was too much. Her fingers inched lower, then she circled him with her hand. He waited, breathless, knowing that her mouth would soon follow, and a deep groan bubbled in the back of his throat. She withdrew her hand, and he squeezed his eyes shut, grimacing in frustration. The bed shifted as she moved. She nestled her body against him, and sighed. Not long after, he heard steady breathing. His wife was asleep.

~

ARLETTE SPENT two days at Leaside with her husband. Away from Greywell Castle and his men, he was a different man, murmuring tender words into her ear as he eased into her willing body at night.

But, during their ride back to Greywell Castle, his demeanor began to change, and the grim, brutish warrior returned once more. His face wore the same shuttered expression she'd seen the day he'd told her that his dead sister was the only woman he would ever love.

Perhaps that was why his stepmother had grown so bitter and resentful. Arlette had heard tales of her jealousy and hatred, but something must have given her cause. Perhaps she, too, had loved her husband once, only to be spurned when she had served her purpose.

*Loved...*

Sweet heaven!

The revelation in her mind issued a shockwave of pain, lacerating her heart as deeply as the whip had torn into her flesh. What had Orson said to her the night he'd offered his hand?

*"Marry for love? You'll have a long wait."*

Arlette was doomed. For she'd fallen in love with her husband.

# CHAPTER 29

As summer came to a close and the leaves began to fall, Arlette continued with her duties, drawing comfort from her relationship with Lillian. The revelation that she loved her husband warred with her conscience. How could she show such disloyalty to her family—to Guillaume, who, if not dead, was lost, and alone, and in need of her?

During the day she turned from her husband, but, at night, she surrendered to her need, and their cries of pleasure echoed around the solar. But, in the morning, the tender, loving man she glimpsed at Leaside had gone, and she turned away from him.

One such morning after he'd left the solar, Esme paused while brushing Arlette's hair.

"Lady—forgive me—are you breeding?"

*Sweet heaven!*

"When did you last bleed?" Esme continued. "You've not asked for extra cloths—I've counted at least two full moons. You must tell the master."

"No!" Arlette cried. "He cannot know."

"He'll find out eventually," Esme said, "and he'll be angry if you don't tell him yourself. Have you been feeling unwell?"

Arlette shook her head.

"Are you sensitive…" Esme said, "…where he touches you —intimately?"

Arlette shuddered. How could Esme speak of such things! But she had to admit that her body—particularly her breasts—had become more responsive to Orson's touch.

"'Tis nothing to be ashamed of," Esme continued.

"Speak no more of it!" Arlette cried.

Esme took her hand. "Do you fear the birth? There's no need—I delivered you and your brother safely."

Arlette nodded. "I remember Mama's screams the night Guillaume was born, and…" She hesitated, recalling her mother's sorrow. After Guillaume was born, once she'd fulfilled her purpose and given Papa an heir, he had no more use of her.

"And what, little one?" Esme patted Arlette's hand. "Do you fear he'll not want the child? All great men wish for sons. Your husband is no different."

"He wants the *child*," Arlette said, "but once he has a child, will he still want his wife?"

"A child needs its mother—and Lillian needs her stepmother."

"My husband has made his opinion of mothers—and stepmothers —clear," Arlette said.

"Marriages among your class are rarely made for love," Esme chided. "You know that."

Arlette's voice caught in her throat, and she nodded, unable to speak.

Understanding shone in Esme's eyes.

"Oh, my sweet lady! Do you love him?"

A tear splashed onto Arlette's cheek. "I've betrayed my family, Esme—for a love that cannot be returned."

Warm arms drew her into an embrace.

"It seems to me you have a task before you, child."

"Which is?"

"Make him love you."

"He's incapable of love."

"You're wrong. He loved his sister, and he often looks at you with fondness."

"Aye," Arlette said. "As a possession."

"Not a possession," Esme said. "A treasure. He's a man, and as such, will never tell you how he feels. But take my counsel—treat him with kindness, for he's known little of it in his life. Give him your love, your loyalty, and a child—and he'll grow to love you."

"What about my loyalty to Guillaume? I cannot forsake my brother."

"If your husband loves you, he'll not deny you anything."

Esme kissed her hand. "I'll leave you now, lady, but think on my words."

After her old nursemaid left, Arlette ran a light hand over her stomach.

*My child...*

She took a seat by the fire, and watched the flames flicker and dance, her heart soothed by the gentle crackling of the logs. The weather was turning cold as winter approached, but as each day passed, she found herself looking forward to sharing a warm bed with her husband.

From now on she would be an attentive wife. When he knew she carried his heir, he would not deny her the chance to find her brother.

A KNOCK on the study door interrupted Orson's discussion with his steward.

"What is it?" he growled.

The door opened to reveal his wife.

"William," she said, "it's time you released my husband into my care."

"Of course, my lady."

His wife and steward exchanged a smile, and Orson eyed them with suspicion.

"What are you about?" he asked.

"I'm taking you for our noon meal, husband."

"It's early yet."

"My husband is sharp today, William," she said, a twinkle in her eyes. She offered Orson her hand. "Come."

What was she about? He'd grown increasingly suspicious of her behavior of late. She seemed to be harboring a secret. He'd heard a rumor from Ulferth that she'd been meeting someone in the village, and since their return from Leaside, her demeanor had changed. Often, he sensed her watching him, though she averted her gaze when he looked at her.

She led him to the stables, where the groom waited with her mount and his destrier, saddled and ready to ride.

"Thank you, Will," she said.

"Where are we going?" Orson asked.

She smiled. "You must show patience to earn your reward."

He helped her into the saddle, then mounted his horse, and they steered their mounts out of the yard. They rode in silence until they reached the forest behind the village.

"Your reward awaits," Arlette said.

She entered the forest and he followed. Despite the onset of winter, the air was warm. The sky was clear and cloudless and the sun penetrated the forest, illuminating the trees, which shone with a myriad of colors. Soon, the trees would shed their leaves to reveal the bare bones of winter.

As they approached a clearing, he saw movement ahead.

"Stop!" he hissed, drawing his sword.

She laughed. "There's naught to fear," she said. "Come, husband, your surprise awaits."

She led the way into the clearing, and dismounted. A fire burned in the center, which one of his men was feeding with branches, while a second roasted a brace of rabbit on a spit. Blankets and furs had been arranged to form a seating area, and two tables had been set, one holding a flagon of wine and two goblets, the other a trencher laden with fruit and sweet tarts.

The men looked up from their work and bowed.

"Brand, Jarvis," Orson said, dismounting. "What is the meaning of this?"

Jarvis approached the horses, and took the reins.

"Lady Wulfson's instructions, my lord."

"You've done well, Jarvis," Arlette said. "See to the horses, then leave us. You know what to do?"

"Aye, lady."

The two men tethered the horses, then disappeared through the trees.

"Sit, husband." Arlette gestured toward the blankets. "Our meal is ready."

"Who shall serve us?"

"I will serve you," she said, "then you shall have your reward, once we've dined."

His manhood twitched at the seductive tone of her voice, and he sat, thankful his tunic covered his groin. But her eyes sparkled with understanding. She crouched by the roasting rabbits, tested them, then, in a few swift strokes, she jointed them with her knife.

"How did you learn to do that?" he asked.

She kneeled before him and held a piece of meat to his lips. "I spent my childhood learning the skills of a man, rather than those of a wife."

"Who taught you to hunt?"

She frowned, and a flicker of sorrow darkened her eyes. "Papa's men—Ernaut and Garret—let me join them. We'd hunt during the day and make camp for the night. I've never felt so free as I did then."

"Did they also teach you to fight?"

"Aye." The ghost of a smile played on her lips. "Ernaut always said that a woman must rely on her wits. A man's advantage is his strength—a woman's advantage is the complacency of men."

"He sounds like a fool."

She frowned, and he regretted his words. This Ernaut must have been one of de Villiers' men—perhaps killed by Orson's own hand.

"He was no fool," she said coldly. "He understood my need for freedom, and taught me to shift for myself until Guillaume was born, and Papa insisted I relinquish my sword and become a lady."

She turned her head away.

"Don't all women aspire to be ladies?"

She snorted. "To be fettered? Imprisoned in finery while there's so much to see and do in the world?"

He took her hand. "Forgive me—I didn't mean to cause you pain. I should know by now that my wife is no ordinary woman."

Her eyes widened at his apology, then she fed him another morsel.

Would he ever understand her? He'd always disliked noblewomen. His stepmother had shown him that ladies were cold, unloving creatures who despised him for his bastardry, and cared only for riches. But this woman he'd married on an impulse, compelled by lust, was the exception.

"Do you regret being born a woman?" he asked.

She took a bite of the rabbit and chewed it, a faraway expression on her face.

"Sometimes," she said. "But had I been born a man, Papa would have left Mama alone—and I would not have had Guillaume. My brother may have been the reason why Papa's opinion of me changed —but I would not have had it any different—I love him so much!"

"You do?"

"Aye," she said. "Guillaume is…" She hesitated, as if warring with herself. "He was…" She shook her head almost imperceptibly. "No matter. He's gone…"

She colored and looked away. Did she have something to hide?

"What if he was not gone?" he asked. "Perhaps your cousin…"

"Please!" she cried. "Let us finish our meal and speak of other things."

"Very well—as my wife wishes." He took another bite of the rabbit, and they ate in silence. But where she had appeared relaxed and eager to please, her demeanor had changed. Each time he glanced at her, she averted her gaze, but not before he caught an expression of wariness —borne of guilt, perhaps?

Why, after months of defiance, was she being so attentive—and why did she react so violently at the mention of her cousin? What was she plotting?

When they finished their meal, she kneeled once more beside him.

"'Tis time for your reward."

"We must return," he said. "It's dangerous to remain here too long."

She placed a finger on his lips. "Your men are within calling distance should we need them."

"You've thought of everything."

"Aye," she whispered. "Now, close your eyes, my love."

*My love…*

He sank back into the pile of furs, and she straddled him, her thighs soft against his hard body. Her hair tickled his chin and the soft silk of her gown rustled as she lowered herself on to him, chest to chest. She brushed her lips over his, caressing her tongue across the seam of his lips before dipping into his mouth as delicately as a honey bee tasting nectar.

"Keep your eyes closed."

Soft hands stroked his neck, and delicate fingertips traced a line across his collarbone, caressing every blemish, every scar. Her lips followed the path of her fingers, and her hot breath assaulted his senses, sending a firebolt of need straight to his groin. A groan of pleasure rumbled in his chest as his manhood surged in anticipation.

"My husband is eager for his reward."

She tugged at the laces of his chausses, and her hand slipped inside. Then she closed her fingers around him, stroking his sensitive skin with her thumb, and a long, low growl erupted from his lips as he grew thick and hard.

"Shhh…"

She tightened her grip, easing his chausses down with her free hand. His manhood throbbed painfully, and the familiar surge in his loins grew stronger.

"Arlette…" he rasped, "…I'll not be able to hold on…I cannot…"

"Patience, husband."

To have his wife's hands cause such wicked sensations was more than he could bear. He gritted his teeth at the strain of preventing himself from spending into her hand.

Then she released him, and his body jerked as the pleasure faded. She pressed her mouth against his, to muffle his cry of frustration, and her lips curled into a smile. Curse her—the temptress!

Then, his wanton wife lowered herself onto him, and he groaned with pleasure as her damp, tight warmth enveloped him. She squeezed her thighs, and his eyes flew open.

She stared back, her eyes dark with desire, surrounded by the chestnut curtain of her hair.

Then she moved, gently at first, letting out a little purr with each rocking motion, and his body surged at the delicious friction. She increased the pace, the purrs turning into mewls. The image of her face, flushed with arousal, as she murmured his name, pushed him over the brink, and he exploded inside her. She cried out, her body shuddering and rippling with the force of her release, then she fell forward and buried her head in his shoulder. He drew her to him and closed his eyes, relishing the scent of their lovemaking that mingled with the earthy aroma of the forest.

A twig snapped, and he stiffened, his senses alerted to danger.

How could he have been so foolish as to lower his guard!

Three men stood before him, swords drawn.

~

Arlette's husband tensed beneath her, and he shifted his gaze and looked over her shoulder. She turned her head. Ulferth stood behind her, his lips curled into a sneer, flanked either side by Brand and Jarvis, the unmistakable gleam of lust in his eyes. She flushed with shame. Her gown was rumpled, her thighs exposed, and the air reeked of their lovemaking.

"What is the meaning of this, Ulferth?" Orson growled.

"Rumors of treachery have reached my ears," Ulferth said. "I wanted to ensure that you—and your woman—were safe." He gestured toward Brand. "This halfwit, with no thought for your safety, said you weren't to be disturbed."

"Yet you disturb us."

"Out of concern for your welfare," Ulferth replied. "I know better than most that wives fail their husbands and cause more harm than good. Anything could happen if your guard is lowered while you are..." he looked at Arlette with a sneer, "...being fucked on the forest floor."

Arlette's cheeks warmed with shame and anger. She climbed off her husband, and lowered her skirts.

"How dare you!" she cried. "Orson—I demand you punish Ulferth for his insolence."

"Don't tell me how to discipline my men." Orson adjusted his clothes, then stood, and pulled her up alongside him.

"Ulferth acts in my best interests," he said. "His duty is our safety, while you indulge in pleasure."

"Don't be a boor," she said, "You..."

"Enough!" he cried. "Have you forgotten the consequences of defiance in front of my men?"

Ulferth's eyes gleamed with triumph. "I took the liberty of having the area searched," he said, "in case anyone unsavory was attracted by the fire."

"Did you find aught?" Orson asked.

"Fresh footprints—two, maybe three men. I'd counsel you to be vigilant. There's treachery afoot."

"What nonsense!" Arlette cried. "Ulferth seeks to disturb us. I insist you dismiss him, so we may enjoy the rest of our excursion in peace."

"From what I saw, you've achieved what you set out to do," Ulferth said.

"Ulferth, that's enough." Orson said. "Arlette, mount your horse—we return to the castle immediately." He turned to the others. "Brand, Jarvis, clear up here, then patrol the forest. Let me know if you find anything."

Arlette took one look at the resolute expression in his face. There would be no reasoning with him in his present mood. Nodding in acquiescence, she approached her horse.

She passed Ulferth, and he spoke in a low voice.

"You think a pair of eager thighs will entice him into your web of deceit? You're nothing but a filthy whore!"

Before she could respond, he moved toward Orson, then whispered in his ear.

How dare Orson treat her like chattel! She'd planned today so carefully—to show she could be a good wife—to give him news of a child, then appeal to his mercy over Guillaume.

But Ulferth had ruined her pathetic plan.

She couldn't tell her husband about Guillaume, or seek his help. How could she trust a man who dismissed her so readily?

# CHAPTER 30

On their return, Arlette dismounted and parted company with her husband. As she crossed the courtyard, she caught sight of Hilda scurrying toward the kitchen. The maidservant stopped and stared at the riding party. Arlette turned and saw Ulferth looking in Hilda's direction. Then he nodded, and resumed his conversation with Orson.

Let them rot! She'd had enough of male company today.

She made her way to the sewing room to join the ladies. At least *there*, she wouldn't be treated as if she were of no consequence.

Edith smiled as Arlette entered the chamber, but her eyes shone with sorrow, and Arlette noticed an array of bruises adorning her arms.

After dismissing the other ladies, Arlette took Edith's hand.

"Edith, what's wrong?"

"I failed my husband."

"Ulferth?" Arlette scoffed. "How could you possibly fail one so undeserving? He's fortunate to have you for a wife, even if he's too stupid to see it."

"Please!" Edith chided. "Don't speak of my husband so disrespectfully. He has every right to punish me."

"Surely you don't believe that!" Arlette cried. "You're a good and kind woman."

Edith shook her head. "I'm a poor wife."

"How can you say that?"

"Because I've failed to give him a son. I…" Edith's voice caught, and she whispered, "…I lost the babe, three days ago."

Dear Lord!

"Why was I not told?" Arlette asked. "I could have taken care of you."

"My husband said I needed to be punished," Edith said, "and he didn't want the whole household knowing of my failure—it reflects badly on him."

Arlette's heart ripped in two. "Oh, Edith!"

She drew her arms around her companion. "I'll speak to my husband. Ulferth cannot continue to treat you like this."

"It's what I deserve." Edith looked up at Arlette, the hope in her eyes tearing into Arlette's heart.

"I pray that I will get with child again soon. Ulferth has forgiven me, and he visits me nightly, for which I am thankful."

How could Edith be so dismissive of her own worth?

And how long would it be before Arlette herself sat in the sewing room, her body covered in bruises, the desperation to please her husband having eroded her self-worth?

As the afternoon stretched into evening, Arlette returned to the solar.

Before she opened the door, a hand touched her shoulder.

"Hilda!" she cried. "Don't creep up behind me like that."

Hilda's eyes narrowed with dislike, then she smoothed her features into a bland expression.

"I must speak with you urgently," she said.

"For what purpose?"

"Your brother has been found."

Arlette's stomach flipped into a somersault.

*Guillaume…*

"Where is he?"

"I cannot say. He's been injured."

"Sweet Lord!" Arlette cried. "I must go to him."

"Morcar will take you, but he demands payment."

Arlette longed to ram her fist into Hilda's face, which had an expression of avarice and triumph.

"A ransom."

"'Tis a trifle to you, lady," Hilda said. "Your brother required treatment, and Morcar had to bribe several men into silence. He risks much, helping a de Villiers, but I've assured him of your gratitude. I, too, risk much in helping you."

"And you want payment, also."

Hilda smiled. "A small price for saving your brother. As a gesture of faith, Morcar is willing to take you to Guillaume tomorrow night. It's an hour's ride away."

"I cannot take my horse without attracting attention," Arlette said.

"You can. Will has agreed to ready your horse. I've paid for his silence."

"You seem very sure I'll go," Arlette said.

"You love your brother, do you not?"

Aye, she did. And she had to take the chance offered, even if her love for Guillaume might be her undoing.

~

THE FOLLOWING DAY, Arlette almost expelled her breakfast. She went about her duties, trying to dampen the anticipation of the night to come—the thought that she might, at last, see her beloved brother again.

Her husband sensed something was afoot. Several times during the day, he asked her if she was sickening for something, and he demanded Freydis brew her an infusion of ginger root. If only his flashes of consideration occurred often enough for her to trust him!

Perhaps, once she'd seen Guillaume, she could petition Orson when the time was right—ask him to show mercy to her brother, the moment she told him she carried his heir.

After they retired, she lay awake, listening to his breathing deepen as he drifted into sleep. He had wanted to make love to her, but he desisted when she feigned tiredness.

When she was sure he slept, she climbed out of the bed, pulled on a woolen kirtle and overgown, and took the purse of coins she'd concealed under the bed. She fumbled for her knife, but it was missing.

She slipped out, into the passageway and listened for footsteps, but the household was asleep.

Her horse waited in the stables, already saddled and bridled, but there was no sign of Will. She led the animal through the courtyard, the echo of its hooves against the stones carrying through the air. But other than the occasional shriek of a hunting owl, there were no other sounds. The mare snorted in anticipation and she stroked the animal's forehead, whispering words of comfort.

The figure of a man stood outside the bailey wall, and he beckoned to her.

His cloak concealed his features, but his frame was too lean to be the rough, squat man Hilda had taken her to before.

"You're not Morcar." Arlette took a step back, reaching for her knife, then cursed as she recalled having mislaid it.

"I mean you no harm," he said. His voice sounded familiar.

"Who are you?" she asked. "I was expecting another."

He drew back his hood, and Arlette's blood froze as the moonlight illuminated his finely bred features—the defined cheekbones, straight nose, and sensual mouth, which slipped into a smile.

"*Mon Dieu*..." she whispered.

His eyes—the color of ice—leered at her. She had always likened them to those of a predator, sizing up its prey before tearing its throat.

It was Fulbert.

"It's good to see you again, little cousin," he said. "As delectable as ever, despite having whored yourself with that Saxon bastard."

He curled his fingers around her wrist. "I'm come to take you home."

"Where's Guillaume?"

He let out a cold laugh. "You always were a fool for your brother. But he served his purpose, in bringing you to me. What's of greater concern is your treachery."

"My treachery?"

"Aye," he said. "You betrayed our family when you fucked the beast who murdered them. But I shall forgive you, once you've been purged of his filth."

"Orson…"

He tightened his grip on her wrist, and her stomach heaved as she felt the bones scrape together.

"Do not speak his vile name!" he spat. "To think…a de Villiers—slut to a Saxon bastard. The only good Saxon is a dead Saxon."

"My father didn't think so," Arlette said. "Neither did yours. Uncle Alexandre said…"

"They were fools!" he snarled. "*I'm* head of the family now—their wishes don't matter."

He spat on the ground. "The fewer Saxons in the world the better. England is ours—and you are mine."

She had always loathed Fulbert, thinking him a strutting peacock who placed too much value on finery. But, as she looked into his eyes, she shivered at what she saw.

Pure evil.

"Let me go!" she cried, struggling to break free.

He lifted his arm, and her face exploded with agony as he back-handed her. Then his fingers curled around her throat.

"You'll soon learn the error of your ways, my dear," he said, "and I'll take immense pleasure breaking you in."

"No!" she choked. "I'd rather die."

"I'm disappointed you value your life so little," he said. "Perhaps you place greater value on the lives of those you love?"

Fear rippled through her. "What do you mean?"

He turned her to face the castle. A light flickered in one of the windows on the top floor, the passageway outside the solar—where Orson slept.

"My man awaits my signal," Fulbert said. "If I don't signal soon, he has orders to slit the Saxon's throat."

"No..."

"He'll then deal with that spawn of his you seem so fond of." His lips curled into a smile. "The brat who calls you 'Mama Arlette'—imagine how her life's blood will look as it stains that yellow silk gown you spent so many hours making."

Cold fingers clutched at her heart. How did he know so much?

"You cannot harm them—please!" she cried.

"Will you come with me?"

She had no choice. Fulbert might kill them anyway—but she couldn't risk it if there was a chance he'd let them live.

There must be a traitor at Greywell Castle—not only Hilda, but another.

It could only be Ulferth.

"Permit me to bind your hands," Fulbert said.

She shook her head, and his smile disappeared. "You wouldn't want to anger me. Think of the brat. My men are virile—imagine what they could do to that sweet, untouched flesh?"

Tears spilled onto her cheeks, and she offered her hands.

"That's better," he said. "Your obedience gives me much pleasure." He tied a rope around her wrists, and secured it with a knot.

Then he let out a low whistle, and a man emerged from the trees, carrying a lit torch, which he waved from side to side four times. The light in the castle window flickered in response.

"Come my dear," Fulbert said, as casually as a man might speak to his wife on an excursion, "we've a long ride ahead."

"You cannot expect me to ride with my hands bound."

"Of course."

His teeth glittered in the moonlight as he smiled. Footsteps approached from behind, but before she could turn, pain exploded in the back of her head and she pitched forward into oblivion.

ORSON WOKE to the sound of hammering on the door. He reached for his wife, but her side of the bed was empty—no trace of her warmth, though it was the middle of the night.

The banging continued.

"Stop!" he roared. "Come in."

The door opened and Hilda entered, her body shaking.

"Oh my lord!" she cried. "The mistress…" She broke off, weeping.

Arlette! God's bones—if anything had happened to her…

At that moment, his heart revealed what he'd fought to deny for so long.

Arlette—his Arlette.

He loved her. Sweet Lord, he loved her!

"Where's your mistress?"

Hilda shook her head, and he grasped her shoulders and gave her a shake.

"Tell me!"

Hilda's voice rose with hysteria. "I—I heard a noise, so I went to see what it was, then I saw her. She's taken her horse and left."

"Where?"

"I don't know, my lord. I tried to follow, but…" She let out a wail. "The stables!"

"What do you mean—the stables?"

"One of the grooms…" She broke off, crying.

"What's happened? Tell me, woman!"

"K-killed…" she rasped.

His blood ran cold. Pushing her aside, he sprinted out of the solar, not stopping until he reached the stables.

"Arlette!"

"Here, my lord!" Ulferth's voice responded, and he appeared at the entrance to the stables. "I'm sorry, my lord—there was nothing I could do."

Orson's gut twisted with fear. He pushed past Ulferth and entered the stable building, blinking as his eyes adjusted to the dark.

A body lay on the floor.

"Arlette…"

But the body wasn't Arlette.

Lying on the floor, in a pool of blood, was the groom. Multiple stab wounds peppered his chest, and a long, thick gash bisected his neck.

His throat had been cut.

Orson clenched his fists as a tide of rage swelled within him.

"Who did this?" he said, through gritted teeth.

Ulferth shook his head. "Poor Will. He must have tried to stop her."

"I don't understand."

"It's better if you see, my lord."

Ulferth led Orson toward the stall where his destrier was stabled. Orson looked down and froze. The body of his horse lay before him, covered in slashes, as if someone had undertaken a frenzied attack. The assailant had finished the job by plunging a knife into the animal's chest and cutting out its heart.

Orson kneeled beside his horse, his eyes stinging. The faithful animal had borne him through battles and tournaments, and they'd ridden together as one. Now, the beautiful beast lay before him, destroyed at a traitor's hands, denied both the dignified death in battle and the comfortable old age.

Rage tore through him—an echo of the fury that had consumed him the day he'd discovered Verona's body.

"Whoever did this shall suffer," he said. "I shall torture them until they scream for mercy before I kill them with my bare hands. There shall be no mercy."

"Aye milord. And I'll help you," Ulferth said.

Orson gritted his teeth. "Who did this?"

Ulferth raised the lamp, until the light fell upon the knife that had delivered the final blow. The hilt was fashioned to fit a small hand, and encrusted with emeralds and rubies that glinted in the light.

*Dear God!*

Hadn't Pearce told him, once, that Arlette had threatened to cut out his horse's heart?

"No mercy," he repeated.

The knife was Arlette's. Orson's wife had betrayed him.

# CHAPTER 31

*B*arton Keep, England, 1086*

"I TRUST YOU SLEPT WELL, COUSIN."

The voice cut through Arlette's dreams and she opened her eyes. Fulbert stood by the door of her chamber, a tray in his hands.

Her head ached, one eye still swollen where he'd struck her.

Swallowing her revulsion, she sat up, and forced a smile as he approached the bed. As soon as he was within reach, she flew at him with her fists.

Dropping the tray, he grasped her wrists.

"Grubby little hellcat!"

"Where's my husband?" she cried. "If you've harmed him, or the child, I'll..."

"You'll what?" he sneered. "You're in no position to do anything, Arlette, except what I wish. But if you learn to behave, you'll find me a generous lover."

"Never!"

He tightened his grip. "I'm not a patient man—take care I don't tire of you too quickly. My men would not be as considerate as I."

"Those barbaric hired hands I've seen parading about?" she scoffed. "They're better men than you, Fulbert. They make no attempt to conceal their baseness. You hide yours behind finery and our family name."

He snarled, his handsome features morphing into an ugly mask. Then he nodded toward the tray on the floor.

"Methinks you need a lesson in courtesy, if you wish to eat."

"I'd rather starve."

His face turned a shade of puce, then he made an explosive noise of rage. He threw her toward the bed, then exited the chamber, slamming the door, the metallic scrape of the bolt sliding into place.

Though she feared him, she took pleasure out of making him lose control. A man with no command over his temper rarely emerged victorious.

A goblet lay on its side by the upended tray, a puddle of wine seeping into the stone floor, next to an unappetizing-looking gray mess, and a hunk of bread. Arlette picked up the bread and nibbled at it. Though unwilling to take anything her vile cousin offered, she needed to maintain her strength.

Fulbert had brought her to Barton Keep, his late wife's ancestral home, almost a fortnight ago. Her chamber had a single window overlooking battlements—too high for her to climb out safely. She had no means of lowering herself out—the bed had a straw mattress and a single blanket, but no sheets to fashion a rope from.

When they'd arrived, Fulbert had tried to force himself on her, hardening while she struggled in his arms. He relented when she rammed her knee into his groin, which earned her a beating. But he hadn't tried to violate her since. Like all bullies, Fulbert was a coward. He feared her—she saw it in his eyes. He believed Orson to be the savage, but Arlette's husband, beneath the barbaric exterior, had a tender heart, though he concealed it well.

Why hadn't he come? He'd roused an army to avenge his sister. Arlette closed her eyes an uttered a silent prayer.

*Please—let him not be dead.*

And what of her child? She needed to escape before her belly began to swell. Her child was half Saxon—Fulbert would never let it live.

She did not have the strength to fight her way out, so she needed to use her wits—play on Fulbert's vanity and convince him of her affection. The notion made her feel sick, but a woman had to choose her weapons well in order to defeat a man.

She would begin tomorrow.

THE FOLLOWING MORNING, Arlette fought the impulse to attack her captor, and sat quietly when he visited her. Patience was the key to victory. That evening, he rewarded her with a bowl of stew. The following day, she ventured to thank him, and his veneer of charm returned.

Pathetic little man! His greatest weakness, other than his lust for wealth, was his immeasurable vanity—the conviction that all women were blinded by his looks.

Almost a month after her arrival, he entered her chamber, accompanied by two men carrying a trunk, which they placed on the floor. After dismissing them, Fulbert sat beside her, and she suppressed a shudder of revulsion as he lifted a hand to her cheek and caressed her skin, where the bruises were fading.

"It pained me to mar your beauty Arlette."

He leaned forward to kiss her. She turned her head to one side, and his lips brushed her cheek.

He chuckled, quietly. "You'll warm to me in time, my love. I can see you softening already. You're clever enough to realize that a little amiability on your part will be rewarded, aye?"

"Aye."

"Good," he coaxed, as if placating a spoiled child. He gestured to the trunk, "If we are to be together you must dress like a lady. We'll be the most admired couple in England—wealthy beyond compare."

"What do you mean?"

"I intend to acquire all the properties belonging to the Saxon bastard—as a blood price for his sins against our family. My plans are coming to fruition."

"What plans?"

"You mustn't concern yourself with such things," he said. "Come and see what I've brought you."

He lifted the lid of the trunk to reveal its contents—an array of gowns and undergarments.

Arlette smiled to herself. They would fulfil a very particular purpose—though not what Fulbert had intended.

"Ah! The lady likes what she sees."

"That I do." She took his hand, and lowered her head to kiss it.

"Oh, little cousin!" he laughed, a note of contempt in his voice. "How easily a woman's heart is turned by a few pretty gowns. I trust you'll wear them for me—perhaps tonight, if I'm permitted to dine with you in your chamber?"

"Of course."

"Then, I'll see you tonight," he said. "But before I leave, would you be so generous as to grant me a kiss?"

Sweet Lord!

He thrust his face close, and she fought back the wave of nausea. Most women would find him handsome, and relish the prospect of his attentions, but evil glittered in his eyes—a lust for power that would never be quenched.

He brushed his lips against hers and she submitted, shifting her mind sideways to focus on anything but the man she loathed.

"There!" he said, pride in his voice. "It pleases me to see that you'd rather be the wife of a nobleman than a Saxon's whore."

He took his leave, and the bolt slid into place in the door behind him.

He didn't completely trust her—yet.

All she needed was time. But was it enough? His manner elicited a sense of dread. If he plotted to acquire Orson's properties, then her husband was in danger.

There was no time to lose. She pulled out the contents of the trunk, setting aside the chemises and undergarments. Though they were fashioned from a fine, thin material, when plaited, they'd make a rope strong enough to hold her weight. She tore a strip off the chemise with her teeth, and set to work.

~

FROM THEN ON, Fulbert visited her more often, his vain little eyes glittering with delight as she wore a different gown for him each day. He began to take her outside, "to show my servants their future mistress."

Each servant they passed adopted the stooping reverence of the terrified. Arlette hid her compassion behind the cold veneer of a noblewoman, but she resolved that once free of him, she'd do everything in her power to liberate the poor souls who toiled under Fulbert's mastery.

Each night, after Fulbert took his leave of her, she set to work, plaiting the strips of the torn garments and knotting them together. Then, as dawn began to break, she concealed her handiwork at the bottom of the trunk, before resuming her efforts the following evening.

After eight days the makeshift rope was long enough to reach the battlements below her window.

Her chance had come. All she need do was wait until the keep was quiet, after supper.

That evening, she ate her meal with relish, and Fulbert didn't fail to notice.

"You seem somewhat animated tonight, cousin."

"No more than usual," she said, stabbing a piece of meat with a knife. "This stew is delicious."

"I shall serve it at our wedding feast."

"Our wedding?"

"Aye," he said. "Once I've secured the Saxon's properties, I shall rid you of him."

Her gut twisted in fear, though she maintained her smile.

"Will my fair cousin mourn the loss of the man she spread her legs for?"

She shook her head, unable to reply, lest she betray her fear.

"If only I could be sure of your loyalty," he said. "Perhaps a kiss would suffice."

She tilted her face, and closed her eyes. His lips moved over hers, and her flesh crawled as he slipped his tongue inside. She dug her fingernails into her palms to resist the urge to bite down. At length, he withdrew, triumph in his expression, then he bowed and exited the chamber.

As soon as he'd gone, Arlette picked up the flagon of wine, rinsed her mouth, then spat on the floor.

*One day, cousin, I'll put my sword in your gut.*

She changed into a plain kirtle, and waited for the household to fall quiet. Then she pulled the makeshift rope from the trunk, secured one end to the window frame, and climbed onto the ledge. She tested the rope, praying it would hold, then, gripping it in both hands, she let herself down, her feet finding a purchase in the indents of the outer wall.

She froze as a roar of laughter echoed through the night. But it came from inside, and she continued lowering herself.

Then she heard the sound of material tearing. The rope ripped apart, and she tumbled through the air, landing heavily on the floor of the walkway.

She lay still, catching her breath, but the distant laughter continued. The torn end of the makeshift rope swung above her head. With luck nobody would see it until dawn.

The walkway led to a door. She opened it to reveal a spiral staircase that descended into a passageway. Keeping to the shadows, she crept forward, then froze as she heard voices from a room at the far end. Her heart almost leaped out of her chest at the mention of her name.

"I'd have the Lady Arlette moaning my name in a heartbeat."

"She's not to be touched. De Villiers wants her for himself."

"Aye, he'll have your cock if you so much as looked at her,

Alphonse. Once he's disposed of the Saxon he's to wed her. But I daresay he'd let you fuck his other woman."

"But *she's* with the Saxon."

"You'll have to wait, like the rest of us, until Michaelmas. For now I'd suggest you take a whore. There's plenty to be had in the village."

Arlette pressed her ear against the door, but the conversation turned to whores and the different methods of taking pleasure from them.

What was happening at Michaelmas—barely a fortnight away? Who was the woman they referred to? It must be Hilda.

Arlette tiptoed past the door, and slipped outside, staying in the shadows of the keep until she reached the stableyard. Her heart leaped with hope as she spotted her mare in the stable building, but there was no saddle or bridle to be found. Shushing the other animals that snorted in restlessness as she passed them, Arlette led her mare out of the stables. Then she hitched up her skirts, gasped the animal's mane, and leaped onto its back. Childhood memories of riding bareback flooded her mind, including Esme's horrified expression on seeing her astride her mount.

She squeezed her thighs, and steered the mare out of the yard, keeping to a steady walk until they were clear of the main gate. Once satisfied she was out of earshot, she applied more pressure, urging her mount into a canter.

Free, at last! How relieved Orson would be to see her return—how worried he must have been!

The night sky was clear, the moonlight illuminating the road. But though a frost lingered in the air, the exercise kept the cold from penetrating her bones. When the road plunged into a forest, her heart leaped with hope, as she recognized the same forest where Orson had killed the boar, and saved her life. She was almost home.

*I'm coming, my love.*

Then, her heart sank. Heavy powerful hoofbeats pounded the earth behind her. She was being pursued—and he was gaining on her. She steered her mount toward the trees, but her mount stumbled on the edge of the road, and slipped. Arlette lost her seat and fell into the undergrowth.

The ground trembled to the rhythm of hoofbeats—the other horse must be enormous. She was in danger of being trampled underfoot, but if she moved, she'd be discovered. She closed her eyes and waited for the inevitable.

But the hoofbeats thundered past, then receded. She lifted her head to see the rider disappearing into the night, kicking clods of earth behind him.

She was alive—but what of the child she carried? The wife of one of Papa's grooms had suffered pains after a fall, and lost her unborn child. Arlette remained still, cradling her stomach, but no pains came. With luck the babe was unharmed.

She struggled to her feet, then cried out in anguish.

The mare was gone.

By the time Arlette saw the battlements of Greywell Castle, dawn had long since broken—thin, watery rays of light stretching across the landscape. Her feet were sore from walking, but she'd soon be home, and in her husband's arms.

As the building came into full view, she broke into a run. A sentry stood by the main gate. He made no attempt to greet her, but merely watched her approach, his expression grim.

"Take me to Lord Wulfson," she said.

"That I will." He took her arm and she winced at his iron grip.

"Is my husband well?" she asked.

"Aye, he's well, considering your treachery."

"M-my what?"

"Speak no more," he said. "You shall answer to the master."

"And so shall you for handling me thus!" she cried. "How dare you!"

He tightened his grip, and led her to the main hall, where Orson stood in the center, speaking to Pearce, his back to her.

Relief flooded through her—he was safe!

"Orson—my love!"

He turned to face her.

Icy fingers clawed at her heart. His expression was dark with hatred—eyes as hard as steel, mouth set in a grim line.

"So," he said. "The traitor returns."

"I'm no traitor…"

"Silence!" he roared, his anger reverberating through her bones. "You think to whore your way back into my bed after what you've done?"

"I've done nothing!" she cried. "I was taken against my will."

"Then how is it that you're here now?"

"I escaped."

He let out a snort. "You expect me to believe that?"

"Do you think a woman incapable of escaping her captor?"

"You once told me that a woman used her cunning, to deceive…" he curled his hands into fists, "…to betray."

"I've betrayed nobody," she said. "Orson, you must listen. You're in danger—we're all in danger…"

"Silence!" He raised his fist, as if to strike her. "The only danger comes from having a murderous wench such as you poisoning my mind with your lies."

"I've murdered no one!"

"Liar!" he snarled, "I saw your handiwork in the stables the night you left. I had no idea you were capable of such evil—but you're a de Villiers, are you not—spawn of the devil!"

She shook her head. "Orson, I swear, on my life, I…"

"Enough!" he cried. "Will's family are calling for your blood, and I've a mind to give it to them."

"*Will?*" Sweet heaven, what had happened?

"You don't deserve a swift death for what you did to Will," he said, "or to my horse."

"Your horse?"

"Don't take me for a fool!" he cried. "Didn't you once say that if you wanted to injure me, you'd cut out my horse's heart?" He glanced behind him. "Is that not true, Pearce?"

Pearce nodded, disgust distorting his usually amiable expression. "Aye," he said. "And you weren't taken by force, madam. I saw you, with my own eyes, leaving of your own accord."

"I was tricked," she said. "Hilda told me…"

"Were it not for Hilda alerting me, I'd never have seen you," Pearce interrupted.

She shook her head. "This is madness!"

Orson spoke through gritted teeth. "The only madness is the fact I ever trusted you—daughter of the man who slaughtered my sister. But 'tis a madness of which I will be purged."

He motioned to his friend. "Get her from my sight, Pearce, before I kill her with my bare hands."

"Aye, my lord."

"The dungeon should suffice. If she resists, give her to my men."

Pearce gripped Arlette by the arms.

"Orson!" she screamed. "Please—I came to warn you!"

But her husband had turned his back, as if she no longer existed. She struggled against Pearce's hold but, weakened by her journey, she was no match for the powerful knight.

"Pearce, you must make him listen."

Before he could answer, a familiar soft voice echoed across the hall.

"Thank the Lord—you're safe!"

A woman with shiny ebony hair, dressed in a blue silk gown, ran toward Orson, and threw herself at him.

"Oh, my love! When I heard that Norman bitch had returned, I feared the worst."

She clung to him, her bosom heaving against his chest.

Kendra had returned.

"Orson!" Arlette cried. But he remained motionless, his back to her, as Pearce dragged her out of the hall.

## CHAPTER 32

*Greywell Castle, England, 1086*

KENDRA SLIPPED her hand into Orson's breeches, and offered her lips for a kiss.

"Leave me," he growled.

"But my love, is it not time I warmed your bed again?"

He pushed her away.

"Go, I tell you!"

She frowned for a moment, and her eyes glittered with spite, then her seductive smile returned, and she strutted across the floor, swaying her hips provocatively from side to side.

All women were whores—playing a part for their own ends. But at least Kendra made no effort to disguise her nature.

Unlike *her*.

What had possessed Arlette to commit such evil acts? Did she hate him that much?

Or had she planned this from the beginning—as vengeance for what he'd done to her family? Why then, hadn't she killed him? Or had she understood that the death of innocents pained him more—his beloved sister, his horse, and young Will. And why had she returned? Surely she didn't think him enough of a fool to trust her again.

The day after her betrayal, he'd expunged her from his home and his heart—destroying the solar they'd shared, and obliterating her memory, drinking himself into a stupor. He'd woken that night to see a pair of lust-fueled eyes staring back, but they were a cold sapphire, rather than the fiery green his weak soul still yearned for.

For what purpose Kendra had returned, the very night after Arlette's betrayal, he knew not. But, faithless his wife may have been, he couldn't bring himself to take what Kendra so freely offered, and he'd pushed her away, oblivion claiming him while she tried to coax his body into submission. She remained at the castle in the weeks that followed, but he cared not. He was done with women. They were all faithless whores, and he took satisfaction from Kendra's repeated attempts to seduce him, because they served to remind him of the folly of trusting women.

The urge to be free—the need for solitude—overcame him. He left the hall, and made his way to the stables.

The groom—barely older than a boy—startled as Orson approached. And well he might. The stones on the stable floor were covered in a dark stain—a memorial to the murders that had taken place. But if the boy were to become a man, he needed to grow a pair of bollocks, and—most of all—learn never to trust a woman.

"Ready my horse, would you?"

"Aye, my lord."

The boy—Lord knew what his name was—scuttled inside the stable building. Then, he returned, leading a young stallion, which bore a striking resemblance to Orson's beloved warhorse. The animal could never replace its sire, but it was training well. A good, hard ride would continue to strengthen the bond between man and horse—and would serve to clear Orson's head, which suffered from his continued attempts to assuage his anger toward Arlette with ale.

She must suffer for her crimes! He wanted to ask her why, but he wouldn't be able to refrain from strangling her with his bare hands.

Gritting his teeth, he steered his mount out of the stableyard, then urged the animal into a gallop.

In time, he would devise a fitting punishment for his faithless wife.

~

ARLETTE STRUGGLED against Pearce's hold.

"Pearce—you must listen to me!"

"Why should I, after what you did?" he said. "You should never have returned."

"You cannot believe me capable of murder!"

"You threatened to slit Lord Wulfson's throat," he said. "I saw your dagger by the bodies."

"I was taken against my will!"

"To where?"

"Barton Keep. Fulbert has kept me there this past month until I escaped."

His expression darkened. "You lie. I sent out a search party—they looked everywhere, including Barton Keep, which they found abandoned, save for a servant who said that a red-haired lady with green eyes arrived with her lover, and left shortly afterward."

"That's not true!" she cried. "I've been there all this time. Did they search the building?"

"From top to bottom."

"They can't have—who dares speak such wicked lies?"

"Seaton."

"*Seaton?*" She gasped. "No…"

"Aye," he said. "We both know that Seaton's incapable of lying—and, of all the men, he's the one most likely to speak in your favor. You cannot imagine how deeply your betrayal has wounded him."

They reached the staircase leading to the dungeons, the entrance a black gaping mouth waiting to swallow her. Arlette's gut twisted in terror. If she descended those stairs, she might never see daylight again.

"Pearce …"

"Be quiet!" he snapped. "You've poisoned our minds for long enough."

A squat man with a pockmarked face waited at the bottom of the stairs, a set of keys hanging from his belt. His eyes widened as he saw Arlette, and Pearce pushed her toward him.

"Put her in the cell at the end."

"Aye, sir." The jailer took Arlette's arm and propelled her toward the cell. He pushed her through the doorway, and she tripped, stumbling onto the stone floor. The door shut with a clang, the keys jangling in the lock, and his footsteps receded.

Arlette struggled to her feet, and checked the door, but it was thick and strong. The only source of light was the window—a thin slit at the top of the cell wall opposite the door, level with the ground outside. She glanced up, her stomach heaving. Mud and waste matter seeped through the window and trickled down the wall to form a glistening trail of slime. It was too slippery for her to gain a purchase and climb to the window—even if she were able to without gagging at the stench.

With no hope of escape, she sank to the floor, succumbing to exhaustion and despair.

~

SHE WOKE, in total darkness, to the sound of footsteps. A faint light picked out the bars in the door as they drew nearer. Then they stopped outside the door, and a face appeared, illuminated by a torch.

Her heart leaped with hope, but the slim fingers that curled around the bars in the door were not Orson's—neither were the cold blue eyes that glittered with triumph.

"I always thought you a traitor," Kendra said. "You're a fool to think he wanted you back."

"He's the bigger fool to sully himself with your company," Arlette replied. "I'm his wife, and I'll always be faithful to him—you're naught but a whore, and a poor one at that. He sent you away once before, and he'll do so again."

Kendra's lip curled into a smile. "You underestimate me at your peril. Wives are easily replaced. I comforted the betrayed husband—I can console the grieving widower."

Arlette's stomach twisted with fear. Kendra's knuckles whitened as she tightened her grip on the bars. One of her rings glinted in the light. It bore the mark of a lion and an oak tree—the de Villiers family crest—surrounded by tiny rubies. Duke William had presented Papa and Uncle Alexandre with identical rings in recognition of their service during the conquest of England.

Sweet heaven! Orson must have taken Papa's ring and given it to his harlot.

How could he have done such a wicked thing!

Kendra stepped back and smiled again, her teeth gleaming.

"I shall leave you to your fate."

The key rattled in the lock, and Kendra retreated, her footsteps receding.

What was she about? Was the woman foolish enough to let Arlette go? Or perhaps she believed Arlette would leave and never return? Nay—Arlette would warn Orson and open his eyes to his folly, if it took her last breath.

She approached the door and tugged at the handle. It swung inward with no resistance, and she peered out into the passageway.

There was no sign of the jailer. The passage was empty, save the torches that illuminated the way out—to freedom.

No matter what Kendra's motives were, or whether she'd set a trap, the urge to flee was too strong to resist. Arlette pushed the door fully open, wincing at the creak of the hinges, and tiptoed out.

Ahead, near the end, one of the torches had extinguished, leaving an area of deep shadow. As she approached it, a shape emerged from the darkness—a huge male shape, with lust-fueled eyes, and a feral smile.

"I'd be forgiven for doing whatever I liked to you, if I found you attempting to escape."

It was Ulferth.

He grasped the back of her head, his thick, fleshy fingers curling around her neck, then he brought his mouth down on hers. She scratched his face, and he withdrew.

"Bitch! You'll pay for that." He lifted his hand to strike her.

"You coward!" she cried. "Would you murder a defenseless woman?"

She raised her arms to defend herself, and he froze, his eyes widening. The bloodlust in his expression turned to horror, and he crossed himself.

"Mother of God!" he cried, his voice tight with terror. "Lady Emmelina..." He blanched, and lowered his arm. "But, y-you're dead!"

Did he think she was her mother's ghost? It mattered not—seizing her opportunity, she grasped his wrists, then rammed her knee into his groin. He let out an airless cry and doubled up. Pushing him aside, she sprinted up the staircase, driven by the need to find Orson. Praying her intuition served her well, she made her way to his study, and almost wept with relief when she recognized his voice. She pushed open the door.

Orson sat at his desk with William and Seaton. The steward remained still, eyes widening, and Seaton frowned. Orson leaped to his feet, thunder in his eyes.

Arlette held her hands out to fend him off. "Please, Orson—you must hear what I have to say. We're in danger. My cousin is planning..."

"Seaton, remove her from my presence," Orson interrupted.

"My lord," the steward said, "perhaps we should..."

"*Now!*"

Arlette reached out to him. "Husband..."

"Seaton, get that treacherous creature out of here before I slit her throat and have you lashed for disobedience."

Seaton moved toward her. "Come with me, lady."

"Orson, please," Arlette cried, "for sake of the love I bear you..."

Her husband's reaction caught her unawares, as he leaped forward and put his hands around her throat.

"Do *not* speak to me of love! You betrayed me!"

"What about *your* betrayal?" she cried.

"I never betrayed you."

"You murdered my family!" she cried. "But, despite all that, I was a good wife, and grew to love you. And now, you've taken that whore back into your bed with no thought for me. She parades about the place, flaunting Papa's ring. Did you give it to her—after you robbed his corpse?"

"I know not what you say."

"Don't lie!" she cried. "She flaunts my family crest at me—I'd recognize that ring anywhere. Papa would never have removed it from his hand."

For a moment, he hesitated, uncertainty in his expression. Then he shook his head.

"Seaton, take her away," he said. "I know not what witchcraft she employed to escape her cell, but have her chained to the wall this time."

"Aye, my lord." Seaton took her arm and pulled her out of the study.

"Come with me, madam."

"Seaton," she pleaded, "you, of all men, should hear what I have to say."

He gripped her arm with unfamiliar strength, his fingers digging into her flesh.

"I am no longer fooled by you," he said. "I searched for you, Arlette. I went to Barton Keep—where you claim to have been incarcerated."

"I *was* there!"

He shook his head. "We searched the building."

"We?"

"Ulferth and I."

"Ulferth? You cannot trust him!"

"I trusted *you* once," he said, "yet you murdered that poor young man."

"I know not what happened to Will," she said. "You cannot think me capable of murder? I'd sooner believe it was Ulferth."

"Oh, how you weave your web!" he cried. "Even now, you seek to deceive me. 'Twas Ulferth who tried to save Will's life."

"He can't have."

"I did," a voice growled.

Arlette's blood ran cold as Ulferth appeared at the entrance to the dungeon.

"You lie," she said. "I'll wager you killed him—as you tried to kill me today. Are you in league with Kendra?"

Ulferth let out a laugh. "See how she tries to burrow her way into our trust?"

"Aye," Seaton said. "But no more. The lady is to be chained in her cell. Help me, would you?"

Ulferth's eyes gleamed with relish, all trace of his earlier terror gone. "With pleasure."

The two men dragged Arlette back to her cell, impervious to her struggles, and locked a manacle around her wrist that was chained to the wall. Before they shut the door of her cell, Ulferth hesitated. Would he try to kill her again?

No—he merely shook his head, a flicker of fear in his eyes, as if he'd seen a ghost, then he followed Seaton out, and locked the door.

All hope for escape was gone. The chain prevented it, as did the fact that she had no allies. If Seaton, of all people, believed her a traitor, then she was doomed.

# CHAPTER 33

The days wore on, and a chill penetrated the air. Arlette woke one morning to find the outer wall of her cell coated with ice, and the cold from the manacle seeping into the bones of her wrist.

She shifted position, drawing the thin, moldy blanket around her shoulders—her senses immune to the odor. Doubtless it was riddled with lice, but her need for warmth had long since surpassed any delicacy.

Her stomach growled and she reached for the bowl of potage the jailer had brought last night. Though it was empty, she ran her finger along the bottom, picking up the congealed remnants.

How long would she be kept captive? Had she escaped her vile cousin merely to swap one prison for another? Fulbert was driven by greed, Orson by vengeance. But it made no difference to the outcome—they each sought to use her for their own ends. But Fulbert, she loathed, whereas Orson...

Orson, she'd loved. Perhaps she still loved him.

But she would never forgive him.

Footsteps crunched outside, and she looked up to see a shadow moving by the window—a pair of feet. Then a voice spoke—a voice she knew and loved.

"Mama? Are you there?"

"Lillian!" Arlette leaped to her feet.

"Hush!" the child cried. "Papa would beat me if he knew I was here. He's saying such terrible things. He told me you killed a man!"

"Do you believe him?"

"No!"

Dearest child!

Arlette moved toward the window, until she reached the extent of the chain, which jerked against the manacle on her wrist.

"Mama?"

"I can't move any closer, Lillian."

A small hand appeared, holding a package, wrapped in linen.

"I have something for you."

Lillian released the package and it fell to the floor. Arlette crouched and stretched as far as the chain would permit, her fingertips reaching the package.

"It's not much," Lillian said.

Arlette opened the package, to reveal the knife she'd lost, and a fruit tart, broken by the fall.

"Did someone ask you to bring this, Lillian?"

"No," came the reply. "Papa would beat me if he knew, and the servants have been ordered not to see you, on pain of death. Elvia tried to visit you, and the Lady Kendra had her whipped. Papa said the next person to defy him would pay with their head, and hung on the bailey wall as a warning to others."

*Sweet heaven!* Had he said such a thing in front of his own child? Was this what he'd become?

"You must go before you're seen," Arlette said. "You've risked much by helping me, and I love you for it."

"I hate Papa for what he did," Lillian said. "I want to help you escape—that's why I stole your knife. Then you can take me away with you. We can go to France, where you once told me you had a castle. We can live there."

Poor child! Arlette hadn't the heart to tell her there was no means of escape.

Or was there?

She held up the knife. If the tip of the blade was small enough, she might be able to prize open the lock of the manacle. She couldn't breach the cell door, but with her hands free, she could take the jailer by surprise next time he brought food.

But, alas, the blade was too wide to penetrate the lock mechanism. She needed something thinner—but she couldn't let Lillian risk her life.

Yet, what greater risk might the child face, if Fulbert were planning to raid the castle? He'd threatened Lillian's life before.

"Lillian, I need you to be very brave for me," she said. "Can you do that?"

"What must I do?"

Arlette's heart soared with pride at the resolve in the child's voice. She had the courage of ten men.

"I need something with a blade that's smaller than my knife," she said. "A dagger—or a thin metal spike."

"I'll see what I can find."

"You must take care not to be seen."

"I will," Lillian replied. "Everyone's too occupied with the Michaelmas feast to notice me."

"When is it?"

"Tomorrow night."

Tomorrow…so little time!

A deep voice called out in the distance. "Daughter! Where are you?"

Lillian let out a cry. "I must go before Papa comes—but I'll return."

"Listen, child," Arlette said. "You must hear what I have to say. Men are coming, tomorrow night, to attack us."

"What men?"

"It matters not who they are. They'll kill you, do you understand? You must hide where nobody will find you."

"Where?"

"In the grain store by the kitchens," Arlette said. "Tell no one. You can't trust anyone, Lillian. Do you understand?"

"Aye," the child whispered. "I trust you, Mama—I'll find you a dagger, then I'll hide until you come."

"Lillian!" the voice grew closer, and Lillian's shadow disappeared.

Arlette sat back, trembling with anticipation.

Perhaps she should have told Lillian to warn others. But, the more people knew, the greater the chance that Orson would discover what Lillian had done. The child's safety had to come first. As for Esme and the servants—Arlette's heart clenched with fear for them—with luck, Fulbert would leave them be.

Orson would have to shift for himself. He had a chance against Fulbert, but Lillian had none.

What would happen tomorrow night? Would Lillian survive—would any of them survive?

Or would tomorrow night bring about a massacre greater than that she'd witnessed at Leaside—and mark the death of everyone left in the world who she loved?

# CHAPTER 34

Orson looked about the hall, his head aching as the excited chatter of the diners assaulted his ears.

"Where's the child, damn her?"

"Don't fret about her, my love," a seductive voice purred. "Have more wine."

The woman next to him thrust a goblet into his hand.

Kendra assumed too much, taking his wife's place at the feast—while Arlette languished in the dungeons below. But Kendra has shown a less cruel streak to her nature of late. She'd even asked that the sentries and servants be permitted to join in the Michaelmas festivities, insisting that several vats of wine be provided for them to enjoy while they worked. She had seemed particularly animated—her eyes bright with excitement.

But Lillian…

The child's behavior had worsened since Arlette had abandoned them. And, today, she'd been stealing fruit tarts from the kitchen, and jumped like a startled filly when he caught her.

And now she'd disappeared.

Perhaps she avoided Kendra. His daughter loathed her—and he

had to admit he found Kendra's company as distasteful as it had always been. No woman would replace his Arlette…

From where had *that* notion come? He was well rid of that treacherous mare. Only when his defenses were weakened, through fatigue, or too much wine, did his foolish heart whisper that she was the only woman to match him.

Curse her!

He stood to address the company. Many of the diners were slumped over the tables. His vision blurred and he drained his goblet, holding it out for a servant to refill. But there were no servants—apart from his wife's old nursemaid, who lay in a drunken heap in the doorway.

His eyelids felt heavy, and his head ached. He closed his eyes and fell forward.

"Is all well, my love?"

A soft voice spoke in his ear, and a hand touched his cheek. He opened his eyes, ignoring the shock of disappointment that the eyes looking back were blue not green.

Saliva flooded his mouth, and the table began to rock to and fro. The undulations increased, and the floor beneath him swirled in a mass of black and gray. He focused on the sharp edge of a flagstone, which rushed toward him—then an explosion cracked his skull and blackness enveloped him.

~

When Orson opened his eyes, a shaft of light assaulted his senses. His tongue, thick and heavy, stuck to his throat, and his head throbbed.

"He stirs, monseigneur."

He turned to focus on the voice, but pain stabbed behind his eyes and he groaned.

"Shut him up, Alphonse," a second voice said. "We're still too close to Greywell."

A dark shape bent over him, and a savage blow returned him to oblivion.

When he regained consciousness his arms burned with pain, and cold seeped into his wrists, penetrating through to the bone. He opened his eyes.

He was surrounded by stone walls, in a chamber that couldn't measure more than five or six feet across. The door in the opposite wall had a small barred window through which a faint yellow light flickered.

He tried to move, but pain shot through his arms.

He was chained to the wall, suspended by manacles. He straightened his legs to take the weight off his arms, and cried out in pain as the sensation returned to his wrists. His fingers prickled, verging between agony and numbness, and he fisted his hands, curling and uncurling his fingers.

Dear Lord—it hurt! What manner of creature would subject another to this?

*You would. You did it to her.*

Arlette...

Guilt gnawed at him. In a fit of anger, driven by vengeance, he'd ordered her to be incarcerated in the same manner. And now, Fate sought retribution.

Or was this her doing—to further the path of vengeance? Would it never end until they had destroyed each other?

Footsteps echoed outside, followed by the jangle of keys. The door swung open to reveal the slim figure of a man, bearing a torch.

"We meet at last, Saxon bastard."

His voice bore the trace of a French accent—a Norman nobleman.

"Who are you?" Orson croaked. "What do you want?"

The man stepped inside the cell, grasped Orson's hair, and thrust the torch into his face. Bright aqua eyes glittered malevolently in a handsome face, which twisted into a smile. Then he released his grip and wiped his hand on his tunic.

"I fail to see what she ever saw in you."

"She?"

Orson caught a blur of movement, then pain exploded in his jaw as his captor smashed his fist into his face.

"Don't take me for a fool!" he cried. "She was mine! Do you hear me? Mine!"

Orson shook his head. "I know not who you are. What do you want with me?"

"My name is Fulbert de Villiers. You violated my cousin—then you and your whore murdered her."

He fisted his hand again, then rammed it into Orson's stomach.

A wave of agony rippled through Orson, and he leaned forward, his wrists jerking against the end of the chains. He expelled the contents of his stomach, which spilled down his tunic. He tried to spit out the acid taste but his mouth was too dry.

His body blazed with pain, but it was nothing compared to the agony in his heart.

"Arlette..." he croaked.

"Do not presume to speak her name!" de Villiers cried. "You have no right. No kinswoman of mine would willingly spread her legs for a filthy Saxon—but you corrupted her. She belonged to me—yet she ran to you and died for her folly."

*Sweet heaven!* Pain stabbed through Orson's heart.

"Died?"

"Aye," de Villiers snarled. "You threw her in your dungeon—chained her like an animal—and left her to die! Can you deny how you treated her?"

"How do you know what I did?"

"So you admit you killed her? Poisoned her in her cell?"

*Poisoned...*

Dear God! What had he done? Arlette—his Arlette. Had she spoken the truth? Had she been taken against her will—and he'd been tricked into denying her?

De Villiers spoke more quietly, his calm tone only serving to heighten Orson's fear.

It was a calmness born of pure evil.

"You killed her," he said, "together with that whore. You'll join *her* in hell, but not before you give me what I want."

"What whore?"

"That bitch—Kendra," de Villiers said. "She murdered my cousin—all because she wanted you. She believed you loved Arlette—as if one such as you would be capable of love!" He spat on the floor. "It's *your* fault she's dead."

"Arlette..."

"I sent that bitch to hell, and you'll join her. But I'll grant you a quick death if you give me what I want."

"I'll give you nothing!"

"On the contrary, you'll bequeath your properties and estates to me."

Orson forced a laugh of derision. "Why would I do that?"

"Because your sister—the delectable Verona—was my wife."

Horror twisted Orson's gut. "You lie!"

"Oh, what a fool you are," de Villiers said. "I made use of you before—I'll make use of you again. You were the means of securing the de Villiers properties—your sister was the means of securing yours. The two of you have made me a wealthy man."

"What do you mean?"

De Villiers laughed. "You Saxons are so weak headed! You secured my inheritance by removing the obstacle—my Uncle Reynaud." He smiled, his teeth gleaming. "I should thank you for disposing of him, but it was most unchivalrous of you to murder my aunt. I'd planned to comfort the grieving widow by marrying her daughter."

Orson swallowed the knot of dread. "You expected me to kill Reynaud de Villiers?"

"Aye." Fulbert's tone was bright with triumph. "An uncouth brute with an ill temper and a reputation for fierce and bloody revenge. I played you, Wulfson—and you did everything I hoped."

*God's bones!* Had he butchered the wrong man in his desperation for revenge? Did Verona's real murderer stand before him now?

*Oh, Verona!*

And Arlette—his Arlette...

His beloved wife—the woman who'd given him her loyalty and her love—who'd endured suffering and torment at his hands. Yet, she had crawled through the harsh winter to warn him of danger, to save his life…

And he'd rejected her—cast her aside and tossed her in a cell, where she was murdered at Kendra's hands.

"You weren't meant to take her," de Villiers said, his eyes burning with hatred. "The night you murdered my uncle, Arlette was supposed to come with *me*."

"What have I done!" A wail of despair exploded in Orson's chest. He lifted his head and howled, straining against the manacles, ignoring the jolt of pain in his wrists.

"I'll leave you to your conscience," Fulbert said, "but I *will* have your properties. Only then shall you earn a quick death. My men possess great skill in prolonging agony, and they're eager to earn their keep." A featherlight touch caressed Orson's face as Fulbert stroked it with his fingertip, leaning forward to whisper in his ear.

"Soon, you will beg me to kill you."

Fulbert brushed his lips against Orson's forehead. Then he retreated, leaving Orson alone in the darkness.

# CHAPTER 35

"By the saints—what in the name of all that is holy did I drink?"

Pearce opened his eyes. Knives of pain sliced his skull, and his throat burned. He lifted his hand to his face—which was sticky and covered with a thick, viscous liquid. He must have fallen, face-down, into the stew. He pushed himself into a sitting position, knocking aside a goblet, which clattered to the floor.

Fighting the urge to vomit, he brushed lumps of meat out of his hair, inhaled, and his vision began to clear.

He was in the great hall. The diners were slumped over the tables, and the floor littered with bodies—mostly servants, but some of Orson's men lay among them. One or two were stirring, soft moans thickening the air. Others lay still, never to stir again.

He glanced toward the high table.

Orson was missing—as was the woman, Kendra.

He reached for another goblet to quench his thirst, then a memory crept into his mind—the potent taste of the wine, a rush of saliva on his tongue, and the world inverting as he fell into blackness.

He pushed the goblet away. The wine might be dangerous.

*"You're all in danger..."*

Where had he heard those words? Who had spoken them?

He surveyed the carnage. Brand and Jarvis lay together, bodies covered in blood. Ulferth lay motionless, a few feet away, together with two men Pearce didn't recognize. A number of servants lay in a pool of blood, including the pretty young Rosa. His heart twitched with a pang of regret—he'd enjoyed a tumble or two with her.

He heard a groan, and a blond head lifted up.

Seaton glanced around the hall, his red-rimmed eyes widening. "What's happened?"

"I know not, Seaton," Pearce replied, "but Lord Wulfson's missing, and Mistress Kendra. We must find the Lady Arlette."

"That traitor," Seaton said. "Do you think *she* planned this?"

"I'm inclined to believe it was another."

"She had an accomplice?"

"Mayhap she spoke the truth when she said we were in danger," Pearce said. "If she were planning a raid, why warn us?"

Seaton shook his head. "Who knew what she was about?"

"Then let us find out." Pearce took his knife and exited the hall, toward the dungeons.

Outside the great hall, they encountered two more bodies. One, dressed in purple silk, had been repeatedly slashed in a frenzied attack. The other bore a single stab wound to the heart.

Seaton let out a cry. "It's the Lady Kendra! Who would do such a thing?"

"Perhaps Lady Arlette has the answer," Pearce said.

Seaton's voice hardened. "Mayhap she's the cause."

But the seed of doubt had sprouted in Pearce's mind. Perhaps he'd been played—perhaps they'd all been played, like pawns in an elaborate game. It was Hilda who'd told him about Arlette's flight—Hilda, who now lay dead, next to Kendra.

But Barton Keep—the building Arlette claimed to have been incarcerated in—Seaton had searched it from top to bottom, and found no trace of her. Seaton was not a man to lie or deceive, unless he himself had been deceived.

Pearce sighed. His head told him that the Lady Arlette had betrayed them.

But his heart said otherwise.

"Come, Seaton," he said. "To the dungeon. But take care. There's treachery afoot."

They followed the passageway, and down a flight of steps toward the bowels of the building until they reached the staircase leading to the dungeons.

"What do you think..." Seaton began, but Pearce interrupted.

"Hush," he whispered. "Follow me."

Most of the dungeons were in darkness, save the flicker from a dying torch. Halfway along, the jailer was slumped in his seat, an empty dish and goblet on the floor beside him. Pearce approached the cell at the far end, taking care to tread quietly.

He peered through the hole in the door, and froze.

The cell was empty.

The heavy metal ring where Arlette had been chained to the wall glinted in the torchlight. But the chain—and Arlette—were nowhere to be seen.

He tested the door, but it was locked.

"Get the keys," he whispered.

Seaton crossed the floor to the jailer, then returned with the key chain. Pearce chose a key and slipped it into the lock, but it didn't turn. Then he tried another with no success.

On the fourth attempt, the key turned and the door swung inward. Motioning to Seaton to remain where he was, Pearce stepped inside.

An untouched bowl of stew was on the floor, together with a full goblet. He kneeled beside the bowl, picked up the goblet, and lifted it, sniffing the contents.

Wine—heavily spiced. And another, sweeter smell he couldn't recognize.

He heard a light footstep, and the clink of metal from behind—but before he could move, a chain wrapped around his neck and he was pulled backward. Choking for air, he clawed at the chain.

The cold blade of a knife pressed against his neck.

"Don't move," a voice hissed, "or I'll slit your throat."

The voice was Arlette's.

ARLETTE TIGHTENED her grip on the chain.

"Are you come to kill me, Pearce? I'm sorry to disappoint you."

Seaton appeared in the doorway. His eyes widened and he took a step forward.

"Don't move!" Arlette cried. She pressed the knife against Pearce's neck, and a fat red droplet appeared on his skin.

"Lady Arlette!" Seaton cried. "Surely you wouldn't hurt Pearce!"

"Wouldn't I?" she challenged. "You believe I murdered that poor young man—not to mention my husband's horse—in cold blood. I'd have no qualms about killing a soldier in a bid for freedom."

"No," Pearce choked.

"Be silent!" she cried. "Do you take me for a fool?"

He shook his head, his body stiffening as her knife slid across his skin.

"I mean…" he coughed, but she held the chain firm, "…you didn't murder them. You didn't murder anyone. I saw you leave that night—but you'd been tricked, hadn't you? Like the rest of us."

Seaton narrowed his eyes. Was this yet more deception?

"Please, lady," Pearce said. "I've done little to gain your trust, but I ask for it nonetheless. I came here to free you."

"Why should I trust you?" she asked.

"Because you know, in your heart, that I'm loyal to Lord Wulfson, above all others," he replied. "I've only ever acted out of that loyalty. I ask for your forgiveness, even though I don't deserve it. I should have trusted you. All I can do now is regret my folly, and swear fealty to you."

Arlette's need for retribution warred with her conscience. Sincerity bled through his words. Pearce was—and had always been—a man of honor. She loosened the chain and released her hold. Still brandishing her knife, she stepped back.

"Stand," she said. "Slowly."

"You believe me?" he asked.

"Perhaps we were both duped."

"What were you doing, lady—the night you left?"

"I was going to find my brother," she said. "Hilda told me he'd been found, and he was injured."

"Why didn't you tell your husband?"

"How can you ask that!" she cried. "Orson declared, many times, that the men of my family had forfeited their lives. He would have killed Guillaume—a mere boy—on sight. My brother is innocent, and I swore to protect him."

Seaton shook his head, his eyes moistening.

"Dear Lord…" he whispered. "Do you speak the truth?"

"You know I do!" she snarled. "*You're* the one who lied. Perhaps you're in league with my cousin—against my husband—planning to raid the castle."

"We've already been raided."

"You lie," Arlette said. "I heard no fighting."

"We were tricked," Pearce said. "The wine was drugged —poisoned."

Arlette glanced at the untouched goblet of wine on the floor. The jailer had brought it that morning, and she'd suspected foul play.

"I passed out during the feast," Pearce continued, "then I woke, to find Lord Wulfson missing."

Cold fingers clawed at her heart.

*Orson…*

Curse him—despite everything, she still loved him.

"What happened?" she asked.

"I know not," Pearce said. "Most lie unconscious—some are dead. I suspect mercenaries were hired to take Lord Wulfson with as little resistance as possible—someone drugged the wine and let them in. Those of us who drank enough to pass out were the lucky ones."

Unconscious, or dead…

A shiver of fear rippled through her. "Was Lillian at the feast?

"No, lady," Pearce said. "I didn't see her. Lord Wulfson was angry because she'd disappeared. Do you think she was taken?"

"No," Arlette said, nurturing a nugget of hope. "I believe her trust in me was rewarded. If I'm right, then we must go to the kitchens—now."

"For what purpose?" Seaton asked.

"Be quiet, Seaton!" she cried. "You've no right to speak to me."

"Why don't you trust Seaton?" Pearce asked.

"Because he lied," she said. "I *was* held at Barton Keep, yet Seaton says otherwise."

Seaton shook his head. "I know what I saw. Barton Keep was empty."

"Had you been there before?" Pearce asked.

"No, but Ulferth led the way."

"Ulferth!" Arlette scoffed. "You trusted his word over mine?"

"We must find him."

"No," Arlette said. "First, we find my daughter."

~

THE KITCHEN WAS USUALLY a hive of activity—servants rushing to and fro, the shout of orders, and steam rising from the cauldron over the fire. But the room was quiet, the fire long since extinguished. Arlette shivered as the cold brushed across her skin. Two servants were slumped over the wooden table—the same table she'd been scrubbing the night she caught Orson watching her. She closed her eyes, imagining him standing in the doorway—desire in his expression, and a knowing smile on his lips. But when she opened them, he wasn't there.

Pearce approached the table and leaned over the two unconscious forms, one of which was Elvia.

"They're alive," he said, "but she's not." He pointed to the floor, where a body lay, and Arlette let out a low cry as she recognized Freydis, her sightless eyes staring upward, the front of her gown soaked in vomit.

"*She*," Arlette said, her voice laced with anger, "was Freydis."

"Where's the child?"

"Hush!" Arlette raised her hand, then approached the door leading to the grain store. She opened the door and peered inside. Several sacks formed a neat row, which disappeared into the darkness at the back of the store.

"Lillian!" she called out. "Are you there?"

Silence.

"Perhaps she was taken, by…" Pearce began, but Arlette interrupted him.

"Hush!" She stepped inside the store, her eyes adjusting to the darkness.

"Lillian?"

A shadow moved between two of the sacks.

"Lillian, it's me—Arlette. It's safe to come out, now. I have my knife—the one you gave me."

A pale face emerged from the darkness.

"Mama Arlette?"

"'Tis I."

The child burst out from between the sacks, and ran into Arlette, arms outstretched, almost knocking her over.

"Mama—I knew you'd come!"

Arlette drew the child into her arms. "Did I not promise to come and find you, my love?"

Lillian began to sob. "I was so frightened!" she cried. "I heard screams—and men laughing—and I thought they were going to catch me."

"They must have swept their way through the castle, killing all who were awake," Pearce said, disgust in his voice. "To think they'd stoop to killing women! Did you see them, child?"

Lillian clung to Arlette and shook her head. "No, sir. I hid, like Mama told me to. I heard voices, then it went quiet—then I heard footsteps, and Mistress Freydis screaming. I was so frightened! But I stayed where I was."

"Good girl," Arlette said.

"What happened?" Lillian asked.

"We were betrayed," Pearce said, his voice grim. "And I know who by. We found Mistress Kendra outside the hall, with Hilda. She must have sold us out."

"You found her?" Arlette asked. "Is she alive?"

Pearce shook his head. "The traitor was herself betrayed."

"And Ulferth?" Arlette demanded. "Where is he?"

"On the floor of the great hall. I know not whether he's alive."

"We must pray that he is," Arlette said. "He might be our only hope of finding Orson."

~

ARLETTE DREW a sharp breath as she entered the hall. It was littered with bodies—many of them slumped over the tables, like the two in the kitchen, but others lay on the floor.

"Rosa!"

She fell to her knees beside the body of the young maidservant, blinking back tears as she stroked her forehead, and closed her eyelids with the tips of her fingers.

"I'm so sorry," she whispered.

*Let her be now at peace.*

"Here he is!" Seaton's voice cut through her silent prayer.

Ulferth lay near the high table, a dark stain on the floor where his lifeblood had soaked into the stones. Seaton prodded him with the tip of his boot, and he stirred.

"You tricked me!" Seaton cried. "You knew if *I* spoke against Lady Arlette, then nobody would believe her. You'll die for this!"

Ulferth coughed, emitting a mist of red droplets.

"He doesn't have long," Pearce said. "I'll deal with him."

"No," Arlette replied. "Stay where you are. Seaton, take Lillian outside."

"But..."

"Now!"

He recoiled at her tone, then nodded and offered Lillian his hand.

"Go with him, child," Arlette said. "He'll not harm you."

As soon as Lillian was out of sight, Arlette kneeled beside Ulferth, and placed her knife against his throat.

"You betrayed us, didn't you?"

Ulferth stared back at her, his expression betraying the knowledge that Death beckoned to him.

"You'll die today," Arlette said, "but help me now, and I'll pray for your soul. Nod if you understand."

Ulferth inclined his head.

"Why did you do it?"

"Lord F-Fulbert promised me Leaside."

"My home?"

"He knew Wulfson would seek vengeance for his sister. Leaside was to be my reward—but he betrayed me."

"What are you speaking of?"

"The Lady Verona," Ulferth said, his voice a low rasp. "Your father didn't murder her—Fulbert made it look as if he had. He knew—Kendra knew—how Wulfson would react."

Arlette tightened the grip on her knife.

"Give me one reason why I shouldn't slit your throat!" she cried. "Was it you who murdered poor Will?"

"Forgive me."

She grasped him by the hair and thrust her face into his. "How *dare* you betray us—you belong in hell!"

"I wanted a property of my own."

"Where's Orson?" she cried. "Mayhap you can redeem your soul if you help us now."

He shook his head. "I don't know the name…east of here…by the sea."

He coughed again, his voice growing fainter. "Be kind to her."

"Who?"

"Edith. She should not be punished for my treachery."

"I will," Arlette said softly. "She is blameless, as are your children. I give you my word they'll not suffer for your sins."

He curled his mouth into a smile.

"Lady," Pearce said, urgency in his voice, "ask him again about Orson. He must know something."

Arlette shook her head. "He'll speak no more now."

Ulferth continued to smile, but the spark of life in his eyes had gone.

Pearce cursed under his breath. "We're no closer to finding Lord Wulfson."

"On the contrary," Arlette said. "I know of only one place beside the sea."

"Which is?"

"Seaforth—Duke William granted it to my uncle. I visited it once when I was a child. It's two days' ride east of Leaside."

"What are we to do?"

"We tend to the injured," Arlette said. "Then we rouse an army and ride east."

Cold determination forged steel into her bones and she stood erect, daring Pearce to challenge her.

"My cousin might have played on Orson's thirst for vengeance—but he shall learn that it's nothing compared to mine."

# CHAPTER 36

"Still stubborn, I see."

Orson flinched at the voice. He hung, suspended from the manacles, his whole body aflame with agony. Echoes of his screams bled from the stone walls at night, the dark recess of his mind his only solace.

With the absence of natural light, he had no idea how long he'd been imprisoned. He'd lost count of the number of visits from de Villiers, each one more painful than the last. His vision had almost completely gone—one eye swollen shut, the other barely able to discern the blurred shapes of the fists and knives his torturer took such pleasure in using.

His captor moved closer, the familiar, hated, smiling face coming into focus.

"Go to hell," Orson croaked, barely recognizing his own voice.

The smile slipped. De Villiers grasped one of Orson's fingers, then a sharp crack was followed by hot, intense agony, and Orson let out a hiss of pain.

"There are nine more, Wulfson. I'll break them all, and remove each one. Then, I shall rip out your eyes. Why not ease your passing and give me what I want?"

Orson jerked his head, motioning his captor to come closer. De Villiers leaned forward, victory in his eyes.

"I said. Go. To. Hell."

De Villiers drew a knife, and pain ripped through Orson as his captor drove the knife into his hand. The metallic taste of his lifeblood burst in his mouth, as he bit down, gritting his teeth to stem the scream threatening to explode in his chest.

"Scream for me—damn you!"

Shouts echoed outside, followed by a clash of steel. De Villiers jerked back and retreated to the door.

A distant voice cried out, "We're under attack!"

Orson slumped forward in his chains, the darkness beyond the pain calling him back to oblivion, while the roars of battle raged in his mind.

Then his blood froze at a familiar sound.

The battle cry of Reynaud de Villiers—the very same cry he had silenced with his own sword.

"It cannot be you! You're dead!" Fulbert's shriek of terror penetrated the darkness. The sounds of fighting continued, until a bloodcurdling cry rang out, followed by silence.

A human form appeared in the doorway, metal armor glinting in the torchlight.

The figure moved closer, and lifted its visor. Bright green eyes stared at Orson, red-rimmed with battle rage.

Raynaud de Villiers had returned from the grave—to avenge his daughter, and send Orson to hell.

*Seaforth Estate, England, January 1087*

"There it is, Pearce," Arlette said. "Seaforth—as I described."

The afternoon sun illuminated the gray stone building, set against the backdrop of a dark, stormy sea. Cold seeped into Arlette's body from the iron-hard ground beneath her, and she shifted position.

"You think I doubted your memory?" Pearce asked.

"No," she replied, her tone sharp, "just my loyalty to my husband."

He let out a sigh. "We should return to the camp. You must rest."

"You think I'm a weak woman?" she asked. "What must I do to persuade you otherwise, if I cannot cast a spell to turn me into a man?

"I don't doubt your authority, lady, but you must think of the child you carry."

Pearce knew her secret.

"Who betrayed my trust?" she demanded.

"Mistress Esme."

Curse the woman! Ever since the raid, when so many had died, Arlette's old nursemaid had taken it upon herself to treat her charge like a frail, helpless creature who needed to be wrapped in furs and watched at all times lest she place herself in danger by merely stepping outside. She understood Esme's love, but it suffocated her.

It felt so good to wear her armor again! And she longed to do something, other than linger and wait, like a lady was expected to do. But she was no ordinary lady—and Pearce, desperate to atone for his earlier mistrust of her, did not dare object.

"Esme shouldn't have betrayed my trust," she said.

"She's told only Seaton and myself—out of her concern for your welfare. A warrior must ensure he's prepared for combat to the best of his abilities, whether that preparation involves training, drawing up strategies—or resting on the eve of battle."

She nodded. "I understand."

"Good," he said. "But you must accept that *I* lead this army. You accompany us on condition that you obey every order without question."

She let out a snort. "Must I accept servitude?"

"This is not swordplay," he said, "and you are not in the comfort of the tourney field. The men you fight will think nothing of killing you. Orders in battle are given with the intent of ensuring success, and for protecting the lives of all our men. A soldier who hesitates is a danger to himself and to others."

"Have you told that to the men also?"

"By the saints, woman—you try my patience!" he cried. "If you wish to fight like a soldier, then you must behave like one. If you cannot accept this, then I'll have you gagged and bound to that tree yonder, until the battle is done."

"But..."

"No!" he interrupted. "I risk much, bringing you with us. Not only is your life at stake—but mine also. If you come to harm, Orson will have me flayed alive."

"Orson..."

Had Fulbert tortured him?

Was he even alive?

A warm hand squeezed hers. "Have no fear, lady. If anyone can survive, then he can."

"I pray you're right, Pearce."

She inhaled, tasting salt in the air, listening to the cries of the seagulls circling above, and the constant boom of the distant waves.

Seaforth stood near the edge of high cliffs—impenetrable, except for a long winding tunnel that ran from the beach at the base of the cliffs to the cellars of the building. Past inhabitants, wearied by invasions, had hollowed out an escape route centuries before.

"The tunnel's the key," Pearce said. "It'll give us the advantage of surprise. Seaton can penetrate the building, deal with the guard, and open the gates, while we attack from the front. From what I've seen, we'll outnumber them."

Pearce was right. The estate, which had thrived with activity when Arlette last saw it, was almost deserted. A handful of peasants scuttled to and fro, occasionally followed by a scrawny beast of burden. The only sign of occupation in the castle was a lone sentry patrolling the ramparts.

"I don't understand," Arlette said. "Seaforth has always prospered—fertile land, plentiful fish from the sea. How dare Fulbert neglect his people like this—damn him!"

"You're no use to me, lady, if you cannot control yourself."

"Have you no feelings?" she cried.

"A solider must set feelings aside. Do not be ruled by your anger."

"I'm merely eager for retribution."

"And you shall have it," Pearce said. "Trust me—I know what I'm about." He smiled ruefully. "After all—I planned the attack on Leaside." He rose to his feet, then offered his hand. "Come and rest now," he said. "We ride at daybreak."

~

PALE GRAY BLED into the heavens, to reveal the horizon, separating sea from sky. Arlette shifted in the saddle, checking, once more, that her shield was secure.

"Be still," Pearce said. "Waiting is the worst part."

"Not just waiting," Arlette said, nodding toward the rest of the company. "Do you trust these men?"

The raid on Greywell had taken many lives. With the exception of Brice and Seaton, the company consisted of hired swords who'd laughed at the notion of a woman fighting among them, until Arlette had held her sword against their leader's groin and threatened to cut off his manhood and feed it to the pigs.

"I trust them," Pearce said. "Mercenaries are loyal to coin—and they were paid handsomely."

"And Seaton?"

"Do you still doubt his loyalty? Or perhaps his ability?" Pearce shook his head. "He's incapable of leading an army, but he's a skilled fighter. And, unlike his lady, he obeys orders." An undercurrent of pride shone in his voice. "I trained him well."

"You're a good man, Pearce," Arlette said. "When this is done, you should take a wife."

"I lost my wife in childbirth many years ago," he replied, the pride in his voice sharpening to age-old grief. "I've no wish to suffer such pain again."

"We must risk pain to win the pleasure," she said. "What think you of the Lady Edith? She's a good woman."

"Aye."

"Promise me you'll consider her as a match when you return to Greywell," she said. "Loving, gentle—she's proven she can survive a birthing. She deserves a loving husband."

"As do you."

Tears stung her eyes and she turned her head away. "He doesn't love me, Pearce," she said. "I shall not return to Greywell."

"Your place is with him."

"Not anymore. Even if I could forget what he did to my family, he had me beaten, humiliated—and he broke faith when he believed me a traitor. He threw me into the dungeon and had me chained to the wall. It would be a weakness to forgive that."

"Don't you see, his anger was so great because he'd grown to love you," Pearce said. "Let us speak of this again once we've…"

"There's the signal!" A sharp cry interrupted him.

The sun had begun to rise from the sea, bright orange streaks rippling across the water. The growing daylight picked out the shape of the main gates, which cast a shadow as they began to open, and the ramparts were empty.

Seaton had succeeded.

The metallic clang of visors snapping shut broke through the song of waking forest birds. Arlette lowered her own visor, and her breathing echoed around her helmet, a thunderstorm of anticipation in her ears.

"Ride forth!" Pearce's roar spurred the company into action, and they charged toward the building. The muscular energy in Arlette's mount released like a coiled spring, vibrating through her body as the animal accelerated into a gallop.

A rush of exhilaration filled her lungs. At last! The chance to finally exact revenge upon the man responsible for everything she'd lost.

Lifting her head, she uttered a savage war cry as she followed the company into the building. A number of men emerged, brandishing swords, but they were outnumbered by Pearce's men, and they retreated into the building, where Seaton would be waiting.

Arlette had little experience of fighting in a confined space—and no experience of a real battle. A melee with men fighting each other at close quarter was completely different to the duels she'd fought with Ernaut and Garret—the gentle, courteous exercises nothing compared to the clash of steel, guttural curses, and the stench of blood, sweat, and death.

The sounds of battle abated as Pearce's men swiftly dispatched the enemy. As Pearce had ordered, Arlette remained at the rear of the party, but a huge figure sprang out of the darkness and advanced on her.

"Ha!" he cried. "A mere boy!" His greater strength and her slight build made her easy prey, but overconfidence dulled his senses, and his right side was exposed.

She hunched her shoulders, feigning exhaustion. He lunged toward her, and she dodged to his right, and her sword hit home, slicing into his flesh.

She withdrew the blade, then thrust her sword into his chest. He staggered back, dark red liquid pulsing from his body, until he crumpled onto the stone, and lay still.

Her first kill.

She had taken a man's life—a mercenary who, had Fate decreed otherwise, might have fought on her side.

Did he have a family? Was there a woman, waiting somewhere, who would never again see her husband—children who would never see their father?

*Forgive me.*

"Lady!" Pearce's cry broke through her prayer and she looked up to see a man advancing on her, sword raised, murder in his eyes.

He towered over her, his bulky frame large enough to flatten her with a single blow.

She didn't have a chance. Frozen to the spot, she awaited her fate.

"No!" Pearce leaped in front of Arlette, then let out a cry as the man drove the sword through his heart.

"Pearce!" Arlette screamed.

He toppled backward, taking the man with him. Arlette struggled to her feet and swung her sword at the enemy. Her aim was true, and he fell to the floor, his lifeblood draining from a gash in his neck.

"L-lady..." a voice rasped.

Pearce lay on his back. The sounds of fighting had abated, replaced with the hiss of Pearce's breathing.

Arlette kneeled beside him. His forehead glistened with sweat, his eyes bright with pain.

"You've been hurt, Pearce," she said. "Let me help you."

He shook his head and held out his hand. "I'm done for."

A dark red puddle had appeared beneath his body, spreading across the floor to mingle with the blood of the man who'd delivered the fatal blow.

"Take my hand," he said, his voice tight with urgency.

She took it, and long, lean fingers curled around hers.

"Promise me, Arlette..."

"Aye," she said. "I'll find him."

"No..." He shook his head and a cough erupted from his chest. "Promise me you'll forgive him, and remain by his side. He's a harsh man, but a *good* man—the best of men."

She hesitated, and he let out a deep sigh and relaxed his grip. When she looked into his eyes, the spark of life had gone.

Pain ripped through her heart. Pearce was a good man—a loyal friend. And she had failed to grant his dying wish—but it was a wish she could never have fulfilled.

Footsteps approached, and she turned, sword at the ready. But it was Seaton.

"Lady—are you well?"

She nodded, and he helped her to stand, steadying her, as if he knew, even before she did, that her legs would fail her. He let out a low cry when he saw Pearce's body.

"He died saving my life," she said. "Loyal to the last."

"Then he didn't die in vain," Seaton replied. "The battle is won—

the building was poorly defended—only a handful of mercenaries. We killed them all."

"I..." she hesitated. "I killed a man—two men."

Her throat tightened, restricting her breathing, then firm hands gripped her shoulders.

"Were you were prepared to die in battle today?" Seaton asked.

"Aye."

"As is every soldier," he said. "As were the men you killed. You must remember that."

She clutched his arm and her fingers met sticky wetness.

"Seaton, are you injured?"

"My arm is cut, but I'll survive."

Brice approached, limping, his visor lifted to reveal a mop of thick black hair plastered to his sweat-ridden face.

"Are they all dead, Brice?" Seaton asked.

"Aye," he replied. "The men are searching the building in case of survivors."

"Have you found my cousin?" Arlette asked.

Brice shook his head.

"Fulbert!" she screamed. "Come out—you evil swine! I know you're here—show yourself!"

A familiar voice rang through the hall.

"Who dares invade my home?"

A slim figure of a man emerged from behind a tapestry, dressed for battle, his chain mail dragging on the floor. His tunic bore the de Villiers coat of arms.

The coward! He must have hidden—spineless louse that he was—and watched while his men were cut down.

Arlette tightened the grip on the hilt of her sword, and pushed past Seaton and Brice.

"I dare!" she cried.

His eyes widened and he stepped back.

"It cannot be you!" he cried. "You're dead!"

"Let me deal with him," Seaton urged, "there's no need for you to fight."

Arlette gritted her teeth. "There's every need. He destroyed my family, and took my husband."

Fulbert moved toward her, and stumbled on the hem of his chainmail.

"Look at you!" Arlette scoffed. "You always preferred prancing about in finery to swordplay. Such a disappointment to Uncle Alexandre! Even his hauberk's too big for your puny frame."

"What about *you*, cousin?" Fulbert sneered. "A woman playing at soldiers—your fool of a papa indulged your fancies but how quickly he cast you aside in favor of Guillaume!"

"How dare you speak of Papa and Guillaume!" Arlette cried. "Their deaths are on your hands."

Fulbert laughed, "Uncle Reynaud may line the gardens at Leaside, but your brother is alive."

Guillaume! Her heart leaped with hope. Her beloved brother...

"Is he here?"

"No," Fulbert said, "but if you promise not to harm me I'll take you to him."

Arlette hesitated, then he lunged at her with his sword. She parried the blow, and he tripped and fell to the floor. She stepped on his hand, and he let out a howl of pain.

"Where is he?" she cried.

Fulbert shook his head. "The devil take you!"

"Tell me now," she said, "and you have my word I'll not kill you."

She pressed her foot down, and her stomach lurched at the sound of bones cracking.

He let out a groan. "V-Villiers castle..."

She released his hand. "Thank you, cousin."

Stepping back, she nodded to Brice. "Finish him off."

"But you promised!" Fulbert cried.

"I promised that *I* wouldn't kill you," she said. "Did you think I'd let you live after what you've done?" She nodded to Seaton. "You, come with me. We have to find Orson. Brice, get on with it."

Ignoring Fulbert's strangled cry, she strode out of the hall, toward the dungeons, Seaton's footsteps echoing behind her.

The dungeon consisted of six cells. The door nearest the stairwell was ajar. Arlette approached it, her shadow from Seaton's torch stretching out before her. She pushed it fully open with her foot, and her heart somersaulted at the sight before her.

A man hung on the wall, suspended by manacled wrists. The tendons in his arms protruded as if they were about to burst through the flesh. His clothes hung off his body in rags. His chest rose and fell slightly, the only evidence of life.

"Seaton, bring the torch."

Arlette approached the prisoner. His face was barely recognizable —swollen, bruised—and a deep cut ran down one cheek, streaked with dark red.

*Orson...*

He opened his eyes.

"De Villiers!" He jerked against the chains, then slumped forward and grew still.

ARLETTE LOOKED OUT TO SEA, where white peaks rippled across the water as the wind whipped through the land. Uncle Alexandre had always said the sea was wild and free—a vibrant, living being that yielded riches, but commanded respect, for it was capable of claiming any man who sought to conquer it.

Closing her eyes, she was a child again, running along the base of the cliffs, Fulbert in pursuit, yelling taunts. She used to hide behind boulders and throw rocks at him. A spoiled and indulged only child, Fulbert had wanted to advance himself only through marriage and inheritance rather than effort or toil. Uncle Alexandre once said Arlette should have been born a boy—and that she'd have made a better son than Fulbert.

And Fulbert had never forgiven him.

Seaton's voice broke through her memory. "It's time to go."

Aye, it was. Seaforth was now the rightful property of Guillaume as the surviving male heir. And she needed to bring him home.

After having reassured the remaining inhabitants at Seaforth village that she'd return, it was time to take Orson home, where he could be properly tended to. His body badly beaten and tortured, there was little hope of survival—but with the herbs and medicines she'd gathered and prepared at Greywell Castle, he had a chance—albeit a slim one.

She followed Seaton to the front of the main building, and her heart tightened with sorrow at the sight of Pearce's riderless horse.

She climbed into the cart where Orson's unconscious body lay. Taking charge, Seaton mounted his horse and the party set off for home.

But Greywell Castle was no longer her home.

~

THE JOURNEY to Greywell took four days. By the time Arlette glimpsed the familiar silhouette, Orson's fever had reached its peak. On her orders, Brice and Seaton carried him to the solar while the household, much depleted since the Michaelmas raid, saw to the rest of the wounded.

A sennight after their return, Orson began to recover. Arlette had kept him sedated while, with Esme's help, she stitched his injuries and reset his broken bones. His right hand was so badly damaged that two fingers had to be removed.

While his fever raged, he spoke incoherent, delirious mutterings. Mostly, he cried for his sister, until, one morning, he whispered another name.

"Arlette..."

She flew to his bedside and took his hand. "Orson?"

He opened his eyes, but they were unfocused, still bright with fever.

"She's dead," he said, his voice flat. "She left me. There's only Lillian, now."

He closed his eyes, and his breathing steadied as he returned to unconsciousness.

The following morning, his fever had gone. It was time for her to leave.

SEATON HANDED Arlette the reins of her mount before checking the fastenings of the panniers strapped to his own horse. They were ready to leave for Normandy.

Esme approached her, sorrow in her eyes. "Won't you reconsider?"

Arlette shook her head. "Once I've returned Guillaume to Leaside, I intend to live there."

"Where will I go?"

"Wherever you choose," Arlette replied, "but I'm going to Leaside, as is the Lady Edith. Brice will escort her tomorrow."

"Then I'll accompany her," Esme said.

The household had begun to recover. Orson's steward had already employed servants and men-at-arms to replace those who'd been killed at Michaelmas.

But the atmosphere had changed. The name of de Villiers was often spoken with hatred—the same hatred that had burned in Orson's eyes the last time he'd looked at Arlette. Ulferth's betrayal clung to the atmosphere like a rancid fog. As his wife, Edith was branded a traitor by association, and she suffered whispers and taunts —especially since discovering she was with child again—the child of a traitor. The desire for vengeance was too deeply ingrained into the people of Greywell.

"Your place is with your husband," Esme said. "You carry his child."

"Hush!" Arlette hissed. "How can I remain here after what he did? He had me imprisoned, chained, and humiliated. He only wanted me as retribution. I've paid my family's debt—his sister's true murderer is dead, and as such, I consider myself free to go. My duty is to my brother and my unborn child. Everyone here is glad to see me go."

"What of Lillian? She doesn't want you to leave.

Arlette looked about her, but there was no sign of her stepdaughter. When she had told Lillian she was leaving, the child accused her of treachery, then refused to speak to her again, seeking comfort in Elvia's arms.

"Lillian has not come to bid me farewell," Arlette said.

"That's because she's hurting!" Esme cried. "She's just a child—she cannot be expected to understand, or accept, what you're doing. She loves you—but *you* are the one who's behaving like a child, thinking only of yourself."

Esme's words pricked at Arlette's conscience. "Lillian will forget me," she said. "She has her father—who believes I'm dead."

"You're a fool," Esme said. "He won't believe that forever." She turned to Seaton. "Do you consent to this, sir?"

"I like it no more than you," he replied, "but I must do as Lady Arlette wishes. I owe her a debt for mistrusting her."

"Then take care of her."

"Aye. I will."

Arlette hugged Esme, then mounted her horse. As she steered her mount across the drawbridge, Seaton in her wake, she glanced over her shoulder, in the hope of catching a glimpse of a familiar face at the window to Lillian's room. But there was no one there.

# CHAPTER 37

*Normandy, March 1087*

"There it is, Seaton, Villiers Castle."

A small, square tower stood on the horizon ahead, its ramparts glowing in the light of the setting sun.

Her ancestral home.

The journey had taken eight days. Though Arlette experienced no ill effects from the sea crossing, Seaton had vomited twice. They had landed at Saint Valery-sur-Somme, a small coastal town within two days' ride of Villiers, and spent their first night on French soil in a small tavern. Arlette had begun to relate how Papa and Uncle Reynaud had helped Duke William amass his fleet of ships there before the conquest of England, but stopped on seeing the horrified expression in Seaton's eyes as she recalled Esme's words.

*I saw ladies and servants alike raped, degraded, and sold into slavery.*

Seaton's family were Saxons—as was everyone at Greywell Castle. Perhaps she'd been a fool to believe she could ever be loved by them. Papa's deeds had seemed so heroic when she was a child. But, over the past year, she'd seen them in a new light—through the eyes of the Saxons.

As they approached the castle, she spotted movement on the battlements.

"Seaton, lift the standard."

"Aye, lady."

He held aloft a square of linen bearing the de Villiers coat of arms, and they stopped beside the moat, across from the main gate.

Arlette cupped her hand to her mouth and called out.

"Lower the drawbridge!"

There was no response other than the hiss of steel as Seaton drew his sword. He was taking no chances.

The drawbridge lowered, with the rumble of metal scraping against wood, then the main gates creaked open to reveal two men on horseback, dressed in battle armor, swords drawn.

"Let me pass," Arlette said. "This is my property."

"You lie," one of the men said, his voice familiar. "This is the property of Fulbert de Villiers."

"Fulbert was a disgrace to the name of de Villiers!" Arlette cried. She removed her helmet. "I am Arlette de Villiers, come to claim what's mine, and free my brother. You are in my way. I advise you to remedy that."

"*Mon Dieu!*" He pulled off his helmet off to reveal a familiar face, weathered by age—kind brown eyes set among strong features, topped by a mop of hair streaked with gray.

A face she knew and loved.

"You always were a hellcat, Lady Arlette."

"Ernaut!"

They both dismounted and she ran into the strong, capable arms of the man who'd tutored her as a child.

"I never thought to see you again!" she cried.

"Nor I you, lady, but if anyone's capable of returning from the grave, you are."

"From the grave?"

"Lord Fulbert told us you'd been murdered by a Saxon."

"He lied."

"And Lord Reynaud—Lady Emmelina? Did the Saxon murder them?"

"It's not that simple," she said. "They died at another's hand, but it was Fulbert's doing. My cousin betrayed us, but he'll not be returning from the grave."

"And the Saxon—does he live?"

"Aye."

"How…"

She raised her hand. "I'll tell you in time but first—is my brother here?"

"Aye, Fulbert tasked us to protect him, and the young woman."

A young woman?

The other rider dismounted and lifted his visor, and Arlette gave a cry of recognition.

"Garret!"

"I'm glad to see you alive and well, *demoiselle*."

Garret nodded toward Seaton. "Who's this—a Saxon?"

Arlette nodded. "He's one of my husband's knights."

"You have a husband?"

"Aye," Arlette said. "We have much to discuss—but first, I'm eager to see Guillaume."

"Then I'll delay you no further." Ernaut bowed and led the way inside. Arlette followed, and Garret brought up the rear, sword unsheathed, his eyes on Seaton. Mistrust between Norman and Saxon ran deep.

~

THE SOLAR AT Villiers Castle occupied the entire top floor. Arlette paused for breath at the final flight of steps.

"Are you well, lady?" Seaton asked.

"I'm a little tired."

"You must take care—think of your child."

"You're with child?" Garret exclaimed. "*Mon Dieu*—what are you about, travelling the length of the country with this…" he eyed Seaton with disgust, "…this *Saxon*."

"Seaton is not the enemy," Arlette said.

"And yet, the Saxon who killed my master still lives."

"He was a pawn in Fulbert's game," Arlette said. "Fulbert murdered his sister, but left evidence to convince him that Papa had killed her. I have forgiven him." She placed a hand over her belly. "I married him…"

"*Mon Dieu*—have you lost your wits?"

"Enough!" Arlette cried. "My husband has lost much at Fulbert's hands. He's a good man. The circle of vengeance must be broken."

"How can you speak so?"

"Thousands of Saxons lost their homes in the conquest," Arlette said. "My husband's own father swore allegiance to Duke William and it cost him his life. If countless Saxons can forgive an entire conquest, then we must forgive this. Let that be the end of it. Until Guillaume comes of age *I'm* head of the family."

"I always said you should have been born a man," Garret said. "If you bear a son, he'll be a handful—a daughter, doubly so. Come, let me help you with these stairs."

"I'm with child," she said, "not dying."

Garret lifted his hands in resignation and led the way, knocking at the solar door. A small voice called out in response.

"Who is it?"

Arlette's heart leaped with joy—to hear that beautiful voice again!

"You have a visitor, Master Guillaume," Garret said.

"Good. I'm bored with this Latin."

Dear Guillaume—he'd always loathed his studies!

Garret opened the door. "After you, my lady."

A boy sat hunched over a table covered in books. Arlette stepped over the threshold, and he looked up, running his hand through a mop of chestnut hair. His brow crinkled with confusion, then large expressive green eyes stared in disbelief.

"Lettie?"

"Guillaume…"

Arlette's knees buckled, no longer able to carry her weight. Guillaume leaped to his feet and ran toward her, arms outstretched, catching her before she fell.

"Lettie!"

She drew in a deep breath, relishing the sweet, familiar smell of her brother as she pressed her face against his.

"Guillaume! My precious Guillaume…" Her throat swelled, constricting her sobs.

Finally, he was in her arms—the object of her every waking thought. Her love for him had sustained her during months of imprisonment and marriage—and it was the weakness upon which her enemies had preyed. But now, her enemies were destroyed. United with her beloved brother once more, she would never be parted from him again.

"Cousin Fulbert said you'd died at Leaside," Guillaume said. "He made me watch it burn. Then he brought me here for my safety so he could avenge your death."

"He lied," Arlette said, through gritted teeth. "He has told many lies —but no more."

She tightened her hold on him as tears blinded her eyes.

"Oh Guillaume, forgive me!"

"What for, Lettie?"

"I swore to protect you, and I failed."

"I'm a man now," Guillaume said. "I can protect *you*."

Dear Guillaume! Arlette laughed through her tears.

"Why do you laugh and cry at the same time, Lettie?"

"I laugh because my heart is filled with joy at seeing my beloved brother again," she said, "and I cry for the months we were parted, when I missed you so much."

She tightened her hold, and he stiffened.

"Lettie, who's that man?"

Arlette released him and gestured toward Seaton.

"Guillaume—this is Seaton, my protector. Seaton—my brother Guillaume."

Seaton bowed. "It gives me great pleasure to meet you, Lord de

Villiers. Your sister has spoken much of you."

Guillaume gave a stiff little bow, then he let out an exclamation. "Oh! The lady—I forgot the lady!"

Arlette shook her head. "What lady?"

"Our cousin brought her here," Guillaume said. "She's in the next chamber. I like her. She embroiders and plays music, and is much better at it than you."

Dear Guillaume had yet to lose the frankness possessed only by children, or those powerful enough not to care what others thought of them. Arlette took his hand.

"I was always too busy tending to my troublesome brother to learn the accomplishments of a lady," she laughed.

"She's in here." Guillaume pulled her across the chamber, stopping at an ornately carved wooden door that led to a suite of rooms, and he pushed it open.

A young woman sat beside the window, bent over a loom, brow furrowed in concentration. She looked up at Arlette, and her eyes widened in fear.

"Mistress!" Guillaume cried. "'Tis my sister!"

"Guillaume," Arlette admonished, "it's unseemly to enter a lady's chamber thus!"

She addressed the girl. "I must ask you to forgive me," she said, gesturing to her hauberk. "Had I known we had a guest at Villiers, I wouldn't have presented myself in such an unseemly manner."

"Who are you?" the girl asked.

"Lady Arlette de Villiers."

The color drained from the girl's face. "Are you here to take me to my betrothed?"

"Your betrothed?"

"L-Lord de Villiers," she said. "Fulbert."

"No," Arlette said coldly. "He no longer lives."

The girl raised her eyebrows, then exhaled, visibly relaxing.

Curse Fulbert! What had he been about? And what had he done to the poor creature to scare her?

"You're welcome to remain here as our guest," Arlette said. "Or do you wish to return to your family?"

"Oh yes!" The girl's mouth curled into a smile, and Guillaume sighed, evidently smitten.

"Is it safe for me to return?" she asked. "Lord Fulbert said...oh!"

She leaped to her feet with a cry of joy. "Seaton!"

"God's bones!" Seaton rushed forward and embraced the girl.

"You know this young woman?" Arlette asked.

"Aye," he replied, a broad grin on his face. He took the girl's hand and pulled her toward Arlette.

"Lady Arlette—may I introduce you to the Lady Verona Greywell —your husband's sister."

# CHAPTER 38

Arlette stabbed at a piece of meat with her knife. Guillaume sat beside her, mouth downturned as he watched Seaton and Verona, who sat across the table, flanked by Ernaut and Garret. Seaton's expressive blue eyes darkened, and he leaned close to Verona as she related the tale of her betrothal.

"He told me my brother was a traitor," she said. "I refused to believe it, but Fulbert said he was an emissary of the king himself. He promised marriage, saying it was the only way I could stay alive." She wiped a tear from her eyes. "Oh Seaton, forgive me! I didn't want to go with him, then when Guillaume told me about his home that Orson had destroyed, I was so frightened! Fulbert said I'd be executed if I was discovered."

"Fulbert has much to answer for," Arlette said. She drained her goblet, then slammed it onto the table. "I regret the swift death I granted him—I wish I'd gutted him. I only hope he burns in hell—curse him!"

Verona gave a little cry, and Seaton took her hand, frowning at Arlette.

"My apologies, Lady Verona." Arlette forced herself to speak calmly. "Many people have died as a result of Fulbert's greed. He's shamed my family. How can I atone for what he's done to you?"

"I only wish to be reunited with my brother," Verona said.

Arlette nodded. "I'll take you to him once I've settled my affairs here."

Verona's face broke into a smile, her soft gray eyes bright with hope.

"Is he well? I've missed him so much."

"Fulbert injured him, but he's recovering," Arlette replied. "His love for you has never faded."

"You know him well?"

Seaton leaned forward to refill his wine cup. "Aye," he said, "the Lady Arlette is..."

"I know him a little," Arlette interrupted, frowning at Seaton.

Now wasn't the time to discuss Orson. Verona's presence already unsettled her—she bore a striking similarity to her brother. Every so often during the evening, Verona's expression underwent a subtle change and it was as if Orson sat before her.

Arlette turned her attention to Ernaut. Villiers Castle was her property, and its management her concern. But the estate was in good hands. She could leave it in Garret's stewardship while Ernaut accompanied her to England.

By the time they finished eating, Ernaut had satisfied Arlette that apart from a brief tour of the estate, there was little for her to do. They could be ready to leave for England in a few days. But, as Arlette watched Seaton and Verona more closely, she resolved to tarry awhile longer. His countenance had changed—she'd never seen him so happy. And, if she couldn't be happy herself, she was determined that the chivalrous young knight who'd befriended her in her hour of need would find the happiness he deserved.

ALMOST A FORTNIGHT after Arlette's arrival at Villiers, Guillaume accompanied her on a stroll through the castle grounds. The gardens had hardly changed since she'd last seen them, but she let Guillaume show her around, smiling at his chatter as he slipped his hand into hers. The memory of similar walks at Greywell Castle with Lillian cut into her heart. But Lillian would soon have Verona to accompany her —the aunt she adored—and she would soon forget the woman who loved her as her own daughter.

"Lettie, you're hurting my hand."

She lifted Guillaume's hand to her lips. "Forgive me, little brother. My thoughts are much occupied."

Guillaume sighed. "Mine, also."

Laughter filtered across the morning air, from where Seaton and Verona sat together at the edge of the garden.

"Poor Guillaume," Arlette said. "Do you fancy yourself in love?"

"I *am* in love."

"You're still a child, brother, and her heart lies elsewhere."

"Is that why you insisted on staying here awhile longer?"

Arlette laughed. "I see no harm in letting a little love blossom before we leave."

He sighed, defeat in his eyes.

"You can take a wife when you come of age," Arlette said. "But take care to love the woman you marry."

"What of you, Lettie? Do you love your husband?"

"It matters not," she said. "He doesn't love me. My place is with you, now."

"When I take a wife, I shall love her very much," Guillaume said, "though she must always do as I bid."

"That's where I erred, brother," Arlette said. "I rarely obeyed my husband."

Guillaume squeezed her hand. "*I* still love you. I'll find you another husband, and will order him to love you."

Arlette embraced her brother. All around her seemed to be bathed in happiness and bright prospects. Guillaume, as Lord de Villiers, would have his pick of the ladies in England. Seaton and Verona only needed a little encouragement to declare their love—with their gentle dispositions and compassionate natures, they complemented each other perfectly.

As had she and Orson. Only he could temper her passion—only he could ignite the fire inside her body and her heart.

The days would be lonely without him, but the nights—how would she bear them?

Arlette massaged her belly and drew in a lungful of sea air. She found the rocking motion of the ship comforting, though poor Seaton sickened again. However, Verona suffered greatly, unable even to sit. Seaton, despite having turned a pale shade of green, insisted on tending to her.

Ernaut appeared at her side. "It's most improper of Seaton to tend to the young woman unchaperoned."

"What harm can there be?" Arlette replied. "They're smitten with each other."

"You think her brother would permit their union? Seaton has told me much of him—and fine a young man as Seaton may be, he has no estate of his own—nothing to give her."

"Not even Orson would deny the man who returned his sister from the dead," Arlette said.

"You think to persuade him?"

Arlette shook her head. "I have no intention of seeing him again."

"A woman's place is with her husband," Ernaut said.

"Why?" she snapped. "Because she's his property? I won't yield to a man who treated me worse than livestock! If he wants me, he must prove his worth."

"What would you have him do?" Ernaut demanded. "Grovel? You're a fool if you expect that. You must pray he forgives your desertion."

Why did men have to be so arrogant? Did they all wish to assert their ownership over everything and everyone in their path?

"My husband is too blinded by his thirst for retribution to look upon me with anything other than hatred," she said. "His lust for vengeance will destroy him. But I won't let it destroy me. His sister lives, while my parents lie cold in their graves. He has lost nothing—I've lost everything. How can you say my place is with him!"

"You wish the Lady Verona were dead?"

"Of course not!"

"It's not your husband who's blinded by revenge," Ernaut said. "It's you. You said yourself—Fulbert's to blame for what happened, not your husband. You're no better than Fulbert if you continue to harbor hatred."

"How dare you speak so!"

"I mean no disrespect. Come—it grows cold. You should go inside."

"Do *you* seek to give me orders?" she demanded. "What would Papa have said if he heard you speak so?"

"He would have commended me for my patience," he said, "then ordered me to whip you raw for such disrespect."

Ernaut was right. Arlette blushed with shame at her petulance.

At length, he sighed. "Ignore my counsel if you wish—you're no longer a child. But you must accept responsibility for your choices."

Before she could answer, he went in search of Seaton. Sighing, Arlette returned to her cabin.

~

After they reached English soil, the journey to Leaside took five days. Guilt gnawed at Arlette for arguing with Ernaut—the old knight had spoken out of concern for her welfare. During the journey she deferred to him, obeying his instructions without complaint.

Having conquered her unease at Verona's likeness to Orson, Arlette made an effort to know her better—the woman Orson loved above all others, and who'd inspired such devotion that he razed castles to the ground to avenge her.

If only he could have loved *her* as much!

But only the meanest soul would harbor jealousy toward Verona.

Kind, gentle, and touchingly fond of Guillaume, she was the perfect mother figure for Lillian, and would make Seaton the perfect wife.

They reached Leaside early afternoon, the smell of spring in their nostrils. Two of Ernaut's men had ridden ahead to announce their arrival, and Esme waited by the main entrance, with a small welcome party.

"Guillaume! My sweet boy!"

Esme let out a wail, then ran toward Guillaume, enveloping him in her wide, fleshy arms. Guillaume wriggled, before relenting, while the old nursemaid kissed him on both cheeks and sobbed over his head. She reached out to Arlette, and pulled her into the embrace, the family de Villiers at home, reunited.

After Esme grew quiet, Arlette bade her take Guillaume inside. There was one last journey to make—one more family to reunite.

~

THE FAMILIAR SILHOUETTE broke through the low-lying mist. Arlette's body tightened as the building came into view, and she reined in her mount.

"This is where I leave you."

Seaton drew alongside. "You're sure you'll come no farther?"

"Ernaut and I must leave now, if we want to return to Leaside before nightfall.

"Won't you come and rest?" Verona asked. "You must be tired."

"I'm quite well," Arlette replied.

"You had no need to accompany us to Greywell," Verona continued. "I have Seaton."

Arlette smiled at the love in Verona's voice. "Seaton will make you a fine husband."

"What of *your* husband?"

Clear gray eyes focused on Arlette, and she averted her gaze.

"Ernaut, it's time we left."

Verona reached out and took her hand. "You owe me an answer, Arlette. Why did you insist on accompanying us to Greywell?"

"I wished to see it one last time."

"And...my brother?"

Heat flooded her cheeks. "I...I wish to assure myself he is well, that is all," she said. "Now, go to him. He needs you, and loves you—more than he ever loved me."

"I think you're wrong," Verona said. "But you must understand that yourself. I only hope that when you do, it's not too late."

Seaton spurred his horse forward, and Verona followed.

Arlette shifted uncomfortably in the saddle as they approached the gates. Seaton's voice rang out clear and true, and the gates opened to reveal a lone sentry.

Then another man appeared, and Arlette suppressed a cry.

He bore a slight limp, and his right hand was still bound—but he stood on the threshold, tall and broad shouldered, and her heart clenched with need. But she couldn't go back—he'd broken her heart once, and she had no wish to risk heartbreak again.

A deep voice cried out and he stumbled toward his sister. Verona dismounted and he fell to his knees as she embraced him. Tears stung Arlette's eyes as his voice, broken with emotion, echoed off the walls of his home.

Arlette wiped her tears, then curled her hands around her mount's reins.

"Come, Ernaut," she said. "My family's sins have been atoned. It's time for us to go."

# CHAPTER 39

*Greywell Castle, England, Summer 1087*

"YOUR SWORDSMANSHIP IS MUCH IMPROVED, my lord. It's good to see you on the field again"

Orson eyed Seaton with suspicion. Did the young whelp seek to flatter him?

But, in one aspect, he was right—it felt good to hold a sword again, even if most of his men eyed him with suspicion, now he fought left-handed.

Only yesterday he'd caught one of the squires crossing himself as he'd watched Orson pick up his sword. But what did they expect? If he were to survive in the world, then he had to learn to fight—and he could no longer use his right hand. De Villiers had broken every bone in it.

*De Villiers...*

Laughter drifted across the air, and he looked up to see Lillian skipping across the field, clutching Verona's hand.

His beloved sister had returned, and he thanked the Almighty every day. But, to his shame, he often found himself wishing that another had returned instead—the woman who completed his soul.

*She*...was not spoken of, and those who dared utter her name in his presence risked a beating. But she occupied his thoughts, and dreams. His soul yearned for her, but he'd destroyed her. To look upon her again would only serve to remind him of his sins.

"My love!"

Seaton sheathed his sword as Verona drew near, and they embraced. She belonged to him, now, not Orson. It was Seaton to whom she looked when she entered the great hall—Seaton she turned to when in need.

And Seaton she'd chosen to wed.

Seeing their evident happiness, Orson had no choice but to consent to the marriage. He would forever be grateful to Seaton for bringing her back, but their impending wedding only heightened his melancholy—their happiness a brutal reminder of what he had lost.

Seaton drew Verona to him and they kissed. A cheer rose up from the watching men-at-arms.

*God's blood, man—must you manhandle her like some rutting boor!*

An audible gasp rippled through the onlookers. Verona freed herself from Seaton's embrace, placed her hands on her hips, and turned her hostile gaze toward Orson.

*Horseshit*—he'd said that aloud.

He gestured toward a servant who stood nearby, holding a pitcher of wine and a goblet.

"Come here."

The servant nodded, filled a goblet and handed it to Orson. He took it, drained the contents, then wiped his mouth with the back of his hand.

"Brother, you're a boor," Verona said. "A miserable boor whose temper is only softened with wine—*so* much wine!"

"Verona," Orson began, "I..."

"In fact," she interrupted, "our cellar will soon be empty if you continue to drain its reserves single-handed."

How dare she!

"You speak out of turn," he growled.

"I've not spoken enough," she retorted. "It's time I did."

From where had his once-gentle sister found such resolve? Perhaps her ordeal at the hands of Fulbert de Villiers had revealed her strength—she'd grown a backbone of iron.

"Cursed woman! You should know your place. *All* women should know their place." He gestured toward the servant with his goblet. "Refill me—damn you!"

A hand slapped his face, sending the goblet flying.

"Rona!" Seaton cried.

"Oh, Seaton, be quiet!" Verona snapped. "My brother's a fool. *I'm* not afraid to say it, even if you cannot. Why do we not speak of her?"

"Speak of who?" Orson asked, rubbing his cheek.

Verona let out a huff. "You try my patience," she said. "Do you think that because we're forbidden to say her name in your presence—we don't speak of her when you're not there to spoil our pleasure?"

Sweet Lord—his sister had turned into a hellion!

"You know nothing of her," he growled. "Be silent."

A sharp crack exploded in his face as her hand struck his other cheek. "Of course I know about her!" she cried. "I know *everything* about your wife—including how you treated her. Who do you think brought me back to you? You believe Seaton did it, on his own?"

"Don't try my patience," Orson snarled. He gestured to the servant. "Bring more wine—to the solar."

He strode toward the castle building.

"Drinking won't solve the matter." Verona's voice persisted in following him. "Neither will shouting at every man and woman in the household."

"Seaton, be a man and control your woman!" he roared. "Tell her not to meddle in affairs that don't concern her."

"You stubborn ox!" Verona cried. "If you wish to wallow in misery and self-pity, then do so—I care not. But if you don't want to die a lonely and bitter man, then know this: the key to your happiness resides at Leaside—the estate you destroyed in my name."

He reached the solar just as Elvia arrived, carrying a flagon of wine. She set it on a table then scurried out, and he slammed the door after her, leaving himself alone, with only the wine for company.

Curse his meddling sister!

He fumbled at the laces of his tunic, but only succeeded in tightening the knots. With a bellow of frustration he yanked the material, tearing it as he pulled the garment over his head, throwing it on the floor. He bent down to remove his boots, and lost his balance. Balling his hand into a fist, he slammed it onto the stone floor.

Curse them all!

And curse *her*—for abandoning him. For not returning to his side, where she belonged.

And for letting him believe she was dead.

He closed his eyes, and once more saw a pair of green eyes, bringing him back from the brink when he'd thought all was lost—soothing his body, and easing his pain.

"Arlette..."

Her name, whispered on his lips, unleashed his pent-up tide of despair.

"My Arlette..."

How he craved her touch—those soft lips, the way she willingly, and eagerly, opened her body to him when they made love, and the little mewling cries she made when he gave her pleasure. She'd said she loved him. But she chose not to return.

*Can you blame her, after what you did?*

He cursed the treacherous voice inside his head, but he couldn't forget the utter desolation in her eyes, the last time he'd seen her.

How she must hate him!

Yet, despite that, she'd brought his beloved sister back.

*The key to your happiness resides at Leaside...*

Verona's voice echoed in his mind.

He should march on Leaside and claim what was his—return her to his home, and his bed.

But he couldn't. To raid Leaside—to forcibly remove her—however much she belonged to him by right...

Such a deed was unthinkable. He'd done it before, driven by

vengeance, and he'd destroyed her family. He couldn't do that to her again.

Perhaps the best way to show his love was to give her the freedom she craved, and let her be.

But there was no harm in going there, one last time.

Just to catch a glimpse of her.

*Leaside Hall, Summer 1087*

Arlette stretched, then rubbed her lower back. Her body ached from the inside. But there was little point complaining to Esme—she knew what her old nursemaid would say.

*A true de Villiers. You didn't give your poor mama a moment's peace while she carried you—nor after you were born.*

Tossing aside her embroidery, she picked up her sword and ventured outside. The gardens burst with summer colors—bright blooms glowing in the sunlight. Closing her eyes, she tipped her face upward, relishing the sun's warmth on her skin.

The estate flourished. Garret had arrived from Villiers and she'd sent him to Seaforth to rebuild the community that Fulbert had destroyed. In time, the name of de Villiers would be spoken with pride, not hatred.

And the family legacy would be safe in Guillaume's hands—he already showed signs of handling responsibility well.

She followed the sound of wooden swords clashing, and entered a courtyard where Ernaut was training a number of squires—young men from neighboring estates—in readiness for the forthcoming tournament at the Wildstorm estate.

"Lady Arlette!" Ernaut cried. "What are you doing?"

The noise stopped, and the men watched her approach. One of the youngest among them—a boy not much older than Guillaume—glanced at her swollen belly, then lowered his gaze.

"I'm restless, Ernaut," she said. "I wanted to feel my sword in my hand."

He rolled his eyes like an exasperated parent. "I've already told you, lady—you're not fit to fight."

"Because I'm a woman?"

"No—because you're nearing your confinement!"

A ripple of murmurs broke out among the men. Arlette gestured toward the youngest, whose face was flushed scarlet. "Will *you* fight me?"

"Don't you dare!" Ernaut roared, as the boy moved forward. "If any of you even thinks about obliging my lady's whims, I'll have you dismembered."

"Then *you* must fight me, Ernaut," she said.

"God's blood, woman!" he cried. "I'll drag you from this courtyard in chains if you continue. Is there no man who can tame you? Didn't your husband…"

She stepped toward him and he broke off, the color draining from his face.

*Your husband...*

Orson was conspicuous by the fact that he was never mentioned. But the memory of him lurked in every corner. Arlette saw him in Esme's eyes, and in the hushed whispers of the household, including the new servants Esme had employed, who looked at Arlette with curiosity—the lord's sister, heavy with child.

Ernaut raised his hand in supplication. "My lady, I meant no offence. I'm merely concerned for your welfare. Your brother commanded me to ensure you rested."

"As he commands us all," she said, gritting her teeth.

"He is lord here," Ernaut said. "Go back inside."

Aye—Guillaume was lord, and by rights, she must defer to him. He took his position as head of the family seriously. He conspired with Esme to ensure Arlette was made to rest, and she always found a servant at her elbow, ready to undertake any physical task she tried to accomplish.

It was as if she were a prisoner again, her freedom curtailed—but not by the Saxon warrior who'd stolen her in the night and captured her, body and soul.

Sighing, she returned inside.

Curse Ernaut for reminding her of—*him*!

The previous night, her dreams had been plagued, once more, by a pair of clear gray eyes. Strong hands played her body like a lute, eliciting sweet music from her lips. But she woke to a cold, empty bed, her body aching for his touch, her breasts tingling with anticipation and hope.

And, even now, in the rationality of daylight, a hungry heat pooled between her thighs—a hunger that would never again be satisfied.

# CHAPTER 40

The summer sun illuminated the stones of Leaside—the building that dominated the horizon. As Orson rode toward the building, he glimpsed flashes of light—the glint of armor as a sentry moved to and fro on the battlements.

The building that he'd largely ignored after he'd rebuilt it—for her—now showed signs of life. Wisps of smoke rose from the surrounding village, the lowing of cattle echoed across the afternoon air, and he caught the distant sound of a blacksmith hammering.

Unwilling to be seen, he veered off the road, and picked his way across the rougher ground. The land stretched ahead, then sloped down toward a small copse of trees, which shivered in the breeze.

A lone rider came into view—moving across the land at full gallop. The horse increased its pace, then veered toward the trees. A distant shriek confirmed Orson's suspicions. The rider had lost control of his mount.

Orson spurred his horse after the rider. The other animal was no match for his warhorse, and he drew alongside the rider before they reached the edge of the copse. He grasped the other horse's reins. The animal, needing only a strong, assured hand, responded immediately, and Orson steered his horse against the other, until both animals slowed to a halt.

"What were you about, you fool," he cried, "riding a horse beyond your skill!"

The rider—a mere boy—shook with fear, but he raised his chin, and gave Orson a haughty look.

"Who are you to speak to me thus?"

"Someone who knows a runaway horse when I see one," Orson said. "You're fortunate I caught you when I did."

"I was in no danger," the boy retorted. "I can do what I like with my horse. Let me go!"

The boy tugged at the reins, but Orson held firm, and gestured toward the copse.

"Look where you were headed!"

Beyond the copse, the ground fell away, almost vertically, toward a river.

"Your horse could have fallen and injured itself," he said. "You might have been killed."

The boy looked sulky, and a knot of anger curled in Orson's gut.

"Have you ever had to give a horse a quick death when it's broken a leg?" he cried. "If you wish to risk your own neck, that's your concern, but how dare you treat the life of your horse so lightly! God's teeth, lad, I ought to flay your backside for such recklessness. I've a mind to take you to your father and insist he beats you."

"My parents are dead."

"Then, who's responsible for you?"

"My sister." The boy's eyes widened and the veneer of bravado crumbled. "Please, sir—don't tell her! She told me not to take my new horse out unaccompanied, though she rides out alone each morning."

"You should listen to her," Orson said. "But, if you let me escort you home, now, I'll tell her nothing of your foolishness. Where do you live?"

Tears pooled in the boy's eyes, as the effects of danger seeped into his consciousness.

"At the castle yonder," he said in a small voice. He released the reins, letting Orson take control, and they set off toward the building that dominated the skyline.

Leaside.

As they neared the building, the boy began to sniff, and a tear rolled down his face.

"My sister will be so angry with me!"

"Let that be a lesson to you, young man," Orson said. "If you love your sister, you must do as she says."

"I love her more than anyone in the world," the boy replied, "though I wish she wouldn't always tell me what to do. Sometimes I love my horse more."

Orson smiled at the boy's frankness—the honesty all children possessed until life taught them not to trust. "I'm sure she only tells you what to do because she loves you."

"Aye, she does. Were she a man she'd be a knight. But I'm glad she's not. If she were, I wouldn't be lord."

Clear green eyes focused on Orson, sending a jolt of recognition through his veins.

"Have you lived here all your life?" he asked.

"Aye," the boy said, "though my cousin took me away last summer. My cousin was a bad man. There was a lady there also."

Orson drew in a sharp breath. "Is that so?"

"I wanted to take her for a wife," the boy said, "but she loved another. My sister says she'll help me find a wife when I come of age."

The boy straightened his stance. "I'm head of my family," he said, pride in his voice. "My sister thinks she can tell me what to do, but she needs my protection." He gave Orson a sidelong glance. "Don't tell her I said so."

He lowered his voice. "Her husband treated her cruelly, and broke her heart. She thinks I've not seen, but she bears scars on her back from a beating, and marks on her wrist where he put her in chains. She cries when she thinks I'm not looking. I want to find her a new husband and make her happy again. Would *you* like to meet her?"

The boy's words tore at his soul, and his gut twisted with shame.

How could he face her after what he'd done? He did not deserve her—and she didn't deserve to be reminded of the pain he'd caused her.

"Perhaps another time," he said. "It's late, and I must return home.

"Oh, very well."

"What is your name, lad?" Orson asked, out of propriety rather than necessity.

"Guillaume de Villiers, at your service," the boy replied. "To whom am I indebted?"

"A stranger who bids you do as your sister tells you next time."

He handed the reins back to the boy. "Go straight to the stables."

"Aye, sir, I will."

"I'll bid you good day, young Guillaume."

The boy gave a stiff bow, then urged his mount forward, and disappeared through the gates in the bailey wall. Once he learned a little self-control, he'd be a fine horseman.

Orson dismounted and approached the wall on foot. He told himself that he wanted to be assured of the boy's safe return. Voices drifted through the air, and he crept closer.

Then he froze. His heart clenched and he stifled a cry.

One of the voices—it was a voice he knew, and loved.

What sweet joy to hear her voice! Even in anger, it ignited a flare of need, deep within his body.

"I care not what you say, Guillaume! I've told you not to speak to strangers!"

"Lettie, I've seen ten summers…"

"Which means you're still a child! God forgive me, Guillaume, sometimes I think I should have Ernaut beat some sense into you."

"Then I'll have him horsewhipped. I'm his lord and he must do as I say."

"Until you come of age, young man, *you* will do as *I* say. You were lucky this stranger wasn't a brigand."

"He was a lord, I'm sure of it, Lettie. I thought he'd make a fine husband for you, but he wouldn't come and meet you."

"Guillaume! How many times must I tell you I'm not looking for a husband."

"'Tis just as well. No man could endure a dragon such as you."

Orson heard a deep sigh, and his heart clenched at the pain in her voice. "Oh, Guillaume! You're the most precious thing in the world to me, can't you see that? You're all I have left, and I don't want to leave you."

Guillaume didn't reply.

Then she spoke again. Though her voice was brighter, it held an undercurrent of despair, only audible to those who knew her well.

"Shall we see what Mylla has for you in the kitchen? What you need after your adventure is one of her sweet tarts."

"Ooh yes!" Guillaume cried. "But I still hope my new friend will visit."

"As do I," she laughed, "if only so I can apologize for your forwardness."

"I only want you to be happy again, Lettie," the boy said. "Like we were before—before Fulbert, before Mama and Papa died."

"I know, sweet boy."

"You deserve a good husband after what—*he*—did to you."

"Let us not speak of it," she said. "We have much to look forward to, you and I—only pain comes from dwelling on the past."

The voices faded, leaving Orson alone, standing in the shadow of the wall. Salty tears stung his eyes. Were they tears of shame? Or merely self-pity?

Young Guillaume was right. Arlette deserved to be happy—happier than he'd ever made her. How could he impose on her peace? She'd lost her family, at his hands, while his sister lived on. The brother she'd striven to find and protect—the brother Orson had once vowed to hunt down in his quest for vengeance—was now home, safe, at Leaside. The boy was her weakness. Others had exploited her love for him to entrap her, leading Orson to believe her a traitor, and break her heart.

However much he wanted her, however much he needed her—loved her—she was no longer his. He'd lost all claim on her—not his claim by the law of the land—but a greater law—that of basic right and wrong.

He made his way back to his horse, mounted it, and set off for Greywell Castle. Verona was right. The key to his happiness—his Arlette—lived at Leaside, and the key to her happiness was in finding peace.

But not with him.

THE DATE of Verona and Seaton's wedding dawned fair and bright. The villagers had lined the road for the procession, cheering Verona to the chapel and back, as she rode alongside her new husband.

It should be a day for joy, but Orson was unable to shake his melancholy—or the memory of his own bride, with her intense emerald gaze, which concealed the fear of her wedding night. He closed his eyes, bringing forth the image of her face when he showed her the pleasures a man and woman could share. But he would never find such pleasure again.

He waved a servant over to refill his cup. The wine might numb the pain, but it also worsened his temper. His stomach churned with envy at the sight of the happy couple. Verona's face flushed a delicate shade of rose at something Seaton said, and she smiled back, turning her head to expose her throat. The jewels in her necklace glittered in the light.

Unfamiliar jewels.

Rather than wear the necklace Orson had presented to her yesterday, she wore another—a delicate chain with a pendant—a single emerald that caught the candlelight and glowed, as if from within.

Verona had spurned his gift.

"What is that around your throat?" he demanded.

Verona and Seaton exchanged a glance.

"A gift," she said, avoiding his gaze.

"Whose gift do you choose to wear over mine?"

She opened her mouth to reply, but Seaton placed a hand on her arm, and shook his head.

Acid bubbled in Orson's throat, and he curled his hand into a fist.

"Whose gift, damn it!"

"Brother, you're in your cups—*again*," Verona said. "Let us not discuss it now. Today is a happy day."

"Then tell me who gave you that necklace."

Seaton shook his head, "Rona, don't..."

"Let him be told," she said, her gray eyes darkening. "Your wife sent it—she who should be with us, to share our joy. The woman who, due to your foolishness, you let slip through your fingers."

"Hold your tongue!" Orson growled, the wine thickening his tongue.

"I shall not!" she cried. "I'm answerable to my husband, not my brother."

"Silence your wife, Seaton," Orson said. "What kind of man are you?"

"More of a man than you, Lord Wulfson," Seaton said, "for I can see past my pride."

*God's teeth*—did Seaton defy him?

"I've heard enough," Orson said. "She never loved me."

"You fool!" Seaton cried. "Do you know what she said when she joined us in battle to free you from Lord Fulbert? She declared that there's nothing more dangerous than a woman fighting for the man she loves."

"Then, why is she not here—why has she deserted me?"

"You betrayed her trust," Seaton said.

"What of you, Seaton? You betrayed her also—you thought her a traitor."

"Aye, but I made peace with her. I resolved to earn her forgiveness, no matter how long it took. And earn it I did. If you loved her, you would do the same."

A small hand tugged at Orson's sleeve, and he turned to see Lillian staring up at him.

"Papa, please listen to Seaton."

"Disrespectful child! Do you want to be punished?"

Lillian slipped her hand in his, "I want Mama Arlette."

"You must learn, child, that we cannot always have what we want." He snatched his hand free, and Lillian burst into tears.

"Brother, please!" Verona cried. "Today is a day for celebrating—for family. Don't spoil it."

"Then I'll retire to the solar, and give you leave to celebrate my absence." He scraped his chair back and nodded to a servant, who rushed to fetch a fresh flagon of wine, understanding his order without needing further instruction.

When Orson reached the solar, he kicked open the door, barely missing the servant who scuttled out of his way. He strode toward the table by the fireplace and picked up the flagon of wine and began to pour, his hands shaking. Wine spilled onto the table, an angry red stain to match his temper. With a roar he flung the flask against the wall. It disintegrated on impact, sending shards flying, and a sharp sting of pain sliced into his hand. Outside, the strains of music vibrated in the air as the entertainment began.

"Oh, Orson—what have you done to your hand?" a voice cried.

Verona had followed him.

"Shouldn't you be with your husband?"

"It seems I must first tend to my troublesome brother."

Soft footsteps approached, and she took his hand, removing the shard of earthenware embedded in the flesh. Then she opened a box—one of the boxes Arlette had prepared—and drew out a bandage and small phial. "When I've treated this wound," she said, "you must return to Leaside and bring back your wife."

She shook out a drop of tincture and Orson winced as it fell onto the wound.

"I went there," he said. "She has no wish to return."

"You saw her?"

"I heard her—she was speaking to her brother. She said I broke her heart, and she wishes to forget."

Verona wound the bandage around his hand. "So you're going to surrender?"

"What would you have me do?" He asked. "Drag her back in chains?"

Verona shook her head. "No, brother, you must *court* her. And don't give up. A warrior must show tenacity when engaging in battle to win his lady's heart."

"She has no reason to return," he said.

"Except, perhaps, the greatest reason of all."

"Which is?"

"Love. Her love for Lillian—who misses her more than she dares admit—and her love for you."

She secured the bandage with a knot, then caressed his fingers. "She's never stopped loving you, but she's a proud woman—proud and stubborn, not unlike someone else I know. A lady must be wooed. And, besides…" She broke off, colored, and lowered her gaze.

"Besides what?"

"There's another to consider."

"You mean Lillian?"

"I mean the child that is yet to come."

"The child…" he whispered.

A child…

His child.

"Aye," Verona said. "Your wife is with child."

His heart leaped with hope. A child to love—as well as his wife…

"H-how long?"

Verona smiled. "She'll be nearing her confinement. She was carrying your child when she brought me home. She carried your child when she rode into battle to free you. What greater act can a woman commit, to demonstrate her love?"

Aye—what greater act, indeed! No man could compare.

Then his gut twisted with shame, and tore at his soul.

She must have been carrying his child when her cousin abducted her—when she'd fought to return to Orson.

And when he'd thrown her into the dungeon.

"Why did she never tell me?"

A voice whispered in his head.

*Because you would not have believed her.*

"Oh brother!" Verona cried. "How you try my patience! If you want answers, you must ask the right person. But if you wallow here in self-pity for too long, you'll miss the birth of your child."

His child.

"I'm going to be a father."

"Aye." Verona kissed him on the cheek. "Sleep off the wine, then go to her. But have a care. Don't expect her to welcome you with open arms. Her pride almost matches yours. You'll need to prove yourself worthy.

Perhaps the greatest battle of his life lay before him—a battle with only one thing at stake. Not his life, his estates, or his pride.

But his heart.

# CHAPTER 41

*Leaside Hall, Summer 1087*

Orson circled the perimeter of the building, his breath sending clouds into the cold morning air. The sun had not long risen—bright orange rays stretched across the landscape, illuminating the dewdrops that glistened like diamonds in the grass.

The gates opened, and a solitary figure rode out on a gray palfrey.

His heart stirred in recognition. What had Guillaume told him?

*She rides out alone each morning.*

Heavy with child, she defied convention, and wore no veil, her hair hanging in two thick braids. Her ripe little body was visible through her gown—full breasts ready for motherhood, and the swell of her belly—a belly that carried his child. In the sunlight, her hair shone like gold. She stroked her belly, her full, rosy lips curving with gentle pleasure.

When had he ever given her occasion to smile so contentedly?

Once clear of the building, she urged her mount into a canter, steering the animal toward the copse of trees where Orson had encountered her brother. He spurred his horse on, in her wake.

She looked untamed and free—a wild woman, passionately loyal, and fiercely protective of those she loved. She had loved him, once, and he'd let her slip through his fingers.

But no more.

He closed the gap between them, and his body thrummed with anticipation at the memory of the last time he'd chased her down after she'd defied him in front of his men. When he'd caught her, she had fought him, but her eyes had shone with excitement. Her cries of passion when he tamed her over his knee were almost his undoing—and when she'd writhed in pleasure at his touch, he was enslaved.

He belonged to her, as much as she belonged to him. And he needed her—now.

"Arlette!" he cried.

She reined her horse, and turned, but the animal stumbled, then reared up. With a scream, she fell to the ground.

"Dear God—Arlette!" He dismounted and ran toward her.

She lay on her side, body shaking, hands curled into fists. Then she let out a wail of agony that curdled his blood, and a dark stain spread across her skirts.

He tried to lift her into his arms.

"No!" she screamed, pulling away.

"Stop struggling!" he cried. "Let me help you."

Eyes closed, face contorted in agony, she drew in a shuddering breath and screamed again. Then her struggles ceased. She had passed out.

Cradling her body, he sprinted toward his horse.

"Forgive me," he said, hauling her over the saddle, then he mounted his horse and spurred the animal into a gallop back toward the building. His wife's swollen body jolted against the saddle but she remained unconscious.

"Stay with me, my love," he urged, "I'm here."

As he approached the building, he let out a roar. "Let me in—I have your mistress!"

The gates opened and he carried his wife toward the entrance, where two sentries stood, swords drawn.

"Let me through," he demanded. "Your mistress is in pain."

The taller sentry held out his arms and spoke in a marked French accent. "Give her to me."

"No," Orson replied. "Let me pass."

"Who are you, *monsieur*, to make such demands?"

"I'm her husband, damn you!" Orson cried. "Do you want her death on your conscience? Tell me where to take her. Now!"

"What's happening, Ernaut?" A boy appeared behind the sentries, and Orson recognized Guillaume. He smiled at Orson, then let out a cry.

"Lettie! Ernaut—let this man in."

"But Lady Arlette said…"

"I care not," the boy said. "I am your master, and this man is my friend. Do as I say."

The sentries stepped aside, and Guillaume gestured to Orson. "Follow me."

The boy led him toward the upper floor of the building, shouting for help. An old woman appeared at the top of the staircase, and Orson recognized Esme, his wife's old nursemaid.

"Maude!" she shrieked. "Fetch the women—the babe comes!"

She flung open a door to a bedchamber. "Bring her in."

Orson carried Arlette inside and placed her on the bed, as a number of women ran into the chamber. She was regaining consciousness, whimpering as her body shuddered. While the women fussed around her, Esme shooed Orson and Guillaume out of the chamber.

"'Tis no place for men," she grumbled. Then she looked up, her gaze focusing on Orson for the first time.

"My lord! You shouldn't be here. You must leave."

"I want him to stay," Guillaume said, clutching Orson's tunic.

Esme raised her eyebrows. "Do you know who this man is, little master?"

A scream came from the chamber, and Guillaume tightened his grip on Orson's tunic.

"I want to see Lettie!"

"Nay, little master," Esme said. "You must wait until she is safely delivered of her child. Go to your room—she'll be hours yet."

Orson took the boy's hand. "I'll take care of him, Mistress Esme."

"Tell him who you are, sir, before he entrusts you with his care."

"I'm a friend," Orson said. "That's all he need know."

She folded her arms and hardened her expression.

"Very well," he sighed. "Master Guillaume—my name is Orson Greywell, Lord Wulfson. Your sister is my wife—and the child she carries is mine."

Guillaume's eyes widened, then his face twisted with distress.

"You're the one who treated her so cruelly!" he cried. "What have I done? I promised I'd protect her, and I've let you in!" He fisted his hands and pummeled Orson's chest. Orson remained still, and weathered the blows.

"Guillaume—stop!" Esme cried.

"Nay," Orson said. "Let him defend his sister."

Guillaume's blows grew weak, then he collapsed against Orson, sobbing.

Orson stroked the boy's head.

"Do not exhaust yourself, young sir," he said. "You must be strong for your sister."

"She mustn't see you here! You have to leave."

Orson took the boy by the shoulders and crouched until their eyes were level.

"You said I was your friend, Master Guillaume, and I am. I love your sister very much—and, like you, I want her safe and well."

"Y-you love her?" the boy sniffed.

"Aye," Orson replied, drawing the boy into his arms. He looked up to see Esme staring at him.

"I have always loved her," he whispered, "though I was a fool not to admit it. I came to tell her before it was too late."

Esme's expression softened, then she nodded.

"Come, little master," Orson said. "Let us wait together."

The de Villiers coat of arms adorned the walls of the solar, together with the light touches of a woman—the vases of flowers Arlette had so often brought to the solar at Greywell. Not long after a servant had brought them a tray of bread and wine, the door opened to reveal a woman, heavy with child. Orson almost didn't recognize her. Unlike the pale, thin creature he'd known at Greywell Castle, her face glowed with a healthy bloom.

Orson rose to his feet, and bowed.

"Lady Edith."

"Join us," Guillaume said. "Lettie's having her baby."

She hesitated, and Orson nodded.

"Please do," he said. "It's good to see you, Lady Edith. I trust you're well?"

"Aye." She took a step forward. "Lord Wulfson, I…I had no idea what Ulferth…"

Orson lifted his hand. "It's in the past. You should not be held accountable for your husband's treachery."

"We're going to find her a new husband," Guillaume said excitedly, "Sir Alain of Wildstorm has paid several visits, has he not?"

"Hush, Guillaume!" Edith admonished the boy, but her cheeks glowed, and she gave a shy smile.

"Are *you* frightened of childbirth?" Guillaume asked, reaching for a piece of bread.

Edith shook her head. "I know there will be pain, but I do not fear it. Your sister will be well, little man. The first child always takes the longest to arrive."

The day wore on, but though Guillaume sent repeated messages, demanding news of Arlette, still the baby had not come. As night fell, Edith retired to her chamber, while Guillaume curled up asleep on a chair.

Shortly before dawn, the door opened and Esme appeared. Guillaume stirred, and rubbed his eyes. Then he sat up.

"Has the babe come?"

Esme shook her head, and cold fingers caressed Orson's neck at the expression on her face.

"What's the matter, old woman?"

Esme wiped her eyes. "My lady grows weak. I've sent for the priest."

"No!" Orson leaped to his feet, pushed past the old woman, and sprinted to the birthing chamber, Guillaume at his heels.

Maude stood in the doorway, her eyes filled with tears. "Oh, little master!" she cried. "You shouldn't be here." She eyed Orson. "Neither should you. This is no place for a man—or a child."

"I care not," Guillaume said. "Brother, go in—you can help her."

"She'll not want me near her, Guillaume."

"It's not about what she wants," the boy replied. "You must do your duty!"

A warm, plump hand touched Orson's arm.

"The little master is right," Esme said. "If you truly love her, then now's your chance to show it."

Finally, he understood. Strength came not from retribution, or glory in battle. It came from love. Weak was the man who refused to acknowledge his love. The old woman was right. This might be his only chance to show how much he loved her—before it was too late.

Arlette lay on the bed surrounded by maidservants, who parted to let him approach. Orson kneeled beside the bed and took her hand. Beads of perspiration clung to her face, glistening in the candlelight.

Her eyes were closed. Her body looked lifeless, then she let out a low moan as a spasm shook her.

"She must push," Maude sobbed, "but she's so weak, now."

Orson squeezed her hand. "Arlette," he whispered. "My love, 'tis I. Orson."

Could she hear him?

Her eyes opened, their expression resigned, as if she had already accepted death. Then, she blinked, and he saw a glimmer of recognition in their emerald depths. A shard of pain dug into his flesh as she gripped his hand.

Then she threw her head back and cried out, as her body shuddered.

"That's it my love," he said. "Fight for our child."

"*My* child..."

Her body shook again, and her face contorted with pain. The tendons in her neck protruded, while she shrieked through gritted teeth.

"*Mon Dieu!*" Esme cried. "The baby comes!"

Arlette bared her teeth, a savage tigress warding off her adversary.

"You'll not take my child from me," she snarled. "I shall give birth to a fine son, who'll stay with *me*." She dug her fingers into his hand, and focused her gaze on him. "Do you hear me, Orson Greywell!"

"Aye, my love. I hear you."

He closed his eyes, praying for her life—offering the Almighty his own in exchange. She let out another cry, which grew in intensity until it became a high-pitched wail. When her grip slackened, he opened his eyes.

Body wracked with exhaustion, she lay silent, but the wails continued, punctuated by the women's voices.

"Oh—*look* at her!"

"Isn't she a beauty?"

Arlette had given birth to a daughter.

# CHAPTER 42

Every bone in Arlette's body ached—almost as if her dream had been real—a dream where she'd fought Fulbert and he speared her belly, splitting it open. Then, strong hands pulled her from the battlefield, and a pair of pale gray eyes urged her to fight, to victory.

She opened her eyes, but those looking back were brown, not gray.

"She wakes!"

Gentle hands lifted her into a sitting position.

"Am I dead?" she whispered. "I heard someone call for the priest."

Someone squeezed her hand. "No, lady, you are most certainly alive." Esme's voice spoke, thick with tears. "You have a daughter."

"A daughter?"

Arlette blinked, and Esme's face swam into focus.

"Aye, my lady—a daughter."

Esme waved her hand toward the door. "Bring her in."

Maude entered, holding a bundle, and she placed it in Arlette's arms.

A tiny creature looked up at her—dark blue eyes in a softly rounded face, with pink cheeks and a perfect rosebud of a mouth.

Arlette ran a fingertip along the baby's face, following a line down her arm until she reached a perfect miniature replica of a fist.

The child uncurled her fingers and wrapped them around Arlette's finger.

"Hello—my sweet little tiger cub."

A rush of love flooded her body. Anger, revenge, redemption—they all meant nothing compared to the new life she'd brought into the world. She might be able to defy men, and wield a sword, but she had no defense against the child in her arms.

Arlette was no longer a warrior. She was a mother.

~

"I'M glad to see you recovered, Lettie."

Guillaume threw another log on the fire, then approached Arlette and placed a fur over her shoulders.

"Are you warm enough?"

"Stop fussing!" Arlette laughed.

Dear Guillaume had taken his position as uncle to heart, and he was anxious to prove his worth.

"What would I do without my brother to take care of me?"

"Esme kept me from you for too long," Guillaume said. "She made me wait two days until I could see you. I'll be glad when I come of age—I won't have to be ordered about by women anymore. I'll have a wife to order about instead."

Arlette laughed again. "Your wife will rule over *you* even if you don't know it."

"It's good to hear you laugh, Lettie. Are you happy?"

She smiled. "I have a beautiful daughter, and a loving brother. I'm very happy here—but when you marry, I'll go to Villiers with little Ursula. Your poor wife won't want to be plagued by your dragon of a sister."

"Not a dragon, Lettie—a tigress."

The door creaked open and Esme appeared.

"Your guest has arrived, Master Guillaume. Shall I admit him?"

Arlette drew the fur close. "A—guest? I'm in no condition to receive guests."

"He's my friend," Guillaume said, pride in his voice, "the one I told you about—who saved me when my horse bolted."

"Then invite him in, so I can thank him."

"Come in, sir!" Guillaume cried.

Arlette lifted her head, and smiled in greeting as the visitor walked in. Then her heart clenched in recognition.

Orson stood before her.

He was a shadow of the powerful warlord who had once swept her off her feet and taken her captive. Dark stubble adorned his skin. His eyes looked hollow in his face, the once-clear gray dulled and bloodshot.

He moved closer then stopped, as if uncertain of his fate. She glanced over his body and her gaze wandered to his hands. His left hand rested on his belt, but the right—almost concealed by the sleeve of his tunic—was twisted and deformed.

"Arlette," he whispered, "don't turn me away."

He glanced at the crib, where the baby slept, and a wave of panic rippled through her.

"You've come to take my child!" she cried. "I won't let you—please leave."

"Lettie!" Guillaume cried. "Lord Wulfson is our guest. He saved both our lives, so you owe him an audience, at least."

"Don't speak nonsense," she said.

"No, Lettie—*I'm* lord here, and you must listen to what I say," Guillaume said. "Lord Wulfson stayed with you, during your confinement, when you'd given up. At the very least you must thank him."

Orson's gaze fell on Guillaume. His eyes shone with pride—and something else.

Love.

Did he care for Guillaume? Perhaps if he had returned for her—and begged forgiveness—she could bring herself to forgive him.

She held out her hand, her flesh calling to his, and he cupped her face in his hands, and brought his mouth close to hers. His warm breath caressed her lips and her body responded, senses coming to life at the intoxicating scent of man and the anticipation of the taste of him.

Then his mouth covered hers and his tongue demanded entrance that she willingly granted, mouths and lips entwining in a sensual dance. Her body began to hum with life, as if it had been sleeping for months, and sweet warmth pooled inside her center.

Then he withdrew, and the heat within her was replaced by a sharp sense of loss.

"I shall consider myself thanked," he said. "Come back with me, Arlette. Return to Greywell."

The time had come for him to beg forgiveness. And she would forgive him.

"Why should I return?" She looked up expectantly.

His brow furrowed, and he gestured toward the crib. "You're my wife, and it's your duty. That child needs a name."

*That child?*

"Is that all?" she asked.

"Is that not enough?" he replied. "You would not have her called a bastard—to live in disgrace, would you? Not when she has a father."

She closed her eyes to stem the tears. What a fool she'd been, for expecting him to show humility! To him she was mere chattel—a slave to be incarcerated within his home, furnish him with children, and bow to his supremacy.

How she had yearned to hear him declare his love—to fall onto his knees and beg forgiveness! But what had he said, months before?

*If you had a heart for me, I would break it.*

He'd spoken the truth—she loved him, and he'd broken her heart.

"Will you grant me one wish, Orson?" she asked.

Hope sparked in his eyes. "Gladly."

"Leave—and never return."

The hope died, then he gave a stiff bow.

"As the lady wishes."

He turned, and exited the chamber.

"Wait!" Guillaume cried, running after him.

Esme folded her arms, and shook her head.

"That was not well done, lady," she said. "It took a lot for him to ask you to return."

"You heard what he said," Arlette retorted. "He only wants my child."

"*His* child."

"Mine!" Arlette cried. "I carried her in my body while he treated me like a traitor—and had me chained. He broke my heart, yet he acts as if he did nothing."

"You want him to love you?"

"Aye!" Arlette's voice caught in her throat. "How can I forgive him, if he feels no remorse?"

"'Tis not a man's province to show remorse," Esme said. "A warrior such as he will never admit fault, or weakness. You cannot expect him to."

"Then I won't go back!"

Esme frowned, as she'd always done when Arlette had lost her temper as a child when unable to get her own way.

"Then you'll be unhappy, my lady, and die alone." She shook her head. "You always were a stubborn child, but I prayed that when you grew up, you'd learn reason. But, alas—you're doomed to suffer for your pride. I only pray your child shows better sense."

Before Arlette could respond, Esme exited the chamber, leaving her alone with her pride.

# CHAPTER 43

Arlette leaned back in her seat, cradling baby Ursula. Laughter filtered through the summer air, and Edith came into view, accompanied by a tall blond man with striking blue eyes—a man who hadn't changed since Arlette had last seen him, three years ago.

"I must say, my dear, Lady Edith seems pleased with my son. More than you were—or so my husband tells me."

Arlette turned to her companion, the diminutive Lady Eloise of Wildstorm. Though her face was lined with age, and her once-blond locks bore traces of gray, she was still a beautiful woman. Her delicate features gave her an elfin appearance. But foolish was the man—or woman—who underestimated her, for her gentleness hid the heart of a lioness.

Her clear blue eyes crinkled into a smile. "Alain is a little afraid of you, still, Lady Arlette—but a fearsome woman is no bad thing, in a man's world."

Arlette let out a laugh.

Lord Harald of Wildstorm had brought his son Alain to Leaside as a prospective suitor for Arlette three years previously. She'd received him dressed in breeches, face smeared in mud and brandishing her sword. Papa had given her such a beating she'd been unable to sit properly afterward.

Lady Eloise took her hand. "I'm glad to see you so happy," she said. "I was most distressed to learn about your family. Your cousin has much to answer for, I understand."

"Eloise, my love," a deep voice spoke, and Lord Harald appeared, Guillaume trotting in his wake. Eloise's husband towered over the boy, who looked up at him with adoration—the same way he'd looked at Orson.

Arlette swallowed the stab of pain at the memory of the expression on Orson's face when she'd asked him to leave, over a month ago. He'd been as good as his word, and not returned.

So, why did she feel so melancholy?

"Lettie—I showed Lord Harald the new trick Ernaut taught me!" Guillaume cried. "Ernaut told him I was one of the best sword-fighters he'd ever seen."

"He spoke the truth, young man," Lord Harald said. "You wield your sword well."

He took his wife's hand and kissed it. They exchanged a loving smile, and Arlette looked away.

Edith and Alain approached, and the young man flushed as he nodded to Arlette.

"It's most generous of you to receive us, Lady Arlette," he said.

"The pleasure's all mine," she replied. "How do you like my friend?"

"Very much," he said. "I fear, however, that she's tired, yet she denies it."

Edith averted her gaze, and the hunted look she'd always worn when Ulferth was alive, returned. The poor woman had yet to learn that asserting her wishes would no longer result in a beating.

"It is a little hot today," Arlette said. "You must be thirsty. Edith, my dear, would you be so kind as to accompany Sir Alain inside? I'm sure he'd like something to drink."

Edith's breath caught, and her eyes widened in alarm—her fear of men conquering her obvious attraction to the young knight. Lady Eloise rose to her feet.

"I find myself thirsty, also," she said. "Edith, my dear, may I accompany you, that is, if my son has no objection?"

"Of course not, Mother," Alain said.

"Would you like to escort me inside, Master Guillaume?" Eloise asked.

"*Oui*, madame." Guillaume offered Eloise his arm. She took it, and he led her toward the building, followed by Edith and Alain.

Lord Harald took the seat his wife had vacated and leaned back, stretching his long limbs.

"Your wife has a perception that many lack, Lord Harald," Arlette said.

"Aye, she does," he replied. "She sees what others do not. I am the most fortunate of husbands—I cannot imagine life without her." He nodded toward the building. "Do you wish to go inside also?"

Arlette shook her head. "I'll stay here awhile. Ursula is at peace, and I've no wish to disturb her."

"She's a fine child," he said. "She'll grow to be a beauty."

"You're too kind."

"And young Guillaume has all the attributes of a knight. He was eager to show me his skills. He wields a sword well."

Arlette smiled at his praise of her brother. "He's a little young yet," she said, "but he's eager to learn. He can already wield a lance—though only for a single run, before he tires."

"As could *you*, or so your man Ernaut told me."

"You disapprove?"

"Not at all. My Eloise is also a warrior—though she wields different weapons. I find that warriors come in many guises. Shall we have the pleasure of seeing your brother at the tournament?"

"Aye. I've told him he can act as squire to Ernaut, provided he forgets his temper and remembers his age."

"And will you accompany him?" he asked. "You're most welcome. My Eloise is fond of you, and a change of scenery would be beneficial for you. We think…" He hesitated, then sighed. "Forgive me, I've no wish to speak out of turn."

He fell silent, the only sound that of the birds singing, and the rush of the breeze in the trees—together with the gentle sound of Ursula breathing. Arlette lowered her head and placed a kiss on her daughter's cheek.

After a while, he broke the silence.

"Lord Wulfson is on the list of competitors."

Arlette's stomach flipped, and she averted her gaze.

"There's much to be said for forgiveness," he said.

"You speak out of turn, sir."

"Perhaps so, but I, of all men, have witnessed the power of forgiveness. And—selfish that I am—I know the happiness it brings."

"I mean no disrespect, Lord Harald," Arlette said, "but you know not what he did to me."

"Perhaps not, but I've committed far greater sins than he. I did not treat my wife well at first. I married against my will."

She let out a snort. "No man marries against his will—that misfortune is exclusive to *my* sex."

"I was ordered by Duke William, after the conquest," he said. "I had no choice, unless I wished to lose my home, and risk the lives of the people within—the people who depended on me."

She looked at him in disbelief, but the expression in his eyes was genuine.

"Perhaps we're not so different, after all," he said. "I mistrusted my wife—saw her as the enemy, and she suffered for it. As did I—for I valued pride over love."

His words pricked at her conscience. "Are you calling me proud?"

"Pride is no sin," he said, "provided it's tempered by love."

She shook her head. "I've never heard a man speak so!"

"'Tis the benefit of having a loving wife."

"And do you love her in return?"

"I grew to love her," he said. "Over the years, our love has strengthened—through overcoming the trials of life, together. But, my wife's a remarkable woman. Even if I had not grown to love her, she had enough love for the both of us."

Arlette snorted. "Are you saying I should return to a husband who doesn't love me?"

"Not at all," he said. "I'm asking you to give him a chance. I understand you turned him away and did not permit him to see his child."

Arlette glanced toward the building. "Your wife has a loose tongue," she said. "She should..."

He raised his hand to interrupt. "My wife says little, and only what is necessary. She's grown fond of you, and though she'd say nothing to you, it distresses her to see you unhappy."

She opened her mouth to deny it, but he turned his gaze on her, and she sighed. She might be able to convince herself, and her household, that she was happy. But the huge warrior who sat beside her, who was, so obviously, utterly devoted to his wife—did not deserve her lies.

"Forgive me," he said. "I spoke out of turn. I did it out of fondness for you, and the love I have for my wife. Nothing would please us more than to see Lord Wulfson wearing your favor at the tournament. If you cannot bear to leave your child, bring her with you."

"You are kind, but..."

"A chamber, and servants, will be at your disposal. Nothing prevents you from coming, other than yourself."

The baby stretched and yawned, then let out a familiar little squawk. Arlette's daughter was hungry.

He rose to his feet. "Your daughter tells us it's time to end our discussion," he said. "Come, let me escort you inside, and we'll speak no more on the matter."

He helped her up, and steadied her as she returned to the building, Ursula in her arms.

Oh—to have a love such as that shared by Harald and Eloise!

But Orson didn't love her, and whether she had enough love for them both, it would be unrequited love—the deadliest form of love.

To be reunited with Orson, only to watch his indifference toward her...

Better to be alone than suffer such a fate.

SCREAMS OF FURY ripped through the night air, rousing Arlette from her sleep.

When would she find rest?

She hadn't slept for two days. Ursula's screams of fury tormented the night hours, and the memory of Guillaume's angry words plagued her during the day.

Since Lord Harald and his wife had left, Guillaume persisted in trying to persuade Arlette to attend the tournament at Wildstorm, but she'd held firm. Two days ago, he left for the tournament with Ernaut. His pleas that she change her mind had turned into bitter words of hatred at her refusal to accompany him.

*You're a coward, Lettie! No wonder he's never returned. I hope he takes another wife. You'll die alone and it serves you right. I hate you!*

She climbed out of bed, and stubbed her toe against a table, and Ursula's screams increased. Arlette approached the crib, and tripped over the table, knocking it over. She fell to the floor, landing on a goblet, its rim digging into her flesh.

"God's teeth!"

Screaming in frustration, she hurled the goblet at the door, narrowly missing Esme who stood in the doorway.

"Curse you, old woman!" Arlette sobbed. "Are you spying on me?"

"Maude!" Esme cried. "Come here!"

Footsteps approached, then Maude's face appeared beside Esme.

"Take the baby for tonight," Esme said. "Lady Arlette is unwell."

Maude bobbed a curtsey and picked up the screaming infant. Ursula settled into her arms, and quietened almost immediately.

Arlette's heart ached to see it. Why couldn't Ursula settle for *her* as easily? Was she such a failure as a mother?

A gentle hand touched her shoulder—a simple act of kindness that breached the dam, and hot tears rolled down her cheeks.

"It's time someone took you in hand," Esme said. "You lack the wit to see what ails you."

"Nothing ails me, Esme. It's Ursula—she won't settle! Why does everybody think something's wrong with me?"

"Because there is."

How dare she—a mere servant—speak to her thus?

"Esme, you've no right…"

"I do," Esme interrupted. "I know what's best for you."

"And what is that, old woman?"

Esme tightened her grip at the insult.

"Your husband," she said, her voice hard. "I know it. Guillaume knows it. Sweet heaven, child—*everyone* knows it! Only you're too stubborn to admit it. You love him…"

"Hold your tongue!" Arlette tried to push Esme away but she gripped Arlette's arms and held her firm.

"For once, my lady, you'll listen to reason."

"No, I…"

"Heavens above!" Esme cried, giving her a shake. "Sometimes I wish your papa were here, to give you a thrashing! Do as I say. Go to him."

"And make myself look weak?"

"It's not weak to stand by your husband. What's weak is to deny that which would make you happy—what you know is right."

"What about his treatment of me?"

"Lord Wulfson was guided by his desire for vengeance, and his refusal to forgive and embrace the future. It nearly destroyed him. I begin to see it in your eyes, my lady. I fear it will destroy you also."

Esme spoke the truth. The darkness, born of bitter hatred, always sat right behind her—waiting to draw her in. And the fear, the crushing fear…

What if he rejected her?

Two warm arms drew her into a soft embrace.

"I understand your fear, little one," Esme whispered, "but what warrior turns away merely because she's afraid? Go to Wildstorm and see him. Give him a chance—and give yourself a chance."

"I cannot go," Arlette said. "Ursula needs me. I failed her tonight—I can't leave her."

"You haven't failed her, my dear, sweet child—you're merely tired. The greatest service you can do for her is to reunite with her father. Say the word, and I'll make the arrangements. Show your courage, and do as I say. I speak out of a desire to see you happy—and you deserve to be happy."

Arlette might be able to weather brutality, but she lacked the ability to withstand Esme's words of reason, spoken with love.

"Very well," she sighed. "I'll do as you say."

A soft kiss pressed against her forehead as Esme issued a prayer of thanks. "Come and rest, now. Maude will take good care of Ursula. All you need do is be ready to ride tomorrow."

# CHAPTER 44

W*ildstorm Hall, Summer 1087*

"I'M glad you finally decided to accept my invitation."

Arlette was already dressed when her hostess entered the chamber, accompanied by a servant carrying a tray of food.

"Forgive me for not coming sooner, Lady Eloise," she said. "It was most disrespectful."

Arlette had arrived at Wildstorm the night before, the moonlight picking out the silhouette of the building and the outline of the pavilion and the tents in the tourney field beyond.

Orson would be sleeping in one of the tents.

"Speak no more of it," Eloise said. "You're here for the final day."

She poured wine into a goblet and handed it to Arlette. "Your gown is very striking, my dear. And my Jeanette has excelled herself with your hair. You'll attract much attention today."

Arlette's cheeks flushed. Her dress—a red sleeveless overgown, embroidered in gold, together with an undergown of green silk—shimmered in the morning light, as if it were on fire. Eloise's maidservant had braided her hair, weaving flowers into each plait. Orson's necklace adorned her throat—his gift on their wedding day.

"I thought of no one in particular when I chose this gown," Arlette said.

"Of course not." Eloise smiled, her violet eyes shining with amusement.

After Arlette had broken her fast, Lord Harald escorted her to the pavilion. The spectators had already assembled, and a number of heads turned, straining to see the newcomer. Perhaps she should have chosen a plainer gown.

Harald stopped beside an empty seat. "I'll leave you to get acquainted with your companion." He bowed, then left to join his wife.

Arlette turned to address the woman next to her and froze.

"Lady Verona."

Her companion did not smile.

"Arlette. I didn't expect to see *you*." Verona's usually gentle voice carried a hard edge, showing nothing of the warmth Arlette had come to know during the journey from Villiers.

"I was detained." Arlette's voice sounded false and hollow to her ears.

Verona nodded, but didn't reply. Then she cast her gaze over Arlette's gown, settling on the necklace around her throat.

"Are...are you well, Verona?"

"Aye."

"And..." Arlette hesitated and Verona raised her eyebrows in expectation.

"...and Seaton? Is he competing?"

"He runs this morning."

"Then I shall cheer him."

Verona turned her head away, and fixed her gaze on the tourney field.

"I've seen Guillaume," she said. "He's tending to Ernaut. I swear he's grown—I hardly recognized him."

"My brother's a handful," Arlette laughed. "It was all I could do to prevent him from competing himself."

Verona didn't smile, and an awkward silence fell, punctuated by the blast of the horn that heralded the arrival of the competitors. Arlette's cheeks burned with shame, and she turned her head to face the breeze as the first competitors entered the arena.

At length, Verona spoke, her voice laced with ice.

"I would tell you that my brother is well, Arlette—should you care enough to ask."

Before Arlette could respond, the herald announced the first run.

Trying to ignore the wall of hostility that had risen between her and Verona, Arlette turned her attention to the jousting, applauding each victor as he unseated his opponent. When the third pair rode out, she recognized Seaton, together with the tall, powerful frame of Alain of Wildstorm. A burst of applause rippled through the crowd as Alain acknowledged his supporters—his parents, Lord Harald and Lady Eloise, among them. Verona drew a sharp breath, and clutched her hands together, her fingers trembling. On impulse, Arlette placed her hand over Verona's.

"Do not worry. Seaton's a skilled rider and Sir Alain is a good man. He fights fair."

Verona nodded and squeezed Arlette's hand. The gesture of friendship breached Arlette's defenses.

"Verona, is—is *he* competing today?"

"Aye," Verona whispered. "He won through to the final yesterday. If Seaton succeeds he'll face him this afternoon."

"Verona, I…" Arlette began, but a fanfare interrupted her, signaling the start of the first run. Verona's grip tightened on Arlette's hand as Seaton urged his horse into a gallop toward his opponent. He raised his lance but Alain deflected it with his shield, and it skittered out of his grasp. Alain's own lance hit Seaton's shield with full force, sending him flying to the ground. Alain dismounted, and ran toward his opponent to help him up, and the crowd cheered his prowess and gallantry.

By the end of the morning, the tournament had its other finalist in Alain of Wildstorm. After felling Seaton, he toppled two others, including a giant of a man who'd clearly been the favorite to win the title.

While the company broke for refreshments, the first raindrops began to fall. Settling back into her seat, Arlette's body began to shake, her stomach churning. Mirroring Verona's earlier gesture, she clasped her hands, which were slick with fear, together.

The fanfare struck up and the herald announced the two finalists. Alain rode into the arena, acknowledging the crowd before holding a silken scarf to his lips—a lady's favor. Then he bowed in Lady Eloise's direction, and she pressed her fingers to her lips.

"'Tis a mystery why so popular a young knight chooses his mother's favor," Verona said, "when there are many young women here, eager for his attentions."

"Perhaps the lady he favors is elsewhere," Arlette replied.

"Aye, perhaps she is. Guillaume told me the Lady Edith fares well, and were it not for her impending confinement, she would be here."

"Aye, she would."

"She deserves to be happy," Verona continued. "I never liked Ulferth—he always treated her ill." She nodded toward Sir Alain, who paraded around the field. "It warms my heart to think that Edith has a second chance at love. You are to be congratulated."

The second rider emerged, his armor glinting in the sunlight, and Arlette's heart jolted in her chest.

His hair had grown—thick and dark, it brushed his shoulders. Her fingers ached to be buried in it once more, and her body yearned to feel him inside her.

He turned to acknowledge the crowd. Polite applause rippled through the company, but it was clear who they favored. His shield was on his right arm. He must fight left-handed, now—no doubt the more God-fearing members of the crowd believed him to be cursed. Arlette spotted one woman making the sign of the cross as he rode past.

As he circled the arena, Arlette spotted a piece of cloth pinned to his chest.

He had taken another woman's favor.

Arlette turned to Verona. "Whose favor does he wear?"

"Why should you care?" Verona replied. "You sent him away and told him never to return. Is he not within his rights to take another's favor after you rejected him?"

Arlette stifled a sob. Had she come here for nothing?

"Forgive me," she choked, "I see I'm too late."

Verona sighed, then took her hand. "No—'tis you who should forgive *me*. I've been too harsh. If I were you, I'd look more closely at the favor he wears."

Unlike the usual brightly colored scarves, Orson's favor was dull—a piece of rag, fraying at the ends, the sleeve torn from a servant's garb at night, in secret, in the tourney field at Greywell over a year ago. Though it had originally been given to Seaton, Orson had claimed it—as he had claimed her.

"Don't you see?" Verona asked. "My brother took no favor here, for he brought one with him. It has earned him the crowd's displeasure, but he wears your favor with pride."

Fat raindrops splattered from the sky as the riders took their positions. For the first run, Orson's starting point was farthest from Arlette. Sir Alain, his back to them, was almost within touching distance. He placed his helmet over his head and his squire handed him a lance.

The crowd fell silent as the herald raised his arm. Then he lowered it.

The two men spurred their horses forward, kicking up clods of earth as they gained speed. The staccato beat of hooves vibrated through the earth. With a great clang, they met at the center, each man's lance striking the other's shield. But neither was unseated, and they continued to the end of the run.

Victory would not come easily—the two men were evenly matched. On the return run, Alain's horse slipped, but he maintained his seat, to the delight of the cheering crowd.

During the third run, Orson's horse lost its footing, and he dropped his lance. Arlette screamed and leaped to her feet.

"Hush!" Verona warned. "You draw attention to yourself."

"I cannot understand why Lord Harald doesn't order them to stop," Arlette said. "The rain's turned the field into a mud bath!"

After reaching the end of the run, Orson steered his horse around and lifted his visor. An invisible hand clutched at Arlette's heart.

He was looking straight at her.

The noise from the crowd receded until the only sound in her mind was her heartbeat, and the rush of her breathing. He snapped his visor shut with a clang, breaking the spell, then returned his attention to his opponent.

At the signal, they set off for the fourth run, spatters of mud spraying up behind the horses' hooves. Halfway along, Orson's horse slipped again, and he lost his shield as he struggled to retain his seat. Alain must have noticed, for he raised his lance. But he was too late. The tip struck Orson's side, and he fell to the ground, his horse landing on top of him. The animal struggled to its feet, then trotted toward the end of the run, where a squire ran forward to catch the reins.

Alain held his lance aloft and the crowd erupted with applause, seemingly unaware of the prone figure lying on the field.

Orson was not moving.

"Fetch the surgeon!" Lord Harald's voice roared through the rain, as Alain dismounted and ran toward Orson's body.

Arlette's gown grew too tight, and a sharp ache spread through her chest.

Why did he not get up?

"Orson!"

She leaped to her feet, and pushed her way to the front of the pavilion. Then she swung herself over the edge, and dropped onto the field, some four feet below. Picking up her skirts, she sprinted toward the cluster of men surrounding her husband's motionless body. One of the squires blocked her path.

"This is no place for a lady."

"Let me through!" she cried. "Sir Alain, please!"

"Give her some space, Geoffrey," the new champion ordered.

Arlette dropped to her knees beside Orson's still form. The squire eased Orson's helmet off to reveal his face. Orson's eyes were closed, his skin a deathly pallor, lips a shade of blue. Arlette stroked his cheek, then pressed her lips to his forehead, tasting salt on his skin.

"Orson—'tis I, Arlette."

He did not respond.

"Orson, please!" She cupped his face in her hands, but still he gave no sign of life.

"Don't leave me!" she cried, pressing herself against his chestplate. "Please—I cannot bear it!" Hot, salty tears mingled with the rain, rivulets of water running down her body, pooling in fat drops at the end of her hair to splash onto his armor.

"What's happening here?" A voice roared. "Get that woman away!"

The surgeon had arrived.

"*That woman* is his wife," Alain said.

"Widow, I'll wager, after the blow you dealt him."

"No!" Arlette let out a wail as despair flooded through her.

She was too late. Her thirst for vengeance had destroyed her chance of happiness.

Why had she sent him away when he'd come to Leaside? All she had to show for her stubborn resolve was a lifeless husband, her chance for redemption lost forever. Her body shook as she clung to the body of the man she'd determined to hate, but had grown to love more than she could have believed possible.

A soft voice whispered in her mind.

"Are your tears for me, Arlette?"

She lifted her head, blinking away the tears and rain. Clear gray eyes looked back at her.

He was alive.

A cry of relief sprang from her chest, and she cupped his cheek with one hand, brushing the other against his breastplate, curling her fingers around the piece of rag pinned to his chest.

"I see you wear my favor."

He placed his hand over hers.

"It gives me great pleasure, Lady Arlette, to accept your token. I wear it with pride, and shall fight for my lady's honor."

Her heart swelled with love. He might not have emerged victorious, but he was her champion.

And he always would be.

"I should admonish you, wife," he said, his voice breathless, "for the unladylike behavior you continue to display at tournaments."

Smiling through the tears, she leaned forward and brushed her lips over his. He grasped the front of her gown, and pulled her close to claim his kiss.

Sir Alain laughed. "Is this the man you rejected me for?"

"Do I have a rival?" Orson growled.

"No, my love," Arlette replied, "you have never had a rival."

A bony hand gripped her arm and pulled her away. The surgeon had lost patience.

"Stand aside, woman, so I may tend to him."

"Here—let me." Alain helped her up, while the surgeon administered to Orson, removing his armor and prodding him through his hauberk. His reward was a curse, and a cuff to the side of his head.

"The bones seem sound, Lord Wulfson," he said, sitting back and rubbing his head where Orson had struck him. "The injuries to your body are superficial, considering the fall you took. As for your temper —I suggest you find another to tend to *that*."

"Just help me up, damn you!"

"Your husband is well," Alain laughed, "and you, lady, have ruined your dress."

Arlette lifted the hem of her gown, soaked and streaked with mud.

"It'll wash," she laughed, "and if it doesn't—what's a gown compared to the man I love?"

Alain lifted her hand and kissed it. "He's a fortunate man, indeed."

"Remove your hands from my wife."

A large hand took her arm in a possessive grip.

"Lord Wulfson, forgive me, I..."

"I *said*—remove your hands from my wife!"

Alain's eyes narrowed, and he withdrew his hand, taking a step back.

"Alain, go to your father," Arlette said. Nodding, he left.

Orson's eyes darkened. "He takes liberties."

"Only in the kingdom of your mind," Arlette replied, "assuming, of course, you have enough wit to possess such a thing as an imagination."

"Saucy wench!" he said. "I should take you over my knee if I didn't know how much pleasure it would give you."

A familiar rush of heat pulsed inside her. "Perhaps you should try it anyway, husband. I know not whether I would take pleasure from feeling your palm against my skin."

His nostrils flared. "First I would know if what you said to Sir Alain was true."

"Aye," she whispered, "a gown is nothing compared to the man I love."

"And am I that man?"

"I ought to spear you on the other side, for asking such a question."

He pulled her close. "I'm glad you came. That young dog may have bested me, but when I lay on the field and opened my eyes to look upon you, I knew I was the true victor."

"A pretty speech for a warrior," she retorted.

"Arlette," he said, "I'm not a man of fine words, but I—I must speak of what I did to your family, to you..."

"Hush." She placed a light finger on his lips. "'Tis better unsaid. I will return to Greywell if you still wish it—for the sake of our child. I have enough love for us both."

His eyes hardened.

"I understand," he said. "You would return, even though I loved you not?"

Her heart withered, and she nodded.

He set his mouth into a firm line and gripped her forearms. She closed her eyes, shutting out his angry gaze, and yielding to the agony in her heart.

"Our daughter needs a father, Orson," she said. "When I return, I'll demand nothing for myself. Forgive me—I always thought you a vengeful man, driven by your need to punish every transgression, without consideration or exception. But I failed to recognize that fault in myself. It matters not that you'll never love me—that's my burden to bear. But I ask you to love our child."

"It this what you think of me?" he asked, his voice thick with pain.

He released her arms and she opened her eyes to see him kneeling before her. He took her hands and drew them to his lips.

"'Tis not right that you're mine, Arlette," he said.

"Orson…"

"God's bones, woman—for once, cease your prattling and let me finish!"

He lifted his head up, an unspoken plea in his eyes.

"I do not deserve you, Arlette. After I lost Verona I thought I could never love again. But then I found you. Your fire and passion gave me something to live for. When you stood in my courtyard, facing me like a warrior as you took a beating meant for others, I knew I'd met my match. When I thought you had betrayed us, it almost destroyed me. In turn, I wanted to destroy you—but I couldn't."

He bent his head as if in prayer, then lifted his gaze. Her heart ripped to shreds at the tears glistening in his eyes.

"Come home to me, Arlette," he pleaded. "You're sorely missed at Greywell. Verona and Seaton chide me every day, and Lillian wants her mama back."

"And what of *you*, my lord?"

"Need I say the words? I cannot live without you, Arlette. I love you—I have loved you from the moment you looked into my eyes in that courtyard."

"You never spoke of love."

"Do you not remember when I gave you the lute?"

"That was a gift from *you*?"

"Aye," he said. "I sent Seaton ahead with it. Coward that I am, I was afraid you might reject it—reject me. But I hoped you'd come to love me. Then, when I saw you with Seaton, and realized you thought it a gift from him…" He shook his head. "I couldn't admit my love for you, thinking you cared for another. Do you not remember that I said it was a gift of love?"

"Aye," she replied. "But you were wrong when you said that love would never be returned, for already I loved you."

"Then I have won my prize today."

His face broke into a smile, radiating love and warmth. He had always been a handsome specimen, but when he smiled, he eclipsed the stars. Her breath caught in her throat at the sight of him, his strong features, the masculine mouth, lips beckoning to be claimed…

She kneeled beside him, her knees touching his, mud seeping into her gown.

"Then, my lord," she said, "the time has come to claim your prize."

He leaned closer until his breath warmed her lips, sending fire coursing through her veins and pooling in her core.

"I wish for a greater prize, little one."

He lifted his hand to her face, and ran a light finger across her lips before tracing a line across her chin and down her neck. Then he dipped his hand into the front of her gown. Her nipples hardened to eager little points, and he chuckled softly. Then he placed his other hand on her belly.

"I would have Greywell Castle filled with fiery daughters and lusty sons. Tell me, woman, with whom should I sire such children?"

He silenced her response with a kiss, his tongue claiming ownership of her—teasing, probing, until her body came to life with the memory of his body filling hers and the promise of what was to come.

She drew breath, her chest heaving, "Perhaps, if my lord's injuries are not so severe, he might claim his prize tonight. Ursula must not be kept waiting for her siblings."

"You named our daughter Ursula?"

"It means she-bear," Arlette said. "I named her after you."

"Oh, Arlette!" he cried, "I am so glad you have returned to me."

"As am I, Orson. I only hope Guillaume will not mind my leaving him."

Orson chuckled, "When we first met, your brother told me I'd make a suitable husband for you. He is Lord de Villiers and you must do your lord's bidding."

"*You* are my lord," she replied, "I'll do nobody's bidding but yours."

He let out a low growl and fisted his hands in her hair, and the swell of passion threatened to break as he slammed his mouth onto hers. His hungry lips marked his territory with a trail of open-mouthed kisses along her neck. Forcing her head back, he nipped her throat—the falcon, claiming lordship over his mate.

"Ahem."

He broke the kiss, and her body deflated with a sense of loss. The fog of passion dissipated until only the cold and the rain remained. Lord Harald stood before them, averting his eyes, Lady Eloise beside him, a knowing smile on her lips.

"Lord Wulfson," Harald said, "You must return to the hall, to have your wounds tended to."

Eloise placed a hand on her husband's arm and laughed. "What my husband asks is would you mind letting him bring the tournament to a close, so we can all come out of the rain. He knows as well as I that you have all you need before you. What better healing can a man experience than a woman's love?"

ON LADY ELOISE'S INSISTENCE, Orson let himself be led away to a guest chamber where a bath had been prepared. Arlette couldn't help laughing at the manner in which he deferred to a woman whom he towered over by almost two feet.

"You have a rare talent, Eloise, to control a man almost twice your size."

"I believe where Lord Wulfson is concerned, that particular talent is exclusively yours, Arlette," Eloise said. "Come, let us follow him."

"My lady?"

"Surely you didn't expect *me* to bathe him?"

Through the chamber door, Arlette spied a maidservant helping Orson into the bath. The candlelight cast shadows over the planes of his hard, muscular back. Orson's hair brushed his shoulders, dripping with perspiration. A large bruise was already darkening where Alain's lance had struck him. Arlette's gaze dropped to his taut buttocks, below which his thigh muscles bulged as he lifted his leg over the side of the tub and lowered himself into the water.

"I'll leave you now, my lord," the maidservant said. "Her ladyship will tend to you shortly."

He murmured a response, and she bobbed a curtsey, her face coloring when she spotted Arlette in the doorway.

"Why does she blush?" Arlette hissed.

"Your husband's a fine specimen as you well know, my dear," Eloise whispered. "Now, I would ask you to respect my hospitality and join him before the water grows cold."

Eloise's mouth curled into a smile of mischief. "I've given orders that you're not to be disturbed."

Before Arlette could reply, Eloise disappeared into the main building, her light laugh bouncing off the walls.

Arlette slipped through the door and closed it softly.

"Ah, lady, I thank ye," a deep baritone murmured from the bathtub.

Since when had Orson Greywell become so civil?

Arlette unlaced her gown, and pulled it over her head. Wearing only her chemise, she approached the bathtub, and picked up the bowl and cake of soap the servant had left. She kneeled behind Orson, dipped the bowl into the water, then tipped it over his head. Then, she buried her soapy hands into his hair, and worked it into a lather.

"Lady…"

"Shhh."

She massaged harder, and he let out a growl of pleasure. Then she ran her hands down his neck, to his shoulders. The muscles were rock hard, but as she worked her fingers into them, the tension began to fade. Digging her thumbs in, she followed the lines of muscle, increasing the pressure with each stroke.

As she stopped to pick up the washcloth, a small sigh of frustration escaped his lips. She dipped the cloth into the water, lifted it, then squeezed the soapy water over his shoulders. With her forefinger, she pushed a small cluster of bubbles down his chest, opening her palm to caress his muscles. She pressed her cheek against the back of his head, and sighed, blowing a soft breath into his ear. His skin tightened, the downy neck hairs rising.

The low throb of his heartbeat pulsed against her open palm. She moved her hand in a slow, slick circle across his chest, tightening the spiral until her fingers brushed over his nipple. His body shuddered as he inhaled, and his nipple hardened against her fingers. Then she took his earlobe between her teeth, and ran her tongue along the little morsel of flesh before giving him a playful nip.

His body jerked, and his manhood poked through the surface of the water, throbbing with unmet need. Groaning, he placed his hand over his groin.

"Forgive me, Lady Eloise, I..."

"Hush, husband. Let me bathe you."

"Arlette!" He sat upright, splashing water over the side, then he grunted with pain.

"Ouch!"

"My poor love," she teased. "I'll leave you in peace."

He took her wrist. "You'll do no such thing. You must pay for tormenting me so."

"Ah—torment is it?"

"Aye, you little vixen. I thought you the Lady Eloise."

He pulled her close until she toppled into the bathtub, sending a great splash of water over the side. "I'm glad 'tis you," he said.

"How glad?"

He held her firm against his chest, sending a jolt of need through her breasts, the nipples hardening to painful points against her soaked chemise. She wriggled against him, and he lifted his leg and jammed his knee between her thighs.

"*This* glad." He eased his hands down her back and squeezed her buttocks.

"And this..." He thrust his hips upward, his manhood hardening against her thigh.

Then, he pulled her chemise up, exposing her thighs.

"I've not finished bathing you," she protested.

"The time for bathing is over." He curled his fingers into her chemise and ripped it apart, before grasping her bare flesh in his hands, claiming his ownership of her.

"Orson, I…oh!" she cried out as his hand delivered a stinging slap on her thigh. A jolt of need shot through her veins, sending a pulse of fire through her body. Her greedy nipples poked insistently against his chest, begging for attention. He curled his lip into a wicked smile.

"Not yet, my love," he said. "You have disobeyed your husband, and I must complete your punishment."

At his last word her body almost burst with passion, forcing the air from her lungs. The steam rising from their bodies thickened the air, the sweet scent of the soap overpowered by the musky scent of passion—a man and his woman ready for each other.

He brought his hand down again, then he dipped his finger between her legs, slipping toward her center, where her flesh pulsed with need. Teasing her with his fingertip, he knew exactly where her body needed him.

He gave her a knowing smile, and raised his eyebrows in challenge.

"Orson…"

She shifted her legs wider, her body pleading for his touch, but he removed his hand, and the rush of cold air on her skin elicited a wail of frustration from her chest.

"Does my wife like her bath?"

Unable to speak, she whimpered, and nodded against his chest.

He plunged his finger inside her, and her body exploded. Luscious sensations radiated from her center, igniting her senses until pinpricks of light burst into fireballs in her mind, and her body rippled and pulsed to the rhythms of her screams.

He captured her cries with his mouth. Before her senses returned, he grasped her thighs and pulled her hard against him, impaling her against his manhood, stretching her deliciously with his onslaught of her body.

Then he stopped moving, still buried inside her, his thick, hard length filling her emptiness.

"Oh, Arlette—long have I waited to claim you once more!"

He moved against her, slowly at first, easing himself out before slowly pushing himself back in, reigniting the spark of life within her, which grew with each long, slow movement, and she rocked her hips to match each exquisite stroke.

She closed her eyes, a falcon soaring toward the heavens, to freedom, the wind on her wings, riding the air until she plunged toward the earth with a shattering cry before coming to rest on her master's hand.

They clung to each other, their bodies melded together as one, while the faint pulses of their climaxes faded. Closing her eyes, she drifted into a delicious doze.

When she opened them again, she lay on a bed, Orson caressing her languid body with a drying cloth. He joined her on the bed, and covered them both with a fur.

There was no need for words—their love for each other was unspoken, but wholly understood, accepted, and celebrated.

A soft smile curled on his lips. Arlette reached up to touch his face, running her fingertips along his cheek to the small indent in the flesh.

"You have dimples when you smile, Orson. I've never seen them before."

He took her hand and kissed her fingertips.

"That, my love, is because only today am I truly happy, because I know that your heart and soul are mine."

He pulled her up and discomfort shot across his eyes. She touched the bruise on his side.

"Does it pain you?"

"Nay, wife. Nothing pains me today."

With gentle hands she took him by the shoulders and pushed him back on the bed, until he lay face up. She dipped her head to kiss his bruised flesh.

"Is that better?"

"Much."

"And this?"

Tasting citrus on his skin, she pressed her lips against his skin, exploring him with her mouth. She traced a line with her tongue along his chest, planting delicate kisses on his body, following the line of his battle scars until she reached his nipple where he gave a sharp little cry as she grazed it with her teeth. Moving her hands toward his waist, she lifted her head, and met his eyes, which darkened as she curled her fingers around his manhood. He came to life again, and a deep growl rumbled in his chest.

"Arlette, I beg you..."

"You wish me to stop?"

"No!" he rasped. She traced a line of kisses down his body, moving her lips closer to her hands while she continued to caress him until he was ready for her again. His body stiffened, little cries of need in the back of his throat while she teased him with her mouth, inching closer to him.

She took him in her mouth and he cried out, her name catching in his throat, his voice hoarse with need.

"Arlette, I cannot hold on..."

He tried to sit up but she pushed him back.

"No, husband, 'tis my turn."

Easing herself over him, she let her body slide onto his rekindled shaft.

"Arlette!" he protested. "We should join the feast. What would our hostess think, if she knew what we were about?"

Arlette smiled. "She would realize, my love, that Lord Wulfson is—most thoroughly and joyously—reuniting himself with his wife.

# EPILOGUE

G*reywell Castle, July 1095*

"MAMA! MAMA!" The voice pierced through Arlette's slumber, and she jerked her head upright. The babe in her arms grunted, but did not wake.

Stretching her legs, she looked out across the garden from her position in the chair Esme had brought out for her. A young woman sat on a blanket making a daisy chain. The owner of the voice, a little girl of eight years, emerged from a gap in the lavender hedge and ran toward them, her skirts flapping around her ankles.

"Ursula!" Arlette cried. "How many times must I tell you, a lady *walks*."

"Papa has arrived," the child cried, "and Pierre's with him. I can see them on the road."

Arlette had missed her son. Six-year-old Pierre had been fostered as a page at Wildstorm, and returned today with Orson, travelling via Leaside where Guillaume had joined them.

The young woman on the blankets held out her arms.

"Come here, little she-bear." She pulled Ursula onto her lap, and planted a kiss on the child's cheek.

Lillian had always been a pretty child but lately she'd turned into a beauty, with her glossy blue-black hair, fine-boned face, and her father's clear gray eyes.

The garden overlooked the tourney field. Already the tents were up and sounds of activity carried across the summer air. The tournament began in less than a sennight. Seaton was competing, though he came alone. Verona neared her confinement with their second child and the ride from Seaforth—which Arlette had gifted them—was long. Seaton had not wanted to leave Verona, but she'd insisted, and, recognizing the true ruler of his household, Seaton had acquiesced.

The party came into view, and the sight of her husband's powerful frame never failed to send a thrill through her body in anticipation of their reunion. He was flanked by a young man and a boy. Guillaume matched his brother-in-law's pace but little Pierre broke into a run as soon as he saw his mother.

"Do not run, sir!"

"Yes, Papa." The boy slowed to a walk.

As her son reached her, Arlette held out her hand.

He bowed and kissed it. "Milady."

"Welcome home, my young knight," she said.

He threw his arms around her neck.

"Careful of your sister," she chided. "Aren't you going to greet her?"

"Hello, Emmelina." Pierre spoke formally but his lip wobbled. "I've missed you, Mama," he said, "but I only cried once while I was away."

Orson and Guillaume reached her together. Guillaume kissed her lightly on the cheek, then settled on the blanket between Lillian and Ursula.

"Go sit with your sisters, young sir," Orson commanded.

Pierre bowed and followed Guillaume, nestling beside Lillian, who wrapped her arms around him and, ignoring his protests, kissed him on both cheeks.

Orson kneeled before Arlette and took her face in his hands. Their lips met, and he ran his tongue lightly along the seam of her mouth until she opened for him. He slipped a hand into her gown, cupping a breast, full with nursing. She shifted in her seat and the babe in her arms gave a little cry of protest.

"Our daughter wakes, husband, and needs me."

"I'm in need of you too, wife," he whispered, giving a triumphant smile as her nipple peaked under his palm. "It seems your need matches mine."

"Are you eager to sire another child?"

"I'm eager to lie with my wife," he replied. "If we were alone I would take you now, in the grass."

Her body pulsed with desire at his words, and she drew in a sharp breath. Chuckling, he kissed her again, then lifted baby Emmelina into his arms, his face softening as it always did when he looked upon their children.

Then he called Lillian over, and she kissed him on the cheek to welcome him home before he handed Emmelina to her. He pulled Arlette out of her chair, then took her place, and settled her onto his lap. She rested her head on his shoulder and he stroked her hair, the tender, absent-minded gesture of a lover.

"At last, I have my wife all to myself."

She relaxed into his warm embrace, the two of them sharing a comfortable, easy silence as they watched over their family—a family once driven apart by greed and vengeance, but now, united by forgiveness and love.

THE END

# THANK YOU FOR READING!

Get *The Saxon Lord's Unwanted Bride*, Book 1 in the *Medieval Brides* available on Amazon.

I hope you enjoyed this book. If you'd like to stay in touch, you can find me on:

Facebook
Twitter
BookBub
Instagram

Fancy a free novella? Sign up to my mailing list, for news, cover reveals, teaser scenes and more. Your details won't be passed on to third parties.

# ACKNOWLEDGMENTS

*There are so many people I want to thank for their support while I was writing this book. Firstly to my Beta Buddies, thanks for all the camaraderie —you really are the best critique group in the world. To Sarah, our zoom chats have kept me on the straight-and-narrow, and your advice has been invaluable, as usual. Thank you to my ARC team for your encouraging feedback, and to Immi, who should be renamed Artemis the Huntress of Typos and, of course, Dar, the Queen of Covers.*

*And, lastly, thank you Neil, Jasmine, and Frankie, for just being there. I love you so much.*

# ABOUT THE AUTHOR

*USA Today* bestselling author Emily Royal grew up in Sussex, England, and has devoured romantic novels for as long as she can remember. A mathematician at heart, Emily has worked in financial services for thirty years. She indulged in her love of writing after she moved to Scotland, where she lives with her husband, teenage daughters, and a menagerie of pets including Twinkle, an attention-seeking boa constrictor. She has a passion for both reading and writing romance, with a weakness for Regency rakes, Highland heroes, and medieval knights. *Persuasion* is one of her all-time favorite novels, and she is fortunate enough to live within sight of a medieval palace.

Printed in Dunstable, United Kingdom

71556103R00208